Secrets of the Shell Sisters

Adrienne Vaughan

Published by

- The -
PARIS
PRESS

Cover design by Trevor Stocks

Author photograph © Jonathan Vaughan

Dedication

In memory of a beloved aunt, Tricia
Broome, a very special and truly
inspirational woman.

Treasured forever. X

About the Author

Adrienne Vaughan writes spellbinding, page-turning romantic suspense.

Her award-winning Heartfelt Series – *The Hollow Heart, A Change of Heart* and *Secrets of the Heart* – is set on an island off Ireland's west coast and features a feisty investigative journalist, and her irresistible West Highland terrier. (Adrienne studied at the Dublin College of Journalism and loves animals, especially dogs.)

Her collection of short stories and poetry, *Fur Coat & No Knickers* was shortlisted for the Irish Carousel Prize for Anthology and her WWII short story, *Dodo's Portrait*, was shortlisted for the Colm Toíbín International Short Story Award at the Wexford Literary Festival.

Secrets of the Shell Sisters – a Rosshaven Romance Book II – is a companion novel to *Summer of Secrets*, a revised edition of the previously published novel *That Summer at the Seahorse Hotel* (2018). It is the second novel in a series of sweeping family sagas, each with a sprinkling of Irish magic.

All Adrienne's books are heart-warming, uplifting reads, featuring her trademark gripping style, and laugh out loud moments.

Adrienne, her husband, and two cocker spaniels divide their time between rural Leicestershire, the Wicklow mountains, and coastal South Devon. Agatha Christie – the cat – (and Lorraine) take care of things while they are away.

Praise for the Author

Irish Magic

What a stunner of a story! Adrienne Vaughan's writing has a definite flavour of Mary Wesley; classy and elegant, with economical prose and yet with such emotive descriptions of her chosen setting that the world she creates lingers long after the book is closed. The characters are well-drawn and their interaction is sparky and realistic. The tension and mystery mounts gradually but everyday life carries on seamlessly throughout, I wanted to go to this wonderful place and stay there!

Stunning Cover, Stunning Book

The stunning cover of this book has to be one of the best I've seen in a long time. The contents of the book don't disappoint either! Set on the East Coast of Ireland, the cast of colourful characters are pretty unique too, from initially-understated heroine Mia Flanagan; her film star mother, Fenella, actor Archie; who might or might not be Mia's father; Leela, the lynchpin of the often chaotic household and many more, including the delectable American, Ross Power and his loveable niece Pearl. The setting was beautifully etched and made me want to visit, especially to meet the characters! The action revolves around something that happened one summer some years before, and this is told in retrospect by various characters, building up to a climatic conclusion. A wonderful book and one I didn't want to end and was sad when I did so.

A great read…I felt I was there in so many ways…

A great read, I loved every minute of it, felt I was actually there, brought back lots of memories of east coast Eire. This is a brilliant story, with a cast of wonderful characters that stay in your mind long after you finish the book. I was rooting for the heroine and fell in love with the hero. Also totally fell in love with the setting – a huge old house on the east coast of Ireland – so want to visit that country now! It sounded absolutely fabulous and the author makes you feel as though you're really there, seeing the sights, breathing in the tang of the sea and hearing the local dialect. Loved it!

Glamour, intrigue, secrets, adventure, and of course, romance – just wonderful!

Adrienne Vaughan has done it again! Another 5* story full of glamour and intrigue, secrets and adventure centring around a rather grand but old family house. I loved the aging Hollywood actor, Archie and the relationship between him and Mia. I think every family needs an 'Archie'! Secrets are gradually revealed as events unfold and the wonderful mix of characters, which have become one of Adrienne Vaughan's trademarks, are carried along together in an adventure spanning the decades as memories are invoked and actions remembered. All set against a backdrop of the Irish coast and its wild and wonderful landscape. This is a must read for anyone who enjoys a good adventure with lots of intrigue and romance too.

Another epic gem from this massively talented author

...a tantalising plot and superb diverse characters – I simply couldn't put it down and am now going to read it again to enjoy all the wonderful subtleties and Irish nuances that lie on every page – it diverted the mind and healed the soul over a weekend when both were badly needed. Could she be the new Penny Vincenzi with both strong and eccentric female characters woven into superb epic plots underpinned by meticulous research?

The best yet!

A delicious combination of romance, mystery and the everyday, with a cast of totally believable and very memorable characters. As with all Adrienne Vaughan's novels there is a strong sense of community and you can't help but be drawn into their lives. Her authentic Irish voice pushes through the easy flowing dialogue with its affectionate humour and there are some laugh out loud moments. The story rattles along at a pace and kept me guessing till the last. Although, inevitably, all good books must come to an end, this mini family saga is one I will definitely miss!

The Shell Sisters by
Adrienne Vaughan

It curved, the bay; a half a moon, of sifted sand, a blue lagoon.
We held a bag, between us two, the way,
when small, we used to do.
And plonking down, we claimed our spot, our
sandals flung, the sun glared hot,
As ocean rushed the rocks close by, to splash
us with its sea-spray sigh.

With turquoise rippling through our toes, sand
pipers swooped and drooped and rose,
We talked of picnics from the past, of
castles built that couldn't last,
And planned our house right on the shore, with
anchored yacht, steps from the door.
And laughing as the wine allowed, we
stared the sky against a cloud.

Then giving voice to dreams we shared and
secrets no one else had dared
Speak, for all the years we'd known strange
ghosts of truths that weren't our own.
We watched them rise from watery tombs and
bate us with their myths and runes,
Yet tempted not our souls away; the shore
held hard, our hearts that day.

And as the cooling shadows grew, we

made a pact, because we knew
The echoes of those times gone by, were
laid to rest, the tears now dry.
And gathering shells voraciously, sweet
mermaid jewels, gifts from the sea,
We let the past just seep away, that glittered
beach, that sunny day.

And though the Sea Witch calls our names,
we'll play not her beguiling games,
For like the treasured shells we keep, our
key to freedom's buried deep.
The darkest sea, with monster's lair, can't
drag us down, gasping for air
The sisterhood we share is strong, the past
is theirs, we've done no wrong.

And when the moon sails through the sky,
as swirling gulls cry last goodbye,
The beach grows still, the waves to hush,
I let the ocean calm the rush.
A sea salt kiss will ease the pain, as gazing at the rippling plain
I sight my sister, swimming free. I'm with
her still, and she's with me.

Secrets of the Shell Sisters

Adrienne Vaughan

Contents

Siren Wails & Fishermen's Tales
An Inspector Calls
A Fragile Truce
Titanic
Mixed Messages
The Sea Chamber
Island Echoes
Memory of a Free Festival
Box of Frogs
Party Animals
Bygones
Old Love Boat
Travelling Companions
A Settlement
And Breathe
Storm Force
Sister Act
Time and Tide
The Familiar
Sea Sister
Moonlight Farewell
The Mermaid's Secret
Family Ties
A Final Swim

Thou rememberest since
Once I sat upon a promontory,
And heard a mermaid on a dolphin's back
Uttering such dulcet and harmonious breath
That the rude sea grew civil at her song,
And certain stars shot madly from their spheres,
To hear the sea-maid's music.

William Shakespeare - A Midsummer Night's Dream

Prologue – Summer 1967

The watcher, eyes slitted against the brightness, tries to focus on the couple in the dunes, nestling amongst the clumps of wispy sea grass, unaware they are being spied upon, again.

A child's laughter drags his gaze to the remnants of a picnic at the edge of the surf. The toddler on a rug throws a soft toy into the air, gurgling as it falls to the sand.

The watcher looks back to the dune, concerned they have abandoned the child, but all he sees is the sea grass stirring as the wind picks up and the sturdy gorse starts to shiver.

Quickly the skies thicken and ropes of charcoal grey choke away the sun as anxious waves swirl and bounce towards the child.

The infant calls out.

The watcher glances left and right, but no one comes.

The child cries loudly now, frightened.

A small dog runs across the sand, alarmed by the cries, and barks, weaving frantically back and forth as the little one wails. It has started to rain, large wet drops of dark water push along the beach in the wind.

A woman appears and racing to the shore takes the child in her arms, wrapping it beneath her coat. She pulls up her collar against the squall and strides off, the little dog at her heels.

The watcher, satisfied the child is safe, crawls out from his hiding place and runs to the spot. The beach is deserted, save for the wind and the rain. At the abandoned picnic, a lone shoe remains, a pretty one, and beside it a doll. A rag doll in the form of a mermaid, her corkscrew hair half-buried in the sand. Taking up the treasure, he stuffs it under his sodden tee-shirt and starts for home. No need to run, he is wet through anyway and will not have been missed.

Minutes later the tide spills angrily along the shore and the pile of clothes, smeared with seaweed and sand, is dragged out to sea.

The men at the nets have stopped working; one of them holds a shoe in his hand, a woman's shoe. Barely giving it a glance, the captain throws it back overboard. He has overheard the young sailor say his wife had shoes like it. Bad luck, women and boats, and they've had enough bad luck. The hold is half-empty, he will barely be able to pay for the fuel let alone the men's wages, and now the weather looks grim.

He refuses to return without a decent catch, sick and tired of being the laughingstock of the harbour. Some said he was not even a proper captain, having won the boat in a card game. He will show them. He orders the helmsman to take them further out, the men looking silently on as he stomps back to the bridge.

The young sailor, distracted with worry, has no choice but to carry on, pray the hold will soon be full and they can motor back as fast as this old tug can go. The sooner the new hotel opens in the town, and he can secure himself a proper job, the better.

He hates the sea, always has.

Nana Morgan is sorting shells with her little granddaughters. The telephone rings.

"Will you get that?" she calls to the young woman at the range.

"It's Mrs Fitzgerald," the young woman says urgently.

"I thought the line might be down with the storm." The voice crackles.

"It's wild up here, alright, they've forecast a bad one."

Nana stops; she hears an infant crying. "What's that?"

"I have the little one, she's alright. I found her on the beach."

Catfish Surprise

W exford, Ireland 2018

Sliding around the building like a shadow, she tried the door. Of course, she knew where the key was kept, but it was high season and with so many people coming and going the side entrance was rarely locked.

Unless things had changed.

Sometimes she hoped they had and yet whenever she did think of here, this place, this house, she prayed it had not. Not that she even prayed anymore, maybe something else she could try again.

The door creaked as it opened. Unusual. This place was always immaculately maintained, five-star in everything but name. A little old-fashioned perhaps but regulars liked that, the familiarity of the well-worn and beloved, newcomers only returning if they fully appreciated the understated elegance, and of course its endearing eccentricities, of which there were many. But she was no newcomer, far from it.

Looking along the corridor, she saw the faded opulence of the Persian runners stretched out before her contrasted gaily against the pale stone flags scuffed and worn, the tread marks of hundreds of years of footsteps. A cool sun threw shadows on the floor.

Still no one.

She glanced at the windows, smeared with sand blown up from the beach. Odd. Everything here always sparkled, regimented polishing taking place early in the morning, especially if the forecast was fair. It had been fair for some time. A good summer.

Built on the very edge of the cliff, this side of the house did not proffer the best view of the harbour or the island, but the sheer drop to the waves evoked a sense of adventure, danger even, as the land fell away beyond each window and guests would walk the length of the corridor in silent awe – especially when the wind was wild, the sea boisterous.

Not today, today was calm. Well, the sea was at least. But she had not yet been seen, and calm was not the reaction she expected to her unannounced arrival.

At the end of the corridor the kitchen door was ajar, so she peered in. The long, polished table stood in the middle of the room. The old cream range at the far end. Two dog beds.

Odd, there was no smell of cooking, no cauldron of soup on the hob or haunch of ham resting on the side. Although the tray of dirty dishes by the sink and pile of linen in the ironing basket gave indication of some human habitation.

Still no one.

Reversing quickly, she was through the door and out in seconds. She started to run, heart beating hard, stumbling down the grassy slope towards the lower gate, calling over and over …

"Cassandra! Cassandra, where are you? Cassandra! Cassandra!"

She threw open the gate, shielding watery eyes against the dull gleam of sea and sky; eyes stayed too long in the city. She looked down towards the beach, a stretch of rocks far below and a slim strip of shale, like a ribbon of silk at its edge, tide pulsing against the shore.

Still no one.

Stepping gingerly now, she started down the cliff walk, a narrow staircase hewn from rock until, familiar with the twists and turns, she abandoned her shoes and took off, scouring the beach as she ran. Until she spotted a lone figure crouched at the water's edge, a woman, wrapped in what looked like a sail, long golden-brown hair falling about her face.

There she was! And leaping from the steps, she waved as the figure stood.

"Look! Look! It's me!"

The woman dragged hair from her eyes, straightening herself. She jangled as she stood, patting the large patch pockets of her sailcloth jacket, weighted and full, and turning at the voice she ran, arms outstretched.

"Greer, Greer, it's me too!"

They flew into one another's arms, hugging as tightly as they could. Then laughing, the same bubbling laugh, ricocheting loudly off the rocks all around. The incomer took a step back to look at the other woman as the laughter died away.

"Orla, it's you? I thought it was Cass, but it's you!"

The woman called Orla furrowed her brow.

"Sure, why wouldn't it be me? I'm not Cassandra, I'm me!" Tears brimmed. Greer leapt forward with a fresh embrace.

"Oh, I so wanted it to be you! Look, look!" She took her sister's chin in her hand and lifted her face to meet her eyes. She widened them making them sparkle, then lowered her lids to gaze through the slits. "Catfish eyes!" she said to Orla. "I'm catfish surprised!"

Orla immediately pulled the same face back.

"Catfish!" she said, grinning because Greer had used their special greeting, tears blinked away. "Tea? Shall we have tea?"

Greer took her sister's hand. It was cold and wet, but Orla rarely noticed such things, not until she was about to pass out with hypothermia anyway. One of the reasons Orla had to be minded. Always.

"Yes, tea, and you can tell me where Cass is. Did she have to go out today?"

Orla nodded, then shook her head.

"No, she's back today and so are you. Both my sisters back."

Greer linked Orla's arm as they strode along the vanishing sand towards the stone steps and the winding climb up.

"Where's she been?"

Orla looked out to sea.

"No, I mean Cassandra, where has Cass been?"

"At the place that fixes things."

Greer frowned. That could be any number of places.

"In Rosshaven?"

"No, not Rosshaven, the one in Dublin, the one for big things."

Greer stopped, finding it hard to breathe.

"Big things?"

"Yes, things they can't fix here, she took the old girl with her." Orla frowned at her sister, hands tightened into white snowballs of flesh. "You must have known to come?"

"I did of course," Greer assured her.

"You're very late." Orla gave another frown.

"Am I?"

"By a few years, I believe."

"Yes. I probably am. Well, you're pleased to see me anyway," Greer said, relieved.

"She keeps saying she's forgotten what you look like. How can she forget, there's pictures of you all over the place?" Orla gave one of her breathtaking smiles. "I'm sure she'll remember you when she sees you."

They were halfway up, and Greer had to stop, she was holding her side, trying to squeeze the stitch away.

"Yoo hoo!" A call from above. "Hello, down there!"

"Come on, Greer, she's home." Orla dropped her hand and took off like a mountain goat, skipping up the steps.

"Right behind you," Greer said flatly.

She gazed back towards the beach. Not too late to change her mind, she could make a run for it right now. And forcing herself to look up, she saw there was no one there; Orla had disappeared, and Cassandra had returned.

Greer pushed back a wave of nausea as she reached the last step. She had no choice but to face the music, again.

There was already a change about the place, lamps lit, curtains drawn. A fug from the kettle hanging in the air, tea brewing in the pot. She tried to slip in, but the top half of the door was unlatched and the breeze following her up from the shore caught it, slamming it shut.

"Make an entrance why don't you?" her eldest sister said, watching Greer's reflection in the mirror as she stood at the far end of the room.

"Sorry, I didn't mean …"

Her sister swung round to face her.

"Sorry you didn't mean to let the door slam and shake the place to its very foundations! Or sorry you've been away for nearly three years and hardly a word?!"

Greer froze, eyes widened.

"Catfish eyes again," Orla whispered to a blond puppy squirming in her embrace.

Cassandra strode the length of the kitchen, the scowling frown transformed to a broad grin making her eyes glint.

"That'll teach you to turn up unannounced!" She clasped her sibling to her. Greer returned the embrace warily; Cassandra could be difficult to gauge.

"I didn't know I was coming."

"That makes three of us!" Cassandra said.

"Two," Orla piped up. "I knew, I just didn't say." They looked at her. "The shells told me, day before yesterday." Her sisters exchanged a glance. "Anyway, Greer doesn't need to be announced, this is her home too, you're always saying so."

Cassandra turned to Greer. "It's so good to see you." Greer looked at Cassandra, something in her tone. "Now, tea? Then food. Are you starving? I bet you're starving. I know I am." And it was gone. "What's left in the fridge, Orla?"

"Half of last night's lasagne and some salad. I didn't have the crumble. I had Rice Krispies instead, that way when I woke up, I'd already had my breakfast."

Greer glanced at Cassandra as she fetched the milk, the

tension in her shoulders easing slightly. She put the bottle on the table. "Whose puppy is that?" She took the wriggling beast from Orla.

"It's Wolfe. Our new baby," Orla told her. They always had two dogs – one called Wolfe, the other Tone – so when one dog remained after a bereavement, its new companion was given the predecessor's name. That way the loss was not too severely felt, a scheme their grandmother had dreamt up for Orla, finding it suited them all.

Cassandra was decanting the milk into a jug.

"When I heard this fella needed a home, I picked him up on the way back."

Greer glanced at Cassandra. "But two empty beds?"

"Tone's with the Nagles, back tomorrow. I bet he's already excited about his new baby brother." Orla stroked the puppy's head distractedly. "Now, I must go and check the shells." She patted her large pockets, making them chink.

"Do, but only twenty minutes, then wash your hands and come in for supper. And don't tell me you had two lunches, so you don't need your meal. I want you at the table with your sister. We can at least try to be a little more civilised now Greer's back from the big city, once again."

Orla smiled and gave Greer's cheek a stroke as she left, closing the door softly behind her.

Sitting in the large wing-backed chair at the head of the table, Cassandra stirred her tea.

"No guests?" Greer asked.

"Not many. I managed a gap in bookings so I could arrange the appointment. Bríd's not too well, Nagle's pulled out of the place with harvest, and I thought Orla could manage for one day and night without me. Fudge was here, of course."

"That's a relief, the place seems deserted," Greer said. Bríd and Fudge, a now elderly couple, had been stalwarts at Manorcliff for as long as she could remember. Bríd and Cassandra shared the cooking, with Bríd managing the housekeeping team, Fudge in charge of maintenance, deliveries, the grounds, and everything else besides. "What's wrong with Bríd?"

"Nothing for you to worry about." Teal-grey eyes gazed unblinking, as Greer buried her nose in the velvet space between the puppy's ears. "What's the story?"

"Why can't anyone bottle this, it's the most delicious scent in the world."

"It is, I agree. But you're avoiding the question, as usual. So, I'll ask again, what's the story?"

"No story, just thought it was time I came."

Cassandra took a deep sip of her tea. Strong, how she liked it.

"Well, you've missed my birthday party."

"Party?"

"Yes, the one you were coming to three years ago."

"Ah …" Greer looked sheepish. "It wasn't a big one though, was it?"

"Every birthday's a big one once you hit fifty, you should know that now, having recently joined the club yourself." Cassandra gave Greer a sweeping look. "The decision to travel was sudden, I can tell that much." Greer was wearing a smart suit, silk shirt and tights, now shredded at the heels. "Still, there's plenty in your wardrobe if you're staying awhile."

"You haven't had one of your famous 'sort-outs' then?"

"To be honest the whole lot is only days from being sent to St Vincent de Paul but with the old dog ill my routine's upset."

This was a rare admission for her eldest sister. Greer watched as she pushed a strand of reddish hair streaked with grey back into place, fingernails unpolished. She also noticed the large, flat ruby ring was missing.

"Orla said you were in Dublin at the 'place that fixes things'. I wondered …?"

"Last resort, I'm afraid, had to see if anything could be done."

"Oh, Cass, how bad is it?" Greer reached out.

"They had to put her to sleep in the end. Loved that ole yoke." She gave the puppy nestling in Greer's arms a soft smile.

"Ah, Cass." Greer passed her a tissue from the box. "The veterinary hospital – for big things – I see now, Orla didn't quite explain …"

"That's why I collected that little fella on the way back, didn't want her too upset. Remember when we lost the last one, she went missing all night and the next day."

"I do, one of the lads at his lobster pots found her, asleep in the boat out beyond the harbour."

"Luckily it was wedged in the rocks near the caves, any later though and the tide would have swept her out to sea." Cassandra blew her nose, and going to the shelf beside the range took down a bottle of whiskey. Greer noticed she was thinner, the moleskin jeans baggy beneath her gilet.

Returning to the table she poured two tots. Greer splashed water from a jug into the glasses. They chinked, said *sláinte* and drank, a shared sigh as they put the glasses down.

"I thought it was you who needed to be in the place for 'fixing things'," Greer admitted, looking away, not wanting Cassandra to see her fear.

"Did you now?" Cassandra poured more drinks. "And I thought you were over in London living the dream, isn't that what they call it?"

"Did you now?" Greer's sea-green eyes shone back at her sister.

"Well, that's what the last 'news bulletin' led me to believe." Cassandra had pronounced Greer's infrequent correspondence 'news bulletins' years ago. She sat back in the armchair, crossing her legs. "Mind you, you haven't written in ages, not even a card."

"I *have* called, a few times."

"Left a message, is all."

"That's what people do, leave a message, it's customary to return the call." Greer pulled a face, an exaggerated downturn of the mouth. Cassandra pulled the same face back.

Suddenly Greer stood, handing Cassandra the sleepy-eyed pup. "I have to go."

"Something I said?"

"No, he's just peed all over my skirt."

Cassandra let out a big burst of a laugh. "Wolfe, where are your manners? We'll have to train you not to piddle on the guests."

"Family's okay though, I suppose," Greer replied, draining her glass before she left.

Bag Lady

Pulling the large oak door behind her, Greer closed her eyes for the count of ten, until opening them she could feast on one of the most wonderful sights in the world; her room. It was a ritual she had practised since the first time she had been sent away, aged only eight.

The sight of it filled her heart with joy and relief in equal measure, for this was her safe place, her sanctuary. And as ever, nothing had been moved or even touched. She could tell by the film of dust on the chest of drawers, the table before the window joined to the wall by a shiver of lacy cobweb and a book upended, left open at the very page she had last read. All was well, here at least.

Drawing back the coverlet, she saw that the bed was just as she left it. Vintage eiderdown on top, soft lawn pyjamas neatly folded beside pillows edged in satin. It looked so welcoming she was sorely tempted to just slide beneath those smooth, cool sheets.

Opening the vast wardrobe door she placed the coverlet on a shelf, relieved to find her 'home' clothes hanging there as they always had. Tweed jackets and thick knits, next to silk shirts and velvet jeans, alongside linen dresses, and cropped pants. The essential layers of the indomitable shore-side resident.

Pulling off her 'dog pee' skirt and casting aside the smart city shirt, she noticed her luggage had been brought up. *Typical Cassandra*, she thought, treating her like a guest, making a point.

Taking the travel documents from her bag, she put them

beside the jewellery purse in the drawer and as she did the 'emergency' dollars slipped from her passport. Here was not quite the destination she had planned. Checking her phone, she exclaimed, cursing softly. It was completely dead and as she put it on charge, changed quickly.

She was just wondering what to do about the other bag – a large lightweight suitcase bearing a designer label – *so like him* – when she heard a muted knock.

"It's your sister," called Orla.

Greer quickly pushed the suitcase under the bed and opened the door.

"I picked out the best of the shells but no messages today." Orla wore a sad smile.

"Maybe I'm today's message?" Greer replied, pulling down the valance, luggage out of sight.

"I didn't think of that, of course you are, you and Wolfe." Orla's smile instantly transformed her soulful face. "Cass has made your favourite, sausage and potato cakes. I think she knew you were coming too, just didn't say."

"What about the lasagne, I thought that was on the menu?"

"Wolfe's having that. He loves Italian. You'll have to make do with the sausages." Orla gave Greer a steely look. People, even prodigal sisters, came second place to puppies.

Greer was helping Orla lay the table, a time-honoured tradition of larking about, putting things haphazardly and blaming each other, giggling as they jarred elbows.

"Don't smash any of the good stuff," Cassandra used to say. "The paying guests want to know we're a cut above, only drop the 'Green Shield'." And Orla would deliberately seek out a piece of delph from the 'Green Shield' catalogue of days gone by to drop on the smooth, pale tiles, making the other two shriek. But there was no 'Green Shield' left and Orla had learned where everything went, so the fun had gone out of it.

Noticing how efficient her sister had become at table-laying, Greer started spinning a plate on the tip of her finger, an old trick.

"I'm a professional hotelier now, Greer," Orla said, laughing, lifting a plate to emulate her sister. "I try not to drop things. Still do, though!" She put the plate gently down. Cassandra would usually admonish them from her default position at the range but tonight she was quiet.

"How many for supper?" Greer asked. Friday evening suppers, 'Changeover Day' as it was known, were always taken in the large farmhouse kitchen.

"Not sure." Cass held her spatula aloft, pointing at the chairs. "Mr and Mrs Montrose were here when I left but might not stay, and Dr James was due in yesterday but if he came Orla forgot to sign him in. And Mrs Crowther and Frances were due to leave but there'd been a mix up, something to do with Frances' job and there was no need to rush back at all. So, as it stands, I've no idea who's staying or going, just hope I've made enough, and sure what's left over we can freeze."

Greer, totting up potentially eight mouths to feed, continued laying the table. Orla, now bored, put out fresh dog bowls, although some might consider the napkins beside them ambitious, Greer mused, smiling. The peat smoke was making her eyes itch, and noticing two aged armchairs pulled close to the hearth, she went to open a window.

"Don't tell me these are for the spaniels?" she asked. Orla was plumping cushions.

"Don't be ridiculous, Greer," Orla scolded. "They're for Mr and Mrs Montrose of course. You remember them, owned a big shop in Dublin, well they did until it went bust. Isn't that right, Cass?"

"I wouldn't repeat that if I were you, Orla, we don't know. Mr Montrose could have sold the business and just retired."

"Oh yes," Orla agreed. "Mr Montrose retired, now I remember. He's having a few years' rest, coming here and being grumpy instead of being grumpy at home."

Cassandra gave Orla a look of reproach.

"Well, that's what Mrs Montrose told me," Orla said, half-laughing. "But he doesn't look too well," she hissed at Greer.

"Orla, how many times must I tell you … please don't talk about the guests and besides he just looks a bit older, that's all," Cassandra grumbled. "Now let it drop!"

"It's dropped," Orla replied, shrugging her shoulders.

By the time the appointed hour for the meal arrived only the sisters and the puppy were present. Greer had gone to check the rooms, finding them in various states of disarray, concluding the Montroses had left, Dr James had not yet arrived, and Frances and her formidable mother had also decided to depart, although they had left their room immaculate. Which was more than could be said for the Montroses who, boisterous as ever, had left bottles on every surface and garments mixed with towels in the bathroom.

"No sign of anyone," Greer reported. "No cars here, either."

Cassandra glanced at the clock, a large cream face encased in veined onyx on a shelf. It was just after half-seven.

"I'll serve so," she announced as Greer brought an already open bottle from the fridge and Orla filled a large crystal jug with water and ice.

Cassandra laid the dishes in the centre of the table. The food smelled delicious, local sausages in dark onion gravy, deep potato cakes browned to perfection and a dish of vegetables fresh from the garden, the last of the peas and sweet baby carrots.

Greer was ravenous, having not eaten since the day before, and noticing she had forgotten serving spoons, went to the drawer.

"Have you moved the silver?" she asked, finding only a mismatch of utensils where the good cutlery usually lived.

"Use what's there," Cassandra replied, sharing out the wine and filling Orla's glass with water. "Your room okay? Everything as you like it?"

Greer nodded, mouth full of food.

"That's a large suitcase you brought, must be staying a while?"

"There was no need to take my bags up, Cass, it's not as if I'm a paying guest."

"No bother." Cassandra sliced a potato cake in half, dousing the fluffy white innards in the gravy. "I recognised the holdall and guessed the big case was yours too. Wasn't sure if you had a man with you though?"

Greer's eyes stayed fixed on her plate. "What makes you say that?"

"Looked a bit mannish for you and your stuff usually matches." Cassandra was still slicing her food.

"I'm not fussed about things like that these days, rather pack a few extra books and a big jumper, you know me."

"I do," Cassandra confirmed, finally placing a sliver of sausage between her slightly smiling lips.

"Have you been long on the road?" Orla asked.

"Left the apartment around six this morning."

"Long time for so short a journey," Cassandra observed. "You'd not long arrived when I got back, was your flight delayed?"

"You could say that." Greer helped herself to more sausages.

"But could *you*?" Orla pressed.

Cassandra shook her head at her. "Greer's tired, love, we'll talk tomorrow, sometimes when a journey's been fraught it's best to forget about it until after a good night's sleep, isn't that right, Greer?"

"You're right, Cass. That was delicious, but it's been a long week." Greer stood, abandoning her meal. "I'll take myself up. I'm no company and can barely keep my eyes open."

"Of course, off you go." Cassandra lifted her face to receive Greer's goodnight kiss, and she stroked Orla's head as she left.

Checking the door was closed, Orla brought the puppy back to the table to sit on her lap.

"Didn't think Greer looked too well either but didn't

comment, I wouldn't want to upset her," she told Cassandra, feeding the dog Greer's sausages.

"Don't make him sick," Cassandra warned, taking the plate away. "He's only a baby, this food's too rich for him." She had already swopped Orla's generous portion of lasagne for puppy food in the dog's bowl.

"She didn't even drink her wine," Orla noted, reaching over for the glass. Cassandra took it from her.

"Probably just tired." Cassandra frowned. She could not quite put her finger on it, but something in Greer's eyes made her think of a surprised deer; anxious, ready to flee. She shook her head, dispelling the image. "We'll put that back in the bottle, save it for tomorrow."

"Will she be here tomorrow?"

"I hope so, she's staying for a while if the size of her bag's anything to go by."

"Could be anything in that," Orla mused. "I watched a film once and a fella had a dead body in his suitcase. Chopped up. Sent it to Scotland on the train."

"I've told you not to watch those sorts of programmes, Orla. Gives you nightmares. Anyway, I'm sure there isn't a dead body in Greer's bag. Just books and big jumpers."

"Well, something's dead. I heard her say something's 'dead' and being upset."

"Did you?" Cassandra stopped at the sink. She turned slowly to gaze at Orla.

"I think she was talking about her phone. That's what was dead," Orla confirmed.

Cassandra gave her sibling a look. "I don't think we need to make things any more dramatic than they already are, do you? We'll let Greer do that all by herself ... as usual."

Orla decided not to comment, feeding the puppy another sausage despite her sister's warning.

Stranger on the Shore

Greer had not slept well, her unconscious mind jangling. Sometimes she woke with the sound of her heart beating hard in her chest, heat burning along her throat, or else she felt cold, as if all the warmth in her had drained away, leaving her fingers bloodless and icy.

Finally sliding out of bed she dressed hurriedly, and slipping the phone into the pocket of her aged sailing jacket, pulled on an old pair of boots to head down to the beach.

Tiptoeing past the kitchen door, she spied Orla and the puppy fast asleep in the winged chair, the fire long since turned to ash. She gazed at her sibling's pretty face; although older than her, Orla looked so youthful in repose, untroubled as she slumbered, nestled with the little dog, safe and content. Greer felt a pang of envy at her peacefulness, as turning the key, she dipped out through the side entrance and was once more on the path leading to the granite steps.

First light was streaking a pale grey crack across the horizon, the tide out and a gunmetal sea glimmered in the distance. She shivered, and pushing back her hood bent to claw up a fistful of seaweed, holding it to her nostrils, capturing the scent.

Greer closed her eyes; grounded at last.

Home.

All would be well.

Letting her catch fall, she wiped her hands on her jeans and looked out across the sand flats, the sea just a shadow beneath the charcoal sky. Even the land looked grey, the rock face behind, the sweep of bay rising to a meander of hills, fields like folds of silver silk; all still, waiting for the morning to move on.

She remembered days like this. Here on this very spot. The low cloud melding sea and sky. A sullen sadness clinging like a shroud. Her mind full of the same unanswered questions, asked whenever she returned, at whatever age. Still unanswered, still the silence. Still.

She looked back at the hotel, barely visible; she always thought mist suited it, a mysterious protective shield, keeping the sisters and their secrets safe.

High on a promontory south of Rosshaven harbour, Manorcliff had been a hotel for many years. Built by their great-grandfather in the mid-1800s, the original family home – a Georgian farmhouse – had been absorbed into a fine Victorian structure, a long three-storey building with an impressive plaza terrace at one end and a glazed ironwork turret on the other.

The turret, accessed via a twisting staircase, led to a steel-framed globe of glass, giving a panoramic view of the harbour and fields beyond. Known as the Moon Room, it was home to one of the first astronomical telescopes in the country and a fascinating architectural quirk which many considered as strange and eccentric as the family who had lived there these many years.

The house had four staircases. As one entered through the large double-doors into the broad stone-flagged hall, one staircase swept up to the left with an identical staircase sweeping down to the right, with doors leading to the cliff-side of the house positioned in between. The third staircase, 'backstairs' ran from behind the kitchen and the fourth, she could just see jutting over the cliff edge, led to the Moon Room, another mysterious unanswered question.

Greer gave herself a shake, dragging her mind back to the here and now; this was not the time to dwell on the past, she had quite enough present-day scenarios to worry about.

Pulling out her phone, she checked again. How many

times had she called? Leaving at first polite businesslike messages. Where was he? He was late, he would miss his appointment.

Then more urgent. *The flight has left.* She checked with the desk, the tickets were transferable, the next flight could accommodate them. *Please confirm you're on your way.* She phoned his business mobile, personal mobile, office landline. Scrolling through numbers, she even called his home. No one picked up and she dared not leave a message, even though they had worked together for years.

Because yesterday was different. *Would* have been different.

Life-changing if they had gone through with it.

But he had not kept his side of the bargain and as realisation dawned, she knew, had known all along, he had let her down, again. And as another flight left for New York with two empty Business Class seats, she wheeled the bags to the Aer Lingus desk and took the next plane home.

All the glamorous, exotic, far-flung destinations in the world glowing enticingly from the Departures Board and she plumped for Dublin. So much for her much-lauded sense of adventure. She ran home. To what?

Greyness.

A humongous heap of grey.

Hands in pockets, she started along the beach. Alone. Not even a solitary gull had braved this dull dawn. The sand stuck to the soles of her boots in clumps as she walked. A bark some distance away startled her. She looked up. A dog ran over the dunes. It stopped. A man appeared, raising his arm. Greer waved back, no idea who it was. Yet the dog recognised her, and twirling in a circle of joy, bounded along the beach.

"Tone! Tone!" she called, running towards the beast. He leapt and as she caught him, her foot struck a rock and she fell backwards onto the shore, laughing as Tone, desperate to lick her face in welcome, wriggled wildly in her arms.

"I thought it was you!" The man was upon them. He

reached out, hauling her up.

"Quiet, Tone, that's enough," she told the spaniel, rubbing the space between his ears roughly, his liquid brown eyes alight with joy.

"What's this? A surprise visit? You haven't been home in a long time."

She slid him a look. "Don't you start!"

"Just saying." He shrugged. "At least Tone's pleased to see you."

Greer laughed. The big burst of laugh he had always loved. "One of the few."

"Well, you can count me in." He smiled, shoving his arm through hers, turning her towards the cliff. "Never a dull moment when you're around. And it's been pretty tedious around here, I can tell you."

"How long have *you* been back?" she asked, seeking out sparkling eyes hiding behind his classic shades; old habits die hard.

"Long enough to run into you again, you little minx." He leant in to kiss her cheek. She squeezed his arm in response. "Here we are." He stood at the foot of the steps as Tone bounced upwards.

"Not coming in?" Greer saw him step back.

"Not quite made my peace with Cassandra."

"Still?" Then changing the subject, she said, "I thought the Nagles were minding Tone?" The dog stood gazing back, tail wagging.

"They were. I called in to see the big fella but some of the herd had escaped in the night, he had his hands full. I was walking this way, so I offered to drop Tone back."

"Were you going to slip in through the side entrance and materialise in the Moon Room?" Greer gave him a knowing look. "You can still perform that trick, I suppose?"

"Don't be cheeky." He laughed, jumping down from the step to stride towards the sea. "Best you don't mention you ran into me though, all the same."

"T'was ever thus," Greer quoted, watching him go.

Archie Fitzgerald, an old family friend. Familiar and favoured, like so much here. He still looked good for his age, she thought, even though that Rolling Stones tee-shirt was long overdue a replacement.

The phone in her pocket pulsed to life. *At last.* She drew it out, staring at the screen.

ID Withheld.

It was the first call she had had since she left.

"Hello? Is that Greer Morgan, project manager, McKeiver Properties?"

"Yes, yes this is Greer."

"Greer, it's Amy, Alistair's wife."

Greer recognised the voice. Amy was a well-known broadcaster, top-flight journalist, hard as nails. In all the years she had worked with Alistair she had rarely spoken to Mrs McKeiver, as Alistair kept his business and home life separate, very separate indeed.

"Is there something wrong?" Greer kept her voice steady, dread beginning to take hold.

"It's Alistair. Thought it best I call."

Greer's ears started to fill with noise, Mrs McKeiver's voice drowned out.

"What's happened?"

"Some sort of seizure. A heart attack, they think."

"Is he in hospital?"

"Yes, intensive care."

"He's going to be okay, isn't he?"

"It's early days." She heard the other woman's breath shudder. "I wanted you to hear it from me."

Greer closed her eyes; she tried to speak but no words came.

This could not be happening. She felt the axis of the earth tilt.

"You'll be written to, all employees will receive formal notification," Mrs McKeiver said coldly. "Things are in hand;

I'm taking care of everything from here on in. Just letting you know where we stand."

"But …" Greer stuttered.

"A lot to take in. Such a shock for everyone." Greer heard the other woman sigh. "Greer, it's best you don't make contact. I'm asking, no telling you *not* to get in touch. Whatever the outcome, we're going to work through this as a family. And now I must go, Alistair needs me."

The call ended. A line had been drawn.

And in a searing flash Greer realised Amy knew, had always known and the future she had imagined was just that, imagined. Amy had taken control, taken him back.

Poor Alistair.

Poor Greer.

In Hot Water

B ack in her room, Greer could barely think. Halfway up the steps she had forgiven him for not letting her down, horrified at what had happened. Two seconds later she wanted to kill him for disappearing from her life on the very day he had promised her a future.

Turning the tap of the ancient roll-top bath Greer started to shake, so violently her teeth rattled in her mouth. She wanted to laugh. Did things like this really happen? This was soap opera, surely? She pulled on an old sweater, trying to stifle her juddering mouth. Come to think of it, this episode, indeed sometimes her whole life, felt like some sort of crappy soap opera.

Trembling, she dragged on tracksuit bottoms, socks, a shower cap. Bloody hell, had she contracted some sort of tropical disease?

She leaned over the hand basin and retched. A ribbon of spittle trailed from her mouth to the bowl. She retched again, the vivid yellow streaking the porcelain. Now there would be trouble, Cassandra was fastidious about bathrooms.

Where was that howling coming from? A weird noise echoed all about her, the wail bouncing off the tiled walls. Sounded like a creature on the edge of oblivion.

Two figures stood by the bath. One turned off the tap, the other proffered a towel, the howling stopped at precisely the same time she closed her mouth. *Fascinating.*

Suddenly very cold, she saw she was fully dressed, lying in a bath of icy water.

"Bath time over," Cassandra said gently.

"Out and into a nice warm bed," Orla interjected. "And soup, creamy chicken soup, the saviour of all things."

Greer tried to speak.

"Shush!" Cassandra took her sopping clothes. "No talking. Not today."

Her sisters towelled her dry, pyjamas and socks on, a turban of sorts wrapped around her head, and without noticing, she had been removed from the bathroom as the glorious bed with the paisley eiderdown stood welcoming before her. She climbed in, hands covered her in bedclothes, pulling everything up to her ears and over her feet. She was safe now, cocooned.

Greer opened her eyes. Cassandra was sitting on the bed with a tray, and the smell of soup made her want to vomit again.

"Here, drink this." She put a glass to her lips.

"What happened?" Greer was bemused. Had she been struck by a car? Spent weeks in a coma?

"You've had a shock, that's all. The tiredness of the journey, bad news coming out of the blue like that. A nasty shock. Now, try to take a sup of this, we'll mind you."

And for once in her life, Greer did exactly as her sister told her. Lying back, sipping soup, as tears, stupid, inexplicable tears dripped from her eyes, running down her cheeks like rain.

"It's Alistair," she said finally, large unblinking eyes dark.

"We know, love. We're here, here with you now." Cassandra pushed Greer's hair back. "You're warm and safe, just need to sleep."

Orla took Greer's hand and feeling her pain started to weep, rocking slowly in the chair beside the bed, never taking her eyes from Greer's grey face.

"He's lost to me now," Greer whispered in the smallest voice, turning her mouth from the spoon proffered. Cassandra widened her eyes at Orla.

Orla shrugged. "Alistair, I don't know about him. The

shells never mentioned him, can't be up to much."

"You know who Alistair is, Orla. He's Greer's boss," Cassandra hissed.

"I thought Greer's boss was that 'feckin' eejit who worked for the British government'?" Orla recited Cassandra's description whenever Alistair's name was mentioned.

Cassandra sighed. "Need you to be sensible today, please, Orla."

"She's very upset over an eejit," Orla confirmed.

Greer opened her eyes. "Cass, not sure if we have guests but we've no hot water," she said sleepily.

"You have to use the tap with the H on it," Cassandra reminded her, as she drifted into oblivion.

Hours later Greer emerged from her room dishevelled, dehydrated and sick with hunger. She needed nourishment, maybe that meant something, maybe she still had the will, maybe …but all she felt right now was sick and tired, so very tired.

Stepping into the main landing that ran the length of the house, she nearly fell over a mound of fur just outside her door. A feathery tail gave a couple of thumps, eyes opened, ears pricked.

"Hello, Tone," she said hoarsely. "What time is it?"

The spaniel tilted his head, knowing he had been asked a question. She slid down beside him. He wriggled towards her, pushing his cold nose into her hand, and warm eyes looked up, the expression of pure love surprising her. Greer wrapped her arms around him, rubbing her cheek against his smooth domed head.

"Thanks," she said, tears rising again. The dog looked unblinking at his favourite sister. Where else would he be when he was needed?

Greer lifted her chin. "Is that bacon?" Tone smelt it too. He squirmed free, trotting away, then stopped, ensuring she followed. "Breakfast," she confirmed and Tone twirled in joyful affirmation before cantering off towards the stairs. There would be a reward for this latest retrieve, he was pretty sure of that.

Surprised to find the door to the dining room locked, Greer stopped but Tone was already making his way to the kitchen.

As they entered Greer sensed all eyes on her, but too hungry to care took the nearest seat gratefully; it had been a long walk from her room to the table. As she ate the rashers with her fingers, Cassandra appeared and wiping her hands with a napkin, signalled Orla fetch a knife and fork. After a couple of swallows of food, Greer gazed about her.

Dr James Butler sat opposite, a regular guest, newly arrived. To his left their neighbour and childhood friend Nagle, known as the 'big fella' for obvious reasons, and at the far end Mr and Mrs Montrose who had either never left or just returned. They were all trying not to stare, even Nagle who had witnessed many unusual Greer Morgan ensembles over the years.

Greer gave him a quizzical look. He indicated scrambled egg on her chin. She wiped it away. He pointed discreetly at her head; she still wore the makeshift turban. She whipped it off. And finally, he tugged at his collar. Greer put her hand to her throat. Tissue paper. She remembered winding toilet roll around her neck to absorb the uncontrollable leakage from her eyes. The song 'Cry Me A River' popped into her head, the Alison Moyet version she had covered with the band.

She shrugged. The loo roll could stay, besides, she had no energy to tear it off. Orla fetched a scarf from the coat rack, placing it gently around her sister's throat as she ate.

"Fresh coffee, anyone? I'm just at the pot," Cassandra said breezily.

"Will we be taking the boat out?" Nagle started up a conversation with the doctor. Mr Montrose lifted his paper.

"I'd love some coffee, Cass." Mrs Montrose took her cup to the range. "A bit of a head this morning, I'm sure that ginger ale in the Shipwrights has too many chemicals in it."

"Not all the brandy that went with it then?" Mr Montrose growled.

The bustle and banter of breakfast resumed, until under the hubbub they heard a strange, repetitive squawk. Orla stopped buttering toast. It grew louder.

Greer was laughing, shoulders heaving, chin buried in her chest as she chortled uncontrollably.

"Not ... the ... brandy!" She wagged a finger at Mrs Montrose.

Cassandra crossed the room, taking her sister by the arm. "A good rest, that's what's needed."

Orla watched Dr James close the door quietly behind them.

"Overworked, like yourself," she said to him.

"Hasn't her boss just had a heart attack? Wasn't there something on the news?" Mrs Montrose asked. Orla did not answer. She could not remember whether she could discuss this with guests or not. Cassandra was extremely strict about keeping their personal business private.

"Must be very close to be so upset," Mr Montrose concluded, dropping the newsprint to glance at his wife.

"I think people often underestimate how close work colleagues can be," Dr James said, taking the toast rack to Orla. "We often spend more time with colleagues than we do with our own families."

Orla gave him a grateful smile, busying herself with the bread. Paying guests were paying guests after all, and disturbing the ritual of breakfast at Manorcliff was nothing short of a cardinal sin. *Greer must be terribly upset, alright. Or worse. She might be going back to the dark place.* The place where it was very hard to find her.

"She'll be fine," Dr James said reassuringly. But Orla was not so sure.

The sun had burned away the early twist of mist, the sea

glimmering murky teal under a clearing sky by the time Greer remerged from her room, showered and by now more appropriately attired.

Tone, sleeping outside her door, roused himself. The heat of the sun through the window and a full stomach of leftovers had prompted a mid-morning slumber. He was enjoying the peace; there was a particularly annoying youngster in the kitchen and as patient as he was, a good nip in the right place was on the cards if the pup was still there when he deigned to descend.

"Come on," Greer ordered, and Tone's decision made, he took off bouncing down the right-hand staircase.

Avoiding the kitchen, Greer strode along the cliff-side corridor, only to find Cassandra rubbing vigorously at a window. She slowed her pace; her sister was perched precariously on a ledge. She waved. Cassandra dropped the window down.

"You look a bit better." Cassandra was brusque. Despite being concerned about her youngest sibling, the episode at breakfast had been excruciating.

Manorcliff, one of the oldest hotels on the east coast, had an exemplary reputation. Rumours of even slight awryness could be extremely damaging. It was the work of only minutes for a guest to leave a bad review, wiping away the years of hard work establishing a blemish-free track-record. Cassandra hoped this morning's performance was the last time she would have to apologise for a family member.

"Why are you doing the windows?" Greer asked.

"It's going to be a lovely weekend."

"Where's our usual window cleaner?"

"Away. Have you had any lunch?"

"Not yet." Greer looked out. The cove looked pretty now; boats in the bay, a couple walking hand in hand along the shore. She turned away. "I was surprised to find guests in the kitchen this morning."

"You were a bit of a surprise yourself!"

All Greer could remember was the smell of bacon and someone laughing.

"The dining room was locked."

"A flood from a bathroom above, some work needs doing."

"Oh, when was the flood?"

"A while ago."

Greer frowned; her sister rarely let things slide. "Unlike you not to ..." A sudden gust scudded along the corridor, slamming the window shut. Cassandra lost her balance, and Greer leapt forward, grabbing her gilet to drag her in.

"Jeez, you shouldn't be out there on the bloody ledge, you're ..."

"What?" Cassandra snapped, white with fright. "Too old? Too fat? Too doolally?"

"Too near the edge is what I was *actually* going to say."

The sisters' eyes glittered at each other.

"Saved you though." Greer smiled.

Cassandra softened. "Must have been your turn, so."

Realising Cassandra's hands were crushed in hers, Greer released her.

"Where's your ring?" Greer asked, pointing at her finger.

"What ring?"

"What do you mean, what ring? The *ruby,* the priceless family heirloom, saved from a pirate raid in 1700 and whenever." Greer was teasing; the provenance of the ring changed frequently.

"Well, I wouldn't wear it to do the windows now, would I?" Cassandra pushed her naked hand into her pocket. Greer pulled a face. Cassandra always wore the ring, cleaning, gardening, sailing, whatever. She adored it, said it gave her energy, a special superpower.

Greer changed the subject. "The windows look clean enough, anyway."

"They do," Cassandra agreed.

"Standards!" they said together and laughed, one of their

grandmother's many mantras.

Greer strode off, Tone trotting at her heels.

"Where are you going?" Cassandra asked anxiously.

"I need a walk." Greer stopped, reminding herself that Cassandra worried. "I'll grab some lunch."

"Where?"

"Muir's, where else?"

"Liquid lunch then, is it?"

They had barely spoken in three years and now her sister wanted to know what she was having for lunch. Greer resisted the urge to snipe back.

"I only meant ..." Cassandra looked wary.

"I know, I'll grab something to eat while I'm out." Greer carried on.

"Greer Morgan!" Cassandra called after her. "You'll have to tell me what's going on sooner or later."

And vice versa, Greer thought, opening the side entrance to let herself and Tone out onto the steps and the well-used track that led to the less salubrious side of the harbour.

There Be Dragons

O rla was on the beach, alternating between shell collecting and puppy training. Wolfe had never seen the sea before and was beyond himself, pouncing on the waves to hold in the froth, barking after seabirds as they rose effortlessly into the sky and dunking his nose again and again, just for the hell of it, the saltiness making him splutter and sneeze.

Eventually Orla wrapped him in a towel, tucking him under her jacket. The wind was picking up and it grew quickly cold out on the broad, blank sand.

Pleased with her morning's work, pockets full to bursting, Orla was convinced more diligence was needed in her particular department. Despite sifting through her haul hour after hour, she had found no indication of Greer's bad news and anxious there was more to follow she was concerned; had the shells, as they sometimes did, stopped speaking to her? Or worse, was the Sea Witch playing wicked tricks and punishing them for whatever misdemeanour she might contrive to displease her?

Orla scowled out to sea.

With his mistress distracted, Wolfe wriggled free to attack a strand of seaweed, chewing as he held it between his paws. Breaking through her thoughts, Orla guessed he was hungry. She was often scolded for forgetting to feed things – including herself – or feeding too much. Who knew Tone would eat an entire sack of dog food when she had merely told him to help himself, and Wolfe was only a baby; babies need building up.

She remembered Dr James said he was working on his

boat today. He would surely have something nourishing on board, and being a doctor, it would be healthy too. She dragged Wolfe away from the seaweed, explaining they were going to see a vet for humans and there was absolutely nothing to worry about.

Greer pulled up her hood, as she and the spaniel made their way around the promontory known as Haven Hook and down onto the lane leading to Muir's Bar.

She took deep breaths as she strode, good strong sea air, clearing her head. She needed to focus, assimilate what had happened and decide what to do. She would not be maudlin, she would not fall into a pit of despair. She was a grown woman, in love with a married man, something terrible had happened but that did not mean everything had to change.

Alistair would recover. He would want her back, the perfect, beautiful life they had planned would happen.

She pushed the sadness away; if their relationship was over, she would hear it from him, her entire future could not be dissolved with a cold dismissal from his frosty wife.

She needed to think.

She needed a drink.

She looked up as the small, squat building came into view, every step lighter the further from Manorcliff she strode. Tone trotted ahead, tail wafting in anticipation; it was a long time since he had enjoyed the sights and smells of one of his favourite haunts.

Pushing open the gate, Greer stopped. The yard, home to barrels shoved against the cellar door and a broken bench beneath a makeshift awning, had been transformed. Now paved in slabs of honey-coloured stone with elegant, upholstered furniture arranged around gleaming glass tables, the whole place seemed to shimmer in the sunlight.

Signs advertising Guinness and Jameson Whiskey were nowhere to be seen, and a trellis bearing a climbing rose interlaced with honeysuckle adorned an oak porch, while tubs filled with geraniums were artfully arranged here and there.

Instead of the familiar hostelry – a haven for the jaded local seeking respite from the relentlessly jolly holidaymaker – she was faced with a nouveau village pub.

Her heart sank.

The interior was even worse. Originally a fisherman's cottage turned into a cosy bar, the building had been extended, the space now filled with tables and the very thing Greer was hoping to avoid – people.

A youngster with piercings and a Celtic tattoo appeared. She wore a bright smile and large black spectacles.

"What can I get you?" An Australian accent.

"A Tardis," Greer replied. The girl squinted through her glasses. "It's a time machine."

"Sorry?"

"Looks a lot different from when I was last here," Greer said, straining to see into the back, hoping Declan Muir would appear and greet her with the usual abuse. A sight for very sore eyes.

"Would you like a drink? Can I get you a menu?" The girl's smile waned.

This was radical. Muir's served food but never needed a menu beyond a scrawl on a board. Fish and chips, toasted sandwiches and soup. *Sure, what more could anyone want?*

"Just a glass of Guinness," Greer said. "When did all this happen?"

"Dunno." The girl tugged at the pump. "Just here for the summer, back to uni in a few weeks."

"Unlike Declan not to be lining up the pints on a busy weekend." Greer looked round.

The girl shrugged, handing over the stout.

"The landlord?" Greer explained.

"Oh, geddit. If you're talking about the old crowd, anyone left drinks up at *The Pirate*."

"Anyone left?" Greer was bemused.

"They'll be there. It's a boat, back of the harbour, down by the old marina. And you'll have to take the dog out."

Greer raised an eyebrow.

"Food." The girl indicated Tone, now sitting at Greer's feet, his scout for titbits futile, the floor spotless. "We serve *food*."

Greer left her beer untouched.

Rough and ready, Muir's could be relied upon for a good night out, a decent lunch and the occasional brawl. Traditional in every way, was how Declan liked to describe one of the oldest hostelries on the east coast.

Outside, Greer gazed along the lane, unsure whether she had the strength to seek out *The Pirate*. Declan, a once successful impresario, still attracted musicians and songwriters, many of whom had been friends in her previous life. Declan would be disappointed if she arrived unannounced, depriving him of his usual fanfare.

No, she was not up to facing Declan today. Besides, at first sight he always reminded her of someone else, alarmingly so, and she was not ready for that either.

At least the grocery shop attached to the petrol station had not changed, although the bold new sign declaring Moore's Mini Market – ALWAYS OPEN was jarringly fluorescent. Thankfully Flossy Moore was behind the counter as usual, with another new addition, a stool. Flossy was a martyr to swollen feet.

She welcomed them with a lopsided grin, warning Tone not to cock his leg on the bale of peat stacked by the door. She passed Greer a packet of Tayto 'on the house' because she only had enough euros for a sandwich, not expecting to be in Ireland or indeed Europe, at all.

"Can I get you anything else?" Flossy asked kindly. Greer looked totally drained, which was odd because Cassandra was always saying how well she was doing in her high-powered job in London. "Not much of a Sunday lunch." The shopkeeper tutted.

"Just a snack, thanks, Flossy. I owe you for the crisps."

"Not at all," replied Flossy, hobbling to a shelf to find a treat for Tone. "Good to see you. Thought you'd have been back before now, though. But Cass says it's big international business you're into over there, isn't that right?"

Greer started reversing towards the door.

Flossy gave Tone his treat, straightening stiffly to look Greer in the eye.

"Stay a while now, won't you? I know people always say they can manage, they're grand, but people can be proud and stubborn. And sisters should stay close, no one knows the secrets like sisters." Flossy gave a laugh as she opened the door – one of seven sisters herself, no wonder their only brother ran off to sea years ago, never to be seen again.

Despite the sunshine Greer was enveloped in a large, dark cloud by the time she found an empty bench looking out at the bright, brittle sea. She had always been good at compartmentalization, indeed much of her success was dependent on it but the news about Alistair was devastating.

Initially just an affair, a fling with a client on a business trip to Cannes, sun, sea, champagne and lots of really great sex, Alistair had been easy to fall in love with. Handsome, clever and very badly behaved, he was the perfect paramour and yet, she later discovered, somehow managed to be the 'perfect' husband and father as well.

Looking back the sun had been shining that day too, but she had chosen to spend it in a bar, a very swishy bar but a bar nonetheless.

Stepping out of the music scene spotlight and desperate to do something completely different, Greer had set herself up as a property consultant, specialising in revamps and restoration, acquiring antiques and sourcing vintage pieces. With her family background and celebrity contacts it seemed an excellent idea. But with a global recession arriving around the same time as her shiny new business cards, Greer feared the worst.

She was drowning her sorrows in the cocktail bar

of London's Savoy Hotel, having just received notice her apartment was being repossessed by the bank, when one of a group of businessmen drinking champagne nearby asked if she was, you know, *the* Greer Morgan.

'Not at all', she told him, 'but I *am* Greer Morgan Property Consultant', handing over one of her shiny new cards. Alistair McKeiver had called the very next day.

If Greer was good at keeping aspects of her life in separate boxes, Alistair was the supreme master; edges never blurred, lines never crossed.

This was *hard*. No one knew her life had just fallen apart – and at the very moment she would have been able to tell the whole world about the man she loved and their future together. And if no one knew, why would anyone care?

Yet someone did know. Amy knew. But Alistair's wife had made it very clear, she was seizing the opportunity to take charge. Reduced to a mere employee, Greer would be written to. Dismissed, in more ways than one.

Pulling the sandwich apart, Greer fed it distractedly to Tone on the bench beside her. A loud blast signalled the ferry setting sail, gleaming in the afternoon sun as it powered through the harbour towards Wales. *Dragonland*, well, that was what she always believed as a child.

Someone sat on the end of the bench. Tone jumped down, grumbling as he sniffed the other dog. It was Wolfe, ecstatic to see him again.

"Are you eating those crisps?" Orla asked. With Dr James nowhere to be found, she and Wolfe were still hungry.

Greer handed the bag over. Orla opened it, sharing them equally between herself and the dogs.

"Ferry's on its way to *Dragonland*."

Greer just kept staring out to sea.

"Haven't seen one in a long time."

"One what?" Greer asked.

"A dragon."

"Do you still keep a log of all the monsters you meet in

that big red ledger of yours?"

"Of course, I'm fastidious where my paperwork's concerned, you know that."

"Seen the Sea Witch lately?"

Orla shook her head, licking salt from her fingers.

"Heard from our mother?"

Orla gave her a look. Greer rarely acknowledged Orla's ability to communicate with their mother.

"Not recently. But I knew you were coming home, I'm sure she sent that message."

"Anything else?"

"Only this." Orla held out her hand. A small slice of pale pebble rested in her palm. It was heart-shaped with a crack running from top to bottom. "This is for you."

Greer took the stone. Smooth, cool, worn by time and tide.

"It's only cracked though," Orla said. "So, although it feels broken deep inside," she touched her chest, "It's only cracked." She lifted the puppy, passing him to Greer. "Here, wipe your eyes with his ears."

A Bit of Piracy

Had Dr James known one of his favourite people was coming to spend a pleasant hour aboard his pride and joy, he would not have accepted Nagle's invitation to lunch at *The Pirate*. But they missed one another by minutes, Nagle roaring off around the bay in his old Boston Whaler with James clinging grimly to the side.

Despite the nausea the short trip on a flat sea had induced, James was looking forward to a restorative pint and a hearty bowl of something solid at the pub. One thing Declan Muir, *The Pirate's* ebullient landlord, could never be accused of was delicacy, his devotion to the creation of impossibly large sandwiches and impenetrable soups was legendary.

Originally a ferry, *The Pirate* had served as the *Maggie May* crossing from Dublin to Liverpool back in the eighties. When it was decommissioned and destined for scrap, the locals banded together to buy her for the community and the ferry became the base for the harbour's sailing school. Sadly, a change in fortune saw the school floundering as funding dried up, but the sturdy old girl was far from sunk.

Ever enterprising, Declan seized the opportunity to sell Muir's Bar, his family's long-established pub to a successful chain and relaunched *Maggie May* as *The Pirate*, a small, no-frills bar for locals and regular sailors. Yet because of its quirky, characterful clientele and eccentric staff, *The Pirate* was becoming a favourite haunt of visitors too, which although financially rewarding, had not been Declan's intention at all.

The landlord was explaining this conundrum to Dr James when, disturbingly, another customer asked for a cocktail, and rather than decline the request, he called behind the bar for assistance. A tall dark-haired man appeared. At first glance he could have been a younger Declan, longer and leaner but the likeness was remarkable.

"Would you ever make those two young ones a Sex on the Beach and a Malibu Sunset," Declan said gruffly.

"You said we don't do cocktails?" the taller, thinner Declan said.

"We don't but with the sunshine we're not that busy," the real Declan replied.

Dr James looked up. "I'll have a Sex on the Beach if there's one going."

Nagle spluttered into his beer.

"Two Sexes!" ordered Declan.

"Two Sexes, *please*, Rai," said the other man, taking down glasses.

Nagle jumped up. "Is it yourself, Rai?! How the divil are ya? Been years, sure, we all thought you were dead!"

Silence.

"Did you now?"

"A figure of speech." Nagle was sheepish.

Rai reached across to pump Nagle's hand. He was nearly as tall as the big fella and dark, very dark. And although Rai looked very much alive, a laser glint to the eye and a twitch of humour about his mouth, there *was* something of the other world about him, always had been.

Cassandra was relieved to see the sisters return arm in arm. Orla had laid the puppy across her shoulders, the way she carried lambs helping Nagle on the farm in early spring, as Tone trotted primly at Greer's heel.

"At last!" Cassandra declared, watching them disrobe in the hallway. "Get a move on, we've paying guests waiting."

A slight exaggeration. None of the paying guests had yet come down for drinks – an early evening ritual at Manorcliff – and supper was well underway, the delicious aroma of a

Cassandra classic wafting out from the kitchen.

"Where's Bríd and Fudge?" Greer asked, pulling out a tray for glasses. She had not seen Bríd at all since her return and Fudge only fleetingly, greeting her with his usual grunt.

"Away. They always take this week. That's why we do a special rate for regulars, they understand we're a bit short-staffed."

"She means they don't expect everything to be perfect," Orla commented, rolling her eyes.

Cassandra lifted the lid off the large oval crock, blowing on the spoon as she tasted.

"Done!" she pronounced. "What was that, Orla?"

"I should have remembered they're away." Greer saved Orla from a ticking-off. "Are they in Menorca as usual?"

"Bought a time-share there, didn't I tell you? Had it for three years now – mind you it's that long since you were here …" Cassandra trailed off.

"We've been invited," Orla announced. "I'm saving up. I'll love it there, the seals come right up to the beach, dolphins everywhere, sea-people too …"

"Orla!" Cassandra warned.

"Well, that's what the shells said," Orla whispered to Greer, who was checking the drinks list stuck to the side of the vast fridge at the far end of the kitchen.

"Are we trying to keep up with the new Muirs? We've gone very fancy since I was last on duty. Gin and elderflower? Organic Prosecco? What happened to a whiskey and red or Cork Dry Gin and Schweppes?"

Cassandra was lighting the large brass candelabras on the kitchen table.

"You *are* living in the past, Greer. We're so on trend, a review last summer called us 'a boutique hotel with a classical twist'."

"If you don't mind dog hairs on the sofa or a plumbing system that gurgles through the night," Orla finished the reviewer's comment. "She only quotes the first bit."

"We only *need* the first bit," her eldest sister reminded her. "Now go and freshen up. I'll finish drinks. Orla, take the seaweed out of your hair please!" She turned to Greer. "And a bit of makeup wouldn't go amiss on you either. Did you spend the whole day in the pub or what?"

Greer went to protest but thought better of it. Wiser to choose her battles where Cassandra was concerned. She steered Orla towards the door, untangling the elaborate seaweed headdress adorning her sister's mass of tawny hair.

A sprawling mansion, Manorcliff had borne witness to the highs and lows of the Morgans' long and colourful history. The family could trace its roots back to England's King Henry VIII. The clan's founding father, an Anglo-French knight named Maurice Saint-Anlais, landed on Ireland's east coast just as the French fleet sank Henry's flagship the Mary Rose in 1545.

A favourite at court, Maurice was betrothed to the King's cousin and looked set for life when he returned to England to marry and take charge of the estate the monarch had gifted them. But while staying with the powerful Irish earl William Fitzgerald, Maurice fell madly in love with the earl's sister Madeleine Morgan, a childless widow battling her deceased husband's family to keep her home south of Hook Haven.

Maurice took up the cause, slaughtering Madeleine's in-laws in their beds and then marrying her in secret – and so the Morgan-Saint-Anlais dynasty was born.

The King was furious, not least because he had to find another fiancé for his ageing cousin, but Maurice had gone native, choosing to remain in Ireland with his vivacious new wife. When Madeleine died bearing their only son, Maurice, broken-hearted, died soon after, and it was Earl William who brought the boy up.

Of course, the Rosshaven version claimed Madeleine – having made a pact with the Sea Witch to give her a child – was last seen on the shore before vanishing, her spirit returning when the moon was full to walk with her son and share her special powers. This was the version the sisters used to whisper under the bedclothes late at night. For they were convinced they had lost their mother that way too.

Greer was in the drawing room, gazing at the coat of arms set above the eaves, recalling the story when Nagle appeared. The big fella was wearing a blazer, his unruly red hair smoothed back.

"Didn't know you were joining us, can I get you a drink?" Greer asked, refilling her glass.

"I'll have something later, thanks. I'd a couple of pints at lunchtime, Cass doesn't like me to have too much, especially when I'm helping out," Nagle told her.

This was another development. The Nagles were close neighbours and both families always looked out for each other but Seamus Nagle – only ever known by his surname – ran the farm, a more than full time job. This was odd. Greer had never known him help at the hotel and although they had more or less grown up together, Cassandra never seemed particularly relaxed in his company, especially if he had been drinking. Something else that had changed.

"How long are you staying this time?" Nagle asked.

The question surprised her. "Why?"

"Cassandra wants to turn your room into another guest suite, you're so rarely here, it's an awful waste when people would pay good money to stay in it."

"Cassandra said that?"

Nagle looked away.

"My room. In *my* home," she said quietly.

"I was only …"

"If you're supposed to be helping, get these doors open." She rattled the handles at the French windows. "It's a beautiful evening, the paying guests can enjoy the sunset. Probably rain tomorrow."

The doors from the drawing room opened onto a broad stone staircase leading to a large terrace. Hewn from local slate, it curved around the east wing of the house, affording the best view of the nearest beach known as the Italian Strand.

Legend had it that during the eighteenth century one of the Morgans had been so enraptured by his tour of Italy that what treasures he could not import legally he paid to have smuggled and delivered to the beach, declaring a ship had run aground and he was merely caretaking the artefacts until the rightful owner could be found.

The exquisite alabaster busts adorning the balustrade indicated no such person ever declared themselves and consequently all the 'recovered' paintings and architectural embellishments had remained at Manorcliff.

With the Morgans' countless forays in support of Ireland's fight for independence, two World Wars and the Irish Civil War in between, there was little left of the collection, but Greer had always loved the Italian busts gracing the terrace, giving them names as they gazed blindly out to sea or stared down their long noses at whatever shenanigans were taking place on the beach. *If they could speak, what tales they could tell,* she often thought.

By the time the sky was streaked with fiery slices of amber and gold, all were gathered, the air filled with the polite conversation of early evening acquaintance.

Greer, slightly fuzzy, having imbibed two hefty gins on an empty stomach, observed her eldest sister moving effortlessly through their guests; animated, relaxed. Cassandra was the consummate hostess, no one would know she had been working flat out since six that morning supervising housekeeping, a team of three women who came up from the town each day. Beds changed, bathrooms cleaned, breakfast served, a list of other chores completed before she attended to the evening meal. She looked bewitching. Russet hair twisted and pinned with pearls, shimmering earrings, and a swathe of turquoise silk over linen pants.

"Come and join us, Greer," Cassandra called to her sister. "Frances has us mesmerised with tales of industrial intrigue."

Greer gave Cassandra a quizzical look. Frances, mousey

and usually dominated into sullenness by her bumptious mother was, as far as Greer could remember, a clerk of some kind.

Crossing to where the normally reticent younger woman was holding court, Greer touched Orla's shoulder as she passed. Orla had changed into a pretty red dress with a floaty chiffon skirt, and although she had painted her nails and put on lipstick, she was wearing wellingtons, meaning a beach walk with the dogs after supper was on the cards.

"I've been put on 'garden leave'. The whole department has. Apparently, there's been a leak. We've been working on a highly confidential case, and it appears the person being investigated has been tipped off by someone in the department." Frances was animated, directing her flashing eyes at Dr James. "I've worked there for over ten years, never put a foot wrong."

"Where is it you work?" Greer asked.

"Revenue and Customs, I'm a manager there."

Greer took a swig of her drink. 'Customs' was not a word that could ever sit happily in conversation at Manorcliff. "Maybe the person being investigated is someone you all know, garden leave in case there's a conflict of interest?"

Frances was wide-eyed, as everyone moved closer. "We *all* know who's under investigation, but I'm sure none of us actually know him personally. He's an international businessman, financial interests all over the world."

Greer felt herself refocus.

"And he's been accused of what exactly?"

"We're still gathering the evidence, but it looks like large-scale tax evasion. Been going on for years. Could amount to millions and it'll be a scandal when it breaks. You see he's working for the government, even linked to some of the royals."

Greer swallowed. "And he's been tipped off about the investigation?"

"It's Katya's fault." Frances pushed her hair behind her

ears. "She was supposed to get to know him, so he would take her into his confidence, infiltrate the enemy, that kind of thing."

"Sounds more like MI5." Greer was incredulous.

"My boss is very ambitious." Frances held out her wineglass to be topped up. "He knows he'll be promoted if he lands this particular fish."

Most of the guests were listening now. Frances was enjoying the attention.

"And?" Greer was finding it hard to swallow.

"Well, she went too far." Frances lowered her eyes. "And Katya's very attractive."

"As in sleeping with the enemy?" Cassandra pressed.

Dr James sighed. "Espionage … so intriguing, so sexy."

"I couldn't say," Frances replied, blushing. "It's all highly confidential, I shouldn't have said anything at all. Must be the wine."

"So, the whole department has been suspended," Dr James confirmed. Everyone was staring at Frances, who had become in the last ten minutes more interesting than she had been in all the years they had known her.

"And I haven't done anything wrong at all. Mother's mortified, she thinks I've lost my job."

"Now, now. It'll all sort itself out, you'll see," Cassandra reassured.

"I'm chilly now, can we go in?" Frances asked.

"Of course, time for something nice and warming." And taking Frances by the arm, Cassandra steered her towards the doors.

Stony-faced, Greer downed her drink, her mind a muddle. Picking a large tray of empty glasses, she started back towards the house. Her pocket trembled as her phone burst into life, Orla ferreted it out. The caller had rung off.

"Did you see who it was?" Greer asked, as Orla replaced the phone.

"Clare Friend. That's nice, isn't it? Having a friend call

you."

Orla was wrong. The caller was Clare *Fiend*. Clare was bad news, Greer named her 'Fiend' to remind her not to reveal anything to this highly manipulative individual, ever. She was also Alistair's sister.

Looking up, Greer missed the step, stumbling as the tray plummeted to the smooth slate surface of the terrace.

Sounded like a bomb going off.

Black Night

R ai Muir was weary, bone tired as his mother would say. He could not remember the last time he'd had a good night's sleep, the dreams always came, and even awake the constant calling to resolve things, make way for the next phase pulled at his consciousness. It was time to settle his account and move on.

He had just finished serving, the last of the late drinkers drifting amiably off, and with everything cleared away and secure, he headed out on what had become his nightly walk. A solid march that took him from *The Pirate*, along Wharf Lane into the town, around the harbour and past the ferry port until he hit a luminous stretch of pale sand; north beach.

The Harbour Spa Hotel shimmered high on the clifftop to his left, its flamboyant awning billowing ghostlike in the breeze, and from here the strand swept back in a deep curve until, striding on he came to the ancient jetty that served Galty House.

The lights were usually on in Galty's eccentric summer house perched on the edge of the shore but not tonight. Once upon a time he would have stopped, called in, shared a glass or two. He wondered would he be welcome there, indeed was there anywhere here that would genuinely welcome him these days and not just treat him as a curiosity, an echo from another time, or worse a bad taste reminding them all of something hard to swallow.

Shrugging deeper into his sealskin coat, he smiled grimly; at least this was one thing that had not changed. How pleased he had been to see it there, hanging on a hook by the door in his brother's pub. As if all along Declan knew he would be coming home. Not everything had changed.

But it was surely going to.

Greer was standing on the balcony, the small patio table and chairs neatly stacked where she had left them, though she could see by the light drifting from the room they were dusty and cobwebbed – it *had* been over three years. She resolved to restore order to at least this small corner of her world.

She loved sitting out here, rain or shine, the wilder and windier the better. As a little girl she would sit huddled beneath an umbrella, a mug of cocoa keeping her hands warm while icy raindrops splodged tears on whichever glorious tome she was devouring, *Treasure Island, Black Beauty* or *Wuthering Heights.*

Reading was her passion, entranced by the magic of being transported to the far corners of the universe, enraptured by the characters she met without moving an inch from her chair. These words, these pages, these stories had been her escape, her other safe place. Where she could be whoever she wished; a pirate, a princess, a horse galloping free, and not the child who was the reason they had no mother, the mother who was taken by the Sea Witch in her stead. This was no legend, she was living proof of that.

"Not in bed yet?" Cassandra came gently through the door. "You must be jaded tired, you didn't sleep last night."

Greer looked up at the black sky, the moon nowhere to be seen. "I'll sleep tonight."

"I hope so." Her sister joined her. "Thanks for helping out earlier."

"Paying guests," Greer replied, the oft cited reason for almost every task the sisters undertook at Manorcliff. "Besides, I needed a distraction, something else to think about."

Cassandra stood at the rail. The sea was still, the shore barely ruffled, not a soul in sight. She turned to Greer; her pretty face looked hollowed out in the shadows.

"When you want to talk …"

Greer moved into the light, eyes shining with unshed tears. "Not now, not yet … I'm … I'm sorry about the tray."

"Ah, no matter." Cassandra reached out, cupping Greer's cheek in her hand. "You're all over the place, don't know what to think or feel, God love you."

"Don't bring God into it!" Greer warned, a phrase she used whenever her sister referred to the Almighty. Greer did not believe in God, any god, she had enough demons, who needed another deity imposing a raft of his own?

"I just meant I'm here." Cassandra made to leave. "And I'm glad you're home, I probably should have told you that sooner, made you more welcome."

"You don't need to make me welcome."

"I know … you're not a 'paying guest'. Goodnight, sis." Cassandra closed the bedroom door just as Greer's phone quivered to life. It was Clare Fiend again. She took the call.

"Greer, thank goodness." Clare's tone was anxious. "Where are you?"

"I'm …" she stopped. "Away at the moment, why?"

The woman on the other end of the phone let out a wail.

"Away? But you *do* know? Know what's happened?"

Greer waited. She would not presume to know what Clare was talking about. It could be anything.

"Oh, Greer, Alistair's desperately ill." The woman started to cry.

"I know, Clare. I'm so sorry." Greer tried to keep her voice steady. "Have you heard how he's doing?"

"What do you care?" Clare sounded drunk. "It's all your bloody fault anyway!"

Greer sighed. "I have to go now, Clare."

"You and that bloody bitch of a wife. Both of you, bad as each other. No wonder he had a heart attack." Clare's voice was rising.

"Where are you, Clare? Are you at home? Is anyone with you? You sound too upset to be on your own right now."

"I'm outside your flat but it's all locked up."

"Like I said, I'm away."

"Aren't you coming back?" Clare was sobbing now.

"Of course I am, why?"

"There's a big bloody 'For Sale' sign outside, that's why."

Greer winced. Andrew's wife had obviously meant what she said, she *was* in charge.

"Clare, I have to go now." Her head was pounding.

"They don't know if he's going to get better, it's so serious. What will happen if ..?" She was wailing again.

"He will, Clare, I know he will."

"But no one is telling me anything, I can't see him, Amy won't speak to me!" She was shouting now.

"I'm sorry I can't be any more help. I think I've been let go."

Greer shut the phone off, gazing briefly at the screen as Clare's details disappeared, and finding a drawer threw it inside. Desperate to clear her head, she stood stock still in the silence and closed her eyes. *Oh, Alistair, please get better, please.* And the tears came anyway.

A pitiful whine startled her. She opened the door. Orla stood there with Wolfe in her arms and Tone at her feet. The hem of her pretty red dress was splashed with sand and her cheeks rosy as she grinned at her sister.

"Black night for a walk. You okay?" Greer asked.

"It's light in my head," Orla replied. "And James came with me, I had to hold his hand, he kept slipping, couldn't remember where to put his feet." She giggled.

"James now, is it?" Greer asked, quickly wiping her eyes. "Some people have to see where they put their feet, Orla, we're not all as clever as you."

Orla shrugged. "Tone's a bit upset. He's worried you're going away again, so we thought we'd sleep with you, so you don't leave in the night."

"I won't need guarding. I'm not going anywhere."

"You don't want us to stay?" Orla was disappointed. Tone

turned soulful eyes up at Greer.

"I don't want to be crowded at the moment." Greer knew Orla would understand that. She looked at Tone. "Well, Tone can stay being as he's upset."

Orla was relieved. Tone was a good guard dog, subtle, discreet. In fact, you could not really tell when Tone was guarding at all, he did it so well, sometimes snoring softly with his eyes closed. The old dog sprang lithely onto the throw at the end of the bed as the sisters said goodnight.

Greer's mood lifted slightly as, moisturising her face, tight from the sun, she went to close the balcony door. The moon had reappeared, hanging silver bright, running a ribbon of grey to the shore, waves fluttering on the marbled beach. Wrapping her robe more tightly about her, she stood drinking in the cool night air like balm. "Good to see you," she mouthed at the man in the moon, an old friend.

Her gaze swept the sand.

Was there movement?

Greer could see the outline of a man striding along the beach. Another midnight walker. She looked again. There was something familiar about the gait. No, it could not be. The moonlight was playing tricks on her sad, tired eyes. She blinked and he was gone, disappeared into the blackness.

Cold now, she quickly re-entered the room, turning off the light. She did not want whoever was out there to know her room was occupied, just in case. Slipping into bed she tucked her feet under Tone's warm body, pulling the eiderdown up to her ears, determined to ignore the flutter in her chest. She was exhausted, stressed, all over the place, as Cassandra said.

And serenaded by Tone's snores, Greer willed herself light as a feather to float far, far out to sea on a gentle wave and soon she was asleep … a deep and dreamless sleep at last.

A Meeting of Minds

Friday. The end of a week racing towards the end of summer. Yet still so much to do. Cassandra gazed at her reflection in the mirror, failing to notice the roses in the vase before her had drooped, the petals turning brown.

With Bríd and Fudge back at their posts, she was able to leave straight after breakfast and, grateful no one asked where she was going, she distractedly reversed the aged Range Rover onto the drive and started along the twirling route to the coast road.

She pulled the visor down as she turned towards the harbour, the sun was already sitting solidly over Phoenix Island, bathing the mass of mossy green in a shimmering glow, making that dark, secret place appear lustrous, as inviting as ever. Lust. She had never noticed those four letters in that word before.

When she checked her good bag for the umpteenth time, the shiny black leather, smooth hand-stitched handles, solid brass clasp, the lock seemed to mock her. *Pandora's box,* she thought. When had she lost the key, she wondered yet again? Orla had probably borrowed it, turning it into a piece of jewellery. She was a magpie, that girl.

A horn blasted behind her. She slammed on the brakes, ribs jarring against the steering wheel, and checking the mirror she saw the green and yellow logo of John Deere. A tractor. Nagle.

"Good God! You frightened the life out of me. What's wrong?" she snapped at him through the window, heart pounding.

SECRETS OF THE SHELL SISTERS

"'Tis you frightened me! You seem to have a death wish this morning. I'm behind you since you left, you were nearly over the cliff twice." He pointed, she was at the crash barrier, which looked decidedly feeble close-up. "Where're you going?"

"Dublin. A few errands. Why?"

"I hope you're taking the train. Don't know if you're up to driving all that way this morning." He leaned into the car, looking at her intently.

"I'm grand, Nagle. Well able and this old thing has never let me down." She patted the dashboard. "But I *am* taking the train today as it happens, I've a bit of paperwork to do on the way. Now climb back in that yoke and let me get on."

She pushed him away as she slammed the car into gear, driving jerkily off. Nagle covered his eyes, looking through his fingers as she left.

"Try and drive on the road, that's what it's for!" he yelled after her.

She lifted her hand, waving two fingers elegantly in his general direction.

"Charming!" He grinned, hauling himself into the cab.

Cassandra checked her watch. She did not want to be late for her next appointment. The young man returned with an elderly gentleman wearing pinstriped trousers, a watch chain across his ample girth.

"Miss Morgan, apologies, it's a big sale today, we're very busy."

She handed him the package, snapping her bag shut. He went to open the ring box.

"*Don't!*" she said. "I don't want to see it again – I might change my mind." She gave a small laugh but there was sadness in her eyes. "Do the best you can for me please, Oliver," she told him, walking briskly out of the auction rooms into the Dame Street sunshine.

Humphrey Beaumont stirred his coffee, the languid movement

swirling the bubbles, the teaspoon dwarfed in his large country-man fingers – though there was nothing frothy about him. Solid, reliable, respectable, these were words used to describe Humphrey Beaumont, Barrister at Law.

Humphrey was also one of Cassandra's oldest friends, always a solid shoulder and here she was again, calling on him to come to her aid, offer advice, help if he could.

He looked at the clutch of paperwork, some of it dating back over thirty years. A batch of covert correspondence delivered to a Dublin PO box number; irregular and spasmodic. But recently there had been a new and urgent flurry, and it was this that troubled her now – a trail to a past not quite brushed over.

Bewley's, the iconic café, was noisy. Shoppers, tourists and businesspeople bustled to and fro, finishing breakfast, dropping in for morning coffee, meeting for early lunch. Waitresses slid by as if skating, courteous and efficient, the chink and clatter of tableware a discordant backdrop to the veil of anxiety wrapping itself around their table.

Humphrey laid the spoon in his saucer, gazing at the attractive woman sitting opposite, her reddish-brown hair twisted through with silver strands, her usually sparkling teal-grey eyes dark today.

"Well, what do you think?" She pushed her cup away, the coffee bitter.

"Not my line of expertise as you know, but it appears the next move is yours. You can write back and say you don't want to take this any further, leave things as they are. Or ..."

"Or resurrect everything. Bring everything out into the open, dig it all up. For what? We did what we did for the best. The best for everyone." She looked round, anxious not to be overheard. "Times have changed, I know that. But what right have people doing this? Appearing out of nowhere. Demanding to know this and that."

"It's the law now, Cass. They do have the right. But you also have rights. The right to remain anonymous. The right to keep it all private."

"Secret, Humphrey, say what you mean. But it's not secret, is it? We're on file somewhere."

Humphrey took her hand, gently squeezing the fingers she had been tapping on the tabletop.

"You've always known there was a possibility this could happen. When you made the decision not to go through with the original plan, which was traumatic enough, there was always a chance the person concerned might, at some stage, seek you out."

"The person concerned?" Her eyes flashed – a myriad of emotion boiled down into a single look.

"The child, Cass. The baby given up for adoption. That person is now looking for her mother. It's a fairly common occurrence these days, people seeking to reconnect with their birth families, for many reasons. And I don't doubt many of these reconnections have satisfactory, and in some cases, happy outcomes."

"What?" Cassandra's mind had gone way back, sucked into that dark tunnel she walked past every day but dared not peer into. "Did you say she's looking for her mother?"

"Yes, that's what I said," he spoke slowly. "That's what this …" He indicated the paperwork. "… is all about."

"Of course it is." Cassandra closed her eyes, pushing her fingers into the lids, freckles bright on her now pale skin. "It never goes away. Never." Humphrey sat quietly, watching her. "That's what I can't stand, and it gives me nightmares. The fact I did the same as my mother did to me – I abandoned her."

"No! You did not abandon her. You gave her over to the care of a loving family and she was cherished. The letters show that clearly."

She gave Humphrey a look.

"I'm not patronising you. It *was* the right thing to do."

"Was it really?" She slumped in her chair. "Then why does it feel wrong, here inside?" She laid her hand on her chest.

Humphrey stood, taking her arm. "Come on, we could

both do with a drink."

It was a beautiful summer's day, Dublin bursting with people, visitors arriving for a city break, locals making good their escape – a heatwave forecast, the whole world heading to the coast.

The atmosphere was effervescent, bubbling to break free and fizzle wildly through the ancient streets, igniting everything and everyone. Even Cassandra felt it as she watched Humphrey power through the scrum at the bar, returning with ice cold beers.

"There's nowhere like it when it's like this," she said, glancing round Neary's Bar, an old favourite. She sat back, tuning into the cacophony of accents. Different languages pinged off the mirrored walls, ripples of laughter, the sheer joy of humanity gathered for a jar, the company, the craic. A sunny summer Friday, a rare and wondrous gift.

They sat companionably with their drinks, the ambience too absorbing for conversation and when after a while the crowd drifted and Cassandra said she would go too, Humphrey made no protest. He considered she had enough against her, pulling and pushing her mind this way and that. And then there was her own conscience. Conscience. That bastard could make a hell of ruckus if you did not stomp on it straight away. He should know, he'd had enough run-ins with his own.

"What're you thinking about?" she asked; his expression had changed, he looked more Monday than Friday.

"The agony of conscience," he replied.

"Ah, Humphrey, now I've put you in a bad mood," she said, signalling the barman for another round.

"I often wonder," he mused, swirling the dredges in the glass. "If we had only ourselves to please, no one else to consider, would we make half the decisions we do?"

Cassandra pondered as their drinks arrived. Sometimes she felt all her decisions were made considering others.

"I often feel I take in so many points of view, I lose my

own." She took a sip off the creamy head. "But with no one else to consider, wouldn't all our decisions be totally and utterly selfish? What kind of world would that produce?"

"A less complicated one perhaps?"

"But not nearly as nice."

"Nice?" Humphrey was incredulous. "You think the world is *nice?*"

"Bits of it are absolutely wonderful." She was serious.

"I'll acknowledge that." He gave her a grin. "And your corner of it is particularly special. Talking of your corner of the world, been a good summer, guess you've been mad busy?"

"Not so much, that new five-star hotel above the harbour is taking a lot of custom away."

"But surely, there's always a market for somewhere exclusive like Manorcliff?"

"Do you mean eccentric?" She smiled. "Needs a lot of investment, more than a bit of an upgrade."

"Aha, I was wondering if you were at the auction rooms today. Anything take your fancy, in terms of investment?"

"A bit too rich for my blood these days." Cassandra hoped he would drop the subject.

"Really? You used to love collecting odd bits and pieces for the hotel at the auction."

"Not a lot of spare cash for frivolity at the moment." She put her hands in her pockets.

But Humphrey had already noticed the large flat ruby was missing and wondered if Cassandra might have been selling and not buying today.

"And now I must be going back to see what havoc the world has wreaked in my absence." Cassandra drained her glass.

"Probably haven't even noticed you've gone."

She gave his well-tailored shoulder a puck. "Don't be ridiculous, I'm indispensable, as well you know."

She picked up her good bag, clicking it shut.

"Walk you to the station?" He stood.

"I'm grand, plenty of time. I'll window shop on the way."
He kissed her cheek.

"Let me know if you want me to recommend anyone, you know, if you need a lawyer, some sort of professional advisor, counsellor, whatever."

"Why would I need any of that? Surely, I just write back and say no. And that'll be an end to it."

"If that's what you want. The offer's there." He placed a hand on her arm. "I believe our mutual friend is making big plans with his birthday looming."

Her eyes narrowed. "We're not really friends anymore."

"Don't blame him, Cass. Don't blame him for something he knew nothing about. He's not responsible."

"Of course he's responsible. We're all responsible. Ignorance is no reason for exoneration."

Same old intransigent Cassandra. Humphrey stood back to let her leave.

"Come and see us soon, yes?" She looked at him earnestly.

"I will." He opened the door for her. The sunshine hurt their eyes. They blinked at each other. No more to be said, for now.

Boarding the train at Connolly Street Station, Cassandra took a seat in the corner of the carriage, away from the windows which would soon be filled with blisteringly bright views of endless sea and ancient coast. A rolling technicolour vista on a day such as this, a late summer's afternoon heading south from Dublin Bay through Wicklow to Wexford; a hazy two-hour journey to the port of Rosshaven.

The carriage was packed. Cassandra looked at the holidaymakers, hearts and heads full of promise. For them, the weekend was a chance to break free, while all she felt was trapped.

Keeping her sunglasses on, she hoped no one she knew would alight and try to engage her in conversation. She lifted the magazine to her face.

Shore Secrets

D usk was seeping into the sky, dripping inky blots over the horizon as Orla and Greer made their way down the slippery steps to the cool sand. The tide had turned, the broad patch of silky land spanned the breadth of the beach, studded with rocks and stones, gleaming as the moon rose.

They carried the basket between them, filled with shiny gems to be returned; part of the ritual. The secrets the sea had shared were given back at each full moon and with the new moon the collecting would start again, the fresh shells bringing messages and guidance for the coming month.

The sisters believed the energy of the ocean recharged the shells, the tides sweeping them away to land upon faraway shores, bringing new messages for others tuned to the ways of the sea.

Not everyone had the gift, the sisters knew that, and as they grew kept the messages more and more to themselves. There was enough they were mocked and pitied for.

It was a warm evening, the breeze barely lifting their hair as they waded knee-deep in the water, drizzling shells from the basket into the surf. The cove was all but deserted, just a family piled high with the remnants of a day at the beach staggering up the track, a lone walker standing watching seabirds dip and dance, feeding in the shallows.

Greer stopped at her task, closing her eyes to hold in the sights, the sounds, the scent, the shore soothing her, the essence of summer seeping in through every pore of her skin to be stored away for the winter. She loved it here, at times like this. She looked at Orla, eyes shining, reflecting the dark green pool about them, and knew that Orla loved this too, being together, like this.

"It's been a long time …" Greer murmured, dunking the basket to rinse it.

"Has it?" Orla's sense of time was odd. Sometimes, when she was little, she could be alone for hours and never make a sound, other times five minutes in her own company and she would scream the place down.

Always unpredictable, Orla had not been at school long before the head nun sent for Nana, describing the middle sister as 'difficult to manage'. Livid, their grandmother simply taught her at home, announcing Orla did not need to be 'managed', she was a child, not a factory.

But Nana Morgan must have despaired at times.

In her forties by the time her only child Miranda arrived, Nana was widowed within the year. Yet somehow, she kept Manorcliff afloat, whilst bringing up the little one alone; no wonder neighbours said the girl was left to run wild.

But the tragedy of losing her daughter to be left with three grandchildren – no more than babies – must have been very difficult. How she had coped with babies, the business, her grief, and everything else besides, it was little wonder she came across as hard. And maybe she was hard, too hard at times but always fair, it was for their own good after all – another of her many mantras.

And although the sisters – Greer in particular – found her difficult, they could see she had always done her best for them and they each had loved her in their own way, there was no doubt about that.

"I feel you're always with me whether you're here or not." Orla took Greer's cold hand and kissed it. "But it's better with the whole of you here and Cassandra likes it too. She keeps saying we need more help and I know when she's checking her phone, saying she's making sure we're not missing any bookings, she's looking for you really."

Greer laughed. It was true, the psychic connection

between them was strong, especially when they spent time together. They each knew what the other was thinking, and tuning into one another's feelings, a mood could change like the flick of a switch. Together, they could be suddenly desperately sad or hilariously happy, with outsiders having no clue what they were laughing or crying about.

It had always been the same and although Greer was pleased to have been missed, she was saddened too. If her eldest sister needed her, why had she not known?

"Cass says you're so busy running huge projects all over the world, she doesn't expect to hear from you. And she's flat out running that place." She glanced up to the cliff, the Moon Room just visible. "And hasn't anytime whatsoever for having her own life, or so she said."

"She said that?" They were walking back, swinging the basket between them.

"She was telling Nagle in the kitchen. They stopped talking when I came in and started foostering at the coffee machine. But I could tell she was annoyed with him. Poor Nagle, when you look at the big brown eyes on him, mooning at Cass. I'm sure he's a spaniel in real life."

Greer was just about to explain *this* was real life when two canines she recognised came bounding over the sand towards them, and Tone, who had been on the boat with Dr James, nearly knocked her back into the sea, such was his exuberance at seeing her again.

They looked up to see Cassandra and James striding towards them, chatting animatedly as they walked. Cassandra shook his hand.

"Good, she's back," Orla said, breaking into a run. "Looks like a deal's been struck."

"A deal?" Greer asked, trotting to catch up.

"Yes, James wants to stay."

"That's good, for how long?"

"Till his life runs out."

Greer grabbed Orla's arm.

"What?"

Orla giggled. "Like Mr Montrose, the way he gave up the big shop for a rest."

"Retirement, Orla, it's called retirement!" Greer was laughing.

And letting go of the basket Orla ran up the beach, dogs at her heels, waving wildly at the approaching couple.

Greer smiled. Dr James Butler looked in rude health and a very long way from running out of life, as he swept Orla into his arms, spinning her round.

"Wait for me!" Greer called out, the eternal cry of the youngest child echoing along the sand.

The next day Greer sought out Cassandra in her office, a large windowless cupboard off Manorcliff's vast, sunny kitchen. It was eleven, the time of day when, fuelled with a cafetière of strong coffee, the hotel director undertook the challenges of the business end of running their faded yet beloved establishment.

The longer she was there, the more Greer realised how much had changed despite her eldest sister's pretence at normality. And apart from a natural concern for her siblings, there was the underlying worry that if all was not as it should be at Manorcliff, what on earth was she going to do about it, bearing in mind she currently had neither home nor job?

Cassandra was engrossed in her work, bespectacled eyes fixed on the computer screen, and she did not look up when Greer slipped in through the half-open door bearing fresh coffee and a plate of Bríd's shortbread just out of the oven.

"How are things in the world of hotels and high finance?" Greer asked, causing Cassandra to spin round, clicking the screen blank as she did.

"Ah, you know, up and down as usual." Cassandra shrugged, pushing papers into a file as Greer brought the tray to the desk.

Greer looked round. "I don't know why you don't use one

of the other rooms, somewhere with a view, we've enough of them. This place is downright depressing."

"Views are for paying guests, Greer," Cassandra quoted their grandmother again.

"There doesn't seem to be too many of them about at the moment, things a bit tight?" Greer asked gently. Cassandra was not the sort to welcome criticism, even if it was meant kindly. Her need to be independent was so strident it could be ostracising. "How's the season been? This weather must have helped."

"You mean actually having a summer must have helped." Cassandra laughed. "It did, of course. Lots of people who normally go abroad stayed at home, which certainly made things feel buoyant anyway."

"Feel buoyant?"

"You know, boats buzzing about the harbour, families on the beach but we need a bit more rain to keep the shops busy and the restaurants full. Too much sunshine and everyone's outside eating takeaways and ice cream, or worse, homemade picnics they've brought with them. Oh, and day trippers, loads of them, coming and going, enjoying the beach and the cliff walks, just doing the stuff that's free."

Greer poured coffee. This was the 'too much sunshine is bad for business' speech, which had alternated with the 'too much rain is bad for business' speech throughout her life. She sometimes wondered if hoteliers and farmers did not have the dire consequences of the weather to consider, what would they talk about at all?

"There seems to be a few repairs and renewals need doing, when are they scheduled?" Greer strolled over to the large pinboard on the wall, examining three sprawling spreadsheets covered in what looked like a colourful secret code.

One was for the current season; guest bookings, events, and special requirements. The second, for next year's forward bookings. Many of Manorcliff's regulars rebooked year after year, requesting the same dates, same rooms. It was one of the reasons the hotel was so successful, returning guests were like old friends coming back to stay time and again, often bringing extended family. As children grew, partners were added and in time babies too; parents became grandparents, wriggling puppies turned into old dogs.

This cycle of life gave Manorcliff its sense of place, that in an ever-changing world, this elegant pile perched high on the cliff remained solid and immovable; the perfect holiday destination, whatever else was going on in the world.

The third spreadsheet was the R&R schedule – repairs and renewals – works to be undertaken throughout the year, ensuring Manorcliff remained a glorious exponent of quality and style, retaining its star rating, the benchmark that not only kept visitors coming but meant the hotel could charge accordingly.

Greer looked closer. Coloured dots on the chart had been moved and others blacked out.

"Schedule of works is slipping a bit," Greer said casually.

"Cash flow, you know how it is. Or was Alistair and his business interests above such things?"

"We had our ups and downs too, you know."

"Ah, had to buy a smaller yacht, did he?" Cassandra closed the file she had been working on.

"Doesn't have a yacht. And besides, his new government appointment is very absorbing, life's not been half as jet-set as it used to be." *Will ever be again,* Greer thought, sadly. *Oh, Alistair.*

Cassandra coughed. "Well, himself and his government appointment seems to have kept you absorbed for the past three years."

Greer cast about, needing to change the subject. Cassandra could be like a dog with a bone once she started. Dog. There was an empty dog basket under the desk.

"The old girl, you must miss her."

Cassandra turned to look at her sister. "I do. They're all

different, like people, I was very close to that particular Wolfe. She-wolf, I used to call her when Orla wasn't around. I often wonder if Nana's idea to protect Orla from grief was sensible, I know she picks up on other people's emotions, but I worry she's never experienced her own."

"Not even when Nana passed?" Greer could hardly remember, having been so consumed with her own grief and shame, bitterly regretting a row that meant she and her grandmother were not even speaking when she received the news.

"Not really, she's always stayed in touch with Nana or so she believes – still talks to the portrait in the drawing room. I do worry though, if anything happens to me or you, what will happen to Orla? What would become of her?"

"What on earth could happen to you? You're our rock, always have been." Greer gave Cassandra a smile, but Cassandra's mouth had a twist to it.

The penny dropped.

Greer turned her sister to face her.

"It was *you* at an appointment in Dublin the day I came back, wasn't it? You told me it was the dog."

Cassandra swallowed. "We both had appointments. The dog at the veterinary hospital, me with a consultant."

"I *knew* it, why didn't you say? What's wrong?" Greer had come to crouch down beside her at the desk.

"A bit tired is all. That's why things have slipped, I've just no energy lately." She lifted Greer's chin to look into her eyes. The sheeny sea-green glazed with anxiety. "They're running tests, they'll get to the bottom of it, you'll see."

"How did I not know?" Greer's voice trembled. "You needed me, and I didn't know!" She felt tears rise again.

"Maybe we needed each other. You've not been having the best time either and I wasn't there for you." Cassandra gave Greer a soulful look. "I follow the news, you know. I see your man's been under pressure. Pressure to resign."

Greer blew her nose in the tissue Cassandra offered.

"He's the one under investigation, isn't he? The one Frances was talking about the other evening, that's why I called you over, so you could hear what was going on."

"Rumours and lies," Greer told her.

"And are the rumours true?"

Greer flashed her sibling a look. "What rumours?"

"The ones about you."

"What do you mean?"

"You know what I mean, Greer, you're his mistress, aren't you? Nobody cared when he was just another rich businessman, but in that weird double standard attributed to anything to do with government, now it's a problem, you're a problem."

Greer had started to feel stifled in the small room; it was airless and cluttered, and Cassandra's eyes were burning into her.

"I can see the attraction," Cassandra continued. "He's a fine-looking fella and you've always said he's great to work with. How long?"

There was a bottle of water on the desk. Greer drank from it.

"How long has he been telling you he's leaving his wife?" Cassandra took the bottle out of Greer's hand. "And how long have you known he never will?"

"Not now, Cass, please." Greer had grown pale.

"Very well, but we'll have to discuss it sometime." Cassandra stood. "It's lunchtime, we need to eat."

Greer nodded, relieved. Cassandra moved to turn off the computer. A picture flashed onto the screen. Cassandra had been watching a news stream. Greer stopped, placing her hand over Cassandra's on the desk. Images of Alistair swam before her.

The room filled with a lump of silence.

There was a photograph of Alistair with his wife, next to another of Alistair with Greer and then a picture of him with a young blonde.

"Don't read that!" Cassandra leapt forward.

"What?" Greer stood her ground.

The headline yelled, '*PM's Special Advisor Under Investigation*'.

Frozen to the spot, Greer pointed open-mouthed at Alistair and the beautiful young woman on his arm.

Cassandra shut the machine down. "Lunch."

The Competition

F udge was loading the Range Rover with luggage when Cassandra and Greer appeared at the front of the hotel. The Montroses were checking out. Longstanding clients, the couple booked every August and always reserved the Island – Manorcliff's grandest suite.

Conran Montrose was puffing heavily on a cigar beneath the glass and iron façade that ran the length of the property. Mrs Montrose, who had an unrivalled reputation for tardiness, was nowhere to be seen.

"We'll miss the train at this rate!" he grumbled, glaring back through the large double doors into reception.

"We're disappointed you're leaving us so early." Cassandra gave his scowl a warm smile. "Have you told reception when you'll be back?"

"No plans," Mr Montrose replied, glancing at his wife as she swept through the doors. "What kept you?"

"I had to wait for the water to heat up *again*." Mrs Montrose's expensively highlighted hair was wet, the hotel's complimentary flip-flops still on her feet.

"One of the joys of owning a period property," Cassandra quipped, helping Mrs Montrose into the car. "Do you mind if we join you? We're going your way." A rhetorical question, as Greer was already onboard.

"Once we're not late," growled Mr Montrose, as Fudge headed down the drive and through the gates, turning left towards the harbour.

"The forecast's good for the rest of the week, shame you couldn't stay and make the most of it," Cassandra said, watching Mrs Montrose applying her sunscreen. "Been a lovely summer, hasn't it?"

"I've an appointment," Mr Montrose interjected.

"New hip," his wife whispered.

"Alright, Betty, no need to put it on the news!" Mr Montrose chided.

"Why don't you come back to convalesce then?" Cassandra asked.

"We might," Mrs Montrose replied, pulling large sunglasses over her eyes.

"We fancy a change, to be honest." Mr Montrose turned to face the hotel director.

Cassandra was taken aback. "You'd have to be careful travelling abroad after the operation, surely, Conran? And we'd take very good care of you while you recover, that's the best idea, isn't it, Betty?"

"To be frank, Cassandra," Mr Montrose continued. "We've booked the other place."

The vehicle lurched towards the cliff edge, passengers thrown against one another with the force of it. Fudge hauled back on the wheel, swerving slightly before continuing more sedately along the road.

"The *other* place?" Cassandra wailed lustily, evoking Wilde's Lady Bracknell.

"The new one, the Harbour Spa Hotel," Mrs Montrose replied. "With Conran having the operation we thought he could do with, you know, a bit extra. Massage, steam room and such, they've a mineral pool and hydration suite too, I believe."

"Plans for a golf course," Mr Montrose enthused. "And the chef has an excellent reputation."

Cassandra nudged Greer, who had been gazing gloomily at the floor.

"Had you heard that, Greer?" She turned to Mrs Montrose. "Greer's boss has a chain of hotels, not sure if he's ever been in any of them, not quite the personal touch, isn't that right, Greer?"

Greer took her cue.

"Don't know if the Harbour Spa is part of a chain, but they're certainly bringing a whole new clientele to the area."

"Is that so?" Mr Montrose gazed out of the window, disinterested.

"Indeed. A lot of younger, well-heeled foreigners. Sure, you hardly hear an Irish accent up there, isn't that right, Fudge?" Cassandra prompted.

Fudge, knowing by her tone assent was required, grunted in agreement, although this was far from the case. The Harbour Spa Hotel was a centre of excellence, nurturing home-grown talent. Greer noticed Mrs Montrose squirm in her seat. They all knew Conran was a complete xenophobe, anyone he deemed foreign – and his deciding who was and who was not was completely random – made him anxious, one of the reasons they holidayed in Rosshaven, not two hours from their Dublin home.

"Funnily enough, Greer and I are going there now." Cassandra was breezy. "The chief executive wants some advice. He's doing themed evenings, you know, waiters dressed up as Vikings, rock bands, fireworks, all likes of that."

"I heard they're going to give bingo a bit of a revival." Fudge scratched his beard, hiding his grin.

"And karaoke!" Greer confirmed.

"Karaoke? Who'd have thought it!" Cassandra gushed, as Conran Montrose glared at his wife.

They drove on in bristly silence. Mrs Montrose spoke first. "It doesn't look like that sort of place at all, does it, Conran?"

Her husband drew in air through shiny teeth. "What am I always telling you about them websites? Don't even be real pictures half the time. Computer-generated. The whole feckin' world is computer-generated these days!"

They lurched around a corner as Fudge pulled into the station car park.

"Here we are and in plenty of time," Cassandra announced. "You can always rely on the Manorcliff team to deliver!"

"That was wicked." Greer gave Cassandra an accusing look over the glass-topped table.

"You mean the Montroses? I don't think so. They've become more and more picky, demanding this and that, and the constant complaining's getting on my nerves."

"Don't want to lose good customers though, they come a few times a year, don't they? And they're big tippers." Greer examined one of the hotel's logo-embossed coasters.

"She would be, if he wasn't so tight."

"I don't think expecting hot water is *too* demanding, do you?"

Cassandra sent her sister a scorching stare. "Don't you dare take their side. They've been planning their betrayal for ages. Bríd spotted them having lunch here the other day."

"But *we're* having lunch here."

"That's different. We're here for research."

"Of course." The more Greer saw of the Harbour Spa Hotel and its cliff-side restaurant, the more impressed she was. Cassandra watched Greer taking it in.

"I know, it's fabulous, isn't it?" She waved a hand at the view. The beach, the harbour, the island basking in a high noon sun, the sky deepest blue as far as the eye could see, wisps of angel hair cloud on the horizon.

Greer looked around the terrace. Beautifully designed wicker furniture, plump cushions covered in creamy linen, huge Asian-style parasols creating cool, shady spots, tassel fringes wafting in the breeze. Every element spelt quality and style, the gleaming rails of the balcony reminiscent of an ocean liner, the billowing canopy a sail.

"We've never had competition like this," Greer remarked.

"It is a worry," Cassandra replied, "And it's making an impact, we're losing custom, make no mistake."

"Is Manorcliff losing money?"

"Not quite yet, but it's getting harder to balance the

books. I keep slicing things to the bone, trying to do stuff ourselves to save a bit, but we're creaking at the seams, we need some real investment if we're going to stand a chance against the likes of this." Her gaze swept the terrace, full of well-heeled diners ordering good wine and expensive food.

"What can I do to help?" Greer asked.

"Ah, no, Greer. You have your own career and more than enough on your plate."

Greer's face fell. *What career?* Cassandra reached out, taking her sister's hand.

"I'm sorry. I didn't mean to blurt all that out." She gave Greer a smile. "Come on, let's order a nice bottle of wine and chill for a while. We're neither of us very good at that, are we?"

Greer smiled back. Cassandra looked tired, her usually bright eyes dull.

"Manorcliff's in *real* trouble, isn't it?" Greer asked gently.

"We've had hard times before, we'll be grand."

"Is that what yesterday's trip to Dublin was about, raising funds? Did the bank turn you down?"

"I wasn't at the bank." Cassandra looked away.

"But you have been to the auction rooms." Greer indicated Cassandra's ringless fingers.

"A conversation for another time," Cassandra said firmly. "Now, what do you know about this place?"

Greer frowned, trying to remember.

"It was definitely something Alistair was interested in. American outfit looking for backers, they were forming a consortium, needed to throw loads of money at it, plans for top class facilities."

"A golf course!" they said together. There had been plans to turn some of the Morgans' less productive farmland into a golf course for years, a joint venture with their neighbours the Nagles, which due to a lack of funds had caused something of a rift.

"Guess our plans have been shelved again?" Greer said.

Cassandra gave the waiter their order of two seafood

risottos and a bottle of Chenin Blanc. "Other priorities, I'm afraid. The estimate for the repairs to the dining room is around twenty grand. The plumbing desperately needs attention and being a period property, that's no small job and again, thousands of euro."

"Can't we apply for some sort of grant?"

"I keep meaning to look into it, but it's hard finding the time, there's always so much to do."

"Isn't that my role? The bigger picture stuff."

Cassandra shrugged. "You're always so busy and like I said, haven't seen you in a while."

"You could come and see me."

Cassandra lifted an eyebrow. Greer raised her hands. "I know, I know, the hotel."

They shared a look, deciding not to revisit the row that had incited their estrangement, Cassandra too proud to admit Manorcliff needed help and Greer too stubborn to accept it was time to finish with Alistair, leave her non-existent career and come home. And because one might sense the other was in trouble, neither of them daring to communicate at all.

From an early age the Morgan sisters were acutely aware of how important the success of the hotel was, the lifeblood of the family. They were a tight unit, and the adjacent farmland was worked to provide food and fresh produce for the hotel kitchen, while paying guests provided funds to keep the place operational. During their grandmother's day anything spare went towards the girls' education but she struggled, their needs were so different.

Cassandra was the easiest. Solid, dependable, and hardworking, Cassandra caused little trouble. While Greer, determined and wilful, battled convention and authority every step of way; a talented, difficult child, yet adored by their grandmother nonetheless.

And finally, Orla, the 'middle one'. Wonderful, beguiling, unusual. Orla was an enigma, coming at everything from a different angle, her vision of the world always slightly off kilter. Throughout childhood she had been sent for all kinds of tests and the results were always different, conflicting, and inconclusive, rather like Orla herself. *'Orla's just Orla',* their grandmother would declare. And indeed, she was.

Cassandra watched Greer gazing out to sea, her pre-set air of concern back in place.

"Eat something, love, you're like a wraith." Cassandra indicated her sister's untouched food.

Greer put her cutlery down.

"Did the article say anything about how he is?"

"Still in intensive care, wife at his bedside. High security too, someone from the hospital leaked the police are there twenty-four-seven."

"Poor Alistair." Greer shivered, despite the heat.

"Poor you, I'm thinking."

"Oh, Cass, I'm such an idiot. I'd no idea about the other woman. I truly believed his bullshit, again. I thought the reason I'd seen so little of him was because he was making the most of his new appointment. I believed all that drivel about him wanting to give something back, doing genuine public service. Aaargh!" She dropped her head to the table, resting her brow on the cool glass. A few diners turned to look. She started to cry.

Cassandra handed her a napkin. The waiter was staring.

"Sit up now and don't be making a show of us. We've always given this town enough to talk about without you having a feckin' nervous breakdown in the restaurant of the competition."

Greer let out a laugh. "You're right." She blew her nose. "They'd say I'd done it deliberately, upsetting the lunchtime trade."

Cassandra reached over, wiping a tear away. "So tell me, after saying he was giving this new job his all, he turned around and told you the pressure was too much, and he was finally leaving his wife?" Cassandra's tone was disbelieving. "Well, you've always described him as unpredictable."

"We were on our way to the airport when he got the call to go back. I was to take the bags and he'd meet me there, our flights booked to New York, all sorted. It got later and later; I couldn't reach him. So, furious to put it mildly, I booked a seat on Aer Lingus and came here instead."

"Well, I'm pleased you did, though I'm sure you'd have told me you were living on another continent at some stage." Cassandra gave Greer a hard stare. "Why didn't you go back and find out what happened? I mean you were supposed to be spending the rest of your life with this man."

Greer sniffed.

"I know, but something didn't ring true. And going back didn't feel right, we'd made a plan to leave together, I thought he'd chickened out. Besides, his company owns the flat and my car, if I'd been dumped, what had I to go back to?"

"A big bloody mess by the sounds of things." Cassandra shook her head.

"So here I am, no man, no job, no home and no future." Greer looked about to cry again. Noting their glasses were empty, the waiter, a little less alarmed, poured the wine.

"Well, that's where you're wrong," Cassandra said, once he was out of earshot. "I'm a great believer in us being precisely where we need to be wherever we find ourselves. So, you have a job, a home and a future right here, right now if you'd care to join me."

Greer blinked at her. "You serious?"

"Deadly." Cassandra smiled, watching Greer take this in, eyes filling again, this time with relief. "As for a man, if that's what you want, I'll leave you to your own devices."

"No thanks. I've had it with men. Finally, completely and utterly." She straightened in her chair, placing her hand over her sister's on the shiny tabletop. "I want it to be all about us from now on, us and the family business. That's the way forward."

"Good to hear. A fresh start, none of the old baggage holding us back," Cassandra said, her grin rigid.

"To the future." Greer raised her glass.

"The future," Cassandra agreed.

Halfway down the second bottle of wine, Greer fixed Cassandra with a look. "Can I ask you something?"

"Anything ... anything at all," Cassandra replied warily.

"Were you ashamed, you know, of my relationship with Alistair?"

"I've never been ashamed of you, only proud, don't you ever forget that," Cassandra told her firmly. "But people talk and although it's none of their business, they think it is, you're from here, 'one of our own' they say, I know it's ridiculous but it's like you're letting them down. I get tired of defending you."

Greer was far from naïve, but this was hard to hear. "Well, don't do it then," she said softly.

"You're my sister, I can't let them go round saying what they like!"

"Ah, don't pay any attention, they're not all squeaky clean anyway, not in this old den of iniquity." Greer flung her arm out, embracing the whole harbour.

Cassandra shrugged. "Not the point. They feel you're representing us, the whole of Ireland some would say."

"That's great. Thanks for that." Greer gave Cassandra a wonky smile. "My whole life is basically a freeze-frame of the one time one of my songs made the top of the charts."

"But your music's been adapted for films, TV programmes, advertising, your work is global." Cassandra grinned, remembering what seemed such an innocent time; Greer only in her twenties when Terrence Hennessy – a well-respected Irish broadcaster – interviewed her on the BBC, declaring the young singer/songwriter had a rare talent and would surely make her stamp on the world.

"Over thirty years ago!" *No wonder I just wanted to disappear,* Greer thought, memories of her brief solo career giving her goosebumps. "Ah, Cass, doesn't anyone round here ever move on, you know, live in the twenty-first century?"

Cassandra sat back, holding her wine glass to her chest as

she closed her eyes drinking in the sun.

"And why would they do that? Far better to live in the past, keep those old prejudices alive, the grudges, the ancient feuds. Something we Irish have always been particularly good at."

Greer shot her sister a look. Cassandra could hold a grudge for years, her feuds never-ending. Reading her mind, Cassandra raised her hand.

"Don't even mention his name." She fixed Greer with a look.

Unseen, an elegant man with wiry hair and twinkling grey eyes behind classic shades stood at the far end of the balcony admiring them.

"Will you be joining the ladies, Mr Fitzgerald?" the waiter asked. "I can bring another chair."

"No, no … not today thank you," he replied, in his beautiful distinctive rasp. "A pleasure deferred." And taking a final puff of his French cigarette he exited stage left, as was his wont.

Ghostly Whispers

After lunch with Cassandra at the Harbour Spa Hotel, Greer had much to think about. This was not the first time she had made a life-changing decision in a split second. Yet the more she thought about it, the more she knew it was the right thing to do.

But before she could move forward, Greer needed to deal with the past; there were reasons why she had left Rosshaven all those years ago and not all the reasons had been resolved or even faced.

And then there was the more recent past, the wrangle of life she had left behind in London.

However optimistic she might be starting to feel, she was not stupid, and there was a distinct danger, elements of what she had been involved in were going to resurface and give her a very nasty nip on the behind.

A good, head-clearing clifftop walk was required. Tone, who had been enjoying a peaceful snooze with Wolfe out of the way, looked up expectantly from his basket as she pulled on her sailing jacket, flicking a glance at his lead on the hook.

"Come on then," she said, and with one swish of his tail they disappeared through the door.

She was standing in a half-moon cavern cut out of rock high on the cliff, a smugglers' den with a large moss-covered boulder at its entrance. Once inside, the soft, sandy floor and smooth walls were womb-like, the wind muted to a whisper.

Greer took up her perch, a raised slab affording a panoramic view of five small bays of blue sea and golden sand, known locally as The Giant's Gems, as if a huge bracelet of shiny turquoise beads had been dropped along the shore. To her left, she could see the luscious curve that formed the natural harbour of Rosshaven, its port and wharfs at the waters' edge with the town nestled comfortably behind.

And out to sea rose Phoenix Island, shining dark and broody, even in the brightest sunlight. The movement of day trippers weaving around the ruins blurred, giving through her half-closed eyes the impression the island was breathing, the sea-beast at rest.

She pictured the granite caves on the far side. The ragged stone, a shark tooth smile, recalling times she and her sisters would steal into the echoing caves, pushing the old rowing boat through the dark water, calling out their mother's name, over and over. Convinced this was the gateway to the Sea Witch's lair, where their mother was locked away like a fabled princess and they were sent 'Famous Five' style to bring her home so they could be a family again, no longer the sad little orphans everyone pitied.

Pulling her jacket closed, she kissed Tone's domed head, a comforting bundle in her arms, gazing at the horizon. For a while they sat still and quiet in her hideaway, the map of her homeland laid out before her, the haunts of childhood days dotted along the coast.

So many plans, schemes and dreams had been hatched here in this secret place, and as she recalled, ghostly whispers of the past started to swirl about her and no matter how hard she tried to push them away, memories of laughter and sunshine drifted through her mind, and she was again a child playing on the sand.

Closing her eyes, she saw the tartan rug and watched her plump toddler fingers grab the rug, squishing the sand beneath the fabric, then smoothing it flat with her palm. She could feel the weather changing, the breeze off the sea turning cool, the waves building, spray on her face. She started to cry, looking round for her mother, trying to see where she had gone, wondering why she had left her alone on the rug on the beach.

And then she remembered, the little dog, barking in alarm and someone running, lifting her up out of the cold, wet sand, burying her head under a coat that smelled musky and sweet. And though she felt safe, still she looked back, trying to see where her mother had gone. She could not remember a witch but knew what she saw, in that split second – a man. A man with wild black hair and blue-black eyes, who swam up through the waves, to wrap her mother in his arms and take her away.

She started to scream.

Even now Greer could feel the panic mounting in her chest, the way it always did whenever she went back to that cold, dark day, and shaking her head to free the memory she saw someone coming towards her. Tall, hair streaked back by the wind, long flapping coat, bold strides as he moved up the cliff path then onto the trail that led to the cave.

The figure slipped behind a fuzz of gorse. Gone.

She wiped her eyes, damp with memories.

The figure reappeared, closer this time.

She caught her breath, recognising the gait.

It could not be.

Not him. Not here.

She jumped up. Tone slid to the ground, and grabbing the lead she started off in the opposite direction, pulling at the hood of her jacket. She could hear boots on the path, crunching the shale, speeding up behind her. She broke into a run.

"Wait!" he called. "Greer, wait!"

She did not look back. Not this time. She could hear him gaining on her. The sound of his boots, breath coming hard through his nostrils.

"Stop!" He ran in front of her.

She had to stop, the path was narrow, the cliff fell sharply away.

She stepped to the side; he matched her stride.

"Let me pass." She lowered her eyes. "*Please* let me pass."

He reached towards her, and she flinched backwards, her foot slipping. He grabbed her arm. She shrugged it free and turning her eyes on his, her blood turned to ice.

He greeted the dog.

"Don't touch him, he'll have your hand off!" Dog and man blinked at each other, wondering which would bite.

"Greer, please, can we talk?"

She had made a vow. Never again. "I've nothing to say."

"We need to talk."

"Nothing to say."

"But *I* have." His eyes held her gaze. Darkest blue, deep as the sea.

"Nothing I want to hear." She looked away. "Now, *please* let me pass."

He stood for a moment, then stepped aside, and keeping a tight hold of Tone's lead, Greer strode on.

Orla and Wolfe were out in the Land Rover with Nagle. Discovering her siblings had hitched a lift into Rosshaven and with Bríd at the cash and carry in Gorey, she was at a loose end. She had missed her chance of a sail with Dr James, because having been up all night going through her precious shell collection, she had overslept. It would soon be Cassandra's birthday and she had decided to create something special.

She had heard her sister on the phone, telling whoever was on the other end that it had been a difficult few years and they 'weren't out of the woods' yet and from 'where she was standing' – which was in the kitchen as far as Orla could tell – she wondered if it was worth it and should she just call it quits and sell.

These events were not unusual; Orla listening to conversations or Cassandra needing to sell something. There had always been a lot of buying and selling at Manorcliff. The hotel was full of antiques and artefacts, with a very fine jewellery collection locked away in the family vault. Though the sisters rarely wore any of it, flaunting one's wealth had always been something their grandmother decried – unless of course she needed to make a point, then she would be espied flaunting with the best of them.

Orla distinctly remembered a diamond-encrusted tiara Nana favoured on very special occasions. Legend had it that Princess Margaret, honeymooning with Lord Snowden in Abbeyleix at the time, remarked on it when their grandmother attended a dinner in the royal couple's honour. Bought off a pirate ship in the early 1800s, it allegedly belonged to Russia's Catherine the Great. Not that unusual, nearly everyone in Rosshaven had something of dubious heritage off a pirate ship – quite the local tradition.

While still very young, Orla asked to borrow the tiara to make a copy out of shells and sea glass. She knew there was a day dedicated to mothers once a year and this year she wanted to be ready, so when the cards appeared in the shops, she could buy one, taking it with her replica tiara to the special rock, where she left her messages. It was a gift for their mother, who would surely be allowed to leave the Sea Witch's castle, just for this one special day to swim with her daughters. But their mother never came, so Orla threw the card and tiara into the sea.

"You're very quiet," Nagle said, pulling onto the lane. Orla often accompanied him on his rounds, checking livestock, water troughs, fences. She particularly loved 'minding the beasts in the fields' as she called them and would jump in and out of the Land Rover seeking a tool for this, a rope for that. But not today. Today she sat quietly, hands in her lap, the sparkly blue evening dress she had been wearing since dinner the night before just visible beneath her raincoat.

She gave him a smile. Orla had the serenest of smiles, Nagle thought, and the vilest of tempers too.

"I'm having a quiet day today. It's been very noisy in my head lately and I was up all night sorting through my stock."

"You couldn't do that during the day? You need your sleep, Orla, we all do." Nagle was remembering the time Orla had camped on the beach for nearly a month because a pair of seals had come into the bay. She stayed awake night after night, making notes of their conversations, the stories they told her. If Dr James had not finally coaxed her home, Nagle was convinced Orla would have succumbed to pneumonia, giving Cassandra a nervous breakdown.

"It has to be done in the moonlight, then you can tell which pieces work best for eveningwear, the light off the water is very different at night," Orla reminded him.

They were heading towards Nagle's boatshed – Orla particularly liked picking over the lobster creels, sorting ones that needed repairing, finding tiny little treasures she could use in her jewellery making – when Wolfe started to bark. There was someone at the boatshed, a woman wearing an old-fashioned mackintosh, silver hair twisted in an extravagant bun.

"Look, it's Miss Finn!" Orla called out.

"She's a long way from home. Can you see her boat?"

The woman gave a wave.

"Maybe she wants a lift back. We could take her in one of yours, it's a grand day to be out on the water."

Nagle groaned. "I hope she doesn't need a lift. I'm very busy and it's a good run over to her place."

"Only an hour there and back," Orla said.

"In a speed boat maybe. No, Orla, not today."

Nagle parked the Land Rover. The woman opened the door.

"What kept you?" she asked gruffly, dangling earrings trembling with indignation.

Shell Shocked

T wenty minutes later Nagle and Orla had loaded Miss Finn's mismatch of bags into a boat. Miss Finn lived alone in an isolated cottage on the far side of the bay and having secured passage to the harbour with a local fisherman, was now stranded. The busyness of the town had left her exhausted, and she had come to find someone who would feel obliged to escort her back.

"I can't come with you," Nagle told them. "I've promised Cassandra I'll look at the boiler, some new people are arriving this evening and they'll want hot water. I said I couldn't get there till later, but I can't let her down."

"We'll be grand, won't we, Miss Finn?" Orla said, taking the tiller as Nagle started the motor. He stepped out of the boat, water whooshing over his boots.

"How will you get back?" Nagle was concerned. Orla's power of concentration was admirable when fully applied but she was easily distracted, and bad weather was forecast.

"I'll take a bike once I've tied the boat up." She nodded towards the boathouse where Nagle kept a clutch of cycles, a kindness for tourists who ill-judged the tide and needed transport back.

"Have you your mobile?" he called after her.

"Of course," she replied, then addressing the woman perched in the bow, "Have you a mobile, Miss Finn?"

Miss Finn, whose face was badly scarred, arched her unaffected brow sardonically.

"Naturally," she said loudly. "Safety first where I'm concerned, you know that. I've a ship-to-shore radio in one of my bags too, just in case."

Nagle glanced skywards. "Well, make haste, Orla, come straight back. Drop Miss Finn off and turn round, yes?"

Orla waved in reply, already scudding the little tender away from the jetty and out to sea. Miss Finn and Wolfe were sitting shoulder to shoulder at the front, as rigidly as a masthead, as he pressed close to the old lady's skinny frame, tail wagging sedately in the breeze. He was clearly enamoured, Orla always felt like that in her company too.

After the teabags and rich-fruit barmbrack had been located in one of Miss Finn's many bags, it seemed rude to rush home. The cottage had certainly not played host to any sort of visitor for some time, if the standard of housekeeping was to be the benchmark.

Despite her gruffness, the old lady seemed pleased to share a brew and slice of cake with her saviours, and besides Orla and Wolfe were starving, because having overslept Orla had yet again forgotten breakfast.

Eventually bringing the last of the logs in for the fire, the cottage damp despite the sunshine, Orla decided it was time to go when she noticed Miss Finn had fallen asleep. She and Wolfe were just tiptoeing out when a gust of wind rattled the door and the old lady awoke with a grunt.

"You off, are you?" she said, rousing from the chair, still in her old mac.

"Better get back, people worry if I'm out on the water in the dark, which is stupid because we see better in the dark, don't we, Wolfe?"

"Wait, I've something for you," Miss Finn instructed and scuttled off into the parlour, returning with a small bundle. She passed her guest a lump of something bulkily wrapped in old newspaper, and Orla opened it slowly to reveal a large conch shell. She gasped as it shone up at her, the smooth, pearly pink, luminescent against the grubby newsprint.

"Is it for me?" she whispered, shocked at so beautiful and

generous a gift. She knew Miss Finn kept her own treasured collection and over the years had given Orla the odd present of a quirky shell or two but never anything like this; this was spectacular.

The woman nodded, her mouth stretched in a scarred grin at her visitor's delight. Orla laid its cool surface against her cheek.

"Warm ice." Orla gave a smile. "I always think shells feel like warm ice." She went to lift it to her ear; Miss Finn stopped her.

"You need to get going or the tide will turn, you don't want to be stranded."

Orla was disappointed, the shell looked like it had lots to tell, but seeing Miss Finn grow agitated, she quickly wrapped the paper back around her gift.

"Thank you so much, Miss Finn. I feel sure it's very special, I'll get loads of messages, probably a direct line."

Miss Finn shrugged. "It's just a shell, Orla. I know you like them." She opened the door. "Go now, I've seen enough people today to last me a month. Fecking tourists, I thought those cheap airlines were supposed to take them all away?"

Orla laughed, clutching the shell to her chest. Miss Finn was always complaining about something, everyone said it was no wonder she never married, who would put up with her giving out all the time and having to look at her scarred, weepy old face. Poor Miss Finn.

Cassandra was just about to send out a search party when a long-eared dog and what looked like a young woman on an old bike came wobbling up the drive. It was Orla, hair flying in the breeze, Wolfe loping along beside her. Tone confirmed their arrival with a loud woof as he charged across the lawn to greet them.

Nagle, lurking in the background, breathed a sigh of relief. Cassandra had wiped the floor with him for allowing Orla to go out in a boat with Miss Finn, despite him explaining for the umpteenth time that Orla was a grown woman, and it was not up to him or anyone else to 'allow' her to do anything. Orla might be unusual, but she was not stupid. And even worse, he had to tell her the boiler was beyond repair, which was now his fault too.

"At last!" Cassandra turned to Nagle who had disappeared into the hotel. "Where've you been?" she demanded as Orla drew up beside her.

"Isn't Nagle here?" Orla asked.

"Yes," Cassandra replied.

"Well, you know where I've been then, because I'm sure he's told you." Orla widened her eyes at her sister. Cassandra widened her eyes back.

"I was worried."

"You're always worried."

"Well, try not to worry me then!" Cassandra made her eyes even wider.

"I'll continue to do my very best," Orla said charmingly, pushing the bike ahead as she strode off, Tone and Wolfe trotting behind.

The entire upper floor seemed to reverberate. Greer was lying in the bath, up to her ears in silky suds as she hummed along to an ancient rock ballad at full volume. Orla poked her nose around the door.

"You probably need to turn that down – the paying guests mightn't like it."

"*What?*" Greer shouted at her.

"*Turn it down!*"

"*Why?*"

"Paying guests." Orla nipped in, closing the door quickly behind her. She had changed into velvet jeans and a silk blouse, her hair piled high and stuck with shell-covered combs, and she was wearing lipstick too Greer noted, grabbing the remote to lower the music.

"Honestly, your life is never your own in this place, it's in hock to the paying guests!"

"Ah shush, will you! You know the rules, if you must play music when we've paying guests, it has to be traditional Irish or classical." Another of their grandmother's decrees. "Anyway, you'd better get a move on, cocktails at half-six, dinner at eight."

"Am I on duty?" Greer's conker-coloured mop was full of conditioner.

"Was I not told you've joined the family firm full time?" Orla was using Greer's mascara. Greer groaned. "Means you're on duty all the time, you know that." Orla turned from her reflection as Greer ducked beneath the water, and a greasy slick floated to the surface. Orla sat on the edge of the bath waiting for her sister to reappear. She broke through the water noisily.

"Need a hand getting ready?" Orla asked.

"No thanks," Greer replied through much nose-blowing. "I won't be getting as glammed up as you, what's the occasion?"

"It's Saturday."

Greer frowned disbelievingly. Orla usually needed a valid reason to don her precious shell jewellery and she looked like she was wearing most of it.

"Hurry up, Cass is in a filthy mood and Nagle's gone home, so he won't be helping tonight." She made to leave. Greer was already in her robe, Cassandra on the rampage was not a pretty sight.

"What's she so annoyed about?"

"I took Miss Finn back in Nagle's boat."

"So?"

"And the boiler's broken."

"Is it?" Greer looked into the bath as the steamy bubbles disappeared.

"Or someone used all the hot water," Orla laughed.

Passing Greer the hairdryer, she noticed the collection of old CDs on the dresser. "That looks like a stroll down memory lane."

Greer shrugged. "I saw someone today who reminded me,

that's all."

"Ah, an enigmatic creature of the night, the irresistible Rai Muir, no doubt."

Sometimes Greer forgot what a brilliant memory Orla had, especially good at reminding people of exactly what they had said, no matter how long ago it was.

Greer switched the dryer off. "You knew! And you didn't think to tell me?" She glanced at the tiny half-moon tattoo on the inside of her left wrist. "Who told you he was back? Was it the shells?"

Orla shook her head. "Nope, Nagle saw him pulling pints behind the bar in *The Pirate*. Just passing through, he said, catching up with a few old friends."

Greer wondered if Rai had any friends left. "Anyone in particular?"

"Archie Fitzgerald, of course, they've always been close."

"Ah, Archie." Greer did not want it known she had met Archie on the beach soon after her arrival. Orla could let it slip and knowing how her eldest sister felt about him, it would be deemed a betrayal not to have mentioned it. News of an innocent meeting would certainly precipitate a confrontation and to be honest Greer had a bad case of battle fatigue, she had been fighting for far too long. "How's he doing?"

"In great form. Coming up to a big birthday and making all sorts of plans," Orla said.

"Plans? Don't tell me he's finally starting work on Galty House, he's always said he needs to do it up before it falls down!"

"Not sure about that but he definitely has a spring in his step, reminds me of years ago."

"Years ago?"

"Yes, when he was madly in love with Cassandra, you remember, always here playing music, taking her out on his boat, inviting us all to watch him at the theatre."

Archie had featured in their lives as far back as Greer could remember.

"She was always laughing when Archie was around," Greer recalled, that was until the time Cassandra came back from catering college in England and announced she never, ever wanted to see Archie Fitzgerald again.

"Is he coming tonight?" Greer wondered if the actor, now one of Ireland's most lauded thespians, was the reason for Orla's glamour.

"'Fraid not," Orla said, leading her sister out. "Cassandra won't have him in the house."

"Still? For pity's sake, how long is this feud to continue?"

"It's worse than ever. She's put all the old photographs in the vault."

"What? Wiped him away?" Greer was dismayed.

"As far as she's concerned, Archie Fitzgerald doesn't exist and never has," Orla confirmed. "Like a body lost at sea."

Secret Stars

The new guests at Manorcliff were a German family, mother and father with a teenage son and daughter. They had flown into Dublin and were exploring Ireland's Ancient East before crossing the country to pick up the Great Atlantic Way, the spectacular western seaboard stretching from Kinsale in the south to Donegal in the north.

The boy was trying to be enthusiastic, asking questions about the history of the hotel but the girl was sullen, barely speaking to her parents and ignoring her brother completely. The Morgan sisters gave one another a knowing look; the Schmidts' stay had 'last family holiday before the kids go off and do their own thing' written all over it.

At dinner, Greer noticed the girl was wearing half-moon earrings and a bracelet of stars, and it gave her an idea. The teenager's angst had struck a chord. Strange but whenever she was home memories of those raw emotions, fuelled by raging hormones, seemed particularly vivid. Or maybe it was just seeing him again, the last person she would wish to encounter while feeling so low. He would know with one look she was vulnerable, unprepared for any sort of combat. Wounded. Disarmed. Beaten.

"I see by your lovely jewellery you like the night sky," Greer said quietly. The girl touched her bracelet, glancing at her mother.

"I think the planets have more impact on our lives than people imagine," the girl replied, her clipped German accent giving her words authority. The whole table looked at her; it was the most she had said to anyone since they arrived.

"I believe that too," Greer told her.

"So do I!" Orla chimed in, breaking away from an engaging discussion about dolphins with Dr James. "The moon rules the tides and our moods, it's all connected."

"If you like, after dinner, I've something to show you, you might find interesting," Greer said.

"You do?" The girl sounded doubtful.

Greer shrugged. She would not push it. The Moon Room was out of bounds, unused for years. Cassandra would be furious if she knew Greer had taken a guest there.

The mother glared at her child. "Thank you, I'm sure she would like that very much, wouldn't you, Ava?"

Ava just nodded, continuing to push congealing Irish stew aimlessly around her plate.

"You'll love it, I promise," Greer whispered.

The moon was full, its face clearly visible, the hinted-at smile plain to see. She loved to watch the silver planet trace its silky path across the heavens, a ghostly galleon plotting a course through the deep dark sky. Moonstruck, Nana used to call it, chasing her out and back to bed whenever she found her there.

This was a journey she and Rai had taken many times, a silent secret shared from an early age, when having found her way into the Moon Room she sought him out, making him follow so she could share this hidden treasure with him, only him.

He was ten at the time, she nearly six and the secret had won his heart, the pact made, never to be broken and she had built her love for him on this. Rai, trusted and adored above all else, beyond every other who tried to win her heart. And deep down, no matter what, that love remained. Always had. Always would.

Now gazing up at the man in the moon, with his half smile, she wondered had he known all along? And if he had, what sort of friend was he not to have warned her that the pact was false and would break her heart in two?

Greer let the telescope fall from her eye, dropping it to rest on its stand. She glared up at the moon, hurt again. But he and his half smile had taken refuge behind a coal-black cloud. *The shivering coward*, she thought and not for the first time.

"Can I come in?"

Greer swung round. Ava had found her.

"Of course, over here. But be careful, the floor has holes in it." She beckoned her across the room to stand beneath the vast glass dome, a window to the night sky.

"Oh!" the teenager declared and finally a smile lit her face. "This is *so* cool."

Greer grinned, enjoying her delight. "Probably my most favourite place in the whole of Ireland. No, make that the world." She stood back to let Ava take hold of the telescope and fall hopelessly in love with the mystery of the sky at night, as she had done in exactly the same spot, so many years ago.

Having seen Ava safely off to bed, Greer slipped into the kitchen. Orla was at the other end of the table laying out breakfast.

"You alright?" Cassandra asked. "Seem a bit distant tonight."

"I'm fine." Greer avoided Cassandra's eyes.

"See anyone out on your walk today?" Cassandra flicked pages of her recipe book.

"Not especially," Greer replied, choosing not to reveal who she had met on the cliff earlier. At the height of their acrimony, splashed across the media for all to see, Cassandra had tried to broker a truce, pleading with them to see sense, come home, start again. Until she had no choice but to walk away and leave them to it, the relationship complicated by their dependency on one another and Rai's dependencies, prescribed and otherwise. It had all come to a head just before the tragedy struck that signalled the end of the band and the beginning of Greer's plans to go it alone, set up home in London and leave everything else behind.

Greer also decided not to mention her visit to the Moon Room. "I was about to ask the same of you. You're very quiet."

"I hope not!" Cassandra was put out.

"No, not with the paying guests but your mind's elsewhere. You're not right since the trip to Dublin, has something else come up?"

"Not at all. Sure, I only did a bit of shopping and had lunch with an old friend."

"Anyone I know?"

"Not especially." She closed the book, changing the subject. "Can you do a drinks order tomorrow please, Greer? And try to keep it under budget."

"Of course."

The sisters fell silent as they finished their chores.

By the time everything was shipshape Cassandra looked exhausted.

"You head up," Greer told her. "Orla and I will give the dogs a quick spin and lock up. Get some rest."

Greer waited until she and Orla were strolling through the herb garden and well out of earshot before broaching the subject.

"Do you know what Cassandra was doing in Dublin yesterday?"

Orla shook her head, the lights from the terrace casting soft shadows on the gravel as they walked, Wolfe and Tone blithely sniffing the undergrowth, unaware their mistresses were anxiously deliberating their eldest sister's sullenness.

"Another appointment, like the last time?" Greer pressed.

"I think that's finished for now, shells haven't said anything anyway."

"Who was she seeing then? Do you know?"

"Could be anyone," Orla shrugged. "She knows loads of people in Dublin and any amount of people from here could be there, shopping, collecting people from the airport, who knows?"

Greer shoved her hands in her pockets as they walked.

Orla was right, Cassandra's trip to the capital might not have had anything to do with what was worrying her, and looking up at the hotel, Greer considered there was probably more than enough to give her sister sleepless nights right here.

"Any news from anywhere you think might have upset her?"

Orla frowned. News was her department after all. Apart from her doubtless mystical talents, Orla had one very practical side to her personality, she was a wizard with technology. Anything to do with the internet came easy to her. She handled all the hotel's online bookings, updated the website, and co-ordinated the social media accounts.

Although Cassandra liked to approve what she posted, Greer knew it was Orla's slightly off-the-wall blogs, photos and updates that helped highlight Manorcliff's eccentric charm. A video of Wolfe trying to capture waves with his paws already had thousands of views on Instagram.

Orla had been put in charge of the mail from a very early age. As she found reading difficult, Nana gave her the job of distributing the post, emphasising its importance for the successful running of the hotel. Embracing her now vital role, Orla's concentration kicked in and she was soon able to decipher letters.

It had worked like a dream, except even now mail did not go directly to the addressee without Orla decreeing it should. And vague as Orla could be, she also knew enough to wield a censorious axe when she felt like it, delaying or declining the delivery of certain items depending on what the shells told her.

Greer remembered, after one particularly horrendous row with their grandmother, finding a pile of prospectuses from far-flung private schools hidden in an abandoned cupboard. The discovery only exacerbated the row, with Nana insisting Orla had been put up to such duplicitous behaviour by the very person the schools were being vetted to admit.

Yet despite her sister's best intentions, Greer had been sent to boarding school anyway, Nana determined the rebellious ten-year-old would imbibe some sort of discipline from somewhere.

But like all these educational excursions, Greer's sojourn at the Grace Dieu School for Girls in darkest County Mayo had been cut short. The result of her writing many letters of beseeching apology home, and both Nana and her sisters missing her desperately.

"There might be something." Orla stopped at the farthest bench, the one perched on the cliff edge, the point of the promontory where Rosshaven swept around to the left and the five coves stretched in lazy loops on the right. The moon had reappeared, streaming a molten ripple across the tumbling sea. The sisters sat, dogs nestling conspiratorially at their feet.

"She's had a couple of letters from England I don't recognise," Orla confirmed.

Greer thought for a moment. "Is that so odd? She must receive lots you don't recognise, what's special about these?"

Orla scratched behind Tone's ears absentmindedly. "They feel urgent. Not in an official 'must do this' way but in a needy kind of way, as if someone's asking a question."

"About the hotel?"

"More personal. The envelopes are typed and say plainly 'Private and Confidential', but they don't come here."

"What do you mean?"

"They don't come in the post but still arrive here anyway."

"How many?"

"Two, so far."

"And have you read them?"

Orla laughed. "Greer, you know I'm not supposed to read correspondence that's not addressed to me." She quoted the official line, declining to mention that while updating bookings in the office, her hands itched so viciously around Cassandra's desk, she opened a drawer and found the file containing the Dublin post box correspondence.

But she was telling the truth, she had not read the letters.

Greer gave Orla a wide-eyed look.

"I did ask the shells about them."

"And?" Greer pressed.

"Nothing yet."

"Why do you say yet?" Greer pulled up the zip on her old sailing jacket; it was chilly beyond the shelter of the terrace.

"Takes time for things to filter through. The shells don't like to send messages too early, things change, and my information needs to be as up to date as possible. The Sea Witch would be really annoyed if I gave out some news before it's ready and you know if we do anything to upset her, messages stop coming all together."

Greer squeezed Orla's hand; it was freezing.

"We'd better wait, then," Greer said. Orla's instincts were usually spot on. They started back.

"I did take a call though."

Greer paused. Orla took a lot of calls.

"It was Humphrey. Haven't spoken to him in ages. We were laughing about something, and Cass took the phone off me, telling him to ring her mobile."

"Ah, Humphrey, that old pirate." Greer gave Orla a curious smile. "You think Humphrey and these letters are connected?"

"I'm not sure. But I noticed the same feeling, a hanging in the air type of thing, like rain coming."

"Or a storm?" Greer looked back out to sea.

"Oh, there's storms coming, alright. The shells are sure about that."

And Orla did that skipping off thing that drove Greer crazy, because no more would be said until the shells decreed the time was right and that could be as close as tomorrow or as far off as Christmas and even Orla did not know when yet.

A Tip-Off

T he door opened a crack. Greer sat up. The general uneasiness of the day was still with her, despite the comfort of her own room.

"Are you awake?"

Greer was very particular about who could and could not enter her room, Cassandra had been barred a few times over the years.

"I am now." Greer slid out of bed, letting her eldest sister in. Cassandra's hair fell in waves to her shoulders, and she wore a classic Iggy Pop sweatshirt over paisley pyjama bottoms. Greer smiled; still her cool big sis.

She closed the door quietly behind her, the extravagant fringed lamp casting a soft glow as Greer indicated her sister take up the time-honoured position at the end of the bed. Propped on a large velvet cushion, Cassandra tucked her feet beneath the eiderdown and took a deep breath.

"I'd a phone call today," Cassandra began. "It was Humphrey. A tip-off if you like."

Greer waited. A tiny tingle of dread fluttered deep in her stomach.

"Apparently, the investigation into the tax affairs of the wealthy businessman Frances was talking about, *is* Alistair." She shot Greer a look. Greer had not mentioned him since their lunch at the Harbour Spa Hotel, but Cassandra had been reading plenty of press speculation about the affairs of Alistair McKeiver, who was still in intensive care in one of London's most exclusive hospitals. "Evidence has come to light he's been involved in something serious, very serious indeed."

The tingle spread. Greer remained tight-lipped. She was not sure where this conversation was going, and saying anything might incriminate her or worse, she could divulge information that might compromise her sister. Cassandra had been head of this household since she was a girl and nothing scared her. Even so, she looked worried, and Greer did not like that one bit.

"I'm right in assuming you know about his business practices?"

"I know Alistair, which also means I certainly *don't* know everything," Greer replied.

"If there was any wrongdoing, anything that might be perceived as criminal activity, you wouldn't be party to that surely, Greer?"

Greer frowned. Cassandra always played it straight, no murkiness, no blurred edges to her way of thinking.

"That depends."

"Depends on what?"

"On what sort of wrongdoing. Alistair is a successful man, Cass, his business affairs complex, I was just a project manager."

"A little more than that, I'd have said."

Greer sighed. "He's very good at keeping everything compartmentalised. Anything he shares is always only on a 'need to know' basis."

Cassandra raised her eyebrows. "No pillow talk revelations?"

Greer tried not to roll her eyes. "What did Humphrey say?"

"The investigators are widening the net," Cassandra whispered, sounding like a character in a TV cop show. "Humphrey says his enemies have the knives out and are determined to reclaim millions in tax and put him away for a very long time."

"Good luck to them. Alistair's not stupid, he'll have the best advisors acting on his behalf and despite what you may think, Cass, he isn't a bad person."

Cassandra kept her counsel. Greer had been fond of Alistair, perhaps even in love with him once, it hurt to see her so wounded.

"I hope he realises how lucky he is to have someone as loyal as you in his life. It would be wrong if all this impacted on your reputation. Bad enough the newspapers implying you're having an affair, calling it a 'close personal relationship'."

"Don't worry, Cass, Amy will have the PR machine jumping all over them, they'll hush up soon enough." Greer's eyes were downcast as she plucked at the eiderdown; she did not want to cry again. "Anyway, no one cares about my reputation, it's different for a woman, you know that."

"Well, it's wrong! It takes two to tango and he's the one who's married, not you."

Greer turned watery eyes at her sister. "What else did Humphrey say?"

"It's likely you'll be called to give evidence or make a statement at least."

"Great. That's all I need." Greer slipped under the covers, pulling the duvet over her head.

"Look, if that's the case, just tell the truth."

Greer resurfaced. "That would be easy if I knew what the truth was. Since his government appointment I've seen very little of him. Dinner dates cancelled, meetings postponed, almost as if he's pushing me away. Which is why I was so surprised when he called, saying he wanted a fresh start." She looked away. "We haven't been close in a long time."

Cassandra watched two large tears roll down Greer's cheek. She scrambled up the bed and kissed her sister's bowed head.

"Listen. Enough of this now. We've loads of lovely, positive stuff to talk about, sure we need to start making plans and use your brilliantly creative brain to *our* advantage for a change. We'll show those blow-ins down at the Harbour Spa Hotel what real class looks like! What do you say?"

She climbed off the bed, tucking Greer in, the way she had been doing all her life. Even at five, Cassandra's job had been to mind her little sisters, and she had always tried her absolute best, however 'un-mindable' Greer and at times Orla contrived to be.

Giving the valance a quick flick, she noticed something unusual. This was unlike Greer; as haphazard as she could be in other areas of her life, her room at Manorcliff was sacrosanct. Everything in its place, nothing changed.

Cassandra pulled out a large designer suitcase.

Greer sat up. "Oh, I'd forgotten about that!"

Cassandra gave her a look.

"Honestly! I had."

"Does it belong to who I think it belongs to?"

"I told you, we were on our way to the airport, he got a call and had to go back to the House."

"Whose house?"

"No, Cass. *The* House. Westminster. Said it wouldn't take long and for me to go ahead, he'd meet me at the airport. That was the last time I saw him." Greer was tearful again.

"What's in it?" Cassandra stared at the bag.

"The usual I suppose, clothes, toiletries. Alistair never did travel light, terrified he'd be invited to something he didn't have the right tie for."

"Well, don't you think you'd better check? I mean it's on our premises."

Greer blinked at her sister.

"We're a hotel. It's a suitcase, how suspicious is that?"

Cassandra gave Greer another of her looks.

Greer knew the combination, it was the code for everything, the date their affair had started on that glorious trip to Cannes. *So long ago.*

As predicted, the case was immaculately packed with elegant clothes, an army of neatly rolled ties and socks. His toiletries, vitamin pills and supplements zipped in a waterproof pocket.

"Impressive!" Cassandra exclaimed. "Did you pack for him?"

"No," Greer replied sadly, running her fingers over her lover's possessions. "Alistair's a control freak did his own packing, ironing, everything. Said it was therapeutic, gave him thinking time."

"What're you going to do with it? Some charity shop would be glad of all that." Typical Cassandra, best way to deal with any unpleasantness, remove it from the premises as quickly as possible.

Greer shoved the case back under the bed. "Not now, Cass. I can't think about that now." And feeling her sister's pain, Cassandra wrapped her in a hug.

"I know it's raw, love, but soon enough you'll be able to let go and like everything behind us, it will be just a memory." She lifted Greer's chin to gaze into her dull, red-rimmed eyes. "Trust me, there's a lot to look forward to, it just doesn't feel like it yet."

Greer knew Cassandra was trying to prevent the sadness turning into a deep fug of depression, the bleakness of the 'black dog' that could only be lifted in time by her favourite things; music, stargazing and of course Tone, the loopy spaniel who had wormed his way into her hardened heart all those years ago. About the same time, she realised Rai Muir was gone from her life forever.

"You can't let this drag you down, Greer, not now, when you've so much going for you." Cassandra was at the door. "Not now, when I need you," she said, almost to herself.

But Greer heard and felt the pull on her heart, the heart that was only cracked. She needed to remember that.

As Cassandra wished Greer goodnight, Rai Muir was saying farewell to his old friend Archie Fitzgerald in the hall of Galty House, the decrepit Georgian mansion that had been the Fitzgeralds' family home for centuries.

The evening had been an intimate dinner for two men

of a certain age, who by dint of beguiling personalities and exceptional talent had risen to the dizzy heights of international stardom in their chosen fields; Archie, a renowned actor and Rai, a legend in the music business.

The fact these two colossi came from the same small town on the east coast of Ireland might be surprising to some, but Archie always pointed out that theatrical legends Richard Burton and Anthony Hopkins hailed from the same Welsh village and as the Irish were generally far more gifted than the Welsh – recounted mainly to annoy his Welsh cousin, a renowned playwright – it was really no surprise at all.

And, while he was happy to indulge in a certain amount of reminiscence, the main reason for the invitation was Archie's revelation that he had fallen hopelessly in love with a wonderful woman who, praise the heavens, felt the same about him and before he grew very much older – his sixtieth birthday looming – he was retiring gracefully to move halfway round the world to be with her.

Rai could not be happier for his friend, a long-time bachelor with a complicated backstory, and someone he felt had spent more than enough time supporting a charming but somewhat dysfunctional family. It was time Archie lived his own life, for himself.

Rai also totally understood Archie's desire not to be claimed a 'national treasure', reduced to opening fetes and hosting game shows. Something he too would dread, if his fate had not been mapped out by a far greater power than the vagaries of popular culture.

Now in the throes of reorganising his life, so he could happily sail off into the sunset with his soon to be Australian fiancée, Archie was determined to 'set his house in order' as he put it, which meant he needed to make peace with certain elements of his past.

A noble ambition, Rai agreed, but one that was proving tricky, especially regarding a certain person who refused point-blank to even speak to him, thereby causing Archie much heartache.

Archie and Cassandra had crossed swords years ago and Archie blamed himself – he had treated her badly. As a typical arrogant youth, he considered practising his charm on the opposite sex fair game. But Cassandra had fallen deeply in love with him and although he too was smitten, Archie was caught in the maelstrom of another heart-wrenching dilemma and in the end left Cassandra abandoned.

Now older and wiser, he longed to make amends. Delighted to discover Greer on the beach only the other day, Archie was convinced that with Rai also in the neighbourhood, their combined efforts could help broker a truce. But Rai and Greer's rift seemed deeper than ever, and Archie was running out of ideas.

"I'm at a loss what to suggest, dear boy." Archie was glum, walking Rai through the vast hall, the Fitzgerald family portraits gazing down from the galleried landing as they strolled. "If Greer refuses to talk to you and Cassandra won't have anything to do with me, we're well and truly scuppered."

"I'm sorry, Archie." Rai drew on the long sealskin coat Archie held out for him. "Beyond booking a room at Manorcliff, how else will we even get close? At least in the guise of one of their guests, they'd have to pretend to be nice to us."

The men looked at each other.

"By George! I think you've got it!" Archie declared, clapping Rai on the back. "That's it, get yourself booked in, give Greer the full-on charm offensive, get her on side and then see if I can 'call in' and finally get to see Cassandra."

Rai gave his host a wry smile. "You have great faith, my friend. The last thing Greer Morgan is, is susceptible to any sort of charm from me."

"Hmm. I've heard she's not having the best of times, wasn't she having an affair with that government adviser fella, McKeiver, the one in hospital? I read they're hoping he'll recover so he can face some serious charges."

"Never made the best of choices where men are concerned,"

Rai said sadly. "I certainly don't want to make things worse for her, but like you with Cassandra there's something I have to share, and I really would prefer she heard it from me."

Archie was thoughtful.

"You'll come up with something, you're nothing if not a genius, I've always said so." And Archie kissed his accomplice on both cheeks in the porch, watching as the light made his dark eyes glint. "I'll await news of the plan. Whatever you do, make sure you don't end up on the menu though, you know they've served up many a guest they didn't like in a stew."

"Bad joke, especially if I'm planning to eat there." Rai laughed.

"Not sure I'm joking," Archie concluded to himself, and closing the large hall door, he stopped. "Rai, you must stop blaming yourself ... you know ... for what happened, you are allowed to be a little bit human."

Rai gave him a hard look – they had avoided the subject all evening – he might have known Archie would not let an opportunity pass without mentioning the tragedy that still haunted him. His old friend had tried to assuage his guilt many times over the years. But nothing anyone did or said could help, ever.

"Am I?" Rai shook his head. "Not when it costs a young life."

"You've always said you know when someone wants to be saved, perhaps he didn't."

Rai's eyes grew darker still. Archie had a point. "I should have saved him from himself."

"'Uneasy lies the head that wears a crown'." Archie quoted from Shakespeare's *Henry IV*. "Take it off, my friend, give yourself a break." And blowing a kiss, Archie watched as he strode off into the black night.

Picture Perfect

G reer's mood was dark as she sat in the morning sunshine, a pot of coffee before her. She ran her fingers over the brightly coloured tabletop inlaid with shells and pebbles, an unusual piece of furniture compared with the rest of Manorcliff's collection, though highly prized nonetheless.

Prized because her mother had made it and for Greer it showed a side of Miranda rarely acknowledged. The creative, artistic side, a glimpse of the fun-loving, colourful character she could hardly remember, yet felt she knew so well.

Of the three sisters, Greer was most like their mother. She had the same eyes, thick chestnut hair turning to springy waves at the merest sight of the sea and a determined chin, pretty enough but stubborn. Greer was also clever yet at the same time volatile and hopelessly romantic. Classic Miranda, according to their grandmother, Nana.

But Greer was told little else, Nana seemingly determined to eradicate her daughter's memory from all their lives. Sadly the same tight-lipped disappointment also applied to their father.

Danny Dwyer was considered a lowly catch for the only child of the well-to-do Morgans. A talented musician, bearing a striking resemblance to the rock star Marc Bolan, Danny was rarely in full-time work, so would 'job' from boat to boat, as he struggled to provide for his vivacious wife and their small brood. Whatever he did make, Miranda quickly spent on beautiful clothes for the babies, fine wine for the table and materials for her projects.

The tiny beach-side cottage they called home played host

to a constant stream of dippy-hippy vagabonds and though filled with music and laughter during the summer, it quickly became a cold, leaky hovel once winter storms hit.

Nana so disapproved of their lifestyle, she could barely force herself to visit, always hoping Miranda would bring herself and the little ones back to Manorcliff to enjoy the comfort and support of the family home. And although the three sisters did indeed return to Manorcliff, it was under the most tragic of circumstances.

Cassandra was five, Orla only three and Greer just eighteen months, when the worst storm on record swept the east coast.

A freak weather front appearing from nowhere had turned a softly rolling Celtic Sea into a cauldron of broiling ocean in minutes. At its height waves tall as skyscrapers crashed against the rocks and as water spilled out of the bay under a low black sky, streets flooded, low-lying fields turning to lakes as boats and livestock were swept away.

Danny and the entire crew of Captain Flanagan's fishing boat were lost a few miles beyond the harbour and Miranda, who had been on the beach with her baby daughter Greer, disappeared, never to be seen again. It was a miracle a neighbour had found Greer crying at the waters' edge or she too would have been lost.

Everyone had a sad tale about that dark day, but Nana never mentioned it, beyond decreeing that after losing both parents the girls adopt the family name, so people knew who they were and where they belonged. Which meant any connection to their father had been swept away too, Greer thought sadly. She sipped her coffee, gazing quizzically out to sea, still unsure, even as she repeated the story in her mind, if it was entirely true.

"Greer! Greer!" Orla came running out of the side entrance in espadrilles and a sou'wester, Wolfe and Tone following in a hurried canter.

Greer did not respond. The haze of heat hovering above

a sea of navy-blue glass had her entranced. The harbour, glittering bays and Phoenix Island in the distance, were picture perfect in every way.

Imagine anyone or anything coming to harm in such a glorious setting?

But it was days like this that proved there was a Sea Witch. How else could everything change so cruelly, making the spirits of the sea turn so bitterly against the humans clinging to their simple way of life on the edge of the land back then?

How could whoever ruled the waves deliver such a crushing blow to three innocent little girls that awful day?

Greer stood, shaking her head to dispel the sadness. She looked down; Orla had taken her hand.

"I can feel it too," her sister said quietly. "It was a day such as this. It will change later. We're to have bad storms this summer and we've not had one yet."

"You've seen the coastguard?"

"No, the shells told me, the moon too, he was odd last night, did you notice that?"

And Greer remembered she had, berating the man in the moon for not being a true friend, for bewitching her into thinking she was in love with Alistair, because Alistair had never been hers, and she knew now, never would. As he came to mind, Orla spoke.

"Clare McKeiver's on the phone, she's been trying your mobile for days and your email keeps bouncing back, it's urgent she talks to you."

"Does she know I'm here?" Greer was in no mood for Clare's alcohol-fuelled hysterics.

Orla nodded. "I told her. It's not a secret and she said you had unfinished business and I know how you like all your business finished."

Greer gathered up her new project book and assortment of pens; it appeared an old agenda needed to be addressed before new business could commence. She followed Orla to take the call at reception.

"Greer. Good. She found you. Are you in hiding?" Clare hissed down the line. "I don't blame you if you are and you don't have to tell me of course, but it's been hell, sheer hell and we've been desperate to get hold of you. Oh, the relief!" Clare sounded remarkably calm and relatively sober for once. "Where are you again?"

"You called me, Clare?" Greer glanced at the handset in disbelief. "You know where I am?"

"Sorry, I've just been phoning random numbers I found in Alistair's desk … is this somewhere foreign, the number looks foreign?"

"It is, Clare, I'm in Ireland." *Another planet,* Greer considered, *in so many ways.*

"Don't tell me any more, best I don't know if I'm questioned under duress, that way I won't be able to say anything I shouldn't."

"Questioned? Why, what's going on?"

"Don't you know? Haven't you seen the news?"

"Not lately," Greer replied, the news and media in general was something she was avoiding. She had abandoned her phone too, having tried Alistair's number one last time and finding it disconnected, realised that was how things must remain, disconnected. "It is Alistair?" She feared the worse. "How is he?"

"Oh, you know Alistair," Clare said. "Came round spitting feathers, saying he was set up and some bastard's trying to kill him." Greer had to laugh, as a huge wave of relief washed over her. "The woman he was with when he collapsed was arrested but she's been released."

Greer's brain went into overdrive; she knew Alistair had been recalled to Westminster, but it looked like Katya had intercepted him en route.

"I thought Alistair had some sort of heart attack."

"He did, but they think it was induced."

"Induced?" Greer's voice was rising, and guests seated on the sofas scattered throughout Manorcliff's spacious lobby hushed to listen. "How?" Greer turned away so as not be heard, the hubbub of muted conversation refilling the silence around her.

"Poison. The police. Special branch. MI5. Whoever, want to speak to everybody – all 'known associates' they call it. They especially want to piece together the recent past, who he saw, talked to and what he was working on." Clare paused. Greer could hear her pull on a cigarette. "Anyway, you're on the list to be interviewed, you'll need to remember when you last saw him, who he had meetings with, that kind of thing. But please, Greer, co-operate and soon."

"Sorry?" Greer's head was buzzing. The last time she saw Alistair was the very day he collapsed. Did anyone know that? Did anyone need to know that?

"Not sure if you can help any more than the rest of us but we need this resolving."

"Resolving?"

"Yes, you know. Put to bed. We need Alistair to be totally exonerated. They've frozen all his assets, his bank accounts, the lot. This is awful, Greer, awful for all of us. Amy, the children, me. The whole family. You'll have to come back from wherever you are and help us out. It's the least you can do."

Despite the impact of what Greer was being told, something in Clare's tone did not quite ring true. Clare and Alistair's wife had not spoken for years. Greer was sure Amy did not know about the regular payments Alistair made to his sister, money that allowed her a lifestyle she could never have afforded without his help. Perhaps Greer was being cynical, but she felt sure one of the reasons Clare wanted things resolving as soon as possible was because she needed her big brother to reinstate her very generous allowance.

"Are you still there?" Clare asked.

"Sorry, Clare, I have to go but no one has been in touch with me and if it's alright with you I'll wait until they are."

Greer was irritated now, no mention of her, how she might be feeling having been well and truly dumped, not only jobless but homeless too.

"You will help though, won't you, Greer? You will explain that everything is above board? Alistair's never been involved in anything criminal. Please, for the family, that's what's important now."

Greer grimaced, replacing the receiver. Still the outsider. The hired help. Yet the very one they needed to vouch for Alistair, assure the authorities he was innocent of any wrongdoing, so he could be released back into the bosom of his family, and they could all live happily ever after.

Before she could assimilate any more of what Clare had said, the sound of screeching tyres outside the hotel stopped everyone in their tracks.

A police car had parked skew-whiff at the bottom of the steps, tyre marks scarring the gravel. The driver's door flung open as a uniformed member of the constabulary emerged, walking briskly to release whoever was in the passenger seat. Everyone watched as he helped her out and straightening herself, the hotel director drew back her shoulders and walloped the policeman across the head with a large sunhat.

"Brendan O'Brien! Frightened the feckin' life out of me," Cassandra laughed, looking up at her old pal's ruddy face. "It can't be safe, driving around like that, they don't teach you that in the guards, surely?"

"Not at all," replied Sergeant O'Brien, taking bags from her. "I went on one of them *Miami Vice* stunt driver courses a while back, comes in dead handy if we've just arrested a couple of gobshites who've had too much sun, sea and sangria. Terror's great for sobering people up, Cass, you should know that in your business." He was halfway up the steps when he spotted Greer.

"Speaking of terror, here's the Vampire Queen herself. Jeez, Greer, shouldn't you be having a nice rest in a crypt somewhere? Sun's not going down for hours yet, you need to be careful or you'll disappear in a puff of smoke."

Greer tried one of her withering looks. He grinned back.

"Such satire, Brendan. Still Rosshaven's answer to Oscar Wilde," she announced coldly.

"I'm delighted to see you too – you're looking fierce well. Is that a slight tan? Take it steady now, you'll end up looking half-human if you're not careful."

"Thanks for dropping my sister back," Greer said sweetly, taking the shopping bags from him. "Tea?"

"That would be very welcome." The officer could barely hide his surprise.

"Well, behave yourself and you might get a cup. I haven't been a Goth since the 1980s so let's make a deal, I won't mention the time you Superglued your hair in purple spikes, if you stop reminding me of what I went through connecting with my artistic soul."

"Oh, is *that* what it was?"

"We all have a past, Brendan, it's called a past for a reason, it's been and gone!" She gave him a tight smile.

"Alright, alright." He made soothing gestures with his hands. "Talking of the here and now, someone's been looking for you, asked at the station if we knew you."

"Oh, who would that be?" Greer forced herself to sound nonplussed.

"Big fella, Scottish accent, left his card said if I saw you, you're to get in touch."

"Did you say I was here?"

"What do you take me for? Betray me own? Never."

Greer knew that was true. Brendan O'Brien was many things, but he was Rosshaven through and through, besides he and his team had enough to do managing the shenanigans of holidaymakers, foreign visitors and any number of smugglers coming in and out of the port. Not all pirates wear the obligatory eye-patch these days, he always said.

He dug about in his uniform, handing Greer a business card. She looked at it. 'Meredith Brown, Special Projects,' an official-looking logo, email and mobile phone number.

"Been busking on the Underground without a licence again?" The officer waggled his eyebrows at her. But Greer had turned pale, reminding him quite vividly of the Goth she once was.

No Room at the Inn

A s is often the case, when something needs to be done and there is no obvious way of even beginning to carve a pathway towards it, good old fate will step in and sweep the whole complicated, conundrum away – just like that.

And this particular conundrum was keeping Rai Muir awake. Lying in his solitary bunk aboard *The Pirate* he was going over the facts.

Estranged from his once close friend Cassandra, Archie wanted Rai to broker a truce. He did not have long before his self-imposed deadline to immigrate to Australia and start afresh with the wonderful new woman in his life. But instead of the feud fading with time, it had deepened, with Cassandra seeming to loathe him more than ever.

Recalling his recent encounter with Greer, Rai understood what that felt like and Archie was right, they knew the Morgan sisters well enough to realise a direct approach would be soundly rejected. Softly, softly tactics were required, a subtle rebuilding of trust, followed by an invitation to meet, talk, make amends. Archie described them as the 'Harbour Queens', remote and untouchable in their fortress on top of the cliff; a kinder nickname than most.

But so far, Rai had failed to come up with a plan. After leaving Galty House the previous evening, he had walked back along the coast, following the path upwards as the hill turned into a steep cliff, eventually coming to the cave where he had encountered Greer only a couple of days ago.

Their cave.

The scene of many secret rendezvous, especially during

the time they had been banned from seeing each other; the age difference considered too wide, too dangerous.

This was where she would hide after one of their screaming arguments, to sit and cry and lick her wounds. Where she would wait, until he came to take her in his arms and declare his love, kissing tears away as anger turned to lust. And after their lovemaking, they would sit wrapped in each other's arms on the bench of stone, gazing up at the star-filled sky as it glittered above the endless sea.

The sea that still reminded him of her. Deep, serene, entrancing yet turning in a flash to tempestuous froth, foaming as it crashed against the rocks in angry waves.

And he would soothe her, hold her close, bring her back, keep her safe.

Rai groaned, fighting the glimmer of arousal brought on by the very thought of those wild, reckless times. Greer, his forbidden first love. Yet, after all this time and all that had passed between them, he still thought of her fondly – too fondly perhaps – and try as he might *not* to revisit the past, still it played like a movie in his mind.

The massive, mind-blowing success of the band. Their band. The tours, the hits, the media frenzy and finally the break-up. Followed by anguish and despair, endless legal wrangles and the near destruction of each and every one of them.

He sighed; surely by now the anger had been spent, the frustration, confusion and disappointment all gone. Rai shuddered, pushing the images away. An echo of another time, a time when they were unstoppable and the whole world was there to be taken.

Yet sometimes, like now, the pain resurfaced, sharp and un-beckoned, leaving a bitterness he could still taste.

The boat started to rock in the water. Rai closed his eyes against the view of the horizon and the nausea that would no doubt follow. He must have drifted off, eyes snapping open as a surge against the side of the cabin made the whole vessel lurch.

A shout, someone calling.

"Rai! Rai, wake up for godsake!"

Declan was beside him.

"It's my day off." Rai rolled away from his brother's angsty face, pulling the duvet over his dark head.

"I won't be needing you for a while if what Mikey McAvoy is after telling me is correct." Declan poked his sibling in the ribs.

"Mikey McAvoy? Now what? Loves a bit of drama, that fella." Rai turned back.

Mikey was the long-time captain of the Rosshaven lifeboat and had always imagined himself a superhero where this particular stretch of coastline was concerned. He took the safety of everybody in Rosshaven personally, often clashing with Finbar Doyle, the revered harbourmaster, for interfering with the legitimate running of the port.

But Mikey, a highly qualified marine engineer, was a close friend of Declan's. He was also a right pain in the arse and being a regular at *The Pirate* had been called to investigate a leak in the engine room.

"He's found where we're taking on water and it's worse than I thought, coming in behind the main fuse box. We're patched up but it won't hold in rough seas, needs a professional repair."

"Didn't look that bad to me, sure he's not bigging it up so he has a job to do come the end of the season?" Rai closed his eyes, hoping Declan would take the hint and leave him alone.

A loud bang. The boat juddered.

"We're going into dry dock. You'll have to find somewhere else to sleep."

Rai sat up too quickly, smacking his forehead against a pipe. "Ouch! Are you serious?"

Declan nodded, unsmiling. Rai collapsed backwards, rubbing at his brow.

"Job and lodgings gone just like that?"

"'Fraid so, bro. Storm forecast later, we're being tugged to the boatyard this morning, lucky Mikey can fit us in."

"Aren't we though?" Rai said sourly, sliding from the bunk to the floor. "What caused it? I suppose 'Aquaman' has it all figured out?"

"He thinks it's something to do with the new hotel, they did a lot of drilling, putting pilings in for the marina, the underwater topography has altered, so Mikey says."

"You mean we hit a rock, like most boats do." Rai was stuffing clothes into a kit bag. He peered through the porthole; a couple of the lifeboat crew were on deck, Mikey in a wet suit, directing operations.

"How long is it going to take?" Rai asked, deciding there was no time to shave.

"Don't know 'til she's up on the cradle and we have a good look." Declan pulled the bedding from the bunk, stuffing it into a locker nearby.

"Could be a long job, especially left to Mikey's mob." Rai turned to look at Declan. "You'll want her back in the water as soon as possible to make the most of what's left of the season."

Declan sighed.

"It's a long dark winter," they said in unison, the oft-quoted chant of the seaside entrepreneur with trade disappearing in September until at least the following May. Most businesses in Rosshaven were seasonal, locals hoping the usually short summer would be profitable enough to stash enough cash away to see them through winter. *The Pirate* had been doing well, building a reputation as a venue for great entertainment, and having to call a halt was a blow.

"Let's keep the pressure on and get it sorted as quickly as we can, eh?" Declan said.

Rai nodded. He would help if he could but his sojourn at *The Pirate* was temporary, he needed to move on and although Declan did not know that yet, he would understand, they were brothers after all.

A thought struck.

"You don't think this was sabotage, do you?" Rai asked.

"I did warn you there's some around here wouldn't want to be served by me, no matter how desperate they are for a pint."

"Are you talking about the Morriseys?" Declan folded his arms. The Morriseys were a family of tough fishermen. He knew well enough that Rai still blamed himself for the fatal accident that took young Mojo Morrisey's life while on tour with the band in the US. But Rai could not save everyone, no matter how hard he tried, and at the time, Rai was in dire need of saving himself.

Declan had been more than relieved when his younger brother sailed through the door only a few weeks ago; hale and hearty and stone cold sober.

What's more Rai had stubbornly assured him that working in a pub was precisely where he needed to be, at least for a while, if only to prove he had left that phase of his life far behind as he prepared for the next – a conversation for another time.

"Look, this is my bar. If they don't like the fact you're here that's their problem. I know the Morriseys are always looking for someone or something to be pissed off about, but they wouldn't do anything like that, what would it gain?"

"Even so." Rai frowned. "I know I'm not welcome in some quarters."

Declan shrugged. "Move on, Rai. This is your home, you've as much right to be here as anyone else."

But sometimes it did not feel like home; nowhere did. Rai gave a bleak smile. "So, which delightful establishment are we going to grace with our presence?"

"Slight problem there. Height of the season, everywhere's full. I've found a bed, but you'll have to make your own arrangements."

"Charming, whatever happened to brotherly love?" Rai gave a laugh. "So, where are you staying?"

"Flossy Moore has a room over the shop she's letting me have," Declan replied. Rai raised an eyebrow. Declan and Flossy had history, sweethearts from way back. Declan, a confirmed bachelor, had never married, and Flossy was long widowed.

"It's not what you think," Declan told his brother.

"I'm not thinking," Rai said, rubbing his chin absentmindedly. "Shame she doesn't have a sister."

"She does, as you well know, six of them actually. But only Leela is single, and lovely as she is …"

Rai laughed. "Lovely as Leela is, all that voodoo frightens the life out of me. And have you seen the 'glow in the dark' teeth she's had done? Come Halloween she'll scare the bejaysus out of any trick or treaters knocking on their door!"

The boat lurched again; the cabin door flew open. Rai needed some air. Declan followed him on deck. Mikey was on the bridge, keeping *The Pirate* straight as a tug towed her towards the boatyard. He gave them a wave, the hood of his wetsuit pushed back and not one but two pairs of binoculars hanging about his neck. Rai rolled his eyes at Declan.

"Do me a favour, Rai, don't piss him off, we need him on side if we're to get this sorted out."

Rai shrugged. "Me? I've never been known to piss anyone off."

Declan's turn to roll his eyes …

Orla decided to respond personally to the invitation to the launch of the new bar at the Harbour Spa Hotel. Upon receipt of the elegant turquoise and gold missive, she diligently marked the date on the calendar and prepared her own handcrafted response, carefully copying the Manorcliff logo onto a piece of parchment and writing in a flourish of green ink, splashed through with silver.

She thanked Ross Power for his kind invitation to the event – jazz, champagne, and canapés – replying that the hotel director, Cassandra, head of sales and marketing, Greer, together with herself – head of everything else – would be thrilled and delighted to attend.

They were looking forward to the event hugely, so they could congratulate him personally on such a great achievement, and she concluded by saying she hoped they could continue to foster the long and mutually beneficial relationship they had always enjoyed.

The invitation also announced that the Academy Award-winning actor, Archie Fitzgerald, was guest of honour at the event, with Orla making a mental note not to mention this to Cassandra when she announced they were all going to a party.

Delivering the reply personally, Orla was striding along the beach with Wolfe when she spotted someone stretched out on a bench. Someone who, despite the heat, was wrapped in a long dark coat, using a battered kit bag for a pillow with dark glasses covering his eyes as he slept.

She pointed, telling Wolfe to 'fetch', and keen as mustard the young dog leapt onto the supine figure, taking the spectacles from his face in his soft spaniel mouth.

"Jeez!" Rai exclaimed, jumping up.

"Good boy!" Orla declared, taking the glasses from Wolfe, who wriggled in delight at having achieved so complex a task.

"Give me those back!" Rai exclaimed.

Orla plonked down beside him, wiping the lenses on her frilly skirt and handing them over.

"You look rough," she told him. "Bit long in the tooth for sleeping on the beach. Well, that's what they tell me when I try to and you're older than me."

"Not much older!" Rai said, stretching as he spoke. "I'm stiff though, and cold, that wind is bitter."

"It's not cold at all. You must be hungry. Blood sugar's low. I get that when I forget to eat." She looked at Wolfe. "Ah, no. I've done it again, I forgot breakfast, we're starving too." She pulled the envelope out of her pocket. "But I've to deliver this first."

Rai gave her a quizzical look.

"Replying to an invitation, party at the Harbour Spa Hotel. It's going to be fabulous!" Her eyes lit up, making him smile despite his ill humour. Orla's enthusiasm was infectious.

"I bet they do an excellent breakfast there." Rai checked his watch – an Omega Seamaster Diver, the one he treated himself to when the third album went platinum. "Tell you what, I'll stand us all breakfast, what do you say?" Wolfe wagged his tail optimistically.

"Sounds perfect." Orla took his arm. "And you can tell me why one of Rosshaven's most famous musicians is sleeping on the beach – I thought you were at *The Pirate* with Declan?"

"Surely, I'm Rosshaven's *only* famous musician and as that was many years ago, amn't I just a 'has been' now?" Rai gave her a slow smile. "*The Pirate's* sprung a leak, I'm currently homeless." He nodded towards the hotel, the glittering terrace visible high on the hill, its awning billowing in the breeze. "Do you think they'll have any rooms?"

"Doubt it. They've been full for months, their advertising is amazing, videos and quotes from famous people who've stayed there." She widened her eyes at him. "Famous people like you, or are you incognito at the moment?"

"I'm just helping Declan out, between gigs as they say." Rai squeezed her hand as they walked. "But I do need somewhere to stay."

Orla stopped. "Why didn't you call me?"

"You're not full?" he asked, surprised.

"As it so happens, the Island Suite has just come free. You can have that!"

"Ah, Orla, I won't need a whole suite. It's not like the good old days."

Orla shrugged. "Good old days? Why don't we ever say 'good now' days? I've heard people tell 'the good old days' weren't that good anyway. Good now days, that's what we need. Anyway, the suite's free if you want it. Locals' rate applies, even though you haven't been a local for years, I still like you."

Rai lifted his shades and winked at her. "Thanks, Orla. I still like you."

"Ha!" She laughed and gave a full circle twirl in the sand. "What's not to like?"

"What about the sisters? Not sure how welcome they'll

make me, been a long time."

"You're coming as a paying guest, that's different, we're always nice to paying guests and anyway, I'm in charge of bookings and Cassandra will be pleased we don't have rooms empty while the sun is shining, it'll be grand."

"And Greer? What about her?"

Orla beamed at him encouragingly. "Greer's joined the family business, so she'll be fine too. It's not as if you two are even friends anymore. A professional arrangement, that's all it is." She took his arm again as they started up the steps towards the hotel. "Besides, Greer thinks you're a sliveen, two-faced, pig-headed bastard. Keep a low profile, she'll hardly notice you're there."

Rai smiled to himself, guiding the woman in the old sailing jacket, frilly yellow skirt and sea-shell earrings up the steps to one of the most fabulous terrace restaurants he had seen outside Monte Carlo.

"It'll be grand," she told him, as they took a table overlooking the beach.

Meanwhile, a woman with a twist of chestnut hair clamped under a baseball cap gripped the rail. She had just spotted her sister with her oldest enemy, the man she hated most in the world.

Jeez! This place never changes, lies and betrayal everywhere you look. As usual there was no one she could trust. It had always been the same. Greer reversed slowly down the steps and fled.

Tête á Tête

Flossy Moore was having coffee with her sister Leela Brennan, a weekly ritual. Leela came into town every Friday to buy supplies for Galty House, where she had reigned supreme as housekeeper for decades.

One of the grandest properties in the area, Galty House, the country seat of the eccentric Fitzgerald family, had enjoyed a rich and vibrant past. During the Second World War it had served as a 'safe house' for escapees from the Nazi regime and some locals still called it that, especially when alluding to its scandalous reputation.

Leela decried this as nonsense, saying the Fitzgeralds were a family like any other and it was only because Archie and his close friend Fenella Flanagan were well-known actors that people imagined all sorts of lurid goings on. But the past casts a long shadow and no one knew that better than Leela Brennan.

Friday was Flossy's day off, the one day each week she did not stand at the counter of Moore's Mini Market, doggedly keeping the business afloat in memory of its founder, her late husband. But recently she had confessed to Leela she was tired, and worse than that, lonely, which had not surprised her sibling, who had long been aware the main driver of the work-alcoholic is often loneliness; sure her beloved Archie Fitzgerald was a prime example.

"So, I've made up the spare room and he's moving in tonight," Flossy announced, avoiding her sister's eyes.

"And how long is he staying?" Leela stirred her cappuccino noisily, irritated that despite her devotion to the Tarot she had not seen this coming.

"Until the boat's repaired. He wants to get *The Pirate* up and running as soon as possible, they were doing well until this happened," Flossy said casually, although two spots of pink had appeared on her cheeks.

"Don't tell me Mikey McAvoy's doing the repair? It'll be Christmas before that's sorted, I've never known a man take so long to do anything. He had that little boat of Archie's for months, in the meantime Archie bought this other yoke – size of a house. His sister went mad when she saw it, but sure why not? He's kept everything going all his life, let the man have what he wants, I say … we're a long time dead." She closed her eyes briefly. "I will miss him, though. Australia's so far away."

Flossy reached across the table to squeeze her hand.

"He came into the garage last week in that ole jalopy. What does he call it? The Great Dame. 'Fill her up' he says to young Conor, 'I'm taking her up to Dublin for a run, I've a few old enemies there I want to poison before I go'. Conor was shook, but I told him, Archie's only being theatrical, sure he can't help it." Flossy sipped her coffee. "In anyway, what else is happening?"

"Just the usual, people crawling out of the woodwork, trying to find out what's happening to the estate when he leaves, which as Archie says is none of anyone's business – but that's families for you!"

"Well, we never had any of that bother, left with nothing only each other." Flossy sniffed. The youngest of the eight Brennans, she was six months old when their mother died, following which Leela, aged only eleven, had taken the whole household under her naïve but nevertheless resourceful wing resisting – with the help of neighbours and friends – pressure to break the family up and rehome them.

The Brennans were a close-knit crew with Leela suspicious of infiltrators, particularly men who appeared suddenly homeless, contriving to charm their way into her sister's very comfortable setup.

"Make sure Declan Muir signs a written agreement with

your terms and conditions, you don't want him getting his feet under the table. A strictly professional arrangement with the rent paid on the dot, insist on three months up front." She pointed a manicured nail at her sister's shopping. "I suppose that's who the new bedlinen is for, *and* you've had your hair done."

"Ah, Leela, I needed a bit of a freshen-up. And don't worry, Declan knows what's what, it's only for a few weeks. It'll be nice to have a bit of company about the place, I've always found Declan very easy, you know that."

Leela tutted. "Easy on the eye, yes. Just make sure he's not too easy in the chair, expecting you to do everything, waiting on him hand and foot."

"I'm just helping out an old friend, you'd do the same." Flossy gave Leela a frown. "Now, his brother is a different kettle of fish altogether. Declan did ask if I'd room for them both, but I made it clear Rai was not welcome. An odd one, that fella, and if what they say is true, he's been keeping a very low profile, lives in a shack on some island in the South Seas, I heard."

"Ah, blame it all on sex, drugs and rock and roll." Leela lifted her sunglasses so Flossy could see the expression in her eyes. "I always take anything in the newspapers with a huge grain of salt and that social medium stuff is a nightmare, sure a Twittering from someone famous just having a laugh, can be taken serious and millions re-twitter it with dire consequences. If half the stuff written about Archie was remotely true, no one in Rosshaven or anywhere else for that matter would even speak to him. Remember the one about him dressing up as a woman to get into a sheik's harem back in the day."

"I thought that was true?" Flossy looked disappointed.

"He was only doing research for a part, not ravaging virgins as the gossipy columns would have you believe."

"He did go to prison though, didn't he?"

"Not at all," Leela said, draining her cup abruptly. "And if he did, sure wouldn't that be research too? He's a consummated professional, you know that." Leela changed the subject. "Anyway, what's happening with Rai? He had dinner with Archie the other night, I know he'd put him up if he was stuck and I wouldn't mind Rai kicking about the place, now he *is* easy on the eye." She lowered her voice. "Flossy, what happened all those years ago was an accident, a tragic *accident* and you and everyone else in this town should leave it at that. Rai was not responsible, Mojo should have never got into that car, the driver was drunk or stoned or both. But these things happen, every family in this town has been touched by tragedy at some stage."

"Well, he can keep himself well away from me. Gives me the willies, that fella, been spotted prowling around at night, sitting on the beach staring at the moon."

"Sure, he's always done that. Old habits die hard but he's not a vampire, Flossy, I'd know if he was. Don't be giving yourself nightmares for no reason." Leela was fully aware of her sister's nervous disposition, another reason she suspected she could be seeking comfort in the arms of her new lodger.

"I don't believe all that rubbish anymore," Flossy announced. Leela raised an eyebrow. "But I do think something's not right. Greer Morgan was in the shop the other day, hasn't been home in years, even when things weren't going too well at the hotel, you know the flood and all the damage it did. Now that's odd."

Flossy bit into her chocolate éclair, throwing it back on the plate as if poisoned. "Ah shite, I'm supposed to be on a diet." She shoved the plate at Leela. "You finish it, I've had enough." Another clue she was preparing for a reunion with her old flame, Leela thought, saying nothing.

"Maybe Greer didn't know about the problems at the hotel. Maybe she had her own stuff going on."

Flossy folded her arms. "You mean carrying on with that government adviser fella and him married with children."

Leela licked her fingers, having finished the éclair.

"What am I after telling you, don't believe everything

you read."

"I didn't read it, Orla told me. That time she was found out on the water, delirious, poor love. Cassandra had been called away on urgent business, so I spent a couple of nights there just to help out a bit and keep Orla calm, she gets very stressed sometimes."

"I remember that now. You couldn't get hold of Greer, isn't that right?"

Flossy narrowed her eyes. "I eventually got through, but she was away, abroad at a conference or something. By the time we heard from her, Cassandra was home and told me not to say anything. She would tell her in her own time, didn't want to worry her." Flossy leant towards her sister. "Well, they seem to have plenty to worry about all over again. Greer's fancy man's been poisoned and now he's under investigation and she's back after years away, in hiding maybe? What do you think?"

Leela suddenly smiled broadly at her sister and sat back, keen to appear less conspiratorial.

"Ask her yourself, she's just walked through the door." Leela stood. "Greer Morgan, as I live and breathe, haven't seen you in a long time."

Flossy leapt to her feet.

"Take our table, we're just on our way, aren't we, Leela?" Flossy gathered her bags. "Must get back, I've a guest arriving."

"I've a bit to do myself," Leela said. "Archie seems intent on entertaining as much as he can before he leaves, which is lovely but I've to keep the place immaculate as always. A big job for a little woman!" She laughed.

Flossy and Greer exchanged a look. Leela's lack of enthusiasm for the more mundane aspects of her role was legendary.

"Let's catch up properly soon," Leela said, gazing at Greer. "Home for long?"

"So it would seem," Greer replied, holding open the door as the sisters bustled out into the sunshine.

"I'll ring, make arrangements," Leela announced, pushing diamante shades over her eyes before delivering her newly whitened smile.

Watching them skilfully navigate the crowded street, Greer was just about to change her mind and cross the road to what looked like a new wine bar when a besuited masculine arm barred her way.

"Did I hear correctly, you're Greer Morgan?"

The Dodger

The man continued to smile. Greer gave him a look but the arm barring her way remained. His smile broadened. A sprinkle of chestnut freckles echoed the soft tones in his hair, slightly frosted at the temples. *Attractive but pushy*, Greer thought. She lifted her gaze to his eyes, warm yet intense.

Perhaps he was a fan from her time in the music business. Even she, occasionally, caught a glimpse of the girl she once was.

"It is you, isn't it?" he pressed. "I've found you at last." She froze. He had a Scottish accent and had been looking for her. "Coffee, yes? Would that be alright?"

She released a breath, giving him her best superstar smile.

"An espresso would be lovely." She nodded towards the counter. "I'll keep the seats."

He seemed reluctant to leave.

"There'll be a queue soon," she told him, indicating a gaggle of tourists streaming in from the street. He moved towards the counter, and in a flash she was gone, the tinkle of the old-fashioned doorbell ringing in her ears as she flew through the door, scooting this way and that, avoiding dawdling day trippers and harried locals.

She was just about to dive into an alley off Patrick's Street when, checking she was not being followed, she slammed into a hard bulk of quilted gilet. The scent of diesel combined with a hefty top note of slurry was familiar.

"Nagle, you nearly ran me down, you great lummox!"

"You're the one doing the running, Greer." Nagle scowled

at her. "Charging through the town like a hare on heat. What ails you? Are you on something?"

She reached up, hauling at his collar.

"I'm being followed," she hissed, as near to his ear as she could. "Someone's after me."

"Ah, the DTs setting in. Paranoia, is it now?" Nagle took her hand in his gnarled paw.

"I'm serious. Some sort of detective wants to interrogate me." She pulled her hand free – she might need to make a run for it any second.

Nagle leaned towards her, a look of deep concern on his face.

"Still as mad as a box of frogs, God help you," he said with a wonky smile. "Tell you what, I'll buy you a drink, you know, take the edge off."

"What edge? I'm not on the edge. I'm telling the truth, he's after me."

"Greer, you can't go around wired to the moon here, you know, it's not London, not even Dublin." He spoke slowly, hoping she would understand.

Greer dug her nails into his arm. He yelped. She was staring at something behind him.

"He's coming! Quick!" She pulled the baseball cap off, shaking her wild mane free, and grabbing Nagle's sunglasses rammed them on as she half-dragged him down the alley towards the strand.

"Greer, stop!" Nagle cried, rubbing his arm as they stumbled along.

"Shush!" she hissed. "My name's not Greer." Slipping her jacket off, she placed it over her arm as she snuggled up to him. "We're a couple. On holiday."

"But I'm in my work clothes, anyone can see that."

"You're a farmer, Nagle, you don't have holiday clothes."

"I do so!" Nagle hated being pigeon-holed.

"Ever worn them?"

"On holiday, of course."

"You've never been on holiday, I'd have heard, it would have been on the news." She was fluffing her hair out, jostling beside him in an odd jaunty sort of walk.

"I'm saving. It's very expensive and I need enough to cover for the money the farm won't make while I'm away." The stock answer, Greer had heard it many times over the years. Real farmers rarely go on holiday, and why go on holiday when the Nagles lived in Rosshaven, they had all the sun, sea and sand they needed right here. But his siblings had long deserted agriculture for an easier life and these days Seamus was the only Nagle left.

"What're you doing?" he asked, despairing of the skipping, and flying hair.

"Footloose and fancy-free, you know, like a holidaymaker."

"Looks more like you're having a fit," he told her, and recognising the side door to *The Wharf Tavern*, levered it open to push her through. "We can hide from your detective in here, only locals and pretty scary ones at that, you'll fit in no bother."

The bar was dark, a clutch of men in sweatshirts and caps gathered around a barrel table playing dominoes, and not one looked round as the door creaked shut behind them. The bar itself stood in the far corner, a semicircle of aged wooden planks holding up a counter with a battered copper top. The bartender was piling coins into towers, his grubby fingers straightening them up. He glanced up at Nagle standing before him.

"Is it yourself?" he asked gruffly. "Long time no see."

"I stay away from town when the tourists are in, you know yourself, Dixie."

"Don't blame you." The man scratched at his beard. "Place is heaving." *True enough, although there is little evidence of it here,* Nagle thought, glancing round the near deserted pub.

"What'll you have?" he called to Greer, still at the door trying to see through its grimy porthole.

"Sparkling mineral water, slice of lime, no ice." Greer

moved from the door, and scanning the room spotted a large booth with the word 'Snug' in faded gold on the panelling. "I'll take mine in there," she told Nagle, who was watching the bartender sprinkle Andrew's Liver Salts into the glass he had just filled with tap water. Then blowing the dust off a jar, he flipped it open with a fingernail and dropped a shrunken cherry into the drink.

"The fizzy water will make it swell out a bit."

"And the lime?" Nagle was sure he had given the correct order. "No ice."

"No ice." He gave Nagle a sneery grin. "No lime, either. Cherry's on the house."

Following Greer into the Snug, Nagle was surprised to find her sitting with an elaborately attired Miss Finn on an aged chaise longue. Miss Finn, surrounded by bags as usual, had at last conceded to the sunshine having donned a pair of massive black-framed sunglasses and a floppy straw hat. She was wearing sandals too, a sort of chunky-soled flip-flop affair exposing red toenails.

"About time!" Miss Finn declared. "I'll need a lift back when you're ready if you don't mind."

Nagle handed Greer her glass, the fizz now a disgusting sludgy froth.

"Sorry, Miss Finn, I don't have the boat and Greer has to get back to the hotel, isn't that right, Greer?"

Greer was not having a good day.

Having just witnessed her sister taking lunch with the most despicable man on the planet and then narrowly escaping the detective sent to interrogate her about Alistair's business arrangements, she was far from keen to leave. *The Wharf Tavern* was not the most salubrious of hostelries yet despite its grotty appearance and substandard refreshment it felt safe; at least for now.

"I was just telling Miss Finn she was always my favourite teacher. Did she teach you too, Nagle?"

"I did," Miss Finn interjected. "Not the most imaginative

of students but he draws a lovely cow. Nothing like you and your sisters though, each different but highly talented. Do any of you still paint?"

Greer shrugged. She had not seen Cassandra at her easel in a long time and if Orla did anything creative it usually involved her elaborate shell art, creating jewellery and decorating picture frames. She had a display case in reception and visitors loved to buy her work knowing it was created by one of the hotel's owners.

"We're all so busy."

"The soul must be fed as well as the body." Miss Finn sucked in a breath. "Music then, are you singing, writing any songs?"

Greer sat up straight; something in Miss Finn's tone took her back to the schoolroom and she felt ashamed, as if she had mislaid her homework or left a project unfinished.

"Not so much." Greer gazed into her sludge. Miss Finn tutted loudly.

"Dixie, bring some wine and another pint." She took the glass from Greer. "Sit down," she ordered Nagle, pulling a chair up beside her. "I can feel a great frazzle of stress wrapped around the pair of you."

Dixie arrived with drinks on a tray, two clean glasses and a fresh pint of Guinness. Miss Finn checked the label on the bottle, indicating he could pour.

"He keeps a decent bottle for when I call in," she explained. "I was just about to leave but I'd a feeling someone was going to turn up, someone maybe needing to kick back, have a bit of a chat, and here you are." She sat back, taking a sip of the Chianti. "Now, who wants to go first?"

"I didn't know they're investigating your boss, Greer. And him so ill. An induced heart attack? Sure, how would someone do that?" Nagle asked, fascinated.

"Poison maybe? Isn't that what these nerve agents do, attack the vital organs?" Greer gazed out of the window; the old Land Rover rattling along the coast road, the stretch of beach bleached blond in the sunshine, lazy waves seeping into the sand like blotting paper.

"I never knew you proposed to my sister," Greer said, checking Miss Finn was still asleep, the floppy hat pulled over her scarred face.

"It was a long time ago."

"Did you ever get an answer?"

He gripped the wheel, staring straight ahead.

"Still waiting, I guess?" Greer looked away, not wanting Nagle to know that she had seen tears in his eyes.

"Never changed, has she?" he said.

"Who? Cassandra?"

"No, Miss Finn. Always wheedles everything out of you. Seems to know what's ailing you, end up telling her stuff I've never told anyone. I hate spending time with her, bloody ole witch." He flicked a look in the mirror.

"Really? I love to see her. Though you're right, she has a knack of getting into the heart of you. Remember when she started her College for Creatives in the barn next to the cottage. We couldn't wait to rush off and be artists, but Bríd wasn't keen – kept trying to give us jobs so we couldn't go."

"Why was that? My mother *made* me go."

"Bríd isn't keen on Miss Finn, thinks she's far too liberal … guh!"

Nagle had given her a sharp jab in the ribs, glancing in the rear-view mirror. Miss Finn was wide awake.

Smash and Grab

"Alright, Miss Finn?" Greer asked, hoping she had not said anything to upset her. She loved Miss Finn. She remembered one evening around a campfire, Miss Finn telling how she came to take up the post of arts mistress at the Mary Magdalene. Sister Martha had seen a performance of *Jesus Christ Superstar* and it had so moved her she had decreed the school needed a new Arts Department.

"The world is changing. Sure, what harm can a few drops of technicolour do?" she would say, in defence of what the Mother Superior considered a radical decision.

No one was sure where Miss Finn came from or how old she was. Whatever hideous incident scarred her had also ruined her voice, and although she could talk, she could no longer sing. Which, she told her pupils, had always been her first love, so if they ever felt the urge to sing – poetry they were learning, answers to maths questions, passages from the bible – they need not ask for permission but merely burst into song. There was nothing she liked more, that and her specialist subject, art.

It was in the teaching of art she became someone entirely different from the seemingly aged before her time young woman. Renovating an old fisherman's cottage Miss Finn created Rosshaven's first arts centre, surrounding herself with painters, poets, and musicians. And children, lots of children, who loved dancing on the sand, grilling fish on the barbecue and generally having a wonderfully liberating time.

In fact, Miss Finn had played a major role in ensuring Greer's childhood had many happy memories. Helping to dispel the ones that gave her nightmares and made her cry out at the moon for turning the tide and sending a giant wave to sweep their mother off to that other place far beneath the sea.

Nagle slammed on the brakes, the force of it snatching the memories away as the old lady's cottage came into view. The tide was out, leaving a deep hem of sand dotted with pebbles and shells like a swathe of embroidered suede, and as the late afternoon sun blurred the view, to Greer it looked beautiful.

"Give me a hand, will you?" Nagle grumbled, hauling out Miss Finn's shopping. "She's gone to put the kettle on and left me with this lot."

Greer dragged herself out of the cab. The bags clinked as she draped them on her arms.

"Is she having a party?" She gazed in at the bottles.

Nagle shrugged. "She doesn't make it into town much these days, not since the guards took her licence off her."

"Driving under the influence?"

"Not sure but certainly dangerous."

"She was always dangerous," Greer confirmed.

"Fell asleep in the car on the beach once too often. Tide nearly took her and the vehicle. Sergeant O'Brien said it was too risky, it's a busy waterway, especially around the harbour, anything could have happened. And then the horse died."

"What horse?" Greer was staggering under the weight of the bags as she followed Nagle to the cottage door.

"She bought a horse to take her and the buggy into town but the poor thing had only ever lived on the farm and died of fright when it came face to face with a bus in Patrick's Street. She tried to take the bus driver to court for murder, saying he deliberately aimed the vehicle at the animal and now she's trying raising money to start a training school for bus drivers."

"To do what?"

"Dunno, learn how to ride horses maybe? You know what she's like when she's on a mission." He swirled a finger at his temple.

Greer glanced at the buildings; close-up the cottage and old barn looked sad and unkempt, not the way she remembered it at all. She thought only of colour, music and laughter whenever she recalled her time here. But she had not been for many years, of course it had changed, and even Greer had to admit her memory played tricks. Nana used to say she 'mis-remembered' things, her phrase for saying she made things up.

Sometimes Orla would argue back, insisting whatever Greer remembered was true and Nana was wrong. Then they would be sent to bed early, favourite programmes banned, treats forbidden, all punished together even if only one had been at fault.

Unfazed, Cassandra would wrap her snivelling siblings in a blanket covered with stars and read them stories by torchlight. *Tales of the Arabian Nights*, *Greek Myths & Legends* and *The Three Musketeers*, and soon the sisters were being carried away on a magic carpet, soaring through the heavens in a chariot of fire or galloping through the forest to freedom. The worst of times and of course, the best of times.

An ear-shattering scream brought Greer up sharp.

"Miss Finn!" Nagle called out, dropping bags as he ran, Greer at his heels.

The door to the cottage was wide open, the frame splintered where it had been forced. They stopped in the hall, listening. Greer looked up at Nagle and putting a finger to her lips tiptoed towards a door, slightly ajar. Someone was dragging something across the floor.

She grabbed an umbrella from the stand.

"Who's there?" she shouted, brandishing the brolly like a sword. Nagle had already whipped a copper warming pan off the wall, swishing it steadily through the air ready to give anyone or anything a good wallop. He stopped when he saw Miss Finn crouched on the floor, head in her hands.

"I've been burgled!" she cried.

Greer cast about; it would be hard to see if a burglar had

been successful, there was so much chaos in the room.

"The safe!" She pointed at the fireplace, where a pale patch of wallpaper above the mantelpiece revealed an opening. Greer scanned the room and saw that a large artwork, the size of the patch, was propped behind the shabby sofa. A small metal door rested against the hearth, prised from keeping the contents of the compartment intact. A discarded crowbar looked guiltily like the weapon used to inflict the damage.

Nagle moved into the kitchen, throwing open cupboards and doors, shouting for the 'cowardly cus' to show himself. He thundered upstairs, going from room to room in search of the burglar.

Greer felt deep in the safe, confirming it was empty. Miss Finn let out a pitiful wail. It pained Greer to see her so transformed from the feisty, opinionated old girl she had shared a bottle of wine with less than an hour ago. She went to her.

"What have they taken?"

Miss Finn looked up, her eyes wide with fear.

"My papers, all my personal papers were in there," she said brokenly.

Greer knelt beside her.

"Valuable?" Greer asked, hoping she could reassure the other woman that whatever was in the safe could be replaced.

"Invaluable," Miss Finn whispered.

Nagle reappeared.

"No sign of anyone, the back door is unlocked though, would anyone have a key to that?"

Miss Finn shrugged. "It's always open. Lost the key years ago."

"You mean they needn't have broken in at all?" Nagle was incredulous. Miss Finn shook her head.

"Not if they'd tried the back door first."

Nagle sighed, glancing at the gaping hole in the wall.

"Just papers," Greer told him.

"*Not* just papers. My personal papers, all of them."

"Anything else?" Greer scanned the room.

"Help me, so I can check." Miss Finn indicated the rug, having already pulled the sofa away. They rolled it back to reveal a trapdoor seamlessly fitted into the floorboards. Miss Finn ferreted about beneath her velvet jacket, withdrawing a long chain bearing a small brass key.

"Has this been tampered with?" she asked, feeling around the edges of the door.

"Doesn't look like it," Greer told her.

As Miss Finn bent to put the key in the lock her hands shook, and reluctantly she took the chain from her neck and handed it to Greer. The lock turned and the trap door sprang slightly ajar.

"Stand well back!" Miss Finn ordered. And then Greer remembered, she had never seen the trap door before but was pretty sure where it led. Beneath the cottage was a large cellar with passages running off it; one led to the barn, one to the beach, others were dead ends, a classic smugglers den.

She and her sisters had discovered it by accident moving some old boxes out of the barn to burn on the bonfire. When Miss Finn found three of her students had disappeared into the bowels of the building she flew into a terrible rage, declaring they had trespassed on private property and would never be allowed back to the centre, thereby officially expelled.

Eventually Miss Finn allowed the Morgan sisters to return on condition they never spoke of the smugglers den they had found. Miss Finn need not have worried; the Morgan sisters were particularly good at keeping secrets, even from one another.

Unsteadily, Miss Finn descended the stone steps, flicking a switch as she went. Greer peered in. Shelves upon shelves were stacked with crates and barrels, frames and pictures propped against every surface. Miss Finn pulled out an object covered in purple tissue, quickly unwrapped it and smiled, turning away to examine it, slowly and with pleasure. Greer thought she saw it glint and then it was hurriedly wrapped back in tissue and stowed it away.

Ignoring their outstretched hands as she climbed the steps, Miss Finn wiped her eyes.

"Lock it and put the furniture back," she instructed, colour returning to her cheeks. Greer had found the phone, an ancient two-tone model with a dial and coiled flex; she started to dial.

"What're you doing?" Miss Finn snapped.

"Calling the police."

"No, I won't have that!" Miss Finn took the phone from her.

"But they'll find out who did this. Get your papers back."

Miss Finn shook her head.

"I won't have those wasters in my house. Back-stabbing scoundrels the lot of them."

Miss Finn's mistrust of any sort of authority was well known.

"But you must report it, let them know what's missing," Greer tried.

"Let's call a locksmith at least," Nagle said, handing Miss Finn a glass of the brandy he had just found. "You've no security here, everywhere's wide open."

The old lady handed him back the glass.

"You drink it, you're white as a sheet, I need my wits about me."

"You think they'll come back?" Greer asked.

"I hope not, they took what they came for but there was something else in the safe, an inventory, a list of precious things. Others would be interested in that, very interested indeed."

"You *will* need the locksmith then," Greer confirmed.

"Ha!" Miss Finn pulled off her jacket and threw it to one side. "The ones I'm talking about won't be put off by locks, keys or anything else you can throw at them. No, they use something else, something far more powerful." She stopped and looked hard at the two of them. "Ah, don't mind me, it's the shock. Now, if you wouldn't mind leaving me to it, I've enough to be doing without you two getting under my feet. So shoo, shoo now."

And with that, saving Nagle swallowing the brandy straight back, they were both summarily dismissed.

Dusk was settling as they drove back towards the harbour, the western sky burned red and clouds of molten gold stretched across a calm, dark sea.

"What do you make of all that?" Greer said.

"Mad ole witch!" Nagle replied. "Could have made the whole thing up, did all that before she came into town, wanting us to go back and be witnesses."

"Why would she do something like that?"

"She'll have a reason, she's a wily old fox. Probably wants to put in an insurance claim."

"For papers taken out of her safe?" Greer was bemused. "How valuable can they be?"

"Think about it." Nagle slid her a look. "You must remember the stories."

But Greer's head was splitting, she could not think straight let alone try to remember Miss Finn's many stories, each tantalisingly told as they sat around the campfire, eating sausages and drinking Pepsi cola.

Greer sat back as the car started the climb. Lights had been lit on Manorcliff's terrace, shining like a tiny trail of stars, as the golden stone of the building glowed warm and solid.

"Nearly home," Greer sighed, eager to return to the orderliness of the hotel. She longed for a hearty meal, a glass of wine, interesting and hopefully unchallenging conversation and then the warm and welcoming sanctuary of her room.

Having witnessed Orla in cahoots with Rai, followed by her narrow escape from the investigator and then the discovery of the burglary at Miss Finn's, it had been a very disturbing day indeed.

Out to Lunch

G reer's assumption that Orla's meeting with Rai was a sure sign of her sister's betrayal was unfounded. They were old friends with a lot more in common than she might remember.

"So, tell me what're you doing hanging around the harbour on a perfect day for sailing, such as this?" Rai broke off some sourdough, slathering it with butter and eating with relish, suddenly realising how hungry he was.

"I missed the boat," Orla replied, large iridescent eyes tinged with sadness.

"Literally?"

She nodded. "We overslept again."

"We?"

She bent to hug Wolfe's damp head. "Yep, and I knew Dr James was leaving early but we'd been on a project, so we overslept."

"What time were you to meet James?"

"Seven o'clock."

"What time did you go to bed?"

"Half-past six."

"Orla, half an hour is not really long enough for a night's sleep."

The waiter brought their food, two hearty bowls of steaming seafood chowder. He nodded at Rai in recognition. The Harbour Spa Hotel had celebrity guests staying all the time, the Taoiseach himself there only last week.

"I know that," Orla replied haughtily, wiping her hands on a napkin before getting stuck in. "But half-past six is morning, I figured if we went to bed in the morning, we wouldn't need a night's sleep at all. Isn't that right, Wolfe?" She fed the dog some bread.

"Logical but not workable, our bodies need proper sleep," Rai explained.

"You can talk!"

"I wouldn't feed Wolfe from the table here, Orla," Rai said, looking round at the well-heeled diners scattered about the terrace, too busy enjoying the food and the view to notice. "Save him something for later."

"Sorry," she whispered. "I forget I've to do the hygienic thing everywhere and not just at our place. But germs have to live somewhere, I mean, they've as much right on the planet as we have. Probably more, bet they were here first."

Rai was laughing now, he had forgotten what good company Orla could be, her unique take on the world so refreshing. He looked out across the bay, boats scudding to and fro, the island in the distance, the sea a crumple of dark velvet covered with diamonds.

"I hope Dr James will be alright," Orla said, following his gaze.

"There's a good breeze out there today, James will be fine, sometimes a man needs to be alone with the sea."

"Sometimes a woman does too," Orla told him. "But you're right, James spent so many years in practice, his head's full of noise. Imagine all that time just listening to people telling you how ill they are?"

Rai considered this. "Poor man," he said, taking a sip of his drink.

"Oh, he's not poor, he's quite rich really. He told me his partner left him very well off when he died, but he doesn't want to be a doctor anymore, so needs to be frugal."

"He sounds very wise, your Dr James, and has he come back to live in Rosshaven permanently?"

Orla was mopping up the last of the chowder, feeding Wolfe the sodden bread from her fingers. She glanced up at Rai. "I'm after forgetting I'm not to do that, sorry."

Rai gave her a knowing look. Orla was well practised at using her eccentricities to her advantage, especially where her favourites were concerned. Wolfe licked his lips lavishly.

"Yes, he's come to live at the hotel," she went on. "But because of his frugality, Cass has worked out a special deal for him, like adding his boat to the hotel's services."

"Services?"

"Yes, sailing trips for guests, fishing, dolphin spotting, that kind of thing. Cass thinks it's a great idea." She leaned towards him conspiratorially, pointing at the hotel logo on her napkin. "This place is very competitive, taken quite a few of our regulars who don't appreciate the genteel qualities of a very nearly stately home like ours."

Rai nodded seriously. "I'm guessing that's what Cassandra says." He was right, it was precisely what she said, to anyone who would listen.

"The problem with James is, he's too beautiful to be let out on his own much," she said, returning to another favourite.

"He is?" Rai asked, signalling the waiter for a menu. He remembered Orla loved ice cream, but Greer had told him years ago she could only have it when someone else was with her. He could not remember why.

Orla guessed what he was thinking. "It's because I like to wear it, more than I like to eat it. It's the smooth coolness, I love the feel of it."

"That's it!" Rai's dark eyes shone, recalling the occasions when unsupervised, Orla did indeed wear ice cream, covering herself in it from head to toe. "I wonder if that's one of things you do to remind people you're a little bit different?"

"Ah, Rai!" Orla grinned back at him. "We're all different, you know that, just like shells, no two are the same, sure where would the fun be in that? Sameness is just another word for boring."

"Well, you're certainly not that," Rai confirmed. "And your Dr James, he's different too?"

"Oh, yes and truly beautiful. That's why Frances Crowther is always hanging about, unbuttoning her top, piling her hair up and letting it down again. Awful creature."

"She has her eye on him then?"

"She has! And anything else she can have on him. She used to come to stay with her mother and sit on a lounger all day reading Jackie Collins but she's not working anymore and keeps coming for long weekends. I don't think James wants to take her on his boat but he's too polite." Orla gave an exaggerated shrug. "Can I have ice cream please? You're not going anywhere, are you?"

Rai was just about to reassure her when a tall, dark-haired man crossed the terrace in easy strides, thrusting his hand towards him.

"Well! I'll be … it's the man himself, Rai Muir!"

Rai sprang to his feet, instantly eye to eye with Ross Power, the hotel's American CEO. The men hugged each other hard.

"How're you doing?" Ross asked, smiling an identical smile back at this cousin. "Declan told me *The Pirate's* out of the water for repairs. You looking for a gig? Somewhere to stay?" And then noticing Orla, remembered his manners. "Ms Morgan, good to see you. Not sure about the company you're keeping though."

"His name's Wolfe," Orla explained. "And he's totally house-trained, even though this is a hotel."

"That's good to know." Ross gave a disarming grin. "But it was your other companion I was referring to. He certainly isn't house-trained."

Orla looked at Rai, unsure if this was a joke. Rai laughed.

"Not looking for either, thanks. Besides, you're always fully booked, I've been told."

Ross started to clear their table. "Always room for one of me own, as Dad used to say."

Rai gave the building an appreciative glance. Designed to echo an oceangoing liner, it was carved from rock with huge glass walls curving towards the bay providing a vista of the beach, harbour and town, the whole scene a living, breathing picture. Ross himself had designed a suite of luxurious subterranean rooms with windows beneath the ocean.

When Orla heard this, she had begged one of the builders to let her see for herself what a room under the ocean looked like, but she had been disappointed. With the lights not yet fitted so the view was just a dense, dark curtain there was no sound, not even a murmur of the beautiful music the sea makes once a being is totally submerged.

"What about a gig then? With *The Pirate* out of action you could come and earn your keep here, we're all set up for entertainment in the new bar. You'll certainly draw the crowds, I know that much."

Rai laughed. "Thanks, but maybe another time. My lovely companion here has agreed to rent me a room in her family establishment, where I know I'll be very comfortable."

Ross frowned slightly. He had heard Greer Morgan was joining the family business and wondered if his cousin might not be as welcome as he hoped. Although whether Greer was back for good was also in question. Dining at Galty House recently, he had overheard Leela telling Archie she was unconvinced Greer had the backbone to stick at anything for long, describing her as flighty, like her mother. Archie had disagreed, telling Leela the Morgan sisters were remarkably grounded, considering they had been orphaned at such an early age. But Leela had merely snorted, saying her family had been orphaned too and they were all perfectly normal, everyone said so.

Ross also knew that Rai's relationship with Greer was the stuff of legend. An on-off passionate affair played out in the full glare of the media many years ago. Rai, a talented singer-song writer, had formed a band with a group of friends and Greer, pretty, spikey and some would say gifted, had been persuaded to join easy enough, at the time she would have followed Rai anywhere.

The Island, as they were known, played mainly in the pubs and clubs scattered up and down Ireland's east coast but when someone had the brilliant idea to host a replica Live Aid music festival during the summer of 1986, the band was discovered, signed a contract with EMI and the rest, as they say, is history.

Rai and Greer's story turned to a fairy tale as the childhood sweethearts soared to the dizzy heights of global fame and of course, once they had been built up, the media took it in turns to tear them down. Sadly, the young and rather naïve couple had been an easy target.

"I don't think I'll have my ice cream," Orla said, pointing out to sea. "That's James coming in now, I'll need to get back, we've a full house too."

"For another time then, I'll make sure we have some of that homemade cherry vanilla you particularly like," Ross the consummate hotelier told her. He looked at Rai; ten years his senior, he had been his childhood hero. He remembered the excitement at being told the rock star was his cousin and meeting him for the first time while on holiday here. They were swimming out to the island but it was too far for the twelve-year-old from New York, so Rai had just picked him up, flipped him over and swum the rest of the way with him on his back.

There had always been something unbound about Rai, Ross considered, watching as he slipped some notes under a plate to cover the bill and although he and Rai looked alike, they were worlds apart, just looking into Rai's eyes Ross could feel the distance between them.

Orla lifted Wolfe into her arms as they made to leave.

"I nearly forgot, the launch party, we're opening the new bar!" Ross exclaimed. "Will you come? Please say yes. Archie Fitzgerald's doing the official opening."

"I'll have my PA check the schedule," Rai teased, those days long gone. "Of course I'll come."

"Perfect. The sisters are coming too, isn't that so, Orla?"

Ross was standing at the top of the steps, the hotel towering behind him, casting a shadow.

"Oh, I nearly forgot, that's why I came." She pulled the envelope from her pocket, handing it to Ross. "Wouldn't miss it for the world," she replied, realising with both Archie and Rai now on the guest list, coercing her siblings to attend could be problematic to say the least.

Surprise Guests

"Where've you been?" Cassandra came flying out of the kitchen. "I've been worried sick, are you alright?" She spun her sister round, examining her. "You've been gone hours, why don't you answer your phone?"

Nagle came in behind Greer.

"You're as bad!" Cassandra wagged a ladle at him. "I must have phoned you a dozen times. Then I phoned every pub in the harbour."

"Charming!" Greer said under her breath.

"It was Dixie Dignan told me you'd both gone off with Miss Finn. Have you been drinking?" She leaned in to eyeball Nagle.

"For godsake, woman, I'm allowed a pint!"

Cassandra gave a dramatic sniff. "With a brandy chaser by the smell of you."

Nagle went to protest but thought better of it. "It's a good job we did go to Miss Finn's she …

"Needed a hand." Greer flashed him a look. They had been sworn to secrecy about the burglary, Miss Finn declaring every crook in the county would be calling by, knowing her security was lax. "Our good deed for the day." Greer took the ladle, tasting remnants of sauce. "Delicious, what're we having?"

"A bowl of fresh air for you two if you don't get a move on and give me a hand. We've a full minibus down from Dublin celebrating a fiftieth, a single fella doing some sort of research and Orla's just showing a late booking to their room."

"Well, we're here now," Greer reassured her.

Cassandra gave them both the once-over. "A quick

freshen up wouldn't go amiss, you look like a pair of escapees from the local sanatorium. Then, Greer in the kitchen and Nagle pre-dinner drinks, everything's ready, you just need to serve, as genteelly as you can, if you wouldn't mind." And retrieving the ladle from Greer, she turned on her heel to leave them gazing after her.

Orla was having difficulty finishing the table.

She had counted the place settings at least six times but kept coming up with a different answer, and much as Cassandra liked guests seated in random fashion, Orla had decided on place names for this evening, having spent hours carefully preparing cards stuck with tiny shells and names in swirly gold ink.

These had been placed on snowy white napkins next to side plates bearing the Morgan coat of arms but even this was not going to plan. Suddenly she realised why. There were some people she could not sit together and some she just had to.

Orla was still in a quandary when Cassandra appeared to check the menu; grilled garlic prawns, fresh crab salad with new potatoes tossed in herb butter, and homemade yoghurt ice cream with raspberries. A delicious Friday evening dinner to welcome guests old and new.

She had, of course, ensured no one was averse to seafood before plumping for the mainly fish supper, selecting a very fine Sancerre to go with it; so important to create a good impression on the first night.

"I thought you were putting out place names this evening, Orla?" the hotel director asked, hastily untying her apron. "Do it now before they come in, I want everyone seated, the prawns must be served sizzling."

Still unsure, Orla waited for her sister to leave and threw the names into the middle of the table; maybe it would just sort itself out.

Disturbed by the scenario at Miss Finn's cottage, Greer was

determined to shake off a distinct feeling of foreboding, deciding a bath and a serious refresh would certainly help. Having changed into olive green palazzo pants and matching tunic with tiny turquoise crystals at the neck and cuff, she descended the stairs.

Strains of a jig drifted across the terrace. Cassandra favoured Irish music on Fridays, it set the tone for new guests. The Morgans were an old Hibernian family, Manorcliff overlooked the wild Celtic Sea and despite whatever modernity Rosshaven had embraced in recent times, the hotel's guests were destined to enjoy a truly Irish experience. Well, Cassandra's version of it anyway.

Entering the large, well-equipped kitchen, watching as Cassandra and Bríd worked in unison to prepare the meal, she realised the task had a rhythm to it. The heat of the day had lessened, the breeze drifting in through the open doors with its calming sea-salt taste seemed to embrace her, so much so, Greer felt a sudden urge to dance.

She presented herself before Orla, who recognising the twinkle in her eyes, bowed slightly and each taking the other in their arms, began side-stepping and twirling the length of the room. They sang as they danced, belting out the lyrics to *Maids When You're Young Never Wed an Old Man*, an irreverent old favourite which still made them laugh.

Bríd stopped to watch, blaming onions for watery eyes; it was a long time since she had seen the sisters dance. It was usually the three of them, Orla between the other two, Cassandra and Greer helping her keep time, remember the words. The three Morgan sisters together, a wonderful, formidable force, not one whole without the other two and whichever two were left, always slightly cast adrift with one missing.

Greer caught Bríd's wonky smile. "Good old days, eh?" she said, spinning her sister to a halt. Cassandra stood stock still, mesmerised as they danced, her mouth in a sad smile. Bríd coughed.

"Ah no, the prawns will be frizzled not sizzled!" she declared, running to rescue the first course.

Now out in the soft evening, Greer was pleased to see so many familiar faces. Nagle serving drinks, Dr James engaging Orla in conversation and making her laugh, telling Wolfe how pretty his mistress looked tonight, and it was a real shame her ears were not as long and silky as his, then she would be a real catch.

The German family seemed far more relaxed too, chatting with one of the new guests in the corner. The man with his back to her looked familiar. As she pondered, Tone bounded over and bending to return the greeting she recognised the man. It was the 'detective' she had so skilfully avoided in town. He was here, in the very midst of the ritual of evening drinks, and this time she had nowhere to run.

Come on, Greer, what's the worst that can happen? She could hear Alistair's smooth voice in her head. *Tell the truth, you don't know anything anyway.*

That's not the point, she argued back at herself. *I need time to prepare, to know what to say.*

"And this is my sister Greer," Cassandra said, bringing him to meet her.

"Hello again." She felt a flush at her throat. "Sorry I had to dash off earlier."

"So am I," he replied.

"Emergency, you know how it is."

"What emergency?" Cassandra was concerned.

"I needed to give Nagle a hand getting an elderly lady home before the tide turned. You know how difficult Miss Finn can be." Greer gave Cassandra their wide-eyed look.

Cassandra did not miss a beat. "She can and the tide comes in very fast where she is, cuts her cottage off in minutes," she explained. "This is Meredith by the way, doing some research in the area, amn't I right, Meredith?"

"Spot on," the man said, still gazing at Greer, who did not

believe that 'research in the area' line for one second. "I was, I have to admit a huge fan. All the albums, posters on the wall, the lot!"

Cassandra watched Greer bristle. She loathed it when people referred to her past career as some sort of guilty pleasure. She had been a singer in a band and a very successful one too. As she opened her mouth to retort, Cassandra steered him away.

"Greer, will you take the dogs, we're about to go into supper." Greer called Wolfe and Tone to heel, relieved to escape. She was also relieved to discover, despite Orla's random place settings, she had been spared their new guest. Instead James, who was already slathering butter on his soda bread, indicated she sit beside him.

Ava, the young German girl, sat opposite, sun-kissed and happy. Orla reported she had been spotted walking on the beach hand in hand with one of the locals down from Trinity College where he was studying German, and although she had not yet forgiven her parents for dragging her to Ireland against her wishes, it looked like a drop of Irish charm had started the healing process.

Nagle passed the wine as the prawns were served, the delicious aroma making everyone's mouth water.

"Keep that place for me," Orla said, pointing at the chair beside the doctor.

"Of course," smiled James. "I want to hear all about your project, the one that made you oversleep."

Frances perked up. "Was Orla coming with us then?" she asked sweetly.

"*She'd* been invited," James replied equally sweetly, implying Frances had not.

"We had a wonderful sail," Frances said. "James is such a skilful captain."

Greer rolled her eyes at Orla.

"Are we all here?" Cassandra asked from the head of the table, ready to raise her glass in welcome. The door opened and a tall, dark figure slipped into the room. "Ah, now we are. Welcome, come and take a seat, there, beside Greer, that's it."

Greer could not quite see who had entered the room, Nagle's large bulk was blocking her view. She squinted at the name on the card beside her as Rai Muir took his place at the table.

A Spy in the Camp

As Rai sat, Greer pushed herself surreptitiously off her chair and slid to the floor. Once there she positioned herself on her hands and knees to crawl the length of the table skilfully avoiding the other diners' legs.

Back on her feet, she closed the door silently behind her, before taking off at speed along the corridor, praying the distraction of supper being served had covered her sudden departure.

Greer accepted that Orla could be slightly off kilter at times, but this really was the limit. Coming up with playschool place names in the hope it would coerce her to sit next to her arch enemy was a naivety too far.

Stepping outside she took as deep a breath of cool, fresh air as her boiling rage would allow and standing perfectly still, forced herself to just breathe – deeply, slowly – willing calm to infiltrate and soothe her, the way she had been taught to, whenever the 'fanciful furies' as her grandmother called them, had taken hold and she had become a 'handful'; another of Nana's favourite sayings.

Finally opening her eyes, she realised it was a beautiful evening. A light breeze from the shore lifted her hair and the scent of the sea made her nose tingle. She looked up; the moon was skulking behind a trail of cloud and although she gave a wary glance, this time he was blameless. A mere bystander, having played no part in the attempt to reunite the soulmates, whatever Greer tried to imply with her steely eyes.

Something brushed against her leg, making her jump. Tone had followed her outside. He gazed at her, querying. No doubt bemused she had left the table during supper, the first proper meal she would have eaten all day.

"You're right," she groaned, her stomach clenched with anxiety. "I need a drink!"

They made their way to the terrace, where the trolley stood replenished, ready for after-dinner drinks beneath the stars. Greer mixed herself a large Cork Dry Gin and tonic, and taking a bowl of Bríd's crumbly cheese straws went to sit peacefully with her companion and watch the darkening view fade to velvet night.

The alcohol had the desired effect and with Tone snuggled beside her, the two soon drifted off, the sound of waves landing on the shore lulling them to sleep.

"Yes, a proper search. She was away most of the day. Nothing." It went quiet, as the speaker listened to the response. "I've tried my best, did as you asked, that's me finished."

Greer struggled awake. Tone groaned. She thought she heard someone; someone in the shrubbery on the phone. She placed her hand over Tone's warm snout, not wanting to disturb whoever was speaking, but all was quiet.

"There you are!" Dr James came towards her. "You disappeared. Not ill, are you?" He placed his hand on her forehead. "Hmmm, a bit feverish. Nausea?"

"You could say that." She removed his hand. "I'm off to bed. I'll be fine."

"Can I get you anything?" he asked. "Might be getting a summer cold, they can be nasty."

"Another one of these should sort it." She waved her glass at him, then looked round. "Anyone else out here?"

"Haven't seen anyone."

"Anyone pass on your way?"

"Nope." James shook his head.

"Sure?" Greer shot him a glance. She liked Dr James, but could she trust him? She decided to change tack. "Are my sisters inside?"

"They were when I left but Orla was tired, she'd had very

little sleep. What's this project she's been working on? Keeping her up all night?"

Greer stood unsteadily, amazed she had slept so soundly on a hard stone bench in the cool evening air.

"Orla always has a project on the go, you don't realise how complex shells are until you talk to Orla. She can name all the different families … Anomiidae, Mytilidae, Cardiidae … there's so many. She may have found the tiniest mollusc and will be tearing her hair out, checking its credentials. Some of her finds are prehistoric." Greer laughed to herself. "Mind you, some of her outfits are too!"

James gave her a look.

"I'm not speaking out of turn, she'd agree with me, she likes old things, she says she can feel the past on them, the layers of time. Helps her understand."

"Understand what?"

"The stories, the legends, you know the kind of thing."

But James did not know and although he tried hard to understand Orla, it was pointless trying to second-guess her, work out what she was up to or what she was going to do next. Yet that was all part of her charm. That and the juxtaposition of childlike naivety with cold-hearted realism.

Orla was an enigma and despite their difference in age and background – James being younger and more widely travelled – there was something that drew them together, Greer could see that now remarkably clearly, despite her inebriated state.

"Fond of her, aren't you?" She smiled into his puzzled frown. Orla said he looked just like Elvis Costello – her favourite singer – but the only similarity Greer could see was the large glasses.

"Extremely," James replied immediately. "She's wonderful."

"Infuriating? Unpredictable?"

"Yes, that too. But her good points far outweigh the bad and her bad points aren't that bad, really."

Greer waggled a finger at him. "You sound well smitten to me, doctor. And if that's what ails you there's no cure, you know that, don't you?"

James did not respond, just sat on his hands gazing pensively out to sea, as Tone and a slightly swaying Greer took their leave.

"Where is she? I'm going to kill her!" Greer stood at the kitchen door, hands on hips.

Cassandra was putting the last of the crockery away, the long table laid for breakfast, a smaller table at the window laid up too, a full complement for the first meal of the day; this had not happened in a while.

"And I'm going to kill you!" Cassandra straightened, placing a hand at the small of her back. "What was that all about? How old are you, ten? Crawling out under the table like a spoilt child."

"You saw what she did! She put her stupid place names on the table and me next to *him!* She deliberately put me in the most awkward position she could." Greer slammed the door behind her. "Bad enough you think it's okay to allow him to stay here but to have to sit with him at dinner. What was she thinking?"

"Greer! If you don't mind!" Cassandra hissed, indicating the door.

"I know, we've paying guests!" Greer said, taking the vodka out of the fridge. She checked the label, recalling their 'tasting sessions'. A few years ago, having one of her economy drives, Cassandra decreed they pick the best match of the cheaper spirits to the top brands. The experiment started well, dissolving into mayhem the more drinks they tried, so much so they mixed up the results, argued and then laughed till they cried. Cassandra had missed breakfast the next morning and Greer had not bothered to get up at all.

Orla, aware her sisters were in no state to prevent her, had slept on a faraway beach that night. Fudge was just about to call the coastguard when she reappeared and without a word, she and Bríd busied themselves disposing of the bottles.

"Sometimes a girl needs to let her hair down," Bríd had said, by way of explanation. Which Orla thought odd, as both her sisters had been wearing their hair up the last time she had seen them. Needless to say, the monumental hangovers meant the hotel director remained loyal to the premium brands, insisting this policy would not only uphold the hotel's reputation but safeguard their guests, being kinder to their livers.

Greer poured a large measure into the glass she still had in her hand. Cassandra glared at her.

"Do I need to remind you we have paying guests and whether you like it or not Rai Muir is one of them? If you're going to play any part in the running of this hotel, you'd better learn that personal feelings should never, *ever* affect professional behaviour."

Greer gave her eldest sister a cold look.

"Have I made myself clear?" Cassandra held her gaze. One of the dogs whimpered.

"Yes, boss."

"Good. Now take your drink and go to bed and don't forget to set your alarm."

"Alarm? Why?" Greer was bemused.

"Because you're getting up early to help Bríd with breakfast. You've been feck all use to me today and I'm exhausted."

"Ah, Cassandra …"

"Don't!" Cassandra said angrily. And then her eyes softened, too weary for war. "Don't let me down …please." And with that she locked the door, checked the dogs had water and switched off the lights leaving Greer alone in the dark.

Suitably admonished and with the threat of early duties, Greer reluctantly left the vodka on the table and slipping upstairs to her room, closed the door quietly behind her. Automatically reaching for the lamp, she stopped, realising there was no need.

A huge moon hung outside, shining its silver light through the French window, drenching the room in a soft, steely glow. The breeze from the open doors shimmered the drapes making the light appear like water, trickling across the furniture and the floor, splashing into corners and streaming over the bed, turning the satin eiderdown into a pool.

This had not happened in years. This was the reason her room could not be altered in any way; the spell might break. This was why her room was so special, the moon made it water.

Not all the time but on rare and wonderful nights, the moon turned her sanctuary into a chamber of water, just as if it were beneath the ocean and she could smell the sea all about her.

Undressing quickly Greer lay in the middle of the floor and closing her eyes, stretched out like a starfish to bathe in the smooth lunar light flooding the room. Breathing deeply, she let the energy seep slowly into every pore of her body, soothing and calming her and as she lay there, feeling her heart begin to slow, the anxiety in her chest eased away, and she felt warm and strong and safe.

Gently, as sleep came upon her, she felt herself falling. Fears floating away as she fell and just when she thought her fall would never end, she was caught in an embrace, strong arms held her, the smoothest skin upon hers, soft as water, cool as silk. Returning the embrace, she wrapped her arms around her lover, burying her face in strands of dark, damp hair and the delicious scent of seaweed.

And as she slept, a name came to her, a name she had not spoken with love for a very long time and Greer whispered, *Rai*. Somehow knowing deep in his heart, he would hear, the way he had always heard whenever they were apart, and she needed to feel the power of his love as much as he needed to feel hers.

Sea Salt

P ale smatterings of dawn filtered through the curtains, as she struggled awake. For half a second, she wondered where she was, her unconscious mind still swimming deep in the depths, and stretching out she felt the cool silk of her eiderdown and knew she was safe in her bed, the beautiful moonlit night passed, leaving her rested and replete. A serenity she only ever felt with …

Greer turned abruptly, half-expecting to see a tangle of dark hair on the pillow beside her, translucent skin stretched across cheekbones, eyes tightly closed – he slept so soundly – and lashes that shone, even in moonlight. The pillow remained unsullied, of course. She pushed an odd sense of something away.

But the feeling would not leave her, even as she stumbled to the shower, she felt he had been here in her room; the room it became when the moon shone in that special way.

"Just a dream," she told her reflection as she brushed her teeth, and wiping her mouth dry, instinctively remoistened her lips with her tongue. She stopped, her mouth tingling, tasting what she might have expected had the dream been real.

Sea salt.

She stared in the mirror, a trace of white, the merest print of a kiss on her lips.

She let the towel fall to the floor.

By the time Cassandra appeared – immaculate in navy sailing trews, red and white striped top and her favourite rope of large freshwater pearls – breakfast was done and dusted with coffee being served at gingham-clad tables out on the terrace.

Bríd was finishing packed lunches for guests heading out for the day and Greer was mopping the hallway leading to the cliff walk, ready for sandy feet and muddy boots coming up from the bay.

"How're things?" Cassandra asked Bríd, glancing towards her busy sister.

"Grand. She ran the show, no problem," Bríd reassured her.

"Any issues with anyone?" Cassandra was checking the vegetable basket, deciding which soup to make for lunch.

"If you're talking about Rai, he didn't show."

"Did he breakfast in his room?"

Bríd shrugged. "If he did, he didn't ask for it to be sent up."

"Still in bed?"

"No, his room's vacant. Not sure he even slept there."

"What?!" Cassandra nearly dropped the basket. "Well, whose room did he sleep in then?"

They looked out to where Greer had been working, mop abandoned, the door to the cliff steps ajar. Bríd closed the door, putting the mop and bucket away.

"Give her a break," Bríd said quietly. "There's enough going on."

Cassandra blinked. "What's going on?"

"Sergeant O'Brien's been on the phone. He's on his way to take a statement from Greer after Miss Finn's burglary yesterday. He wants to talk to Nagle too, he's down in the lower field, fixing the gate, Greer's gone to fetch him." Bríd went back to slicing the boiled eggs.

"Miss Finn burgled? They never said. Well, keep O'Brien in the kitchen and tell him to take his bloody hat off, don't want people saying this place is crawling with police. Where's Orla?"

"Sailing with the doctor. Frances Crowther wasn't too impressed with her lonely breakfast, said her bacon was too crispy, tea too strong, you know the kind of thing."

"Funny, nothing ever wrong when I serve her."

"She's always having breakfast with Dr James when you serve her, that's why everything's perfect." Bríd gave Cassandra a tight smile. "Anyway, she's checking out, says she doesn't feel as welcome here as she used to."

The bell on reception rang. Cassandra went to attend to their guests.

"Not much to tell, usual thing, front door jemmied open, everywhere a bit of a mess. Picture taken down, safe wide open and Miss Finn's papers gone." Nagle was leaning against the range, long legs crossed at the ankles, thick socks with a hole at each big toe on full display.

"Did she say what the papers were?" Sergeant O'Brien asked.

"Just precious," Greer answered. "She said they were precious."

"Was anything else taken? Touched even?"

Nagle shot Greer a look. She pulled a face.

"Don't think so. Didn't mention anything else, did she?" Greer asked Nagle.

Nagle shrugged. "Nope. Nothing."

"No clues? Car tracks? Cigarette butts? Abandoned boat, that kind of thing?" The policeman pushed his spectacles onto his forehead; he had seen a fella in a classic English detective do that, gave him an air of inscrutability.

"Oh, for godsake, Brendan, you sound like something off the telly. Miss Finn probably took the papers out of the safe herself and forgot where she left them." Cassandra placed a tray of homemade whiskey cake on the table. Sergeant O'Brien helped himself. "She may have had a couple of glasses of wine, no harm to her but at her age it makes her forgetful." She gave Greer their wide-eyed look.

"We'd had a glass together earlier," Greer confirmed. The policeman glanced at Nagle. He held his hands up.

"A pint! I had one pint!" Nagle shouted, his face on fire.

Cassandra went to him. "Alright," she whispered, putting

a hand on his arm. "Brendan isn't asking about you, just if Miss Finn had a few drinks on her."

"Well, it certainly looked like she'd been burgled and not just forgotten where her stuff was." Nagle was adamant.

Sergeant O'Brien closed his notebook. "We found a jemmy in the barn. Looked like paint from the door on it."

"Whoever broke in probably threw it away as they left. What about fingerprints?" Greer suggested.

"Sadly, any prints on the jemmy have been smudged."

"Has she told you what the papers are?" Cassandra asked the sergeant.

"No, won't give any details, just that they're private."

"So how do you know what you're looking for?"

"We don't."

"Well, what could they be used for?" Greer pressed.

Sergeant O'Brien picked up his hat, fixing her with a stare.

"Blackmail, Greer. Miss Finn said her papers contained information, the sort of stuff people might not want made public. But as we all know, the poor old girl's not right in the head and could easily have set the whole thing up for a bit of attention. It's a lonely ole place out there, doesn't see a soul for weeks on end."

"Ah no," Cassandra protested. "It's a bit wild alright but she's artistic, she loves to be inspired by the remoteness."

"I'll get to the bottom of it, you know me." And much to Cassandra's chagrin, Sergeant O'Brien put two more pieces of cake in his pocket, thrust on his hat and made to leave. "Greer, see me out, will you?"

Greer raised an eyebrow at her sister as she left.

The police officer waited until they were on the steps leading from the main entrance. "I'll need you to call into the station in the next day or so. A detective inspector, Crosby Jones, his name is, from Scotland Yard is coming over, wants to interview you. He's handling the investigation into Alistair McKeiver's affairs."

Greer knew it was serious, he was using his 'official'

Garda voice, the one he saved for rowdy tourists or local farmers who might have 'accidently' moved some sheep belonging to someone else.

"But I thought I'd dodged that, wasn't that Meredith fella looking for me earlier this week?" Greer had consulted the hotel register that morning, relieved to see the man she thought was the 'detective' from England had checked out.

"He was looking for you, because he *was* doing research. Told me he's making a film about the band, the fame, the accident, the break-up, all that kind of shite."

"You never said!" she flashed angrily.

"You never asked, and besides, I didn't tell him anything, didn't have to. Unfortunately, this is different, I'm obliged."

"You don't have to mention I'm here."

"No choice. European-wide police policy. We all co-operate with one another. I'll ask a female officer to come from Gorey if you'd prefer it."

"Why?"

"In case you want a woman with you, I've to offer you that."

"What for? Have I to take my clothes off for him to question me?" Greer was incredulous.

Sergeant O'Brien sighed. Greer was the most strident of the sisters, and they all had their moments.

"I'll make the arrangements and let you know when the DI arrives." He opened the car door. "Don't worry, Greer. It'll be alright, I mean you're not in any real trouble, now are you?"

Greer did not answer.

"Just don't leave town, okay?" he told her, still using his serious voice.

Approaching from the garden, Rai lifted an arm in recognition, and the police officer waved back as he drove off.

Gazing after the squad car in puzzlement, Greer did not realise Rai had come to stand beside her.

"In trouble again?" he whispered. And caught off guard, she looked up into those deep, dark eyes, the ones that bored straight through to her very soul and wondered, in that instant, if indeed she *was.*

Call to Action

S he stepped back; he was too close. She caught the scent of
him, the briny, sea salt smell, his hair damp, bending into
curls on his forehead. He was smiling and she noticed the
slight chip in his front tooth which, despite pressure from the
band's stylist, he had never had fixed.

"We need to talk," Rai said gently, his voice as soft as a
ripple on the shore.

Too much detail. Why did she always notice every tiny
nuance, everything thrown into sharp focus, hungry eyes
seeking out all she could find to keep and remember?

"What can we have to talk about?" she replied,
exasperated. First Sergeant O'Brien, now Rai. "We've paid
lawyers thousands, no, tens of thousands to do the talking for
us over the years. So, if you have something to say, put it in
writing and get your solicitor to send it to mine."

"It's not that kind of talk." He reached for her hand. She
took another step back. How dare he presume he could place
his skin against hers?

"You've nothing to say I want to hear," she told him.

There was a kerfuffle on the steps, guests were leaving,
Fudge helping with bags. Greer looked up, relieved at the
interruption.

"I work here now, so if you don't mind, I need to get on."
She gave him a stern look, and as the guests neared, smiled.
"Let me know when you're ready to check out, Mr Muir, I'll fast-
track your departure, I can assure you of that!" And with the
smile still frozen, she made haste back into the hotel.

Fudge glanced at Rai as he loaded the luggage.

"Staying long?" he asked.

"It's my home too," Rai told him, nodding towards the bay.

"If you say so," Fudge replied. He had known Rai since he was a small boy and had always liked him, despite the 'wilderness' years, as Rai himself called them. Rai was different, individual, never ran with the pack. Yet sometimes, even as a child, Rai was scary, there were glimpses of a strangeness in him, something not quite …

"He's gifted," Bríd always said. "A true genius is never quite belonging of this world, they can't see it like us, sure where would be the beauty in that?"

And Fudge would scratch at his throat. For as long as he had known his hardworking, practical wife, sometimes she said the weirdest things and rather than question the meaning, it was easier to just respond, "True enough." Which is what he had been doing now for over thirty years.

As Fudge drove away Rai caught his reflection in the window, and frowned. He looked wild. He needed a shave and a haircut, the rugby shirt he wore was faded and the Levi's hung off him. He tightened his belt; he could do with some food.

He had been too busy to eat. Having cooked breakfast for Miss Finn, he helped her clear up, rearranging the cottage until it was back to her liking. And as usual, once a task was completed, she sent him away. Giving him no time to assess how she was, beyond her blustering that she had put a good, strong curse on whoever had done this, so they had better watch out.

In truth he had been shocked when he saw her; she had aged, frailer in herself and smaller, as if her bones were shrinking from the inside.

"I'll be back tomorrow, see how you are, check if you need anything," he told her.

"No, no," she said, examining the door he had made secure. "I'm grand. Need a rest, that's all. You'd serve me better finding my papers, Sergeant O'Brien wouldn't see them if they were stuck to the peak of his cap!"

"Any clue who might have them?"

"I can't see as clearly as I used to." She peered at him, but he knew it was the second sight she was talking about. "It's something to do with the sisters. Trouble there, I think."

"Which sister? What trouble?" Rai asked.

"Like I said, I can't see deterunes, she said, "No boat?"

"I needed a swim today," Rai said quietly.

"Hmm, too long on the land dries up your soul," she admonished. "The time is coming to go back, I've done all I can here. I'm thinking you'll be going soon too; you're badly needed in the other place." She stood for a moment, staring at him. "Try not to break her heart again, Rai. Let her know, no matter what, that you love her. Let her feel held, even when you're gone." And shooing him out she went to close the door, giving him a sweeping look from head to toe. "So like him," she whispered, raising her hand to stroke his cheek, then she pulled her hand back, shutting the door. "Go now, I've enough to do."

Rai shuddered, the wind off the sea was cold. Miss Finn was right, the time was coming, he could feel it too.

The day had reached the late morning lull most hotels encounter. Breakfast cooked and cleared away, guests checked out, rooms cleaned, lunch prepared, and the evening menu agreed.

After dropping his passengers at the ferry and the station, Fudge had a list of errands to run. Bríd was having a lie-down – a regime Cassandra had enforced when her weak heart was diagnosed – and Greer had not been seen since her conversation with Sergeant O'Brien, followed by a brief encounter with Rai Muir at the front of the hotel.

Cassandra was sitting at the long table in the kitchen, coffee in her favourite mug beside her, Wolfe and Tone slumbering by the range. Nagle had gone about his business and for once the house felt still.

The foolscap daybook, leather-bound in olive green with two silk page dividers, lay open before her. The hotel's itinerary, daily schedules, weekly plans and monthly accounts were all computerised these days but still she kept her log of lists and tasks, neatly catalogued in her tight handwriting on every page, with important contacts and email addresses stored in a separate compartment inside the back.

She was looking at it now, gazing at a telephone number under the letter G. A number she knew as well as her own. The quandary hung heavily. The choice was hers. She could stick to the decision she had made all those years ago, when she was frightened and alone and had no choice.

Or she could – given the imminent departure of a particularly significant figure in the scenario – spill the beans, make a clean breast of it and once it was out there, let it take its own course.

At the very least she would be free. Free of the awful dread nagging away at her, the fear of doing the wrong thing for all the right reasons, yet again.

The phone beside her sprang to life. She stared at it, its incessant ring like the bleat of an abandoned lamb. Her eyes widened, the number calling lit up the screen. Galty House. As if she had willed it.

"I heard about the burglary at Miss Finn's." Leela Brennan was on the line. "Have you spoken to her? Do you know what was taken?"

"No, not yet. I'll take a run over there this afternoon. Papers, she's saying, papers out of the safe."

"Nothing else?"

"Nothing else she's admitting to, but she's getting terrible forgetful. Who knows what could be gone? At least she wasn't hurt or worse."

"Thank heaven! You check on her today, I'll go tomorrow. We're expecting guests, Fenella's coming, and Archie wants me to produce a banquet as usual, so I'm off to fetch supplies."

"That's good news, not just a flying visit, I hope?"

Cassandra was genuinely delighted. Fenella, something of a national treasure these days, was not often in Rosshaven and to reminisce with old friends – real friends – was a rare treat.

A thought struck.

"Archie's not leaving yet, is he?" Everyone knew one of the town's favourite sons was relocating to the other side of the world.

"Not yet," Leela told her. "He's making the most of his goodbyes though, you know how he loves the house full, everyone up till all hours, playing jazz and drinking port in the summer house."

Cassandra did not reply. She did not need to. She remembered all too well the wonderful parties at the 'Safehouse' recalling sun-kissed sailing trips, barbecues on the beach, late night singalongs in the library with Archie pounding the ivories to the latest Elton John. Her love affair with everything to do with the place was still vivid.

"Have you heard about the boat?"

"A boat? He always loved being out on the water," Cassandra said wistfully. It was a long time since she had been sailing. "Will he take it with him, I wonder?"

"Probably, he said he's making a fresh start, but the list of things I'm to pack is ridiculous."

"A fresh start … lucky him," Cassandra said quietly.

"What was that?"

"Nothing."

"I saw Greer in town yesterday, you must be delighted to have her home. I believe she's giving you a hand running the place. About time too, you take on too much, always have."

Cassandra smiled. Leela tried to mother everyone, particularly protective of those orphaned the night of the terrible storm all those years ago; the Morgan sisters, Fenella Flanagan and the Muir boys to name just a few.

"I said to Greer, we'll come over. Have one of our evenings? I'll bring the cards, what do you say?"

Cassandra was wary. Leela had the gift. She could read

the Tarot and a lot more besides. Sometimes her visionary intervention was welcome, providing a guide, helping to influence a decision. But sometimes she saw too much, and her razor-sharp memory combined with her connection to Rosshaven's oldest families meant she knew things most people would rather forget.

"Great idea," Cassandra replied tactfully. "Get back to me with dates."

"I will," Leela confirmed. "There's a new moon next week, that would be best, the cards will be with us. Most useful."

"For what?"

"Guidance, Cass. A bit of guidance from the universe can be very helpful, especially when we don't know what to do for the best."

She rang off. Sometimes Cassandra wondered if Leela really could read her mind.

The door swung open. Greer stood there, scowling.

"Someone's been in my room," she said. "You'd better come."

Closing the daybook, Cassandra gave her 'To Do' list a baleful glance. The costs against her list of repairs and renewals were mind-bogglingly prohibitive. She sighed, and slipping the phone into her pocket followed her youngest sister as she stomped up the right-hand staircase to the next floor.

A Case of Keys

R ai was grateful that Bríd, discovering he had risen early to go and check on Miss Finn, had left sandwiches and soup on a tray in his room. She had also left half a bottle of Chablis in a wine cooler and a glass on the table.

There was a time when he would have been disappointed – offended even – at just the half bottle. His reputation for devouring at least half a case in a session was well known. There was also a time when he would have gazed at it longingly before feverishly opening it to immediately pour it away.

Nowadays, he was both wary and respectful. Rai had been clean for five years and although he had spent most of that time away, in a safer place, it had been time enough to help him change his attitude to the problem. Giving him the key to start to understand it, the strength to accept it and the determination to deal with it; so far so good.

But being back was a test in itself, the whole environment was testing, never mind Bríd leaving the wine.

Rai showered and changed into the identical outfit he had been wearing ever since he arrived back in Rosshaven, this version freshly laundered. He always wore Levi jeans and a plain navy rugby shirt with a white collar bearing the logo of the RNLI, putting new clothes through the same process, first he swam in them – a good long swim in sea water – and then he stretched them over a rock to dry. So, whenever he had to pack, there was nothing to think about.

However, the promised invitation to the cocktail party at the Harbour Spa Hotel was proving a little tricky in the wardrobe department. No matter how laidback his hometown appeared, if there was a full-on party with red carpet and VIP guests, the good citizens of Rosshaven would don the glitz and glamour with the best of them. As the locals said, if a harbour town could not be relied upon to 'push the boat out' who could?

Rai caught his reflection in the mirror. His recent heavy physical workload meant he had dropped at least a stone. And his skin was pale, an odd shade of luminescent pearl, indicative of too long spent underwater. He touched his shoulder where the skin was dry, frowning as he withdrew his hand, his fingertips coated. He looked closer; tiny, miniscule flakes of flesh shone back at him, sheeny like scales.

Wiping his hands on a towel, Rai reached for a bottle of seaweed oil, moisturising hastily, his flesh drinking greedily until the skin was soothed. He scowled in the mirror. He should be less neglectful, he would not have been able to put clothes on without the oil, the chafing of the fabric unbearable.

As he dressed, he contemplated his outfit for the party at the Harbour Spa Hotel. Raiding Declan's wardrobe was not an option, any dress-wear he owned would have last been worn by a seventies' showband, complete with flares inset with glittery triangles. Declan would insist he only wore it for karaoke these days, his rendition of 'Love Me Tender' had to be seen to be believed. So no, Declan would be no use whatsoever.

Hoping Rosshaven's one and only gentlemen's outfitters might have something marginally more acceptable than Declan's Elvis suit, Rai heard raised voices overhead, possibly – *no, definitely* – Greer's room. He grabbed his keys, taking the stairs two at a time to the upper floor.

Listening at the door, he pushed it gently open, standing to one side so he would not be seen.

Greer's neat bottom clad in denim dungarees protruded from beneath the bed. She wriggled out.

"It was definitely here!"

"You've moved it, you must have!" Cassandra's voice from the dressing room. "Seriously, Greer, there's things here you've had since school!"

"Don't touch my stuff!" Greer shouted, darting across the room. She noticed the door ajar. "Who's there?" she demanded. Rai slipped into view. "Oh, joy of joys. What now?"

"Heard voices, just checking you're okay?"

"Really? About thirty years too late for that, I might suggest!"

Cassandra appeared, a small collection of gowns over one arm.

"Rai! You missed breakfast and your bed hadn't been slept in, is everything alright?"

"Absolutely fine," he reassured. "I went early to check on Miss Finn. The break-in doesn't seem to have upset her too much, but she's a bit frail to be out all that way on her own, guessing there'll be no moving her, though?"

"If she moved that would be the end of her completely," Cassandra said sadly. "And she'd never come into town, she doesn't like being with people, it upsets her. No, she's best where she is, I'll take her some soup later, just so she has something if she doesn't feel like cooking."

"Now, if you don't mind, we're busy," Greer dismissed him.

"What're you looking for? Perhaps I can help?" Rai suggested.

"No thanks, family business," she replied, pointing at the door.

A sudden gust from the shore lifted the curtain, causing the French window to slam. Greer struggled with the handle and as she reached up Rai's hand was there, releasing the door, the fabric blowing free as he stepped outside.

"I'd forgotten how spectacular the view is from here. All the way round to Phoenix Island, glorious isn't it?"

"If you don't mind!" Greer closed the doors.

"Yes, of course, but we still need to talk, and I won't go away until we do. I can't." He reached for her hand. She snapped it away, thrusting it into her pocket, glaring at him.

But Rai was immune to Greer's glares. He turned to look at the view before he left. "Do you want a hand bringing that case in? Rain later, it'll get drenched."

"That's okay, we'll deal with that," Cassandra said, dropping the clothes on a chair as she went to the window.

"Going somewhere nice?" Rai asked, indicating the gowns.

"A very smart party, if you must know," Greer told him. "Some of us are still welcome in civilised society, I'm pleased to say."

"And some of us wouldn't be seen dead in so-called civilised society. Each to their own, my love." He smiled at her.

"Don't 'my love' me!" she hissed as he left.

"I won't, my love, I promise."

With Rai gone, Cassandra wheeled Alistair's case into the room.

"Who on earth put it out there?" Greer asked.

"I did!" Orla appeared at the door. Cassandra beckoned her in, finger on lips.

Greer closed the door behind her. "What's the story?"

"I heard Frances talking on the phone, saying she was going to check your room out. I remembered you arrived with Alistair's case, so I came up here to hide it. Anyway, someone followed me into the room, so I nipped out onto the balcony with it, closed the door and held on to the handle so they couldn't open it. They poked around for a bit then left."

"Did you see who it was?"

"No, but must have been Frances, nosey old crow."

Greer vaguely remembered a conversation she overheard when she was on the terrace last night. That was surely Frances confirming she had looked but did not find anything.

"How did she get in?"

"She had a key."

"Come to think of it, how did you get in?"

"I've a key to all the rooms," Orla confirmed. "So does Cass."

Greer caught Cassandra shaking her head at Orla.

"What?" Greer demanded.

"We'd a bit of a problem with locks and keys a while ago," Cassandra said, giving Orla a look. "Had to have some changed."

"Don't tell me." Greer looked from one to the other. "All the rooms have the same key?"

"Only the ones we had to change," Orla confirmed.

"How many was that?" Greer was incredulous.

"The guest rooms and your room too, I'm afraid," Cassandra said.

"What on earth happened that all the locks had to be changed?"

"Someone poured Superglue into the keyholes." Cassandra continued to stare at Orla.

"I had to do it!" Orla glared at them both. "The spirit of the house was seeping away. I had to keep it here or it would have gone, and we wouldn't be here anymore. I'd no choice!"

Greer looked at Cassandra.

"I was putting the place up for sale. The estate agent had been round taking pictures. Orla thought if she sealed the rooms, the spirit of the house would stay put and prevent me from putting it on the market."

"Orla!" Greer exclaimed.

"Worked though, didn't it?" Orla replied.

"No, Orla. The bank worked. A re-mortgage, that's what worked," Cassandra reminded her.

Great Things

T he rain which was forecast came in quickly, darkening the bay and Greer's mood with it. The grave implications of her sister's revelation hung heavily as she sat in the large turquoise chair gazing out across a deep, grey afternoon. Sky, sea and rain merged into one rippling sheet of gun metal as far as the eye could see.

Tone, who had been spending mornings with Nagle learning how to be a gun dog again, had found his way to her room, slipping in to lie at her feet as she sat saddened and dismayed staring into the distance.

How had she become so removed? She had no idea what was happening here. No wonder Cassandra had failed to return her erratic and infrequent calls. No wonder her eldest sister had been cool and distant. She was going through a terrible time and Greer, the precious one, the one destined for great things, was totally and utterly oblivious.

"Great things," she told Tone, casting about the room, viewing the trappings of her supposed greatness. The platinum disc on the wall, acknowledging the band's biggest hit. The framed picture of her, sparkly and surprised, accepting an international award for the most promising newcomer of 1987; a still from the fashion shoot she did for *Vogue* and finally a massive poster of the new image a famous designer had created for the band for the cover of *Rolling Stone*, not long before they broke up.

The early days had been a wild and rocky road and she had loved it. She and Rai inseparable, writing songs in the back of the van, sharing chips and wine at the end of a gig, laughing and loving their way around Europe. Yet after their first few hits, the pressure had started to build; gruelling tour dates, endless interviews, photoshoots, so many TV and recording studios she lost count. She felt displaced; those she cared about and trusted either drifted off or were being pushed away.

And Rai changed. His dependency on alcohol and drugs to help him sleep, stay awake or even just cope becoming more and more prevalent. His mood swings deeper and darker. Sometimes staring at him, slumped in a chair, she would push his hair from his eyes and whisper, "Come back to me, Rai. Please come back."

And taking her hand away she would see the scales on her fingertips, the tell-tale sign he was losing the essence of himself, his soul shrinking before her eyes and there was nothing she could do. Rai did not want to be saved and finally Greer realised she had no choice but to save herself.

Her decision to bow out, just when it looked like the wheels were about to fall off, was a wise one. Who knew if she would have even survived without Cassandra turning up at the discreet private hospital on New York's Upper East Side, to literally wrap her in a blanket and spirit her home? *Greatness indeed.*

Tone whimpered, feeling her pain.

She looked at Alistair's suitcase, standing centre-stage in the middle of the room. Expensive, irrelevant, it seemed to mock her, forcing her to acknowledge that she had exchanged what had become one hollow lifestyle for another. The so-called 'consultant' to a property developer with an international portfolio was, in reality, nothing more than a trophy mistress.

Looking back, Greer's stellar career had been almost accidental; a pretty girl, with a good voice and a talent for songwriting, she had happened to be in the right place at the right time. And Cassandra had been so proud, pushing her on, encouraging her, dissolving anything that might stand in her way – no ties, no responsibilities, no worries.

Determined that despite the tragedy of losing both parents, their grandmother's strictness and her troubled teenage years, Greer would show the world that a young girl from a small town on the east coast of Ireland could be a global superstar.

Cassandra's dream. Not hers.

She remembered suggesting to Cassandra she came home, London was expensive and if the truth be known, she was lonely.

Cassandra was bemused. "But London is where you need to be, it's all about contacts, Greer. You see, you'll land something big, you're so talented your star will rise again."

And when her agent's calls lessened and the contracts to host TV shows or sing on backing tracks dried up, her genius idea to become a property consultant resulted in a long-running affair with a successful man who had fallen for an ageing pop princess. Basically, Alistair had been a safety net, an easy option – in truth the *only* option.

She buried her face in her hands.

Why had she not been where she was needed ... so disconnected from real life, *this* life, she had not even realised she *was* needed.

Greer felt a lump of despair lodge like a weight in her chest. This was bad, very bad and this feeling of dark despair could quickly turn into something beyond her imagining, it could become reality, it *could* happen. But she could not let that happen, she was going to have to fight it. Feeling anger rising, she leapt out of the chair, causing Tone to yelp.

"And you!" she cried, grabbing the handle of the case, hauling it towards the door. "Can get out of my life once and for all!" And flinging open the door, she dragged the bag into the corridor, reaching the top of the stairs at precisely the same moment as Orla.

"Where are you going with that?" Her sister indicated the case.

"I'm going to dump it in the sea where it belongs, why?"

Orla blinked. Any sort of dumping at sea was anathema to her.

"I wouldn't do that if I were you," she said.

"I don't mean it literally, I'm just getting rid of it."

"I still wouldn't do that."

"Why?"

"Because it's here for a reason. I know it is. That's why I came up to your room yesterday, there's something the bag is trying to tell us."

Greer sighed. There was no doubt her sister was truly special and at times it seemed the shells did speak to her. But a suitcase? Greer went to protest but Orla was already wheeling the bag back to her room.

Rosshaven's unpredictable microclimate meant the skies had quickly cleared to crystal blue, giving the beach and garden the appearance of being freshly laundered. Bríd was busying herself opening windows, while Fudge raised parasols over tables as guests filtered back outside.

Cassandra, having checked all was ready for the evening meal, loaded her basket into the Range Rover and lifting Wolfe in beside her, headed off to check on Miss Finn.

As it was now late afternoon, the comings and goings of visitors had eased, and her usual route via the back lanes beyond the harbour was relatively traffic free. She opened the windows, letting the breeze ruffle her usually tidied away hair and Wolfe – sensing adventure – stuck his head out, ears flapping. Cassandra leaned over to scratch under his chin, as his tail thumped happily.

Simple pleasures, she thought as they rounded the bend, and had she not grasped the wheel with both hands at that precise second, they would have careered straight into an old, very beautiful vintage car parked diagonally across the road.

The Range Rover screeched to a halt with millimetres to spare.

"What the ..?!"

The bonnet was up, and a skinny be-jeaned bottom protruded from beneath glossy metal. Cassandra did a double take as she recognised the car and – if she was not mistaken – the rear end of a once very close friend.

Slamming the vehicle into reverse, she prayed there was a gateway she could swing round in and drive away as quickly as possible.

As she turned the wheel, an arm sheathed in crumpled linen rested on the door; she tried to close the window, but elegant fingers held the glass firmly in place.

"Cassandra Morgan, a vision of loveliness as always," he said in his beautiful voice, a little more rasping since she had last heard it but exquisite nonetheless. "Haven't seen you in a long time." And he gave her that smile, as easy as the wash of a wave and she had to fight the fear of drowning. Again.

Cassandra gathered herself to give Archie Fitzgerald a bold look.

"Broken down?" she asked.

"Only the car. A minor issue, nothing to worry about." He winked at Wolfe and the traitor wagged his tail.

"Well, if you could just move it out of the way, please. I'm on an errand."

"Going anywhere interesting?"

Where she was going was none of his business. She just needed to go.

"Move the car, Archie," she told him coldly.

"I'll need a push."

"I really don't have time for this." She checked her watch. She was making a quick visit to Miss Finn and then back to prepare for the evening sitting at Manorcliff.

"Look." She started the engine. "I'll just shunt you out of the way until a mechanic gets here, okay?"

"Shunt? Shunt? You can't shunt the Old Dame, that car is a classic, I love it as if it were my own child."

Cassandra closed her eyes for half a second.

"You're blocking a public thoroughfare! I'll shunt that

fecking thing out of the way, with or without your say-so, Mr Fitzgerald. Now remove your arm and let me get on!"

He stood back as she wound up the window, then quick as a flash whipped round the other side and opening the door hopped in, pulling on the handbrake. Cassandra reached to release it and grabbing her hand, he held on to it.

"Gotcha!" he said, laughing. "You were always difficult to hold on to."

She dragged her hand free. "Archie, I mean it. I really don't have time for this today. Please let me go."

"Would you have time for it another day?" he asked quietly, not looking at her. The question hung in the air. "Just a little bit of time … for me?"

Cassandra sighed. "Not really, Archie. Not now."

A blast of a horn made them jump. It was Nagle in his truck. The big man came towards them, opening the passenger door as Wolfe leapt out.

"Well, this is cosy," he said, leaning against the car, dog in his arms. "But I'm going to have to move you two lovebirds on. A chance reunion in the middle of the road is one thing, but people have to go about their business and let's face it..." He looked directly at Archie as he spoke. "You're in the way!"

"Nagle, the very man!" And Archie was himself again, out of the car, taking his old neighbour over to the Daimler to see what could be done.

Cassandra had no choice but to sit and watch as they poked under the bonnet. Nagle gave her a scowl as he passed, going back to the truck for his tools, and in less than five minutes she heard the engine of the Daimler fire up and with his foot on the accelerator Archie gave the thumbs up, hauled on the wheel and drove away.

And as he left, she felt it. The agony and ecstasy of his closeness and of letting him go without saying a word.

Not one word.

Open and Closed

U npacking Alistair's suitcase was initially unsurprising. A complete control freak, no one except the man himself ever did his packing. Alistair was a perfectionist, fastidious in every way.

It was exactly as she expected. The contents of his suitcase a faithful representation of the man she knew so well. Highly organised, immaculate, faultless.

Taking the last of the garments to place on the bed, she considered this summing up of the man she had once imagined she loved to distraction. And as she did, she began to realise what she had suspected for some years to be true.

The things she had loved to distraction about Alistair were in fact the things that did indeed distract. The trips, the exotic locations, fabulous hotels and restaurants, penthouse suites, yachts, cars, clothes – in short, the trappings of success, the accessories that represented the man he was, or more accurately, the man he tried to project. There seemed very little of the real Alistair she truly knew and loved.

Because the real Alistair had managed to disappear beneath his own image. The essence of him so diluted by ambition it had overtaken him and he had all but vanished.

She flumped on the bed, leaden with sadness.

Orla was watching her. Reading her mind.

"Did you not think it was odd, considering you had seen so little of him recently that he suddenly wanted to go away with you?" Orla asked. "I'd have wondered what he was playing at. He doesn't strike me as the kind of man who acted spontaneously, everything looks very calculated." She indicated the neat piles on the bed.

As usual, Orla's ability to see straight to the heart of the matter hit a nerve.

"But we'd been together for years," Greer said.

"Had you though? Or were you just a travelling companion for trips his wife couldn't make? Someone for him to come home to when she was away on the holidays which rarely included him?"

Greer looked at her. "How do you know all this?"

"Social media. It's what I do. If you put the pieces together, Alistair was a workaholic who had so little time for real relationships he didn't really have any." Orla shrugged. "Perhaps that was deliberate too, filling his day with business, big deals, huge contracts making sure he didn't have to deal with the mundaneness of being a real person – a father, a husband or even your boyfriend."

"We had a good relationship," Greer defended. But she could not deny Orla's summing up felt disturbingly accurate.

"But how much time did you actually spend together, say over the last two or three years?"

Greer went to retaliate but stopped, mulling over her sister's words.

"Not loads if I'm honest. There were a few trips, but Alistair always had such a heavy workload I was often left alone to go shopping, visit the spa, sit by the pool."

She glanced sadly at the piles on the bed, so pristine they could have belonged to anybody. Or nobody.

"So, you were surprised when he rang, said he wanted you to go away with him?"

"Staggered is how I'd describe it," Greer replied. "I was heading in a completely different direction. I knew the lease was coming up on the flat, I'd already starting packing."

"Why? Where were you going?" Orla was poking at the lining of the bag.

"Well, that's the weird thing, I was coming home. Alistair had a new career, a wife, a family and as far as I could tell another girlfriend. I was feeling more or less redundant – that's not to say I was being treated any differently, my salary went into my bank account every month, he still called me at the same time every week."

"He called you every week, was that all?" Orla was shocked.

"I'd been in denial, Orla. The writing was on the wall, I needed to move on."

"Oh, Greer." Orla sat beside her sister on the bed, taking her hand. "I could feel something was wrong, but I didn't know your relationship was over. You must have been very lonely over there in London with all those millions of people and no one to love." Her eyes filled with tears. And yet again, in the simplest terms, Orla had summed up the whole situation.

"I'd made friends over the years, of course, I had. But they seemed to drift away, had their own lives, their own relationships. I started to feel as if I was standing on the side-lines all the time, waiting for a bloody phone call. Stupid or what?"

Greer gave a sad smile. "Do you know, it was once I started getting ready to leave that it hit me. The stuff I was packing to come with me were things that belonged here anyway. Pictures of us as girls, photos on the beach with the dogs, the painting of this place I did at Miss Finn's summer school. There wasn't anything I'd acquired over the years I really wanted to keep."

They sat shoulder to shoulder, an echo of loneliness uniting them, the same tears shining in their eyes.

"And then Alistair phoned, saying he'd had enough, telling me to organise tickets to New York and he'd pick me up in a couple of hours. I thought, this is it, one last chance, this will make or break us." She started putting Alistair's clothes into a bin bag. "We were on our way to the airport when he got the call. It was the Prime Minister's office, he stopped the taxi saying he'd meet me at check-in, nothing to worry about."

"How did he seem?"

"Quite stressed, now I come to think of it. Understandably I guess, he kept saying 'this is for the best, remember that, Greer, for the best'. Then he took the call and was gone." She was holding one of his shirts aloft. "Come to think of it, he must have been very stressed, his choice of outfits is odd, it would be hot in New York, but these are winter things."

"I thought that," Orla agreed. "And I found some notes in one of the pockets, look." Orla spread her find on the eiderdown.

"Roubles?"

"He *was* stressed then," Orla said. "Taking the wrong currency to America."

"Unless …" Greer started rifling through the clothes. "This bag wasn't packed for America at all, it's packed for Russia."

"What?"

Greer emptied Alistair's toilet bag onto the bed.

"This is the bag he took to Russia. It hasn't been touched since his last trip." A couple of items had labels in Russian, a shower cap bearing the logo of the Grand Hotel Europe - one of St Petersburg's finest.

"Must have been very stressed then, hey?" Orla said, frowning at the plethora of containers on the bed.

"No, no. This is too odd. If I know Alistair this was deliberate, this was coming with us for a reason." She swung round to face her sister. "Orla, you said the bag was calling to you. Tell me what was it saying? Can you hear it now?"

Orla shrugged. "No, nothing."

"Think! Remember! What was it saying?"

"I … I don't know." Orla looked concerned. "You know I can't understand things if I'm being shouted at."

"I'm not shouting." Greer lowered her voice. "But what can you remember? Anything?"

"I just remember a message, one message. *Don't tell anyone about the bag.* Just that. No one else is to know."

"Ugh!" Greer threw herself back on the bed in frustration. "But it's just a bag, admittedly the wrong bag for the trip we were planning, but still just a bag, nothing remarkable about it."

Orla started putting the contents of the washbag back.

"Took a lot of medication, didn't he?" she said, rattling the plastic containers.

"Mainly supplements, he was a bit of a fitness fanatic."

Orla tried reading the labels, but they were in a variety of foreign languages. Alistair travelled a lot. "No Viagra?"

"Sorry?" Greer sat up.

"I'm surprised there's no Viagra. Dr James says it's ever so popular, especially with middle-aged men too busy to relax and enjoy the good things in life without needing an instant solution to an age-old problem. Well, that's what James says anyway."

"Do you know what it's for?" Greer asked, wide-eyed.

"Of course I do, I'm not stupid."

"Should you be discussing Viagra with James, though, I mean it's very personal?"

"Very personal to who? I can discuss what I like with James." She stood. "James doesn't treat me like a child, Greer. And for your information James and I are very close, we discuss lots of things."

Greer was at her side. "Does Cassandra know you and James are 'very close' as you put it?"

"What on earth has it got to do with Cassandra?" Orla threw the pill bottles onto the eiderdown. "Or you for that matter? Am I the only one not allowed a relationship?" She went to the door.

"But …"

"Other than with my sisters!"

"But, Orla …"

Orla stuck her head back into the room. "And the dogs!"

And with that she closed the door, stomping along the corridor till she reached the staircase.

Orla could hear voices below. It was Sergeant O'Brien, talking with Cassandra at reception, Cassandra saying she would try Greer's room, as she lifted the phone. Sensing Orla was there Cassandra looked up. Orla shook her head, disappearing back onto the landing. She had to warn Greer, quite what about she was not sure, but she had to warn her nonetheless.

She stopped. Her hands were itching like mad. She turned them over to look at her palms. Bright red. Another message. A very strong and disturbing one at that.

Siren Wails and Fisherman's Tales

M iss Finn and Leela Brennan made a fascinating picture as they sat side by side on a pair of ancient steamer chairs, perched on a piece of scrappy lawn leading to a shale beach and the sea beyond. A rickety table draped with a wafting silk throw bore a mismatch of glasses and jugs.

As was common for this unusual summer the sun was high in a cloudless sky, and with very little wind, the deep cove with Miss Finn's ancient cottage at its edge was littered with becalmed vessels, rocking gently in the sun.

"We haven't had a season like this in many a year," Leela said, pushing the broad-brimmed yellow hat back, diamante-framed sunglasses on the tip of her nose. She squinted at her hostess, who was making a fist of slicing fruit for their sangria.

A swirly kaftan, streaked in ribbons of turquoise, green and gold, draped Miss Finn's long, thin frame. Her hank of dark silver hair was twisted and piled on her head, wispy tendrils drifting at her face, softening the vivid scaring on the left side.

She wore a pair of sunglasses even larger than the ones worn by her guest, the lenses so badly scratched they did little for her vision, seriously curtailing the delivery of the long-awaited Spanish cocktail.

"Let me do that," Leela offered. Miss Finn gratefully passed her the knife, sinking back into her chair as Leela splashed another large slug of brandy into the jug. *Truth juice.*

"So, nothing else gone, only the papers that were in the safe?"

Miss Finn nodded, drinking from the now full glass.

"Odd, that. Why only papers? You've plenty of valuables.

Silver, paintings, some lovely porcelain. When they all came here as children, I remember you let them play with everything, nothing put away in case they broke it."

Miss Finn, less agitated now the cocktail had hit the spot, looked out to sea.

"I can't be doing with all that nonsense," she said. "So-called valuables are worthless in the scheme of things, don't you think? And if things are valued for the craft that has created them, the love and detail that has gone into them, they should be touched, held, stroked, not just looked at from a distance." She took another drink. "Sometimes you have to hold something to know its true worth. Real value can only be felt here in the heart!" She thumped her chest.

Leela nodded in agreement, well used to Miss Finn's higher thoughts and deeper meanings. The jug empty, she went in search of more wine.

The whole break-in affair seemed rather half-hearted to Leela's way of thinking. The door had been forced but someone had re-secured it easily and although Miss Finn said nothing else was taken, many of her usual treasures were nowhere to be seen.

The walls, always covered with her surreal interpretations of the area – vast sweeping seascapes, dramatic sunsets and dark night skies, with her trademark lone figure, standing beneath a tree or beside a rock, gazing out, small, fragile and alone – were now blank.

And then she realised the vast display cabinet filled with 'precious trove' as Miss Finn called it, was also empty. The pirate's casket dripping with jewels, the Sea Lord's dagger with the mother-of-pearl handle, the luminescent dragon egg – all disappeared.

Miss Finn stood peering in through the kitchen door.

"But where are all your things?" Leela indicated the empty spaces.

"Stored away for now."

"Why is that then?" Leela opened the bottle at the large

kitchen table, spattered with so much paint from the 'art school' days it was a work of art in itself.

"Big storm on its way," Miss Finn replied.

Leela stopped at her task; there was something ominous in her tone. "Are you sure about that?" But Miss Finn's face was closed.

"Has Sergeant O'Brien any idea who did it?" Leela changed the subject.

"Did what?" The mention of the storm had her distracted.

"The burglary!"

Miss Finn peered over her glasses. "Hardly Poirot, now is he, Leela?"

"He suits us," Leela defended her old friend. Another who knew many secrets and always kept his counsel.

Besides, the port was the busiest on the east coast and although some natives maintained a healthy trade in anything that could be bought or sold – proud of their long-standing tradition of skulduggery – serious criminal activity was uncommon and Sergeant O'Brien had to be thanked for that, even if his methods were unorthodox at times.

"Have *you* heard anything?" Miss Finn asked her guest.

"No, not yet. But what use could those papers be to anyone? Whatever was in that safe is ancient history, it can't affect anyone now, surely?" Leela took Miss Finn's arm, guiding her back outside, the cottage unusually gloomy for such a bright day.

"You'd have thought so," Miss Finn sighed. "But we can never be sure. I did my best, I know that much."

"We all did, sure isn't that all we can do, our best." And they sat companionably gazing out to sea.

Miss Finn pushed scarlet toenails beneath the pale sand and closed her eyes. Leela gave her wellingtons a grateful glance. Odd for a shore-dweller to hate the sand so much but Leela had plenty to be odd about and her oddness was nothing compared with Miss Finn's.

But as they often agreed, there are some things no one

understands and some things are not meant to be understood, best left alone; a bit like the past.

"How long is it now since Nana Morgan died?" Leela asked Miss Finn, languidly stirring the ruby liquid in the jug.

"Why do you ask?" The question had jarred Miss Finn.

"I was thinking about the Morgan girls, all back together again. Cassandra must have been only a teenager when she took over that place and the responsibility of the younger ones, she's been doing a big job these many years."

"Not unlike yourself, weren't you only eleven when you lost your parents?"

Leela stopped stirring. "I was. Flossy still a toddler. Neighbours offered to take us, but I wouldn't have us split up, I'd promised Father, you see."

Miss Finn remembered Leela's father, a kind man with crinkly hair and huge hands. A fisherman, as most were in those days. He died the same year Leela's mother had been found drowned, inexplicably tangled in trawler nets and cast up on the beach after a storm. No one knew what happened but the tragedy haunted the poor man. Some said he died of drink; the kinder ones said his heart had been torn in two.

Whatever the cause, the eight young Brennans were orphaned and though they all lived on the coast, none of the girls ever took to the sea again.

Leela looked at Miss Finn, wondering if she remembered. Miss Finn turned away; it was difficult to decipher what she could remember, and indeed how much she was allowed to remember, given the circumstances of her coming to live in the cottage all those years ago.

"Cassandra never married." Miss Finn gazed at her ringless fingers. "None of us seem the marrying kind."

"I beg your pardon!" Leela exclaimed, lifting her superstar shades to blink at her companion. "There's plenty of time yet!"

Miss Finn laughed, her odd crackly laugh.

"Not for me perhaps, not now," Leela said, smiling at the

remembrance of proposals past. "But Cassandra's still a young woman."

"She is compared with us," Miss Finn replied, laughing again.

"You don't think we'll end up a pair of old maids, surely?" Leela asked seriously.

"We might," Miss Finn replied with equal gravity.

Leela let out a guffaw; both now in their seventies, their spinsterhood looked well settled.

"But Cassandra?"

"While she still holds a candle for Archie Fitzgerald, sure who would get a look in?" Miss Finn finished her drink. "And that's just an excuse not to bother with anyone else. She's convinced herself she's still in love with him to save having to carve out a relationship with someone who might actually be in love with her."

"You mean Nagle," Leela confirmed.

"He's always stayed the course."

"Often the case when someone's too close and you can't see that they're really Mr Right."

"And sometimes someone's so far out of reach, you can't see that they are *so* Mr Wrong. You imagine they are the love of your life, but you hardly even know them." She slumped into silence and Leela wondered if she was talking about herself.

"Ah, but people have to follow their dreams, don't they? Sure, what would life be like if we didn't do that?" Leela was wistful, emptying the remains of the jug into their glasses.

"There'd be a bit less heartache for one thing. Fewer children left abandoned. Little ones who should be out playing in the sunshine, instead of worrying where the next meal is coming from." Miss Finn finished her drink, slamming the glass on the table.

"On the other hand, sometimes dreams don't have to be followed at all, they can be right under your nose, there for the taking. Sometimes you just have to come back to it," Leela remarked sagely.

Miss Finn was quiet for a moment.

"Ah, you mean Greer and Rai."

"Always been a match."

"They're just not good together. She's so intense, when you love someone too much it's easy to lose your sense of self."

Leela glanced at Miss Finn; she was surely talking about herself and Rai's father. "Ach, she just needs to calm down a bit. Always up in arms about everything, flying here, chasing off there, running away from everything."

"Trying to catch sunbeams, Greer's always done that," Miss Finn said, a note of regret in her tone.

Leela gazed at the water, ripples sparkling like diamonds. "Plenty of sunbeams around here at the moment, maybe she'll stay awhile."

Miss Finn sighed heavily. "And then there's Orla. What would become of her if the sisters did finally marry? Where would she end up?"

"Orla will be fine. I think the universe has its own plan for Orla," Leela confirmed.

Miss Finn sat up to look at her.

"Do you know, I think you're absolutely right. Orla could surprise us all."

They chinked glasses in agreement.

"Will I get the cards out, see what's what?" Leela stood, a trifle unsteadily. She and Miss Finn had not enjoyed an afternoon with the Tarot for ages.

"Good plan, I'll get us another drink," Miss Finn announced.

"Shall we just have wine, though?" asked Leela, recalling the major operation the sangria required under Miss Finn's auspices.

"Not at all, I'll make us Black Russians," her hostess declared. "You know your problem, Leela Brennan, no fecking sense of adventure."

Leela rolled her eyes. She did not need a sense of adventure, it had always found her, no need to go looking.

An Inspector Calls

S atisfied everything belonging to Alistair was well hidden, Greer and Orla descended the staircase into reception.

The scent of beeswax mixed with lavender drifted headily up from the busy vestibule. The first of the month was 'spit and polish' day and the early morning housekeeping team had been busy; crystal and surfaces shone, cushions were plumped, and the pale stone floors gleamed.

It was hard to spot the frayed edges on days like this, with its windows and doors flung wide in the balmy sunshine, palm trees gracing the long drive. Today Manorcliff looked rich and regal.

Only one small element jarred. Sergeant Brendan O'Brien in full uniform was leaning against the reception desk, arms folded, his patrol car visible through the grand double doors parked at the base of the steps.

"About time!" Cassandra declared as her sisters arrived. Greer shot her a look, but the eldest of the Morgan clan was in no mood to be placated.

"Brendan's been here so long he's taken root. Now, can we get this sorted once and for all." She leaned towards her sisters, lowering her tone. "As much as it's agreeable to see an old friend, the police constantly visiting the premises is hardly good for business."

The guard indicated the grandfather clock centred between the staircases.

"Better get going, the boat's in." He looked at Greer, who gazed back blankly. "You've had notice?"

"About what?"

SECRETS OF THE SHELL SISTERS

"The inspector from England. Appointment in an hour." He checked his watch against the clock. "Did you prepare a written statement?"

Greer glanced at Cassandra. "I wasn't aware."

"I've been trying to call you." Her sister indicated the house phone. "Greer's been very busy helping us here," Cassandra defended. "I don't think we received any communication. But that's Orla's department. Orla?"

Orla pulled a face.

The sergeant replaced his cap. "We've sent emails, left messages. Greer, I've come to take you for the interview."

"Take her where?" Cassandra demanded.

"The station. Let's at least get a statement typed up before he arrives, get this over and done with, eh?" Sergeant O'Brien was not happy. Rosshaven was his patch, he ran things here. The very idea that a high-ranking police officer was arriving from England to conduct an interview in *his* Garda station was anathema to him. And besides, Greer was one of their own. She might have a chequered past but she was home now and it was his duty to ensure she was protected.

Greer looked down at her grubby denims. "I'll be two minutes," she told them, racing back upstairs. Cassandra gave Sergeant O'Brien a watery smile. The thought that Greer, defiant in the face of any sort of authority, might not return at all, had crossed both their minds.

True to her word, Greer reappeared in minutes, chic in a smart skirt, shirt and good shoes. Cassandra flashed a look of relief at the police officer; if he was surprised, he hid it well.

"Orla, mind the shop!" Cassandra ordered. "And check Bríd has the Emerald Room ready, it's booked for later."

And with that all three of them left.

Garda Regan was disappointed. Sergeant O'Brien had made an almighty fuss about the VIP visitor he was expecting at the station, he had even had his mother in on her 'not usual' day to give the place a good clean.

The coffee machine had been reinstated, and he had been sent to buy biscuits, not just boring old Rich Tea or Fig Rolls but those great lumpy yokes that looked like geological samples, all stuck over with Belgian chocolate and hazelnuts.

You would have thought the President himself was paying a visit. Yet despite the big build-up, Inspector Richard Crosby-Jones of Scotland Yard 'with special attachment to the Foreign Office' was a small, slight figure in a too big tweed jacket, with thick-lensed spectacles and a streaming cold.

Hardly James Bond.

As for Rosshaven's answer to Madonna, the youngest Morgan sister, apart from being a nice-looking woman of a certain age, there was nothing remarkable about her at all. She did have those eyes though, quite startling if you were not prepared for the colour of them or the fierceness of the look they gave you.

She even smiled when he brought her coffee, another disappointment. No display of the wild temper, the furious flamboyance renowned as her trademark.

He braved a question.

"Are you still recording, Ms Morgan?" He held a lumpy biscuit towards her.

"No, no. Long retired these days."

"You must miss it then, touring the world, the fans, the buzz?" the young guard ventured, nibbling at the rejected confection himself.

"I had a wonderful career, made many great friends, I was very lucky," she said gloomily, in no mood to discuss her past, with the present so pressing.

The door opened.

"You made it!" Sergeant O'Brien pumped the hand of the tall, casually dressed man. But even in chinos and a soft linen shirt, Humphrey Beaumont had presence. Cassandra's face crumpled in tearful relief at the sight of him.

"I'm due a visit anyway, thought I may as well swing by today, not sure if I'm needed, but I'm here anyway."

Greer looked up, her gloom evaporating. She adored Humphrey, all the sisters did. The big brother they never had. Humphrey Beaumont always stood firmly in their corner. Why Cassandra never married him, who knew? But they did know or thought they did.

When it came to it, it was all pretty painless. The inspector made no comment on the entourage – Cassandra, Humphrey and Sergeant O'Brien all present – seeming to assume that the once famous Greer Morgan still required a quota of attendants, and besides, his wife was a massive fan and would expect no less.

Greer had prepared her statement following Humphrey's advice; stick to the facts, make it succinct and try not to appear emotionally involved.

She wrote she had been given instruction to arrange a business trip to New York. They were travelling to the airport when Alistair took the call to attend an urgent matter and she was to go ahead; he would meet her at the airport. Nothing unusual in that, she was one of his project managers, after all.

"Did you know what the trip to New York was for?" the inspector asked.

They often went to the States, she told him, Alistair usually briefed her on the plane. He had business interests there; three restaurants, hotels and a casino.

Did she know what the urgent call asking him to return to Westminster was about?

"No," came her response. "Kept his government work completely separate, his parliamentary private secretary handled all that."

"Ever accompany him to Russia?" the inspector asked casually.

Greer opened her mouth to reply when a shot rang out.

Glass shattered.

"What the feck?" Sergeant O'Brien ran to the window.

The inspector had disappeared under the table.

Garda Regan poked his head through the hole. "Me Da's hunting rifle, just giving it a bit of a clean. I didn't mean ..."

"To kill the inspector from Scotland Yard?" Sergeant O'Brien asked, wide-eyed.

"What?!" The young guard blanched.

Greer crouched down beside the inspector, hunched in a ball beneath the table. "You weren't hit, were you?" She was anxious, looking for signs of blood.

"No harm done, absolutely fine." He emerged, white with fright. "Just an accident, I'm sure."

"More expense." Sergeant O'Brien indicated the damage. "Out of your wages, me laddo."

"Hope he has a licence for that," the inspector said, colour returning to his face.

"He does of course," Humphrey soothed, showing the inspector back to his chair.

"Now, where were we?" The poor man looked askance, papers in disarray.

"Finance, I think finance is next," Humphrey said, pointing to a page he had placed on top.

"Of course," the inspector agreed and asked Greer about her knowledge of Alistair McKeiver's finances. This was not part of her role, she told him, she had a separate bank account for all her business-related expenses and compiled regular reconciliations for Alistair's accountant, that was it.

"The accountant has all the statements," Greer said.

He nodded. She was only confirming what he already knew.

"And your bank account? Did Mr McKeiver put anything into that?"

"My salary. An annual bonus, oh and a thousand pounds on Saint Patrick's Day."

"Really?" the inspector frowned "May I ask why?"

"Alistair went to a convent school as a child. The money was for me to distribute as a donation. He loved his Irish nun, a teacher called Sister Immaculata. I give it to the school here, it pays for extra lessons for kids who need them. Alistair always said he would never have made his millions without the grounding that little school gave him." She stopped and swallowed hard.

"Thank you, Ms Morgan, you've been very helpful."

Humphrey, who had been sitting a discreet distance away, coughed. The inspector looked up. "Can you advise Ms Morgan what will happen next?"

"Ms Morgan's statement concludes my part of the investigation. Nothing that impacts on what is suspected."

"Which is?" Humphrey asked.

"That Mr McKeiver was the victim of an assassination attempt."

There was a communal intake of breath.

"Assassination how?" the barrister pressed.

"Some kind of chemical injection, designed to implode an artery at its weakest point and cause the heart to arrest. Luckily, he's a fit man and his medical team second to none." The inspector had started gathering his papers, the proceedings coming to a close. "Been used before but never in the UK. Well, not to our knowledge anyway."

"But why?"

"I couldn't possibly say."

"But if you might speculate? For Greer's sake, help her understand what's happened, it's been a terrible shock, very difficult for her." Humphrey had managed to make it sound as if the man was being unreasonable. The inspector looked at Greer, her face grey, a lost look in her eyes.

"We're not sure. Maybe he made promises he couldn't keep to the wrong people. Who knows?" he said softly.

"Has anything been proven?" Humphrey asked.

"I don't think it can be," the inspector confided. "All supposition, I don't wish to appear insensitive but the longer this goes on the more the media make of it and quite frankly we don't want that."

"I'm sure you've enough to be doing, like myself,"

Sergeant O'Brien said. "Sometimes a lot of this job is tidying up, so a line can be drawn."

"That's about the truth of it," the inspector agreed. "My recommendation will be that the results of the investigation are inconclusive, and my department will step back." He glanced at Greer. "The other affairs in question, thankfully not my department. But it really would be best that Mr McKeiver takes some time to fully recover."

"If they let him," Greer said quietly. Humphrey gave her a look. He knew she was referring to her own experience, the relentless agony of being caught in an unfavourable and unforgiving media spotlight.

The inspector stood. "We're all rather jaded with these Russian conspiracy theories the media enjoy so much. We're stretched enough, without being sent on wild goose chases." He picked up his file. "Thank you for your time, Ms Morgan, we won't be needing you again. But if I could make one small request?"

Greer frowned.

"A picture? My wife will kill me if I go back without a photo, I had a real battle stopping her from coming with me, she was desperate to meet you."

"Regan, get in here and take a picture of the inspector with Greer," Sergeant O'Brien ordered. "Then we'll have a spot of lunch, we can't have you come all this way and not enjoy a bit of good old-fashioned Rosshaven hospitality, now can we?"

"That would be most welcome!" The inspector smiled at last.

Photo-call over, Sergeant O'Brien guided everyone out into the sunshine. The inspector shrugged off his jacket, hauling at his tie.

"Where's the rain?" He gazed up at the sky. "It always rains in Ireland, doesn't it?"

"Not your first visit, surely? I'd have had you down for doing a spell in the North." Sergeant O'Brien was surprised.

"The Falklands, actually."

"Aha! Thought you were a military man, you fair shifted when that gun went off."

"Thought we were under attack." He gave a thin smirk. "Didn't realise you're an armed force."

"We're not," assured Sergeant O'Brien. "And then again, sometimes we are."

"Isn't that er … a little irregular?"

"So is this incessant sunshine," Sergeant O'Brien said, indicating the bright blue sky. "But it happens now and again, you know yourself."

A Fragile Truce

Orla was not happy, disturbed at being left in charge while her sisters went into town to meet someone important; this was another scenario the shells had not foretold. She waited until reception was empty, shut down the computer and propped a sign on the large walnut desk.

'We're attending to another guest's needs – back in ten minutes'

Sensing a shift, Wolfe and Tone who were dozing by the door, perked up and followed their mistress, shell bracelets jangling as she strode, descending into the bowels of the building.

Orla's quarters were below stairs. Her suite ran alongside the hotel's cellar, a long, cool space divided into bedroom, bathroom and work room. The walls were painted in as many shades of blue as could be imagined and although windowless, it was surprisingly bright and airy, filled with an eccentric collection of lamps, each covered with shells and sea glass collected over the years.

Orla was only three when she decided this would be her special place. Despite having a perfectly pretty bedroom upstairs she refused to sleep in it. When Nana found her wrapped in a blanket in the cellar for the umpteenth time, she decided to get to the bottom of the problem.

"I don't like the dark," Orla explained.

"But this is the cellar, darling one. Not a bedroom for a beautiful little girl like you and besides it's dark here."

"It's a different kind of dark." Orla had looked at her with those glittering green eyes. "And this is the nearest room to the sea. I want to be under the ocean."

Nana was shaken. How did she even know the word ocean?

"Why do you want to be under the ocean?" she had asked gently.

"Because Mama's there, there with the Sea Witch. I want to be with Mama."

"But it would be even darker there, come back to your pretty room, I'll close the curtains, that will keep the night out."

Orla shook her head. "I can't sleep with that dark outside the window. I want to stay here."

And half-afraid that if she did not get her own way she might indeed contrive to be under the ocean, Nana decreed she could sleep there but only temporarily. Orla had been there ever since.

Wolfe and Tone trotted beside her, noses in the air. Orla's room was wonderful, so many different scents; fish, seaweed, glue, all the things she used to create. And then there was the music, she sang all the time here, a safe, happy sing-song kind of place, the canines liked that a lot.

Sitting at her worktable, littered with boxes and sets of drawers filled with finds from the shore, Orla would carefully label and catalogue her collection. It must have numbered in the thousands, and she knew every one; where she had found it, what it was called and which family it belonged to. Because shells had families too, another reason why she loved them so much.

She had cleared a space, and the large gleaming conch Miss Finn had gifted her sat sheeny in the lamplight; its cream and gold shell rippled like the surface of the sea, the inner chamber smooth as silk, gleaming, iridescent pink in the lamplight.

Orla was only a toddler when the shells had first sent their messages. She could not remember precisely when, but she did remember how. Whenever she was on the beach, the wind would drop and she would hear voices, barely whispers but voices nonetheless.

As time went by, she learned to decipher them. Not every shell had a message or story to share but many did. Sometimes it was something simple like the echo of a family enjoying a holiday on a faraway beach, the shell arriving from the warm waters of the Mediterranean. As she became more adept, she could make out different languages, even accents. And soon she was picking up messages from the past. Disturbing messages, the frightened cries of men and women being taken under the waves, sucked below by the Sea Witch, just like her mother had been.

She would hear the mournful music of the slave ships during the long crossing from Africa to the Caribbean, the voices of these shells so homesick and anguished it upset her deeply.

Or she would come across a clutch of shells from the sixteenth century, bringing the noise of warships, embattled fragments of flotillas, as dying soldiers sent farewells to their loved ones before they too were drowned.

Orla learned to deal with these messages by writing the names in her log book and when the moon was full she would light candles for the souls who had come to her, setting them free and returning the freshly washed shells to the sea, their rightful place.

Her sisters had always known this was Orla's special gift and they would go to the beach to help collect her shells, hoping there might be one, among the thousands that lay there, with a message for them.

When Orla did hear their mother's voice, she would race back to share the message. But often the message would be gone by the time she returned, the voice barely a whisper, drowned out by everyday noise, the parallel reality of another life.

Whenever this happened Orla would weep for days, uncontrolled sobbing that would break all their hearts, especially Nana's, because Orla was convinced the messages said their mother was coming home, she would be back, to watch over them. But she never came.

As Orla wept Cassandra would retreat into a cocoon of silence, never even mentioning their mother while Greer, quite the opposite, would scream and shout at everyone and everything, for no reason and every reason she could think of; the poor broken-hearted shell sisters.

Now, Orla took a deep breath and closing her eyes lifted the beautiful conch to her ear, sure this would bring a very important message indeed. At first, all she heard was the sea, the wind and the waves, and then a deep silence, her ears filling with water as if she were swimming, swimming beneath the ocean, down into the warm velvet depths that led to the other world.

And then she heard it, her mother's voice, singing softly, a lullaby so warm, so comforting, she felt immediately safe and happy. Straining to listen, Orla caught the words and as they became clearer, she picked up her pen and wrote them down.

There is another child, or there will be
Another little sister, of the sea
She needs my family now, for she has none
So, take her in your arms and bring her home.

And once she had written down the words, the voice lessened, and the sound of the sea rushed in the way it did whenever a message had been successfully delivered.

Laying down her pen, Orla collapsed into a chair, suddenly very cold, as if she had just come out of the water with the sun gone and the beach turned to grey.

Her ordeal over, Greer left the others to walk back alone. The wind had picked up and there was a pleasant freshness to the air, clouds scudding across the sky promising a change that would be welcomed by some at least.

Climbing upwards, she unbuttoned the collar of her silk

shirt, the stress of her encounter with the inspector easing away with every step, and reaching a slab of rock jutting out towards the sea she climbed onto it, shuffling out to its furthest tip as it balanced like a springboard over the beach.

She looked down, remembering a time when the tide was in and the wild sea had crashed below. When in the moonlight he had taken her to the very edge, diving off, hand in hand, the air rushing past her skin so fast it felt like scorching and then her body breaking the surface, cool as ice as she dived.

Feeling her fear, he had wrapped his arms around her as they swam, deeper and deeper, anxiety turning to wonderment, realising as he cut through the water like air that he was home, home in his special place and she had never really known him before this and wondered would she ever really know him again, now he had shown her something she could not understand and could never be part of.

Greer shuddered, stepping back from the edge, because whatever had happened since, nothing could dull the excitement of the memory of those far-off days, when her love had been so raw, so deep, she would have followed him anywhere and indeed she did.

"No regrets," she said to herself, breathing in the clean, fresh air. "Let it go, what's done is done."

Climbing back down onto the track she strode up towards the cave at the very top, her special place near the stars, so far removed from his. Yet so like his, dark and warm and safe.

She could not wait to be there now, feed her soul with the glorious view and rest, renew. The time for making plans would come soon enough. It was time to enjoy the here and now and what better place to enjoy it.

She noticed a swoop of gulls, diving, swirling and calling at the entrance to the cave. And then she heard it, music, a soft melody layered beneath their cries. The gentle strumming of a guitar. She stopped. Disappointed. She did not want her special place invaded by strangers. But as she listened, she recognised the song. One of her own. One she had written when she was in the band, and they could do no wrong. She walked on.

Rai was sitting at the mouth of the cave, half in, half out of the sunshine, bent over his old guitar, bare brown feet tapping the beat in the dust. He looked up, sensing her there and smiled. The sweet, sad smile she always felt was just for her. Something cracked inside, like the shell of an egg and all the bitterness seemed to seep away as she stood before him, the music creeping into her soul, smoothing the frazzled edges the way it always had.

Rai played till the end, and she clapped. He nodded his thanks, placing the guitar on the ground.

"Humphrey said it all went okay. You alright?"

"You've spoken to Humphrey?"

"I was waiting outside, you know, just in case."

"Just in case?"

"You needed me. Couldn't see you hauled off to an English gaol and you only just back. Humphrey and I planned to hijack the car as they drove you away and hide you on the island till the charges were dropped." He stood and struck a pose. "Superhero style!"

She laughed. "Eejit!"

He patted the space beside him.

"Join me. Nice cold beer in my bag, we can celebrate."

"Celebrate what?" She was tempted.

"Freedom. A great thing to celebrate, don't you think?"

And Greer Morgan found herself, after more years than she cared to remember, sitting beside the love of her life turned arch enemy, drinking cold beer, as the sun shone, the sea sparkled, and the gulls called the news of their truce far and wide around the bay.

"Any plans?" he asked eventually.

"Nothing beyond staying a while. I've signed up to help with the hotel. Things aren't easy, we're losing custom." She indicated the Harbour Spa Hotel, the cream awning billowing out to sea.

"Certainly makes everything else around here look slightly shabby."

"Slightly?" Greer declared. "I don't think anything's been spent on our place in years. The dining room is still waiting to be redecorated, the boiler needs replacing, and the Moon Room is so dangerous it's out of bounds."

Rai looked at her. "I wondered why we hadn't had drinks there, especially with how beautiful the night sky has been lately, nowhere like the Moon Room, it's one of the hotel's USPs, as they say, needs promoting!"

"Don't!" Greer put her head in her hands. "So much to do!"

They sat silently sipping their beers.

"Caught up with any of the old crowd?" Rai asked, changing the subject.

"Not really had time with all the Alistair stuff going on."

"Of course. I'm sorry, Greer, officialdom often forgets real people are involved and hearts get broken. Word is you two were close?"

"Close?" She gave him a look. "Not for a while."

"You loved each other though?"

"We did. Once." She could have been talking about them. She stood, smoothing her smart skirt, picking up her heels.

"Thanks for the beer." She went to hand the bottle back. "No alcohol? You're drinking no-alcohol beer?"

"Changed man." Rai gave a wry grin.

"That bit needed to change," she said seriously.

"I know. I was a mess, and then after the accident ..." Rai's dark eyes grew darker still. He had been so out of it the night the band's drummer Mojo Morrisey had died, he had been blaming himself ever since. Convinced that if he had been *compos mentis* Mojo would still be alive. Sadly, Rai's response to this tragic event was to try to block it out with anything he could lay his hands on, resulting in Greer's near nervous breakdown and Cassandra having to fly out to New York to bring her distraught sister home.

Greer was watching him, reading his mind, fighting the

urge to take him in her arms, tell him it was alright, it was not his fault, it *was* an accident.

"You doing okay?" she asked in a small voice.

"I am," he replied firmly. "One of the reasons I like to celebrate freedom, it comes in many forms." He put the bottles away, turning to give her a bright smile. "So, are the Morgan sisters going to the party at the new hotel?"

Greer was relieved at the change of subject. "Yep, good excuse to check out the competition. You?"

"Happy to give Ross a bit of support, I'm sure he'll refer customers to *The Pirate* when we're back in business, and he *is* family."

"Any idea when you'll be afloat?"

Rai shrugged. "Declan's dealing with it, it could be a long job."

They exchanged a look. Rai's older brother had been the band's manager in the early days, but they had parted company after an impossibly gruelling tour had taken its toll. When their ageing camper van burst into flames near the border with Northern Ireland, the entire band had been arrested on suspicion of terrorism. It had been a nightmare.

He stood. "Walk you back?"

She wanted to say yes. She wanted to be with him. He was easy company when he was like this; sober, sane, safe.

"I'd prefer not. You know."

"I do." He gave her that smile again. "We still need to talk though, Greer, it's important." And although he did not want to put her under pressure, he had a deadline he could not miss.

"You're still full of yourself, aren't you?" She rounded on him. "It's important! *Is it?* Is it really? Some bloody stupid something of total inconsequence, Rai, and you think it's important. All I'm going through and whatever *you* need to talk about is important!"

Rai shrugged, picking up his guitar. Same old Greer, turning on a sixpence.

"Another time." And dusting off his jeans he started

downwards towards the beach.

"Give me strength!" She stopped. "Go on then, tell me, tell whatever it is that's so important."

"Later," he replied, raising a hand in farewell.

"Jeez!" she growled. "Infuriating bastard! Drives me absolutely bloody mad!" And as ever, Greer stormed off in the opposite direction.

Rai did drive her mad, always had and when she found out what he had to say, she would be madder than ever because yet again the enigmatic Rai Muir was about to turn her whole world upside down.

Titanic

C assandra guessed something was amiss when, calling Fudge to collect them from the Garda station, there was no reply. She tried reception, the call went straight to voicemail, and finally having to disturb Bríd, and no reply there either, her heart started to thud in her chest.

"Make haste!" she told the taxi driver, ignoring the 'slow' sign as they swung through the gateway. "Something's wrong, put your foot down!"

The scene was chaotic. Piles of luggage littered the hotel steps, vehicles jerked testily in and out of parking spaces, while clutches of people stood about in anxious groups. In minutes they were out of the car, running towards the entrance.

"What is it, what's wrong?" Cassandra asked Mrs Van Heusen, one of the most elegant women on the planet, who was in slippers and bathrobe, hair in disarray. She pointed at the roof.

"Someone's up there. That man said it's a suicide attempt." She pointed at another regular, Neely Brody. Neely was a notorious busybody who loved a bit of drama.

"Nonsense." Cassandra forced a smile. "It'll be workmen, that's all."

Humphrey was at her side. "Why are all these people leaving?"

"You wouldn't stay in a hotel wit' somebody's brains splattered all over the front steps now would ye?" Neely Brody declared. "Sure, that would spoil the holiday mightily, wouldn't it?"

"Not helpful, Mr Brody," Cassandra said through clenched

teeth. "I'm sure it's nothing to worry about."

Bríd was at reception, with a face like boiled bacon.

"What is it?" Cassandra demanded.

Bríd indicated Cassandra come closer so she could whisper.

"Orla. She's on the roof. Fudge is up there but she won't come down. She's been standing on the edge, you know." She gave Cassandra a wild-eyed look, holding her arms out behind her.

"*Titanic*! Oh my God, what's brought this on?"

Bríd shrugged.

"Someone must have seen her, set the fire alarm off and then this ..." A straggly queue stood at the desk, people were on their phones, others strutted in and out of the doorway. Everyone was either preparing to leave or waiting for something dreadful to happen.

"Will I go up? Fudge doesn't seem to be having much success," Humphrey offered. He knew Orla well, this could be tricky.

"He's not the best, to be fair," Bríd said. "He's afraid of heights."

At the same time as Greer arrived through the front door, Dr James appeared at the top of the terrace steps, cutting through the crowd.

"She's on the turret at the far end of the building," he hissed to Greer.

"We can get out through the roof, I'll show you." Greer stopped at the desk. "We'll sort it," she said to Cassandra, and glancing at Humphrey, "Use your barrister voice to get everyone back into the bar for a nice drink on the house, tell them it's a false alarm."

"I'm on it." Humphrey gave a quick salute, striding outside to restore order.

Cassandra turned to Bríd. "Teas and coffees please, Bríd. I'll get a couple of bottles of whiskey open on tables so people can help themselves to a drop."

"Good idea." Neely Brody had overheard. "Very calming when we've all had such a terrible fright."

"Now, now, Mr Brody. Nothing's happened, has it?" Cassandra took him by the elbow to the farthest corner of the room. "Sit yourself down there and I'll bring you a glass and the newspaper. Isn't it *The Mail* you take? Nothing like a few headlines of 'we're all going to hell in a handcart' to reassure you all's well with the world." She smiled sweetly, bustling away.

Half an hour later, the rescue team were in the kitchen and Orla was tucked up in bed. James said he would stay with her until she was properly asleep. Wolfe and Tone were providing backup, curled up beside the small sofa the doctor had requisitioned for his vigil.

"It was James brought her down," Greer told them as Bríd poured tea. "Masterly he was, she never batted an eyelid, calm and cool as a cucumber, none of the usual stuff we have to put up with when she's having one of her turns."

"Such a relief," said Cassandra, who seemed to have shrunk, collapsing into the wing chair at the end of the table.

"Bríd, have you anything stronger than tea? It's already been a bit of a day without all this carry on," Greer pleaded.

Bríd gave Cassandra a look.

"A bottle of wine, Bríd, fetch one from the cellar if you wouldn't mind. Nothing too good though, we know Greer can't tell the difference between a decent old-world vintage and some of that muck they send us from down under."

"I wouldn't malign the entire Antipodean wine industry, Cass." Greer hid a smile; her sister was feeling better. "It was weird though she couldn't hear me. Completely lost in her own world. But when James spoke, she could hear him. It took a while for her to understand but he climbed up behind her, ran his hands along her arms until he was holding her and then slowly guided her back down onto the roof."

Bríd poured the wine. Cassandra took a large slurp.

"Did you ask her what was wrong?"

"She said all the souls had called out to her and the noise was deafening, she'd gone up to the roof to clear her head. That's all she could remember." Greer's turn to gratefully take a sip of wine.

"Poor love," Bríd said quietly, watching as Cassandra and Greer stared at each other, feeling Orla's pain.

Humphrey coughed. They had forgotten he was there.

"I think the natives will get restless if we don't present a united front at dinner this evening. Is there anything I can do?"

He glanced around the kitchen; no sign of anything being prepared and time was marching on. Cassandra hauled herself upright. Taking her lead, Greer finished her wine.

"Make It Up Stew?" her eldest sister asked, a slight smirk about her mouth.

"Call It What You Like Casserole – the choice is yours." Greer grinned back.

"Bríd, let's get the 'specials' menu up, we'll have cocktails on the terrace as usual," Cassandra decreed.

"Maybe Nagle will make a vat of his Rosshaven Rum Punch," Greer said. "You know, his olde pirate recipe, the one that makes you want to walk the plank, your hangover's so bad the next morning."

Cassandra was already pulling ingredients out of the fridge. "Give him a ring, tell him Humphrey's here, I'm sure those two old seadogs will be delighted to spend some time together. How long is it since you've seen each other now?" she asked Humphrey, who was preparing to leave the women to it.

"Ah, too long," he replied, standing. *Although forever would be long enough*, he thought. Despite a longstanding veneer of friendliness, Humphrey and Nagle did not get on. A disagreement that went way back. Rather more than that, if Humphrey remembered correctly. There had been a fight, he and Nagle had literally tried to kill each other, and Cassandra had been at the heart of it. Cassandra and Archie to be precise.

Mixed Messages

T hings settled down remarkably quickly at Manorcliff once Dr James explained to everyone gathered at dinner that Orla, discovering a gull trapped in some old netting on the roof, had gone up to release it and having done so, found the trap door stuck so could not get back down.

Typical Orla, everyone said, a saint, a true champion of all animals, and so the fractiousness of the day was soothed away, with positive thoughts and bowls of Call It What You Like Casserole. A stroke of genius that tonight's meal was a vegetarian Turkish hotpot, served with sultana flatbread, goat's cheese and homemade berry chutney. Not a hair or feather had been harmed in the making of the entire meal.

They were just clearing away when the door opened and Leela Brennan and her sister Flossy Moore poked identical noses into the room. Cassandra had to hide her surprise.

"You forgot we were coming, didn't you?" Leela declared, pulling off her waxed drovers coat; the evening had turned squally, the air full of misty drizzle. She helped Flossy out of her anorak.

"Not at all," Cassandra replied graciously. "Just couldn't remember what time." Greer gave her the wide-eyed look. "New moon," Cassandra told her. "And we haven't had a girls' night for so long, Leela's promised us a reading."

Greer raised her eyebrows. "Glad you haven't given up any of the old traditions, Leela. But we've all moved on a bit since tea leaves and Tarot cards. Sure, people get their horoscopes on email these days." She was taking glasses from the cupboard.

"Indeed, that's right," Leela agreed, pushing her hair behind her ears to reveal a pair of exotic crystal earrings, and a necklace of extravagant amethyst joining an Egyptian ankh at her throat. "But it makes no difference how the messages of the universe are delivered, it's what we do with them when they arrive that counts."

She gave Greer a steely look. Leela had known the Morgan girls since they were toddlers, they were all highly tuned to otherworldliness and Orla had the gift. Greer might think she could deny her inherent connection with the forces of nature while she was over there in England, but not here in Rosshaven, one of the most mystical places on the planet.

Flossy pulled a couple of bottles out of her recycled carrier bag. "Rhubarb wine and damson gin!" she announced. "You can get sick of that foreign muck, can't you? Russian vodka this, German lager that. I've gone completely natural, if it's not home grown, I don't want it. No air miles for me."

"Admirable," remarked Cassandra, returning the Prosecco she was taking from the fridge. "Apple cake then. That'll go nicely with your very generous gifts."

"Good old 'soak it up' grub." Leela laughed. "I'll just have tea though, I need to keep a clear head till I see what's what."

"No Orla?" Flossy scanned the room.

"Out with Dr James and the dogs for a walk. Been a trying day, wouldn't want her any more upset." Greer indicated the lavishly illustrated cards Leela was shuffling expertly, her navy-blue high gloss manicure shimmering in the candlelight.

"She can feel the new moon too," Leela said.

"We all can." Cassandra pulled out a chair to sit opposite their guests.

With everyone settled at the table and Greer hovering in the background pretending to be busy, Leela dealt Cassandra's cards deftly. No one said a word until the cards were dealt in the spread of the Celtic cross and Leela with eyes closed, hands on the table, took a deep breath before the reading began.

Turning the cards over, she fixed her gaze on the

fantastical illustrations, saying not a word. The tension in the room caused Greer to tiptoe behind Cassandra's chair. Leela turned another luminously illustrated card. Still no words.

"For heaven's sake, Leela," Cassandra hissed. "Nothing?"

Leela raised a hand.

"Be patient." Greer poked Cassandra in the back.

At last, the hand was fully revealed.

"Interesting," Leela announced, sipping her tea. "Some very strong messages here, Cassandra, and change, lots of change."

"That's what you always say, Leela. No change there then!" Greer laughed.

"I hate change!" Cassandra took her glass and knocked back the tot of gin so fiercely it made her cough.

Flossy immediately refilled her glass. "You'll need it."

"Change is inevitable, just needs managing, like everything." Greer glanced around the vast kitchen. The range at the far end, the plethora of utensils hanging above, the dog beds either side, ancient gaily patterned delph on the mantelpiece, nothing had changed here in a long time.

Leela started going through the cards in order. Judgement first. "This indicates renewal and revival, dormant matters coming back to life, health matters improving, a time to be happy, new beginnings in the offing."

Next the Six of Wands, a bearer of great news, then Justice, a card of balance, legal documents, marriage agreements for instance. She looked around the table with raised eyebrows.

"Hmmm, now the Five of Cups, you think you've been let down or betrayed in some way and the Magician, he's saying you've all the skill and ability you need, this is a time for action and new ventures."

"Well, that's positive at least," Cassandra said, leaning towards the cards, hoping to glimpse some of what Leela saw so clearly.

"Who's this fella then?" Greer pointed at the Knight of

Pentacles, sitting astride his fabulous horse resting in the meadow, a rabbit in the foreground.

"Represents a man. Could be quite a big influence. Not the most exciting of knights but reliable, trustworthy, you know the type."

"At last!" Greer cried out. "Someone to come along and sweep her off her feet. This I have to see!"

"Not sure about that." Leela looked hard at Cassandra. "Depends if she's open-minded, he's part of the immediate future anyway."

"A man? At my time of life! No thanks. Now that would be a change too far!"

They were all laughing now. Leela raised a hand; these were serious issues to be considered.

"I see the careful knight is followed by the King of Wands. He represents your fears, Cassandra," Leela told her. "A strong, dynamic personality usually very good at his job. Might come across as overconfident, a bit controlling even, but he has a way with words and his energy makes him very attractive."

The room fell silent. Everyone was thinking the Knight of Pentacles could be Nagle and the King of Wands sounded very much like Archie Fitzgerald.

"I think that's enough," Cassandra said, pushing her chair back.

"Not quite finished, Cass," Leela said firmly, indicating her hostess stay put. "Now concentrate." She tapped the next card. "The Queen of Pentacles can run a household as well as a business. She's very practically minded. On the downside, likes things done her way, can be stubborn and self-indulgent. Some people think they can take advantage of her, because she's very generous but she's no fool."

"A lot like yourself and meself," Flossy told Cassandra.

"Yes." Leela looked warily at her sister. "Neither of you need be taken advantage of, if you just keep your wits about you."

"And your knees together!" Greer added.

They started laughing. Leela called them to order.

"The next two cards are well placed; the Four of Swords means it's time to rest and recuperate after a period of struggle and the Three of Wands shows your initial goals have been realised but more planning and moving things in the right direction is needed."

Greer aimed a reassuring smile at Cassandra, who just pulled a face back.

"And finally – and this is one of my favourites – the Two of Cups. The main theme of the whole reading in one card!" Leela announced dramatically. "The blonde woman and brown-haired man are opposites. They represent an important union, a relationship surrounded by harmony and balance. If there has been misunderstanding or quarrels this card brings reconciliation and the rediscovery of a union that is meant to be."

"Ah, Leela, for goodness sake!" Cassandra declared, reaching for her drink.

"*Meant to be!*" Leela repeated with feeling and joining her hands closed her eyes to thank the universe for a truly inspired reading. "None of this is ominous, Cass, it's just saying be prepared and when whatever comes, go with it."

Having been left in charge while still very young, Cassandra had always been desperate to avoid change, determined everything remain the same.

She had to be rock solid. Something for Orla to cling to when all the voices in her head were too much to bear, and a safe harbour for Greer, wilful, passionate Greer, who over the years had loved and hated everything about their home in equal measure.

Cassandra had always been there for them both yet sometimes when she looked in the mirror, she could not see who she was anymore.

"You're next, Greer," Leela said. "Who's going to sweep you off your feet, I wonder?"

"No, no, *no!*" Greer replied. "I've had enough sweeping to

last me a lifetime. Those knights are all the same. Sweep you away and once they have you, they've no idea what to do with you, so they just go off and find someone else to sweep away. Useless shower of shites!"

"Ah, Greer," Flossy said, reaching over for the last piece of apple cake. "Don't damn all them knights. My knight was a great fella."

"You were very lucky then, Flossy," Greer said snippily.

Cassandra gave Flossy a smile. "Not that lucky. I'm sure you'd have liked to have had him for longer." She flashed Greer a reproachful look.

"Sorry," Greer acknowledged, annoyed with herself and her big insensitive mouth.

"And how long are you with us, Greer?" Leela asked, gently changing the subject.

"She's joined the family business, I'm delighted to say," Cassandra interjected.

"Oh, a change of direction. We heard that fella you worked for has been very ill," Flossy said, wiping her mouth with a napkin.

"Yes, heart attack, poor man, making progress though. Isn't that right, Greer?" Cassandra said. Greer nodded.

"Has he family, Greer?" Leela had obviously decided she had enough messages from the universe because she had poured herself a large glass of rhubarb wine.

Greer nodded again; she did not want a conversation about Alistair and his family with the Brennan sisters – the whole harbour had enough to gossip about where her personal relationships were concerned – besides, she had nothing to say.

"And a lovely wife," Flossy offered. "Isn't that right?"

Greer sat quietly. Leela spread the cards before her.

"Take one."

Greer shook her head.

"Ah, go on, just for fun," Cassandra prompted.

Greer sighed, pulling out a card.

"Interesting." Leela found all the cards interesting.

"The Ten of Pentacles, meaning?" Greer asked.

"Security and stability. It particularly refers to the family home and traditions, values you can lean on when you need a bit of guidance." Leela smiled into Greer's face but Greer's mind was elsewhere. Leela's summing up only served to confirm something she had been considering for some time. "It's telling you to rely on those who mean the most to you, and that, even if things are difficult now, you're not alone. It can also represent inheritance or money, but whether it comes with money or not, it indicates harmony could be just around the corner."

"Ah, Leela, why didn't you give her one of them knights," Flossy bemoaned. "Someone passionate, you know, a fling kind of a fella."

Greer laughed. "Come on, Flossy, I'm hardly in the market for that kind of carry on and besides, there's no one vaguely attractive, never mind single in this neck of the woods. I'd have to do internet dating and what chance would I stand, can't even get a signal round here!"

"What about the flatterer, you know, the one laying it on a bit thick because he just wants to get his leg over?" pressed Flossy, always slightly obsessed with sex, which Leela put down to her being widowed so young.

"You mean someone like the Knight of Cups?" Leela laughed. "I can't just magic him up from nowhere ..."

"Am I interrupting?" The door at the far end of the room opened. Rai stood there, the lamp from the hall forming a halo of light around him. A faint waft of Eau Savage mixed with sea air drifted towards them, his silvery dark hair combed back in thick waves.

He held something towards Greer. "For you, I signed for it, came a while ago."

The women at the table collapsed into howls of laughter. Not one word was intelligible as they alternated between pointing at him and shrieking at Greer.

"This place gets madder," he said, placing the envelope on

the dresser. Rai had not missed the tell-tale bottles and cards spread on the table and there was a new moon tonight, which would account for a lot, especially where Leela Brennan was concerned, because Leela was a witch, no doubt about that.

The Sea Chamber

L ess than two minutes later the door opened again. Rai had returned with an extremely anxious Dr James. The women, laughing as they cleared away the remnants of their evening, fell silent.

"It's Orla," Dr James said, glancing worriedly at those gathered.

"What's wrong?" Cassandra asked quietly.

"She's in the water. We were on the beach. She'd woken, agitated, said she needed a walk. One of the dogs distracted me, she let go of my hand and before I knew it, she'd slipped into the sea."

"Where is she now?" Greer was at Cassandra's side.

"A long way out. I can't really tell, it happened so quickly."

"It's getting dark," Rai said, but the night made no difference, Orla loved the sea turned black.

The sisters exchanged a look.

"You go," Leela told them. "We'll finish up here."

Cassandra and Greer were through the door and onto the cliff steps in seconds, Rai and the doctor following. They could hear the dogs in the distance.

"She went ..." Dr James called as they ran towards the waves, but the sisters already knew which direction Orla had taken. She was in the slipstream, swimming out towards the island. They were undressed by the time the men reached them. Wolfe and Tone had stopped barking, standing still at the spot where Orla had disappeared.

"I'll come," Rai said, shrugging off his jacket. Greer stopped him.

"We don't want to scare her."

Rai knew well enough upsetting someone while they were submerged could be dangerous.

"You know what to do if you need me," he told her. Telepathy, they all used it when they swam.

A splash. Cassandra was in, instantly disappeared below the surface.

Greer followed. The cold slammed into her as she dipped under the waves, rigid at first, anxiety stiffening her body as she pushed against the current, straining her eyes to seek out Cassandra. Adjusting to the gloom, she saw her. Instinctively, Cassandra glanced back, urging her on, radiating the energy she needed to cut through the water. In minutes she was with her and finding her rhythm nestled in behind.

Cassandra arched her back, legs together as she swam. Following, as she swerved left and right, Greer could see a ribbon of soft turquoise slicing the blue. The slip stream, a warm river of water that mysteriously appeared every new moon. A secret path of smooth, tropical sea leading to a deep cave. An underwater chamber. A secret sanctuary where the sea-people would restore 'beachers' they saved to send back to live above again. But only after they took away all memory of the place, leaving only a vapour of a dream, a reminder of having stayed too long beneath the waves.

"She has to be here."

Greer read Cassandra's thoughts, widening her eyes in answer. Despite Dr James's care, Orla had not settled. Her sisters needed to know what was wrong. They needed to bring her back. Ground her. For she could so easily be lost, and they could not bear to lose her. Not again.

Cassandra reminded Greer to fill her lungs with oxygen, her ability to breathe underwater less practised, and they pushed on. The waterfall at the end of the tunnel appeared impenetrable but where the dark shimmered electric blue, Cassandra and Greer knew to slip through into the chamber.

As they scanned the room there was no sign of Orla.

Everything was as they remembered, although it had been some years since they were here. The last time had been horrendous, Orla so devastated by the death of an aged Tone, had run away, refusing to come home, insisting she would stay until their mother found her, still convinced Miranda would return, despite being missing for over half a century.

"Their time isn't the same as ours," Orla told them. "A year on land is merely a moment in the deep, where time can stand still if you want it to."

This was not quite true but because the worlds were so different, there was no common ground for comparison. In a place where if time did exist it could only be measured by seismic change, a few hundred years was nothing.

And of course, sea-people did not die. Their spirits merely merged with something or someone who needed the extra energy and could helpfully use whatever was left of the other being.

Cassandra said this system was true of all things, humans had just been taught the wrong interpretation of the transformation, making people sad because someone had gone. Instead of rejoicing that this wealth of spirit lived on, having been absorbed by another, giving strength to a new soul in a special way.

Greer reached out to Cassandra; she could hear her sister's thoughts, a cacophony, swirling through her brain like a storm. She shook her head. Orla had not passed. Orla was here.

They heard a noise. A scrabbling sound at the far end of the chamber, and crossing the floor of seaweed they found Orla on her knees, digging with her bare hands at the shale, weeping softly.

"Where are you? Where are you?" she sang, in her sweet, sing-song voice. "We must go back, before they cover the track."

They ran to her. Her eyes were closed. Face wet with tears.

"We're here," Greer told her. "We've come for you."

Orla immediately relaxed, becoming weightless as they held her.

"Be careful now, don't wake her," Cassandra whispered to Greer. And slipping their arms into hers, the sisters carried her gently out of the chamber, through the waterfall and into the tunnel. Finding the slipstream they swam, the three together, a tiny shoal of human fish slicing through the water with ease, landing softly on the shore in the moonlight.

Rai and Dr James held Orla between them, Cassandra and Greer followed, the beach strangely silent save for the far-off call of gulls.

Once their mistresses were safely ashore the dogs ran ahead, and by the time the men were through the side entrance with their catch, Bríd was stirring soup at the range. Cassandra saw her tired eyes fill with tears of relief as they settled Orla by the hearth. They wrapped her in blankets, while Dr James fetched his bag.

"Blood pressure's low," he announced. "Temperature's up."

"A fever?" Cassandra asked.

"Not quite." He looked down at Orla, still drowsy but breathing more easily.

"This has happened before, I gather?"

They nodded.

"Not for a long time, though," Cassandra offered. "We thought she'd grown out of it. Was it a panic attack?"

"A bit more than that, I'd have said." Dr James was kneeling before his patient, holding her hand in his. "She was so long in the water and so far out, it's a miracle she wasn't drowned."

"She found a safe place," Greer said quickly. "Near the caves, out of the water."

"You both seemed to know where she'd be?"

"Lucky guess," Cassandra told him, drying Orla's hair gently. "We'll get her off to bed as soon as she warms up."

Greer glanced at Rai, who had not said a word. He had been here before too; more than once.

"Thank you," she mouthed at him. He gave her his sad smile. It had taken a lot of willpower for him not to go after them, forcing himself to stay by the shore with the doctor and the dogs. They were fine, fit women but they were not young girls anymore and as far as he knew spent most of their time out of the water. Their strength and special skills would be diminished with disuse. He knew that once the rush of relief at having brought Orla safely home had ebbed away, they would be totally drained.

"You all need a good night's sleep," Rai said, going to lock the door. "We were lucky to make it back before the storm."

"Storm?" the doctor asked, closing his bag.

"Big storm on its way," Bríd confirmed, taking the bowls Wolfe and Tone had emptied greedily to the sink. "You're all back just in time." As if to underline her words a rush of wind swept through, slamming a door, making them jump.

The sisters stood watching Orla as she slept. A glimmer of perspiration on her forehead, her lips dry but she was calm, lost in a deep sleep, safe in her own bed.

"She looks so fragile," Greer said, smearing balm on her sister's mouth.

"I know. She has the nicest skin, don't you think? She looks like a young girl lying there," Cassandra whispered, smoothing strands of Orla's hair across the pillow. "Our little shell sister."

"I couldn't understand what she was saying, could you? Why did she go there? Who was she looking for?" Greer took the mermaid doll with the spaghetti wool hair from the bedside table and tucked it in the crook of Orla's arm. A special treasure, they each had one, made by their mother, one of the few keepsakes Nana allowed.

Cassandra shrugged. "No idea, made no sense."

But the episode disturbed her more than she let on.

Who was Orla looking for, surely not their mother after all this time? Yet she knew, they were all still searching, blaming themselves for the loss. Was it their fault she had gone and nothing to do with the Sea Witch at all?

The wind had started to whip around the building, making it groan. Greer looked upwards.

"Sounds like we'll lose a few more slates off the roof tonight." She folded her robe across her chest.

"Bits of this place all over the beach in the morning, I shouldn't wonder." Cassandra stifled a shudder. "Maybe the Moon Room will fall down and we can claim the insurance. I could do with it for more pressing repairs."

Greer realised her sister was not joking. "Don't say that, Cass. The Moon Room is special, we were always going to restore it to its former glory."

"We were, but what with?" Cassandra said. "It would serve us better if it fell down, and preferably in the winter, when we've no guests."

Greer was about to protest, defend the Moon Room's restoration yet again, but she was tired and Cassandra looked done in.

"I'll stay, Cass." She indicated Orla, now snoring gently. "You get to bed, a long day."

Cassandra smiled gratefully, stopping at the door to look back into the room. Orla in her big blue bed, Wolfe at her feet, Tone curling up beside Greer in the armchair; the night watch.

"You were good tonight, long time since we swam together like that, you did well."

"I'm a bit out of practice." Greer grinned back. "But I'm a natural, must be something in the genes."

"Must be." And Cassandra laughed, closing the door, more than relieved she had not lost both her sisters tonight, because that was her biggest fear. Always had been

Island Echoes

C assandra could not sleep, the heart-racing adrenalin she experienced throughout Orla's rescue refused to subside, and she found herself wandering the hotel checking doors and windows, turning off lights as the wind rattled anxiously about the building.

As she arrived at the staircase to the Moon Room, she noticed the sign declaring it 'Out of Bounds' had been moved. Peering upwards she saw a flicker of candlelight, and taking the torch from her pocket began to climb, the metal structure creaking as she went.

Pushing open the door she found two bodies wrapped in a duvet in the corner of the room, a candelabra dripping wax onto the piano. The couple, so buried beneath the folds, were only just visible. Cassandra drew breath, recognising the young German girl Ava and her boyfriend, the local lad home from college.

She was just about to wake them when something caught her eye. There was a hole in the floor, a glimmer from the joist below. She reached to pluck it out and held aloft an earring, a clutch of pearlescent shells gathered on a gold hoop.

Cassandra recognised it immediately, she had played with it as a child, fascinated as the shells shimmered in the light, glimmering beneath her mother's beautiful hair, long like a mermaid's.

She closed her hand, holding it in her palm, glancing around to make sure no one had seen. For this was proof, proof she had not been dreaming and this explained everything, her mother had left because Cassandra had witnessed her with her lover in the Moon Room. The lover her mother had smuggled in while her father was away at sea. How could a small child be relied upon to keep such a secret?

And Cassandra remembered, something she had trained herself to forget.

Watching him take her mother in his arms, they danced in the shadows as music played, and her mother's laughter turned to moans.

She could see her on the window seat, the rich velvet of her dress stark against her pale skin as he pulled fabric from her shoulders, mouth at her throat. She unbuttoned it slowly revealing more flesh for him to kiss, her legs draped around him as his greedy mouth made her cry out in pleasure. The little girl in the doorway stood transfixed, unable to make a sound.

"Cassandra!" her grandmother called. "What're you doing out of bed?"

The spell broke. Cassandra started to scream. Her grandmother flew past, slamming the door in her face. She remembered sitting on the stair, calm now. Surely her grandmother had stopped the man biting her mother, either that or he had eaten them both.

Her tummy rumbled; she decided to go and find Bríd, she was pretty hungry herself.

"I bet you read them the riot act!" Bríd said, smiling after the young couple, who had sheepishly sipped the hot chocolate Cassandra had placed before them with a scowl.

"They said they didn't know it was out of bounds."

Bríd shrugged. "Always been a magnet for romance, that place. The views across the bay take your breath away, and as dusk falls the night sky wraps you in a cloak of mystery. Beguiling, isn't that the word for it? Sure, where would that leave anyone but beguiled?"

"You seem to know a lot about it!"

"We all have a past, Cassandra," Bríd replied huffily.

"Fudge Molloy hasn't always been the cranky old shite we know today!"

Cassandra laughed. "Nor, I hope, have we." And Bríd laughed too.

"Are the sisters okay?" Bríd handed Cassandra strong tea in her old china cup.

"Both fast asleep, the doctor gave Orla something to relax her, she was very anxious once she realised she was back."

"You mean back on dry land?" Bríd said bluntly; she normally only ever alluded vaguely to the sisters' strange gift.

Bríd was barely a teenager when Nana Morgan took her as a trainee, and one of her earliest duties was to help with the girls. The first time she discovered Orla playing happily with her mermaid doll while totally submerged in the bath had scared her witless, but the hysterical child she had to deal with once she hauled her out was even more frightening.

As they grew to trust her, she witnessed time and again instances of the three being able to breathe under water. She had watched them plunge into a pool, dip beneath the fountain or lie flat on the bottom of the large copper bath and just stay there. She had even found Cassandra hiding in the water butt once, the only clue her hair floating on the surface.

Bríd's heart had been put crossways in her often enough but the first time she saw the three of them dive beneath the sea together, she felt sure keeping this secret would be the death of her.

Yet as promised, they returned in time for supper with Bríd silent as she served, nose twitching at the sweet sea salt scent drifting from their strangely dry hair. But she had gasped at Cassandra's eyes, shining electric blue as if lit from within and seeing her surprise Cassandra blinked and the light was gone, if it had been there at all.

"You're very early," Cassandra commented, changing tack as if she could see Bríd's memories. It was only five am.

"I wanted to get ahead." She had not slept a wink either. "Why don't you three go off for a while. Get the boat out, take a picnic. A change would do you all good."

Cassandra cast about. Breakfast was laid out, trolleys with towels, toiletries and bed linen ready for the housekeeping team. She caught sight of her gauntness in the mirror, and her back ached, really ached if she would but admit it.

"Go back to bed for an hour," Bríd instructed. "Tide will be perfect around ten, I'll deal with everything here." And for once Cassandra did as she was told, too weary to argue.

Greer had to look twice at the thick envelope on her dressing table the next morning, trying to remember where it had come from.

Of course, Rai had delivered it to her in the kitchen. She turned it over; registered mail, London postmark. It was with a sense of trepidation she opened the envelope, spreading the contents on the eiderdown, credit cards, cheque books, insurance policies and a letter from Alistair's accountant.

Dear Ms Morgan

I am writing in relation to the winding up of the McKeiver Group of Companies.

I am to inform you that all Mr McKeiver's business interests have been ceased with immediate effect and to this end, regretfully your services are no longer required. As you are no longer retained by the company, the lease on your apartment has been relinquished and we have recovered the vehicle you had the use of while on company business.

As you are currently out of the country, the McKeiver family has kindly taken it upon themselves to ensure all your personal belongings have been removed from company premises and placed in storage, details of which are enclosed. You have 30 days to reclaim your goods and chattels. If you have not repossessed them or arranged for them to be removed and/or delivered elsewhere they will – according to our terms and conditions – be destroyed.

Remuneration covering statutory notice as per your contract

has been paid into your bank account as of today.
Yours sincerely, for and on behalf of the McKeiver Group
Graham Pincher, Accountant.

Greer read the letter twice. Amy had certainly taken charge of things and without even a 'by your leave' she had been summarily dismissed from their lives. No personal note, no acknowledgement of how hard she had worked for the company, not even a hint of what Alistair had meant to her and she to him.

She could almost hear Alistair's sister, Clare. *Don't be naïve, Greer, you were his mistress, nothing more, nothing less.*

It was Clare who had told Amy that Greer had accompanied Alistair to Cannes at the very beginning of their affair. Greer remembered the call well.

"*But, Clare, you shouldn't have told Amy, for goodness sake, she'll think something's going on.*"

"*You mean she'll know something's going on because I've told her you're going, and Alistair hasn't. Grow up, Greer, everyone knows you two are at it like knives and if you're not, you soon will be.*" Clare *Fiend*, alright.

Putting all the paperwork back in the envelope, she slammed the drawer shut. So, that was that. *Goodbye, Alistair.*

Then glancing at the Post-It stuck to the mirror, she laughed out loud. It read ...

'*We're sailing. 10am sharp. No scurvy, no skivers. Captain's Orders.*'

She checked her watch, she had better get a move on.

The Lady Godiva had been the family boat for years. A sturdy twenty-six feet with foresail, mainsail, and all-weather cuddy, it had a small well-equipped galley and a cabin, comfortable accommodation for two, a cosy squeeze for any more.

She had been their grandmother's boat and they had spent happy days chugging along the coast, fishing over the side and diving off the stern. A familiar sight in Rosshaven's sunny, safe harbour, three little girls, the matriarch, and ubiquitous spaniels.

Like much of what they owned, the boat had fallen into disrepair, yet as she watched it bobbing on the quayside *Godiva* looked as welcoming as ever and seeing her sisters aboard Greer was deeply moved. How she had missed this, it had been such a long time?

Tone spotted her first, leaping from the pontoon, racing to greet her. Wolfe barked after him. Cassandra looked up.

"Here she is!" she called to Orla, making ready to cast off. Orla stopped to wave, her huge smile beaming.

Greer lifted Tone into her arms, pushing her face into his soft spaniel ears, not wanting her sisters to see her tears.

An hour later, having skilfully circumnavigated Phoenix Island, *Godiva* was securely moored at the new jetty and the three were heading up the track towards the ruins of the old seminary, its crumbling walls, and turrets of golden stone at the highest point of the island.

Cassandra led the way, bottles clanking in her rucksack. Orla and Greer carried the picnic basket between them; it weighed a tonne and the sooner their sister decided to make camp the better.

"She won't stop till she gets to the well," Greer advised Orla.

At last they reached the perimeter, the remains of the church visible through the ragged hedgerow. Cassandra was working the spaniels along the wall, sending them on; if there was a gap, they would find it.

A shout.

"We're in!" she called, squirming through, ducking beneath the sign declaring trespassers would be 'Persecuted' clinging to the fence.

Before long they had laid out the picnic in the dusty, overgrown courtyard, the circle of pale gold stone in the centre marking the well, as crumbling gothic arches faced them, a reminder of the chapel that had once been filled with student priests.

"A penny for them." Greer sat beside Cassandra on the rug. "You're miles away."

"Just listening to the echoes," Cassandra said, handing Greer the corkscrew. "I forget how special it is here."

Greer sat back in the sunshine, the warmth of the old stone wall seeping through her shirt, easing away the tension of the last few days.

"Seductive I'd call it," she said, closing her eyes. "*Fantasy Island*, did a lot of my dreaming here."

Cassandra sipped her wine, watching Orla play chase with the dogs, scooting this way and that around the well, giggling when they caught up with her; happy to be back.

"I wonder will Archie be at the party." Greer had been admiring the view of the Harbour Spa Hotel from their vantage point, glass walls glittering in the sunshine, like a vast liner ready to set sail.

Cassandra kept staring at the horizon.

"Nagle said you nearly ran him off the road the other day, how is he?"

"Same as ever," Cassandra said. "Arrogant, full of himself, no thought for anyone else as usual."

The Archie Fitzgerald Cassandra described, if she could ever be persuaded to speak of him at all, bore little resemblance to the gregarious, generous fun-loving *bon viveur* Greer had known most of her life.

"I saw him on the beach when I first arrived, not changed a bit."

Cassandra turned to look at her. "You never said!"

"He wouldn't come in. Said he wouldn't be welcome. That's not like you, Cass, especially given the circumstances."

"Circumstances? You mean I'm to be nice to the old goat because he's moving away and I'll never have to see the self-centred, up his own arse, fecker again? That would be false, Greer, I couldn't be false."

"You'd give him a chance though, surely, if he wanted to make peace?"

"Peace? We're hardly at war, we're neighbours who don't get on, is all," Cassandra scoffed.

Greer raised an eyebrow.

"Remember when he used to bring his records over and you'd escape to the Moon Room, 'Maggie May' and 'Brown Sugar' blaring out across the bay. I was in total awe, such a glamorous couple, so cool."

"Nonsense! We were never a couple." But that was a lie, they had been a couple. Here on this very island after the festival, that wonderful, glorious day of sun, wine, and music.

Cassandra closed her eyes, trying to fill her mind with the here and now, but Rod Stewart's rendition of the wrong kind of love played in her ears and Archie, tanned in his chambray shirt and Wrangler jeans, chased her up to the ruins.

Laughing she ran, bracelets of shells jangling, heart beating as he swept her into his arms and his mouth found hers and all the tender teasing of their childhood years melted away.

She recalled gazing into his eyes, questioning, and he had dropped to his knees with a look of such adoration she just froze.

And then he whispered, "Darling Cassandra, make this the happiest day of my life and let my dearest friend become my lover, my beautiful, precious girl. I want you so much, I can hardly bear it."

And looking into those glittering grey eyes, she wanted him too, more than anything and undoing her cheesecloth blouse as slowly as her trembling hands would allow, she had taken his hands to place them on her warm, exposed flesh, saying:

"I love you, Archie Fitzgerald, always have, always will."

And wrapping her in the strongest embrace, words of love blurred against her throat as his lips, never ceasing, kissed every single inch of her and she, so crazed with lust for him, could have eaten him alive.

And every night thereafter they had made love wherever and whenever they could, until the very last day of that long, hot summer.

Memory of a Free Festival

G reer woke with a start. Someone had thoughtfully placed a straw hat over her face. The remains of the picnic lay abandoned. They had devoured Cassandra's delicious courgette, olive and mozzarella flan, homemade Scotch eggs and chunky coleslaw followed by Bríd's jammy ice cream – a frozen yoghurt concoction laced with fruit liqueur. No wonder she had slept.

Shielding her eyes, she could see her sisters with the dogs in the distance, bobbing up and down on the shore, shell collecting a time-honoured tradition. So many traditions remained, yet so much had to change, she thought, gazing up at the sky.

The island remained unchanged, a few bins for tourists, a sturdier jetty for boats, but little else, yet it was a day such as this that had changed her life forever. She recalled how, once the date of the festival had been announced, the logistics of getting the equipment ashore was such a mammoth task it appeared insurmountable. It was Rai who persuaded the whole community to help.

She cast about, remembering.

The harbour had been full of boats, laden with supplies; food, barrels of beer, cases of wine, gallons of water. She could picture it now, seating erected to form an amphitheatre against the backdrop of the ruined church, gantries of lights, generators wheeled into position. A concert on a massive scale for such a tiny place.

It was 1986, the summer after Live Aid, the global fund-raising effort to bring relief to famine-stricken Ethiopia. Rock stars Bob Geldof and Midge Ure had pulled off an amazing feat, their brainchild of two live concerts, one in the UK and one in America had galvanised people on both sides of the Atlantic, raising millions for the cause. Rosshaven did not want to be left behind.

There were five members in the band – The Island – back then. Rai, lead singer and songwriter; Bryan D'Arcy – cool and moody bass player; Mojo Morrisey – totally bonkers drummer; Sly Jackson – gifted lead guitarist, and Greer Morgan, quirky and talented keyboard player.

But Greer and Rai had been virtually inseparable since the first time they met, Rai ten and Greer only five. A relationship so close one seemed to know what the other was thinking and as a child, if Rai was not around, Greer appeared so cast adrift it was heartbreaking. They needed each other, always had.

Today Greer's memories were tinged with justifiable pride. The festival had been a huge success, The Island had headlined with an impressive list of performers turning up to do their bit. The sun shone, wine flowed, and vast sums were raised for famine relief. A triumph. The perfect launch pad for the next phase of the band's career.

Except there was one fly in the ointment.

Herself.

The band's new manager was a hard-nosed New Yorker, Melissa Malachy. Melissa loved The Island, they were talented, edgy, and different. And she *adored* Rai.

There was something ethereal about him, she used to say and if she could bottle it, she would make a fortune.

Rai had mass appeal and it went right across the spectrum, his intangible otherworldliness making him utterly irresistible; even an alien would fall for him, Melissa decreed.

And then there was Greer.

Greer and Rai were conjoined, and Melissa needed to change that. She needed an unencumbered protégé, someone she could manage and manipulate. Someone only she could control. She needed Greer gone.

Greer was packing away the picnic, humming to herself, songs from the old days drifting in and out of her mind, the set they had performed, the tumultuous applause, the enraptured crowd swaying, cigarette lighters aloft; a truly magical time.

And then she recalled the conversation she overheard through the flimsy awning of the makeshift dressing room, a situation she had been half-expecting but was shocked by nonetheless.

"The contract, Rai, the deal, it's not straightforward. It's something we have to work through, there'll be changes, it'll all be for the good, trust me."

"Yeah, yeah." *Rai was only half-listening, lost in the afterglow of the gig, exhausted yet happy having given his all.*

"Just let me take care of everything, okay. I'll make sure we get the best deal for everyone." *Melissa's tone changed.*

Rai stopped as he zipped his precious Gibson into its case.

"What changes, Melissa? What changes are you talking about?"

"The thing is not everyone makes the grade."

"Not someone in the band, surely?"

"I'm sorry, Rai, it's Greer, she's the one not in the line-up. The company thinks it's time for a change, to harden up the appeal, make The Island a real rock band, on par with The Who, Queen, U2, that kind of thing."

"But Greer's part of the band – always has been," *Rai protested.* *"We write the songs."*

"I think you write the songs, Rai, and anyway we'll find you people to collaborate with – big names. Elton John, Prince, Bowie, just think of it, every song a major hit!"

"But what about the chemistry?" *Rai was bemused.*

"Don't you worry about the chemistry, sweet thing," *Melissa purred.* *"There'll be plenty of that going down, I'll make sure you get all the chemistry you need."*

Greer could feel heat rising in her chest even now. Still raw. The beginning of the end began right here, where the

SECRETS OF THE SHELL SISTERS

dream had started to dissolve into a nightmare.

She did not know whether to laugh or cry. Melissa had already approached her with what she said was a tantalising proposal. A solo career. Same spiel, collaboration with some of the biggest names in the business, a complete relaunch, backed by a massive marketing campaign. She already had tour dates lined up, talk of a cameo movie role, the Bond franchise had even been mentioned. But Greer knew a fairy story when she heard one.

That was when she opened the door to find Melissa attached to Rai, arms wrapped around him. Greer tapped him forcibly between the shoulder blades. He swung round, dislodging the other woman.

"Greer ... I ..."

She raised her hand. "Helpful finding you two together like this."

Melissa just blinked.

"I can let you both know at the same time."

"Know what?" Rai asked. Melissa's livid purple lipstick stained his mouth.

"I quit."

"You what?"

"You heard me. I quit."

"But you can't quit. This is nothing." He indicated the woman standing open-mouthed beside him.

"My decision is nothing to do with that nothing." Greer nodded at the manager she had just sacked. "I quit. That's an end to it." She went to the door, but before she did she wiped Rai's mouth with the back of her hand. "All of it, Rai. I mean it."

And replicating his sad smile she left, going in search of Cassandra, hoping she had not yet made for home, she needed a lift back, she needed to get away from here as fast as she could. She had made her decision.

A foghorn sounded out to sea, dragging Greer back. Cassandra and Orla were waving at a tug towing *The Pirate* towards its mooring. Declan and Rai would soon be back in business. Rai's stay at Manorcliff would be over and he could take himself and his disturbing presence back to his brother, or better still, return to the South Seas where he worked for some obscure charity, no doubt doing his best to assuage his guilt and cleanse his soul.

Folding the rug, Greer lifted the backpack. There was a rustle at the fence and she looked up, expecting to see Tone bounding towards her, coming to fetch her before the weather turned.

A man stood there instead. Tall, waterproof jacket, expensive trainers and shades hiding his eyes.

"Hello, Greer." He gave a grim smile, folding his arms. "Had a nice picnic?"

Greer pulled on sunglasses, hoping to hide her surprise. "What're you doing here?"

"Oh, I think you know the reason," he said lazily. "Let's not be beating over the bush, the sooner you give me what I've come for the better for all concerned."

Greer straightened to look at him and although she could not see his eyes, she knew he was glaring at her. He put his hand in the pocket of his jeans and drew something out slowly.

She saw the blade of a knife glint in the sun.

Box of Frogs

"Here she is!" Orla called out. "Oh look, she's with the scowly fella with the accent. The one who checked in this morning."

Cassandra watched the pair come towards them. The 'scowly fella' had insisted on taking the picnic basket, Greer carried the rest, there was no need to go back to where they had made camp. Cassandra was relieved, she was tired now. There was much to do when they returned, the hotel full and nearly everyone booked in for dinner. She looked at the couple as they walked. There was something odd. She sensed a familiarity, yet Greer had stiffened, the ease of the day gone out of her.

Greer cut to the chase. "Janis Petrova, my sister Cassandra."

"We've met," she said, wearing her hotel director smile. "Mr Petrova is one of our newest guests. Tell me, how do you know each other?"

"Janis is Alistair's private secretary," Greer told her.

The man gave the women a melancholy smile. "More than that, like brothers," he said. "I am very worried for him and I pray."

"You didn't bring bad news, did you?" Orla asked him accusingly.

"The last I read, he's making good progress, but such an awful thing to happen."

Cassandra looked him in the eye. "I hope you're not tempting my sister back to those bright city lights?"

The man raised his hands. "No, no. Just here on holiday like everyone else. Greer always told me what a beautiful place it is, thought I'd find out for myself."

Greer gazed at him. She had never mentioned Rosshaven to Janis. Their relationship was strictly business, his constant shadowy presence a necessary irritation. And although she and Alistair were going away together, she had been expecting him to appear at the airport, surprised he was not hovering in the background as usual. Maybe that was when she realised something was *really* wrong.

Her pulse started to throb; the knife episode had disturbed her. Watching her closely he had slipped it from his pocket, taking off his shoe to remove a pebble with the point of the blade.

"There!" He had given a sly smile. "Neatly done, no one would suspect a thing."

Greer gave him a steely stare as he stood with her sisters.

"Is that where I get the ferry back?" He pointed at a small queue on the shore.

"Every half hour, the last one six o'clock, in plenty of time for dinner," she told him as her sisters climbed aboard *Godiva*. "We'd offer you a lift but we've some errands on the way back and besides the ferry takes the scenic route, with you on holiday after all."

Tone trotted over and gave him a cursory sniff, glancing at his mistress. The slight shake of her head was imperceptible, but Tone sensed it and trotted back.

"See you later then." He raised a hand in farewell.

"You're not a fan, I can see that," Cassandra announced as they cast off. "What's he after? Do you know?"

Greer shrugged. "Not sure. He and Alistair were thick as thieves, but what he wants with me, I've no idea."

"Unfinished business?" Cassandra asked, pulling up the hood of her sailing jacket, the misty drizzle turning to rain.

"I'm sure there's plenty of that where Alistair's concerned," Greer said, more to herself, nestling into the cockpit, Tone snuggled beside her. She shivered; Janis was a nasty piece of work. More henchman than private secretary,

Alistair had taken him on at the same time as his government appointment. And since then, he had never been more than a few steps behind; in the next row at the theatre or at a nearby table in the same restaurant. Always alone and never off duty, Greer knew that much.

But what he hoped intimidating her would achieve, she could not fathom. Alistair might not have always played with a straight bat, but he had been careful never to involve Greer in anything underhand. She and his family were sacrosanct, kept safely in their separate compartments. No blurred lines.

Greer tucked Tone under her jacket, his warm damp fur smelling of sea and sand, and she sniffed deeply, a rich comforting aroma, and closing her eyes tried to empty her mind, the sound of wind and waves doing little to soothe her, as *Godiva* powered home.

Dinner that evening was a subdued affair. The hot sunny day had turned squally and after-dinner drinks on the terrace were abandoned. Some of the guests had remained at the table while others mooched moodily about reception.

The Moon Room would come into its own on an evening like this, Greer thought, resolving to argue more stridently for its restoration. A storm could be spectacular up there, clouds threaded with lightning swirling in the twilight, the sea crashing in angry white breakers against the rocks; a monochrome vista filled with drama and mystery.

She was relieved that Janis, although a lurking presence, had kept a discreet distance, making small talk with other guests. Although she did not doubt that she would discover his purpose soon enough, for now she had enough on her plate.

Looking about for familiar faces to ease her anxiety, Greer was disappointed. Nagle had called Dr James to the farm, one of his prize heifers was struggling to give birth and with the local vet away, he wanted the doctor to give him a hand. Rai was staying with Declan, to ensure the newly repaired *Pirate* was securely moored against the forthcoming storm and similarly, Fudge had left to check the outbuildings. While Bríd, having done an extra shift so the sisters could have their picnic, abandoned her post as soon as she could. Orla had also disappeared; the new shells had to be catalogued, of course.

Noticing her eldest sister clutch at her side as she bent to put the last of the plates away, Greer persuaded the remaining guests to take coffee in the bar, closing the door firmly as they left.

"Cass, this is no good, we need more help." She took her by the elbow to sit her back down at the table.

"Ah, we can manage, another couple of weeks and the season's nearly over, there'll be hardly anybody here."

Greer sat before her, noticing smudges of grey beneath the teal eyes.

"No, we can't manage. I've put a proposal together. Costs for refurbishment and at least three new members of staff, two in the kitchen and one front of house."

Cassandra went to protest. Greer passed over a file of paperwork on her way to the cupboard, returning with two glasses and the decanter.

"You've been busy," Cassandra said, taking the drink gratefully.

"Just doing my job." She gave her sister a reassuring smile. "I've a meeting in Dublin next week, I'm going to see the bank about another mortgage, get funds in place and draw up a proper programme. We may well have to close for the winter while work is underway, but that's fine, we'll factor that all in."

Cassandra looked shocked.

"We can't do that, Greer! What about the staff? We can't lay Bríd and Fudge off, they'll have no income, we'll lose them and there's hardly any work here in the winter, you know that."

Greer shrugged. "You can't make an omelette …"

"Without breaking a few eggs, I know but, Greer …" Cassandra looked on the brink of tears.

"Early days," Greer said, knocking the whiskey back. "Lots to sort, just keeping you in the loop, so you know what I'm up to."

"Well, that's a first." Cassandra gave a weary smile. "Making sure I know what you're up to."

"We're a team now, Cass, and although it might be hard to believe, I'm really not that headstrong teenager anymore. Honestly."

Cassandra gave her a look. It was an ongoing debate. Whenever Greer did something that displeased her, Cassandra trotted out the same old line, Greer was impulsive, reckless, inconsiderate – always had been – and Greer would bridle against the image of a still immature girl who had joined a band, left home, toured the world … made mistakes.

"Cass, I know you've never put a foot wrong in your life but … don't dwell on the past." Greer leaned over to take her sister's hand. "Another nightcap and then bed, yes?"

Cassandra smiled, her cheeks turning slightly pink.

"Did you ever get to the bottom of what upset Orla so much the other day? Why she took off to the other place?"

Orla and Greer shared a different kind of closeness. Greer was not afraid to delve into Orla's specialness, she was not as restrictive as Cassandra, less fearful of what Orla might say or reveal.

"Just that the shell, you know, the conch Miss Finn gave her, brought her a message."

"Who from?" Cassandra poured them out another tot.

"Our mother. She's told her there's another sister."

"*What?*"

"That's what she said, why she was so upset. Another sister with no family and we're to take her in, mind her. That's why she went there, she was looking for the other sister." Greer sipped her whiskey thoughtfully.

"Well, she's come up with some nonsense, but that takes some beating. I worry about her more and more, I really do. What if she's going a bit … you know … doolally … and we can't tell, because she's Orla, if you see what I mean?"

Greer started to laugh.

"It's not funny, Greer, I'm serious."

"You could say that about all of us, Cass. Who's going to have any idea if we go doolally? Sure, we're all mad as a box of frogs – always have been!" She gave the big, loud guffaw all the Morgan sisters had in common, and Cassandra started to chuckle too, forcing the laugh back into her throat.

"Sp…speak for … you … your … yourself," she stuttered. But it was too late, and the laugh came out anyway, along with the whiskey, spattering her good white skirt in shiny damp spots. "Oh dear." Cassandra held her face in her hands and then, laying her cheek on the table closed her eyes. In less than a moment, she was asleep. Greer squinted at her, gave her a poke but she was gone, dead to the world.

"Never could hold your drink, I've always said so," she muttered to herself, half-dragging, half-carrying Cassandra to one of the armchairs where she took off her shoes, easing a cushion behind her head. Cassandra moaned slightly as Greer took up her position opposite; her sister would wake in a couple of hours and would need a hand getting to bed.

Greer's blurry gaze rested on her sister's still pretty face, the face she had always known and loved. She noticed, even as she slept, the slight frown between Cassandra's brows, a twitch of concern about her mouth, almost as if she were clinging to wakefulness for whatever reason. Slipping from her seat, Greer went to sit on the floor and taking her sister's hand kissed the space where the ruby ring – Cassandra's superpower – usually shone.

"I'm sorry if I made you ashamed, Cass. I never meant to. I know you've always wanted the best for me, always wanted me to be rich and famous, and wildly successful but they were your dreams, not mine. I'd have been quite happy staying here, writing songs on the beach with Rai, swimming in the sea with my sisters." Greer sniffed, as a large tear rolled down her cheek. "I've missed you, Cass," she whispered, nestling into her sister's legs as she slept. "And I'll never let you down again, I promise."

Party Animals

Manorcliff's staffing problem needed addressing sooner than Cassandra seemed to appreciate. A major event she and her sisters were expected to attend was imminent. Yet Cassandra appeared to have completely forgotten about it, which was surprising, because not only was it the main subject of conversation in the town, Orla had written all the details in flamboyant swirls on the large blackboard in the kitchen.

The grand opening of the new bar at the Harbour Spa Hotel was almost upon them and everyone in Rosshaven had been invited. As long-established local business owners the Morgans were special guests, requested to attend a private champagne reception before the main event, followed by a guided tour of the hotel.

But Orla and Greer knew their sister well, surmising that the combination of lack of help and Archie Fitzgerald's purported headline appearance would provide Cassandra with the perfect excuse to bow out.

Greer considered this. The new hotel might be a rival but a strategic alliance with a first-class establishment like the Harbour Spa Hotel could only be of benefit. Manorcliff needed to raise its profile; not everyone was aware she was back, and the presence of all three sisters would leave no one in any doubt they were a force to be reckoned with.

Orla's ambitions for the evening were less business orientated but resolutely focused even so. She could not remember whether it was the shells or Leela who had told her, but Nagle was planning to sell the farm and move away. His brother managed a forestry plantation in New Zealand

and had been asking Nagle to join him for years. This was worrying, because not only was Nagle one of their dearest friends, but she felt sure that somewhere in her seemingly impenetrable heart, Cassandra loved him deeply and would be devastated if he finally went to join his brother nearly twelve thousand miles away.

Time was running out – Nagle had started selling livestock. Perhaps the party would provide Nagle with an opportunity to tell Cassandra his plans, making her realise how she felt about him and how broken-hearted they would all be if he left.

All this aside, Orla had another special intention for the evening. She loved to dance – in fact she danced all the time – on top of cliffs, along the terrace, at the beach. She could hear music all around and whenever she felt like it, she would dance to it. Tomorrow night at the party, she particularly wanted to dance with James. When she asked the shells if she had met her own true love, the shells had told her yes – and he was a healer just like her, with kind eyes and soft hands. He was lonely too, for he had lost a love which had left a hole in his heart, just as losing her mother had left a hole in hers.

"So, you see, Cassandra, we're covered. Bríd, Fudge and Flossy in the kitchen, Ava and her boyfriend in the bar. We've agreed menus, have numbers for dinner and breakfast – all sorted!" Greer placed the clipboard with the paperwork on the table. "I think we should offer Ava an apprenticeship. She's already asked to stay while her parents and her brother finish the rest of their tour and with her boyfriend being bilingual too, they make a great team."

Cassandra looked distracted.

"What's the weather doing?" The sun was already high in a cloudless sky. "I mean tomorrow."

"Looks good."

"Is Nagle doing drinks on the terrace then?"

"No, Ava and her fella can do that. Nagle's at the party with us."

"Ah, Greer, I don't know ..."

Greer picked the clipboard up, shoving it officiously under her arm. "Well, I do know. We've discussed it." She nodded at Orla, who sat up straight and folded her arms. "And we're all going. It's time the Morgan sisters looked this town in the eye, too many rumours flying about the place and us sitting up here in our ivory tower doing nothing about it!"

"What do you mean?" Cassandra asked, pushing away the coffee she had forgotten to drink.

"You know what I mean, we've always been the talk of the town, they call us 'The Coven'. Nagle said the sight of us sailing across the harbour the other day had the place agog. It was reported the shells told Orla there was buried treasure on the island and we'd gone to find it. You know the sort of mad stuff they come up with."

"Did anyone see the sister?" Orla asked quietly.

"For goodness sake." Cassandra heaved herself up. "There *is* no sister, Orla. The message was wrong."

"But the room under the sea, I was waiting ..."

Cassandra glared at her.

Greer stood between them. "A dream, Orla love," she said softly. "Just one of your dreams. Now, no more of this from either of you. We've a plan, let's stick to it."

And with that Greer gave a dramatic sweep of her paisley shawl and left the room.

Orla descended the left staircase first, looking like a Pre-Raphaelite representation of Queen Guinevere, hair in tiny plaits, entwined with beads of shell and sea glass. Her empire line dress fluttered in waves of tie-dye gossamer as she tripped towards reception. Wolfe and Tone sat at the bottom of the stairs gazing at her. Wolfe wagged his tail expectantly but Tone, more attuned to human foibles, knew this was no 'walk on the beach' ensemble, despite Orla's eccentricities.

Greer followed, opting for a beautifully cut silk suit. Long-line jacket with mandarin collar and three-quarter sleeves, muted jewels in sea glass studded the cuff and hem of the cropped slimline trousers, a favoured pair of handmade evening shoes encrusted with the same jewels in her hand, the heels too unforgiving for running downstairs.

"Where's Cass? We'll be late," she told Orla. Fudge had the Range Rover at the door, engine running.

"She's trying not to come." Orla gave Greer their wide-eyed look. "Every dress she owns is on the floor and her hair's wet."

Greer looked at the clock. "I don't want to miss the tour, do you think we should go and help?"

Greer turned back to the stairs. Orla stopped her.

"Nagle's up there. Said he's come to escort her, whether she likes it or not."

Greer was shocked by Nagle's uncharacteristic temerity; he rarely challenged her sister.

"He said we all had to go and show a united front, as pillows of the community."

Greer was just about to tell Orla they were in fact 'pillars' of the community when Cassandra and Nagle appeared at the top of the stairs. Her sister wore a rich green taffeta cocktail dress, the deeply curved neckline displaying the traditional three strands of pearls beautifully, especially as she wore the large emerald and diamond clasp to the front. The necklace was part of Nana's exquisite collection, one of the few items, Greer suspected, that had not yet been sent to auction

Nagle had made an effort too, and although his dinner jacket was shiny with age, his sparkling shirt looked new. Orla gave Greer a nudge. Not a word was said as the handsome couple descended the staircase and although they could see Cassandra had been crying, she was smiling now, and so was Nagle, albeit grimly.

The fifteen minute drive 'over the back road' was filled with chatter as the sisters – Orla and Greer in particular – speculated wildly about who would be at the party and with whom, and of course what they would be wearing.

"I love a man in a well-cut dinner suit," Greer said, brushing dust off the back of Nagle's jacket. "Makes even old farmers look elegant."

"Do you think so?" Nagle twinkled at her in the rear-view mirror, having ousted Fudge from behind the wheel to take over the driving. Fudge was delighted to be replaced and not have to wait until all hours for the women to decide to come home. The Morgans were renowned for never leaving the floor until every last note had been played.

The setting sun streaked plumes of orange across the sky as the Range Rover rattled up the driveway towards the elegant sandstone building. The domed entrance was reminiscent of an ancient temple glowed, as well-heeled guests spilled out of vehicles, polished in honour of the occasion.

As Nagle pulled up alongside the red carpet, doormen in powder-blue uniforms magically appeared to release his passengers.

"I'll park it, sir," one of them said, holding his hand out for the keys.

"Why would you do that? Sure, how will I know where it is when I come to go home?" Nagle asked, bemused.

"As soon as you're ready to leave, sir, I'll bring it right back," the porter replied, smiling steadily.

Cassandra handed the keys over. "Thank you."

"No trouble, ma'am, all part of the service." The young man swung into the driver seat.

"Now," she said, taking Nagle's arm. "Why don't you enjoy yourself tonight, let your hair down. I'll drive home and if I have to leave early, I'll send Fudge back for you."

Nagle stopped.

"No. You're the one to let your hair down for a change, be loads of old friends here, enjoy yourself. I'd like to see you dance the buckles off your shoes, it's been a long time." He looked her in the eye. "And I'll be right by your side, okay? You don't have to worry about a thing."

Cassandra took a deep breath, moving quickly along the red carpet, past the flame-filled bowls either side of the shining gold and glass doorway and into reception, a huge circular room carved out of rock. The cool marble floor made a pathway to where Ross Power stood welcoming guests with chilled champagne and a slightly strained smile. Spotting Cassandra, the smile broadened, and he took both her hands as she reached him.

"I'm so glad you came, Ms Morgan, it's an honour to meet you, it really is." Cassandra looked up at the handsome young man, his words genuine, she could see that. "Now, before all this kicks off and I forget, I'd like to invite you to a luncheon I'm holding for people like us. Please say you'll come."

He was so disarming and charming that Cassandra could see that Ross Power would be very difficult to refuse.

"People like us?" She frowned.

"Yes, people like us trying to run establishments like this," he indicated the hotel. "And making it look easy. I need to know all your secrets and the sooner the better."

Cassandra let out the loud Morgan guffaw, causing her sisters to look up.

"I'd be delighted," she confirmed. "I just hope you won't be too shocked."

"Too shocked?" Ross was curious.

"At the secrets." Cassandra gave him a wink.

"Is Archie here yet?" Nagle asked, bringing up the rear as the ladies moved onto the terrace.

"Not yet but he's promised, so I'm keeping everything crossed," Ross replied.

Cassandra overheard. "Well, I certainly hope he doesn't let you down. Has a habit of breaking promises, that fella."

As soon as she said it, she regretted it. It made her sound bitter and now she was annoyed with herself because she *was* bitter and had no reason to be.

What happened was in the past.

She was as much to blame as Archie and anyway, Archie

did not know the outcome. He did not know what she had done and the more she thought about it, *was being forced to think about it*, the more she realised that if anyone had a reason to be bitter, it would be Archie himself. More than bitter, he would feel betrayed, because what she had done was unforgivable. And now she felt dreadful and wanted to cry again.

Greer was at her side with a fresh glass of champagne.

"Here, drink this," she ordered. "And stop going around looking as if the sky is about to fall in. Can't be that bad, can it?"

The hubbub intensified as guests parted like the waves and Archie Fitzgerald arm in arm with the beautiful actress Fenella Flanagan appeared on the red carpet. They really were a most striking couple; she every inch a star and he, eccentric, beguiling, a national treasure. Cassandra swallowed, her throat constricting even now, after all this time.

Bygones

T he arrival of another guest created a welcome diversion
for Cassandra at least. Greer knew it was him, she could
feel it; her skin prickled and all the noise in the room muted
as she, on tenterhooks, strained to hear his voice. Because
although she dared not admit it, she missed him. Having him
around had reconnected her somehow, making her feel less of
a stranger here in her own hometown.

He greeted Cassandra with a kiss, Orla with a hug and
having shaken Nagle firmly by the hand, turned to face her.
She had been practising one of her many inscrutable looks
for just such an encounter but smothered a smile instead. Rai
stood before her, steely black hair slicked back, midnight blue
eyes sparkling in an off-white dinner jacket and classic black
tie. The jacket had wide shoulders and broad lapels, the letters
RM sewn in sequins on the breast pocket. A vintage piece.

She recognised it immediately; he had had a dozen made
for the US tour and worn it on the photoshoot for the cover
of their last album. Although, adding a modern twist, he had
now ditched high-waisted pleated trousers for a pair of black
chinos.

"Before you comment." He fixed her with his gaze.
"There's no rule in the fashionista handbook that says men
can't wear vintage too. And" – he gave her that smile – "It was
all Declan had left, one of the few items of memorabilia he
hasn't sold."

"Suits you." She tried to keep a straight face. "What time
are you on?" She nodded at the small stage.

"Don't be cheeky," he warned, as their host came to greet

him. Greer saw the likeness immediately.

"I'd forgotten you're cousins, the apple didn't fall far from the tree where you're concerned, did it? Right ugly-looking pair of bowsies." She grinned up at the handsome men. Ross gave her a quizzical look, unused to the vernacular.

"The lady refers to us being a most unattractive pair of ruffians," Rai said. Ross laughed.

"I do my best," Ross assured her. "But my family's legacy goes before me. The past casts a long shadow." He gave a familiar smile, eyes twinkling.

"It does," she agreed. "Especially around here. Best stick to running a hotel, that way the pirates can keep you topped up with swag and you stay out of gaol."

Ross laughed again. But Greer was only half-joking. Old habits died hard in places like Rosshaven, where one bad storm could sweep away a barn full of grain, drown livestock, destroy homes, and ruin families. Difficult to imagine how tough life could be on a warm summer's evening, the setting sun turning the sea to molten gold, the laughter and chink of glasses giving the impression no one had a care in the world.

Rai watched her. Greer could so easily slide into the dark.

"Had the grand tour?" Rai asked, hoping she would uphold their truce.

"Very impressive. State-of-the-art kitchen, fabulous guest rooms. Quirky too, highlights of harbour history dotted about, art, sculpture, old photos, the whole place tells a story."

"I'm pleased you approve," Ross said. "I want it to be a haven."

Rai and Greer glanced at each other. He was pleased she remembered.

Haven.

A word they used to describe one another at the height of their fame. A haven to bask in the glory yet keep the madness at bay. They were a haven for each other, until it all fell apart.

"The rooms beneath the sea are amazing." Orla, wide-eyed with wonderment, had joined them. "I could stay there all day."

"Welcome, anytime," Ross declared. "We're just putting the finishing touches to a café below sea level at the harbour end. You'll love that."

"Will there be a way out?" Orla asked. Ross frowned. "So I can swim the other side of the glass walls."

The men exchanged a look.

"Not everyone is as good a swimmer as you, Orla," Greer said. "The last thing Ross wants is people coming in and out of his glass walls, flooding the place." Greer made a mental note; this side of the harbour needed to be out of bounds for any future sisterly expeditions.

Ross checked his watch.

"Excuse me, Archie's speech." He strode through the crowd to where the actor was holding court.

Unsurprisingly, Fenella had swept Cassandra into an embrace, declaring it had been far too long, and they were well into some hilarious reminisce when a tap on the shoulder made Cassandra swing round. Archie gave a small bow.

"You're not going to ask me to dance, are you?" Cassandra was shocked, he had caught her off guard again.

"Not if you prefer I didn't." His delicious voice was a whisper. "But I *would* like to ask you something."

She gave an exaggerated sigh, then stopped herself. Her petulance was childish. Unreasonable.

"You'll have to excuse me." Fenella dissolved into the crowd.

Cassandra forced her lips into a tight smile.

"Please hear me out." His usually dancing eyes gazed at her steadily. "Whatever I've done to make you despise me, I beg your forgiveness. I know this is utterly selfish, but I would prefer not to leave my homeland with someone I once loved hating me."

A flash of heat scorched her chest.

"You're so dramatic, honestly..."

But his eyes bored into hers, pleading. "Cassandra,

please."

She tried to speak but no words came. For in truth, it was she who should be apologising to him.

She looked down and taking his hand in hers, squeezed it briefly, walking quickly away.

Archie watched her go, tears of relief in his eyes. He had broken through. It was not over yet.

The lights strewn across the terrace shimmered like low-slung stars, trailing the steps to a small, private beach. The last of the Chinese lanterns had been released into the sky and a smooth jazz quartet joined the piano player on stage.

Although Rai's bad habits were in the past, he still allowed himself an occasional cigarette, and taking the opportunity for some quiet time had made his escape. But there was someone else on the beach, sitting on an upturned boat, gazing at the sky as the lanterns melded with the stars before drifting back to earth.

"Not given everything up then?" Greer had taken off her beautiful shoes, burying her toes in the cool sand. He smiled when he realised it was her, he had been hoping their paths would cross again before the evening ended. He held the cigarette towards her.

"Nothing more than a few strands of tobacco. Care to share?"

"No thanks," she replied. "It's still poison."

Rai shrugged. "True enough. And your body's a temple, of course."

"At least it's not a bike shed!" A reference to the legendary many lovers he had taken over the years.

"Not entirely fair, Greer. The last article I read on the subject reported I slept with hundreds of women. If that were the case, I'd still be in bed!"

"With a woman?" She gave him a look.

"Not at all, with a broken back!"

She started to laugh. Rai had never taken that aspect of

stardom too seriously. The music, yes but not the trappings; the limos, the groupies, the endless supply of booze and drugs. He had always been serious about his work though, genuinely enjoying the pleasure it gave.

That is, until Greer left.

After that, it all seemed to spiral out of control. Ending in that dreadful night when Mojo Morrisey, their drummer, had been killed in a car crash in Los Angeles and the whole band had been arrested.

The darkest of times.

"Are you going to enlighten me about the meeting I've been invited to attend next week?" she asked, changing the subject. She knew he had been thinking about Mojo. This was where they used to rehearse in the early days, long before it belonged to a smart hotel. It was safe on the beach, no one could hear them play out of tune, sing the wrong words, argue over nothing. Happy days.

Mojo had been in the original line-up and there were many in Rosshaven, including Mojo's family, who blamed Rai for what had happened. Rai was in charge. He should have taken care of him, Mojo was young, impressionable. But worse than that, Rai blamed himself. It should never have happened. Not on his watch.

Rai took a deep draw of the cigarette, clipped it and put it in his pocket.

"Just tying up loose ends. You know, legal stuff."

"There's still stuff needs tying up? Stitched up more like," she said, half under her breath, and reaching down, shook the sand from her shoes. "Well, I certainly hope it isn't going to cost me anything because I just don't have it. I was the one who was ripped off, don't forget, the one who never got paid."

"Let's wait till the meeting, Greer, you can have your say then." He started towards the steps. "Right now, I'm due on stage."

"Seriously?" she called after him.

"Yep. Special request. Archie wants a song before he goes,

SECRETS OF THE SHELL SISTERS

can't let him down."

"This is I have to see!" Greer said, running barefoot to catch up with the once love of her life.

Rai was a total professional; Greer could tell he had rehearsed with the band as soon as they played the opening bars of one of their biggest hits. She was impressed, the songs had new arrangements, softer acoustic versions more suited to a one-man show. She was even enjoying it until Archie sidled up beside her and said loudly,

"Why don't you give him a hand, my darling? It would surely gladden this old fella's heart to see you back together again, if only for one song."

"Not even for you, Archie." She smiled into his mischievous grey eyes. "Those days are long gone. Besides, he's doing fine without me."

But someone close by heard Archie's request and in seconds the crowd had started chanting her name. Ignoring her protests, the swell of people propelled Greer forwards and when Rai leaned towards her, hand outstretched, the old excitement fluttered in the pit of her stomach and suddenly she was on stage. The sea of expectant faces took her breath away, and in that instant, she realised this was still one of her favourite places in the world.

"'Remember'?" he said into her ear above the roar of the crowd. "Shall we do 'Remember'?"

Greer nodded as Rai handed her the mic and taking his guitar counted her in.

The audience fell silent as Greer's exquisite voice filled the night air and the poignancy of the lyrics, telling of a long lost love, cast a spell over all who listened. Rai played the haunting theme beautifully, harmonising the chorus, lips close to hers as they shared the mic. He stood back to let Greer sing the final lines, as she always had, without accompaniment.

"And when nothing else is left,

And all I loved is gone,
Your home is in my heart,
The memory lingers on."

A half heartbeat of silence and the place exploded, applause, cheers of delight and whoops of joy. Cameras flashed as people held their phones aloft, capturing the moment when Rai Muir wrapped Greer Morgan in his arms and whispered,

"You're still amazing."

And she pretended not to hear, taking her bow and blowing kisses to Archie, who decided now was a very good time to steal quietly away.

Declan was still clapping as she walked towards him, grinning broadly, eyes alight.

"Awesome, just awesome. Jeez, your voice is as good as it ever was no, actually better. The rest has done you good, you look amazing too – haven't had any 'work done' have you?"

"Watch it!" She punched him playfully on the shoulder.

He opened his arms for an embrace, Rai stepped between them. "Don't mind him, the old flatterer, never changed."

"Seriously, Rai, that was amazing. Look at everyone." Declan's glance swept the crowd. "They're buzzing, can't stop talking about it, you two, back together, up there!"

"It was a one-off, Declan. A song for an old friend," Greer said.

"Okay, but what about this for an idea ... let's do a farewell gig. We never did one, so it would be genuine, just look at this crowd, it would be a complete sell-out!"

Rai shook his head.

"No, wait," Declan insisted. "A fundraiser, we'd raise millions for your favourite charity!"

"Or your pension scheme?" Greer rolled her eyes.

"I'm serious!" Declan was exasperated. "It's a brilliant idea, come on, you'd make so many people happy."

"And you rich!" Greer teased.

"Ah, stop!" Declan ran his hands through his hair. A few of the guests were hovering, autograph hunters back in the day, fans requesting selfies now. "Look at them! The time is *right!*"

Greer glanced at Rai. His eyes were dark, shut down.

"We've had our time, leave it now." And giving Greer a look that made her heart clench, Rai left.

While Orla had availed herself of her sister's beautiful rendition to dance blissfully with a most delighted-to-be-danced-with Dr James, Cassandra excused herself from Nagle's watchful eye to repair her face. This penchant for tears was becoming expensive, the amount of eye makeup she was getting through.

"Look at me," she told herself. "Dabbing my eyes at the sight of those two on stage together. Thought I'd be long past that kind of sentimentality." And relieved to be alone she stood for a long moment, wishing she had danced with Archie Fitzgerald and wondering for the thousandth time if she should just get everything off her chest, tell him the truth about their child. The one that she had given up. The one not even her sisters knew about.

"Oh, stop it!" she barked at herself. "You made your decision, no good would come of him knowing now. Leave it, for pity's sake." And willing her anxiety away, Cassandra repaired her face and painted on a smile, little realising that this particular secret would be revealed soon enough – except perhaps to the most important person of all, Archie himself.

Old Love Boat

When they returned to Manorcliff in the early hours only Wolfe and Tone stirred at their arrival. Nagle, an early starter, was pleased to bid the sisters goodnight and Cassandra equally relieved to see him go, her head too full for convivial conversation.

Undressing in her immaculate bedroom, Cassandra took fright at the sight of herself in the mirror. And little wonder, how else would she look, her heart sore with the memory of old jealousies, her soul bereft, mourning a lost love.

What a waste, what a sad and wasted life she and her stupid pride had forced herself to lead.

The waning moon cast a cool glow on the throw across the bed, wisps of cloud drifted by, reflected in the moonlight, the night was soft and calm, but it did little to slow the rumble of rage in the pit of her. Too strong to be quelled it grew to a torrent and burst from her in a violent roar and by the time her fury was spent, every book, picture and ornament had been hurled to the floor.

Greer sat up in bed, listening as the rampage took hold, crash after crash and wailing, like a banshee caught in the eye of a storm; she feared it would never end and although she wanted to go to her, she dare not. Whatever her sister was dealing with was private, an expulsion of her own demons, something Greer understood perfectly well.

Finally unable to bear it, Greer threw back the covers and as she did the whirlwind abated and the house grew still. She waited. Silence. And feeling her elder sister's pain she lay in the dark, silent tears of pity wetting the hair of the little mermaid

SECRETS OF THE SHELL SISTERS

doll on the pillow beside her.

Cassandra left for Galty House at first light. Leela, unsurprised by her early arrival, pointed to the jetty beyond the summer house.

"He's taking the boat out, be quick."

"I can't go with him. I need to get back."

Leela arched an eyebrow. Within seconds she watched as Cassandra raced through the kitchen garden, the little gate and down to the shore, looking for all the world like the young girl she once was.

He waved her aboard, as if he had been waiting for her to arrive before setting sail. They were on the water now beyond Phoenix Island, motoring at a gentle pace, enjoying the warm breeze, the heat from the sun.

"I was saddened to hear … you're leaving … you know," Cassandra said, wanting to acknowledge it somehow.

"Liar!" Archie exclaimed. "You've wanted me out of your hair for years!"

She flashed him a look. "That's not true!"

"It is so true! You can't stand the sight of me, everyone says so." He was laughing now he had her riled. "You have me cursed, leaving is my only escape."

"Stop that, Archie Fitzgerald! I've never put a curse on any man or beast."

"You don't have to, just a flash of those glittering eyes could turn a mere mortal to stone. I should know, I've had enough of your withering looks over the years." His smile was sad now. "I've tried to apologise, make reparation, many times, you do know that, don't you, Cass?"

She softened, gazing at him with affection, remembering a time long ago when a garrulous, gangly young Archie would call up to Manorcliff, the latest Rolling Stones single barely off the boat from the UK – ordered through the *Melody Maker* – and beg to give it a turn on the record player in the Moon Room. The acoustics were brilliant up there and so remote, you could get away with full volume, providing the 'paying guests' did not complain.

She always said yes, Archie was impossible to refuse, so charming and downright fascinating, and different from the others. He would ask about *her,* what was she reading, cooking, where had she been sailing, swimming – there is nothing more seductive than someone being interested in you.

He enquired about the shells, where were they from, were there any messages? And she would rebuke him, insisting he should not mock what he could never understand, and with a twinkle in his eye, he would tell her how he would love the chance to understand her, inside and out. And she would chastise him for being too forward and to please stop trying to slip his hand up her top, especially when she closed her eyes to Mick Jagger's version of 'Ruby Tuesday'.

Archie would laugh, totally unabashed, and tell her all the things he dreamt of doing if she would only give him half a chance and 'for pity's sake leave something hanging off the balcony so a poor fellow, half-crazed with love could climb up and steal a kiss'.

"You read too many plays," she would reprimand him, "Half-crazed with lust more like!" pinching the front of his jeans to make him jump. "It's more than a kiss you're after and me just a slip of a girl!"

Which was true, although she thought herself a very grownup fifteen-year-old and Archie every inch the man of her dreams at just eighteen.

He was looking at her now, under his eyelashes, his tangle of strawberry blond hair threaded through with silver strands blowing wildly in the breeze. A half-smile teased his lips.

"Oh, Cassandra, how I loved you!"

"A crush was all it was, for both of us really."

"Never!" he declared. "I adored you. I'd have sailed the seven seas, fought dragons, slaughtered pirates, you only had to say the word!"

She was laughing now, his swashbuckling antics along the deck causing him to stumble. He grabbed at a stay to steady himself, missed and fell back, landing heavily. Cassandra flew to him; he lay twisted, she tried to move him, he cried out.

"What is it?"

He stiffened, regaining his composure.

"Sorry, my love. Awkward fall. Fucking dragons, sneaky bastards, swat you with their tails when you least expect it."

She helped him up, eyes watering as he winced in pain. She settled him beside her, placing cushions around him, pulling a jacket over his shoulders.

"You're getting on a bit for those kinds of antics." She handed him a beaker of red wine.

He rubbed his elbow. "I probably am a bit." And resting against the side of the boat, he pulled her to him to kiss her and she felt the kiss against her scalp, searing into her, igniting her senses, taking her back to her very first love and the very first time. And snuggling up against him, she let herself relax, moving gently with the ebb and flow of the water, her natural home.

"If only, Cassandra," she heard him whisper. "If only ..."

"Stop now." She took his hand in hers.

"I know I hurt you. I know you've held it against me all this time, but it was never meant, Cass."

"Hush, Archie. A long time ago, leave it now."

"I may have, back then, given you the impression I didn't care."

"Impression? Archie, you didn't care and why would you? You were on the precipice of your career, lauded by the world, the press, celebrities, everyone wanted to be with you, in all the papers, tipped to be the next James Bond."

"Landing that would surely have sent me over the edge, I was pretty full of myself as it was."

"At least you didn't make a show of the whole country!"

"Really?" Archie sounded disappointed. "I hoped I had!"

"You had your moments, but you were relatively well

behaved compared with the carry-on of others I could mention!"

She was talking about Rai and Greer. At the height of their infamy, she had asked Archie to intervene; could he persuade the warring pair to reconcile, come home, lick their wounds and start again? It was not to be, and Archie had enough going on.

"Ah, a lot of that was hype, being a 'bad boy' all part of it."

"And a bad girl too, I suppose?" Why she still felt the shame of it she had no idea, everybody else had moved on. "Anyway, you were too busy to play Bond."

"Or get married and have a family. I regret that now, Cass. To be too busy for that was wrong."

Cassandra closed her eyes briefly, battling her conscience yet again. But she had made her decision all those years ago, now was not the time.

"You should have few regrets – and now a new beginning, with a new love. Is she truly wonderful?"

He looked at her. "She is. I'm swept away by her. She's easy, she's difficult, she's fabulous and it's all truly terrifying." His eyes shone. "And I have to give it a go, my best shot. I want that precious thing, one last time and forever."

Cassandra took his hand and kissed it. "I understand, I really do. We all deserve that. You're a brave and lovely man and I'm proud of you and your bold decision." She sat up, the sun glimmering on the horizon, the breeze causing waves to flutter against the boat. "And now time to get you and your beautiful boat home, Mr Fitzgerald," she said, placing glasses and crockery in the cooler bag.

He went to move.

"Stay where you are," she ordered. "I'm well able to take her in."

"It's a long way." He gazed towards the harbour, Galty's beach and boat house out of sight. "We could move closer to shore." He indicated the island. "Drop anchor, spend the night. Very comfortable down below and a long time since I gave you breakfast."

She burst out laughing. "Archie Fitzgerald, you've never changed! Incorrigible, so you are."

"Not so much," he smiled. "I'm very selective these days, true loves only."

"But you had so many." She busied herself coiling stays, checking the sails.

He tutted. "Come below, see for yourself. I won't pounce, I promise."

It was warm in the cabin. Archie turned on the lamps; sheltered from the elements, all was quiet. They snuggled into the settee, the gentle movement of the boat rocking them.

"I heard you," Cassandra whispered. "That's what hurt the most. You told Fenella you only slept with me to make her jealous. That's why you made a great show of giving me the famous Fitzgerald ruby for my eighteenth birthday, it was all for her."

"No!" Archie jumped up, shocked. "Not true!"

"You can't deny what you said."

"I was a fool. A young fool. Fenella and I have always had a turbulent relationship and yes, we love each other but not as lovers, siblings, close as siblings. I was vain, immature, stupid. I never, *ever* meant to hurt you."

"I tried calling the house, but knew I was wasting my time. It was when Fenella ran away and you'd gone to find her and the baby to bring them home. I'd put the phone down whenever someone picked it up, I was making a fool of myself and needed to leave you alone."

Archie sighed. "Oh, the things we do ... things we believed."

"Some people thought Fenella's baby was yours."

Archie poured them both another drink, the cosiness of the cabin warming them.

"Another great Rosshaven myth." He shook his head. "We know, the ones who count anyway. The fact that this has never been confirmed or denied is what it is. If Fenella insists it remains one of life's mysteries, that's up to her." He gazed unseeingly into his glass. "All I ever tried to do was make sure those I love know they are loved, and Fenella and her child could always make Galty their home, no matter what."

"You've always been praised for that, Archie, and you've a special relationship with Fenella's child, don't you?" She bit her lip.

"Indeed." He smiled. "Her mother can be slightly self-obsessed."

"Most actors are, I believe." Cassandra poked him in the ribs.

"That's true," he agreed. "But I've done my bit, had my day. Good God, if they turn me into a 'national treasure' I'll throw myself in the drink!" He started to laugh. "I suppose I look like one now too?"

"Never!" she told him. "You'll always be a scene-stealer!" And as she squeezed his hand, he lifted her fingers to his lips.

"You're being kind, Cassandra, so like you. Kind-hearted, hard-working, still running the old place, Nana would be very proud of you – cantankerous old bag that she was. They should all be grateful we never ran away together, it was always my plan. Do you remember when I asked you to run away with me?" Archie was gazing at her intently, a wicked glint in his eye.

"I do not!" She grinned back.

"Yes, you do, I asked you where you would go in the world if we could run away together and you said ..."

"I want to go to all the famous places in the world to swim."

"A most unusual request but that's what I always loved about you, Cass, so different, so special."

"Niagara Falls, the lake in the middle of Central Park, the Black Sea, Lake Como, Amsterdam's canals, imagine swimming around Venice, backstroke under the Rialto Bridge ... heaven!"

"Did you ever go?"

"Of course not."

"Ah, couldn't bear to go without me, eh?" Archie smiled.

"Not at all, I couldn't go, I had to run the hotel and besides I couldn't leave my sisters, what would they have done without me, and me off on a grand tour, not a care in the world."

"Well, Greer was always so wrapped up in herself, she wouldn't have noticed and Orla, collecting her shells and singing on the beach, sure she wouldn't have cared, not till she was hungry anyway." He kissed her hair. He meant no malice; he loved her sisters too, she knew that. "I was genuine, when I asked you to run away with me and the next thing I knew you'd gone off to some college in England, without so much as a 'by your leave', I was devastated!"

"You were not! And I needed to get on with my studies – you were a very bad influence."

He propped himself up on his elbow. "I often wished you'd said yes, I felt as if we were unfinished somehow ..."

"Ah, Archie, you had your whole life to get on with, your brilliant career, imagine if that hadn't happened, the world would be a lesser place."

"Really? Do you believe that?"

"I do. I've seen your Hamlet. Haunting, it was."

"I could still have been Hamlet with you, Cassandra."

"I was tied, Archie, you know that."

"Ah, the tyranny of responsibility, I do understand."

"Maybe now you do," Cassandra wanted to say. *"But not when you needed to be wild and free, to be Hamlet, Aramis, Sherlock Holmes and all the other glorious characters you've played over the years."* She touched his much-lauded cheekbone. *How I loved you, Archie Fitzgerald,* she thought but did not say and as usual in Archie's company, he had her bewitched.

He leaned across, brushing back strands of hair from her face. "Oh, what a glorious union we'd have made, Cassandra. The joining of two ancient warrior tribes, the legendary Fitzgeralds and the indefatigable Morgans!"

"I think you'll find we're far more legendary than you. You're only blow-ins compared with us."

Archie laughed so hard he nearly fell off the couch.

"Come on, enough now." Cassandra stood. "Time to get back."

Now on deck, she went to the helm and started the engine.

"Ah, Cass," Archie pleaded. "Stay on the water with me tonight. Just one more time. You always loved the lull of the sea, the stretch of endless sky."

"Wind's getting up," she insisted, turning the wheel as they pushed through the water.

"No, it's not," he replied. "Besides, there's a sky light in the captain's quarters, so many stars to see, then the glorious dawn just there for the taking."

He put an arm about her.

"I'm sorry, Cass, truly sorry, I didn't mean to abandon you," he whispered. She continued to steer towards the harbour.

He sighed. "It was a strange time for all of us."

Cassandra did not comment. Unsure if she was included in the 'us', although she ought to be, but Archie would not know why, of course.

She pushed the engine up a gear; it was a fabulous boat, went like a dream, she had never been in control of anything so powerful.

"I'd forgotten how at home you are on the water. A natural, on it and in it, I seem to recall." He slipped his other arm around her.

Dusk was seeping into the corners of the sky, charcoal clouds edged with amber light as the last of the sun trembled on the rippling sea. She gazed up, the moon rising, a pale gold stain hanging low, stars glittering not far behind.

"It's so different out here, the sky's so close and we're so small, it's as if we don't count at all."

"We don't," Archie said softly.

Cassandra gave him a grin. "Okay, you asked for it! Strap yourself in, big boy, I'm taking you for a ride!"

And they sped away, the long-lost lovers beneath a starry sky, a final turn around the bay.

Travelling Companions

S earching for a window seat so she could follow the curve of the coast to the city, Greer wondered if Rai was on the train too. Irked she had not heard from him since their impromptu performance, she was even more annoyed with herself for being bothered. Even so, she checked her phone. No calls, no messages.

The train was due into Connolly Street Station at eight forty-five, meaning she had some time to bask in the bustle of the city. She had been in such a rush to get to Rosshaven when she arrived, she had barely acknowledged the capital and was so exhausted by the time she boarded the train heading south, she slept most of the way, missing the glorious scenery the winding journey threw in for free.

She checked the list of attendees; apart from Rai, there was a representative from the record company, an accountant and two lawyers, including the band's solicitor Anthony Mayhew and a specialist in intellectual property. That is what these meetings were about, why the creative force behind their most successful songs had never been properly paid for her contribution to the band's fortune.

Greer sighed. The battle for lost royalties had raged for years and she had long ago stopped attending such meetings, mainly because Rai rarely did and if he was there, his version of events varied so wildly from her own it was a farce. Of course, their versions were different, Rai had spent most of the 1980s on another planet, was the truth of it.

Relieved to find a seat, Greer took a file from the briefcase borrowed from Cassandra and started to read. As well as an appointment with the bank manager, ahead of meeting Rai and the legal team she was seeing Humphrey for lunch. This meant she could catch up with an old friend while seeking advice – because whatever the outcome Humphrey could always be relied upon to proffer some much-needed wisdom.

Now settled, Greer realised her seat was free because the man reading the newspaper opposite had his feet on it. Removing them as she sat, Janis Petrova lowered the broadsheet to fix her with a grim smile.

"Business in Dublin?" he asked.

"If I have, it's nothing to do with you," she replied, recovering quickly.

He folded the newspaper slowly.

"Oh, I think it is. Especially if you have property that does not belong to you. Perhaps you are in the hope that the heat has died down and it will be easier to move on."

"I've no idea what you're talking about."

She felt a thud on the seat. She looked down. Janis had thrust his boot between her legs.

"I searched the office, his London home, the cottage in Norfolk and then it made sense, he gave them to you." He was still smiling. "Hand them over and there won't be any trouble, they just want them back, not any harm done."

Greer swung her leg over his foot, pushing it roughly off the seat.

"You've lost the plot. Why don't you piss off back to Latvia and leave me alone," she said equally pleasantly, eyes glaring.

"You know what I'm talking about. The last trip. Payment for services to be rendered. The trade deal that cannot now happen, now your boyfriend is no longer in high office. Maybe best he does not recover." He crossed himself, his cold stare never leaving her face.

She did not flinch. "As I said, no idea."

Yet something was beginning to jangle. Something Alistair said, just before he stopped the cab and disappeared into the black Jaguar with the official number plate.

"If I'm delayed, carry on. I'll be there as soon as I can."
He had kissed her briefly. A *see-you-later kiss*. But then he said
something odd. "Whatever happens, take care of your smile,
Darogaya."

Darogaya – Russian for darling. His pet name for her
during their last trip to St Petersburg.

Greer had visited the historic Russian city with the band
years before and had jumped at the chance to return. Today
the former Russian capital was a celebrated tourist destination
and Greer was enthralled, delighting in the grand ballrooms
of the Winter Place, the historic artworks housed in the
Hermitage and the elegant waterside home of the notorious
Rasputin, complete with private theatre.

She bought hand-painted boxes and a fabulous fur hat
at the market beside the church of The Saviour on the Spilled
Blood, where she had stood in candlelight, inhaling incense as
a guide explained the ancient paintings and relics and asking,
even though it was now a museum, if she wanted them to pray
together, moving her almost to tears.

She had adored the luxurious Grand Hotel Europe with
its subterranean pool where she stole a secret late-night swim
in its smooth warm water. Breakfast there was a veritable
feast; smoked fish with caviar, pickled eggs and wafer-thin
ham taken with a shot of fiery vodka, setting them up for a
day of sightseeing. And before dinner, diamond earrings – a
surprise gift from her lover – sparkling in her ears, combining
with the discovery that the Russians made their own excellent
champagne, only added to the glamour of a truly memorable
trip.

Greer loved everything about the place, except perhaps
the lurking presence of the ever watchful Janis, and however
romantic Saint Petersburg had been, the trip to this wonderful
city was to herald the beginning of the end.

Known as the 'Venice of the North' St Petersburg is built
on a myriad of canals and waterways, giving the city a real
sense of the sea, something else she adored about the place.

They had been invited to a cocktail party, hosted by a well-known oligarch on board his luxury yacht, which would give Alistair a chance to network with diplomats from some of the lesser-known Baltic states, an opportunity to forge the ever-important strategic alliances. She could see it all so vividly …

Greer was dancing with their host, who despite an education at one of the UK's most lauded public schools spoke in a heavily accented monotone when Alistair cut in, remarking he rarely had the chance to dance with his charming colleague. The other man gave her up reluctantly, leaving them with a leery grin. She nestled into Alistair's shoulder, falling into an easy rhythm, their slow dance long practised.

"It's like the 1960s, don't you think?" She eyed the waitresses, all cleavage and eyelashes.

"Don't be rude. Our host has his faults but he's a very generous man, a very generous man indeed."

"Sounds like you've made a deal you're particularly pleased about."

Alistair, a workaholic, was already hugely successful but his role in government had given him new ambition, another area in which to shine.

"Let's just say he's made the trip very worthwhile."

"Well, that's good news, isn't it?" Greer asked, for there was something unnerving about Alistair that night.

"You're right. However, it's bad news for us, my darling." He pressed his lips against her forehead as they swayed. She pushed back, looking him in the eye.

"I'm letting you go."

"Letting me go?" His words left her winded. "You're dumping me in the middle of one of the most romantic cities in the world?" she asked, her voice rising.

"Don't make a scene," he said coldly. "We need you out of here as soon as possible."

"But why?"

He continued to smile sweetly. "It's complicated. I had no idea how well-known you are here. Quite the celebrity."

"I did tell you. We were huge. One of the few bands who came here."

"I appreciate that now we've been all over the media, Greer Morgan, the pop star back in Russia. Something I had not envisaged, an unwelcome spotlight in many respects but luckily your former career has provided you with insurance."

Greer's eyes widened. "What on earth are you talking about?"

"Our host has proposed you stay on while I return to the UK and fulfil my part of the deal."

"You mean I'm to be a hostage?"

"Not quite, let's say your visit has been extended ..."

"Surely, you haven't agreed to such a thing?"

"It's ludicrous I know but I had no choice. Our saving grace is you're famous here, they like you, which means we have people on our side. That's why I'm going to very calmly dance you towards the exit and when the band stops playing and everyone stands to applaud, you slip out on the deck, ditch the heels and run as fast as you can to the bow of the boat. Janis will be there, when you get to the marina, someone is waiting to take you to the airport."

"To go where?"

"Back to London. You'll be safe there – I'll make sure of it."

Alistair carried on dancing, moving her across the floor. Greer's heart started to flutter. He could not be serious, surely this was a bad joke. She glanced up at him, eyes closed, a half-smile on his face, as if lost in the music.

"Just do as I say, all will be well," he whispered.

Less than two minutes later, shoes abandoned, Greer was racing along the deck. The superyacht glowed in the darkness, she heard the engine of the rib firing up and looking down into the black water, saw Janis at the helm. For a split second she was tempted, tempted to dive into the deep and swim away, hide in an underwater cave, search out a slipstream and when the coast was clear head for home.

"Quick. Come." He gestured abruptly. She dipped under the

294

rail and gripping the sides of the steel-cold steps, descended into the boat.

"You in?" Janis barked.

She barely replied before he slammed the vessel into reverse and they were away, bouncing over the water at breakneck speed. She clung to the side, the wind whipping through her silk gown, spray wetting her face like tears. But she was too stunned to weep, silently grateful for Janis's expertise as a boatman, swerving through the waves until they arrived at the pontoon. A man she recognised from the Embassy was waiting for them.

"Your bag's in the car, Ms Morgan, you can change on the way."

She was trembling with cold, teeth rattling. Janis had already turned the boat back towards the yacht.

"Do you know what's going on?" she asked, pulling on jeans as they screeched through the city streets to the airport.

"Just following orders, ma'am, you're on the next flight to Heathrow. A colleague will meet you there. Get you home safely. Nothing to worry about." He gave a tight smile. They all looked pretty worried to her.

The week following her return to London had been odd to say the least. Greeted at the airport as promised by one of Alistair's many assistants – who clearly spent a lot of time in the gym – once inside the car with heavily tinted windows, she asked what was going on.

"I'm to take you to your apartment," he told her, not taking his eyes off the road.

"And?"

"That's it."

"No other instructions from Mr McKeiver?"

"Nothing I'm at liberty to discuss," came the reply.

Greer shrugged. If Alistair had arranged her 'protection' it would be discreet and impenetrable. He was a man of his word.

And then, at the end of a week in which her emotions

ranged from feeling she was being watched every minute to being convinced she had been totally abandoned, Alistair called.

"Sorry about all that unpleasantness. You're okay, aren't you?"

She did not know what to say or think, he sounded so calm.

"Unpleasantness? I've been terrified nearly out of my mind. What the hell is going on?"

"Just business, Greer, I'll make it up to you, I promise."

"Alistair, have you gone completely mad?"

He laughed.

"Wouldn't like to run away with me, would you?

"You *have* gone mad!"

And the next thing she knew, she was packing again, this time going west, New York to be precise.

As the train pulled into Bray, Greer checked the time, wondering if she could jump off and grab a cab to Dublin. It would be expensive, but anything would be better than sitting opposite the melodramatically menacing Latvian with the bad breath.

Janis was still glowering at her when the door at the far end of the carriage opened. An extraordinarily tall man, arms folded across his broad chest, started walking slowly towards them. Greer watched as Janis's face changed, first recognition, then fear.

"I hope you have what they want," Janis snarled, standing. "For all our sakes." And when he joined the man, she watched as they sat huddled over a map of Dublin, eyes shielded by dark glasses, their words blurred by the rattle of the train against the tracks.

A Settlement

Bemused as Greer was by the disturbing encounter with Janis on the train, she needed to focus. It was her turn to put family affairs first.

As for Rai, the business with the band should have been dealt with years ago, filed away in a drawer labelled 'Do not open', a Pandora's box of painful memories, and if there was more bad news to come, she would simply walk away. She needed all her energy to save Manorcliff.

As she moved swiftly through the station, the breeze fluttered the scattering of seahorses on the pale green silk of her favourite dress, making her realise she had been so busy being hands-on at Manorcliff since becoming a full-time member of the team, she rarely dressed up. Catching a glimpse of herself in a window, she flicked her thick mane back behind her ears, admiring the shell earrings Orla had insisted she wear to the city; today was going to be a good day, she would make sure of it.

The city was already hot as Greer followed the boundary wall of Trinity College curving left, crossing the road she turned right into Dawson Street and then into Fitzwilliam Place. Cool cream awnings stretched out from elegant Georgian buildings shading the pavement, the rich aroma of fresh coffee and almonds drifted up from bistro tables filled with workers and shoppers, the hubbub soothing her, slowing her stride.

She had an hour before meeting Rai and the record company lawyers, enough time to go to the bank, then take a stroll through St Stephen's Green, a ritual she had embraced since childhood, acknowledging the glorious day Miss Finn had taken her little art class up to the capital to paint and picnic beside the lake with the swans.

The time she and her sisters had disappeared beneath the water, Cassandra and Orla keen to discover if they could breathe in the lake as well as they could in the sea and her sitting on the bank, too frightened to stay too long beneath the surface for fear she had not the gift. And when they returned, drawings and remnants of picnic splayed out on the grass, Miss Finn with not a word of reprimand simply brushed out their hair to dry, almost as if she had expected them to swim deep in the lake, as she herself might have done once – perhaps.

Moira Williams-O'Brien seemed startlingly young for a bank manager, Greer considered, as she was ushered into a room the size of a confessional.

"I hope you haven't come out of your way to see me," the young woman in the linen suit said. "So much easier to do everything online these days, we're geared up for it, you see."

She spoke as if Greer's visit was an irritating interruption.

"I appreciate that," Greer replied. "But as a long-standing client, I thought it best to meet you, especially as I've some very exciting plans to discuss."

The young woman gave Greer a stiff smile, reluctantly clearing files from a chair to offer her a seat.

"Of course. We're pleased to have ..." She checked the name on the screen. "...the Morgans as clients for so long. Now, you want to talk about the business, The Manor House, isn't that it?"

"Manorcliff Hotel," Greer corrected.

"Oh yes, in Kinsale."

"Rosshaven, County Wexford."

"Ah," the young woman turned back to the computer. "Did I get a copy of the latest accounts?"

"I've a copy here." Greer passed the papers across the slice of grey desk.

The woman's French manicure tapped the keyboard urgently. "I thought I had them on email?"

"Better to look at them together, so I can explain, yes?" Greer said hopefully.

The manager's face darkened. Greer was not sure if it was the information or the fact it was presented on paper that she found displeasing.

"Now, what I think …" Greer offered. The manager raised her hand.

"If I could just finish," she said sweetly.

She read on, turning the pages without comment. Greer could feel the atmosphere change. If it had been cool to begin with, it was icy now.

The manager looked up, removing her designer spectacles to gaze sincerely at the older woman.

"Based on these figures, Ms Morgan, I'm afraid the proposal's just not viable."

"Oh, but it is, you see …"

The woman raised her hand again.

"The business is making a loss, that loss has increased year on year for the past three years and some mortgage payments have been missed."

"We do have *some* capital," Greer insisted. "Just need to reinvest, make the improvements and we'll be back on track, that's why we need to re-mortgage."

"Re-mortgage, again? But there's no way you'll be able to make the repayments. I'm sure this has been dealt with." She was at the screen. "Yes, your application was declined, we sent you an email to that effect last week, I can see it here."

Greer sighed. It appeared her email address had been made redundant along with everything else.

"I'm so sorry, we're unable to help." The bank manager moved to the door, time for her long-standing customer to go.

Greer appreciated there might be some difficulty persuading

the bank to support her plan but to be irrevocably turned down was a blow. She stood on the granite steps of the building, the ebb and flow of passers-by merging before her.

Shit.

Nothing for it but to activate Plan B.

Problem. There was no Plan B.

Shit again.

Greer still had three quarters of an hour to kill. She could either walk to St Stephen's Green, park herself on a bench and gather her thoughts or find the nearest pub, invest in a very large vodka and see if that helped inspire a solution.

Davy Byrnes was in Duke Street, the scene of many a night of gaiety and laughter. Hostelry of choice for the in-crowd, Davy Byrnes played host to musicians chasing a gig, agents and record company executives sealing deals, and models and photographers either just flying in or just flying out; the buzz was always intoxicating.

She pushed the door. Two well-dressed ladies with Brown Thomas carrier bags were having coffee in a corner, and a man in a pinstriped suit sipped a lone pint at the bar. It was still early.

"Looking for someone?" A voice behind her.

She swung round. Rai Muir gave her a grin. She let the door close.

"Great place, wasn't it?" He glanced up at the sign, gold lettering on a blood-red background, tables and chairs studded the pavement. "Such memories."

"You can remember? Well, that's something."

"Some things I'll never forget," he said, and she felt it again, the warmth of his voice stirring her blood.

"Shall we go?" He offered his arm. "If we get the meeting over early, I could take you to lunch?"

She took his arm as they walked along Grafton Street, past the street musician strangling Bowie's 'Golden Years', past the flower sellers, the scent of lilies heavy in the air, and she softened, it felt so natural.

"I'm seeing Humphrey after," she told him.

"I know," he said. "So am I."

The meeting took place in what had once been a gracious family home facing St Stephen's Green. It had all seen better days, even down to the shiny suit of the elderly man ushering them in.

"Everyone's here," he announced, opening the door to the library, Joe Sweeny's office for over twenty-five years.

Joe was the first to greet her, face weathered from foreign golf courses, his balding pate and stocky frame little resembling the youth once considered the 'wild man' of the music industry. Then Anthony Mayhew shook hands, another member of the backroom team. Anthony was an ally but without any real evidence to support her claims, he had been side-lined over the years, so much so that at the last meeting she attended Anthony had said nothing at all.

Greer did not recognise anyone else. Having withdrawn from the spotlight long ago, she wondered if any of the others were even born when their biggest hit was number one in the charts, and they appeared on *Top of the Pops* every Thursday evening for what seemed like forever.

She took her seat.

"I'll get straight to it," Joe said, sitting beside her, chairs arranged in an oddly shaped circle, so everyone appeared on equal par. "As you know, we're winding everything up. Rights, intellectual property, shares in other businesses, the apartment in Los Angeles, the lot. It's been a long, slow process but we're nearly there."

She looked at Rai. "I didn't think there was anything left. Nothing that had anything to do with me, anyway."

He sat back, crossing his long legs at the ankles, the way he did when he wanted to appear relaxed.

"Hear me out, Greer," Joe continued. "We need to make sure everyone is treated fairly and that includes you."

She gave Rai the wide-eyed look usually reserved for her

sisters. He pulled a face back. Anthony coughed. They needed to take this seriously as there was quite a lot of money involved.

"Greer, when you left the band it was done in haste, things could've been handled more equitably." Joe spoke again.

"I didn't leave, Joe. I quit but I couldn't leave until we'd completed our tour dates, then I was sacked. Didn't even have access to the bank account." She said this in a monotone, having used these words in similar scenarios many times before. She looked at Rai again. "What's changed?"

"Let the man speak," Rai told her, joining his hands together as if in prayer, lips against his fingertips thoughtfully.

"Proof you wrote a large proportion of the band's early material has come to light," Joe confirmed.

"Come to light? I've been telling you that since the 1980s."

"Greer," Rai said gently.

"So?" She scanned the faces in the room.

"As part of the winding-up process, royalties due to you have been recalculated and backdated," Joe said.

"At last!" Greer exclaimed. "But what's …?"

Joe raised his hand. "This added to your shares means there's a sizable payment due to you. We just have to complete the formalities. Sign the acquisition agreement and we're done."

Anthony leaned across, handing Greer a document. She gave him a quizzical look.

"It's good news, Greer. A happy ending." He smiled.

As Greer read her hands started to tremble.

"Jeez. We made a lot of money," she said softly. She looked up. "But what's changed, why now?"

"Rai found demo tapes from way back," Joe told her. "Just you, laying down some tracks."

"That time you'd been sent away again. You must have written over twenty songs. You made tapes. The lyrics are in an old schoolbook. Remember?" Rai was staring at her.

Of course she remembered. It had been one of the most traumatic periods of her life. Her grandmother, determined to end their relationship once and for all, had sent her to a boarding school in the wilds of the Scottish Highlands. A strict, academic crammer with an unrelenting policy of intense classical education, enlivened with gruelling mountain treks.

Forty miserable teenage girls made to run through treacherous terrain in freezing conditions for the good of their health and the fortitude of their souls. Greer had been so lonely, so broken, she had contemplated ending it all. She missed her home, her sisters and most of all, her soulmate, Rai.

And just when she was at her lowest, an unlikely hero came to her rescue. The caretaker, an elderly man with whiskers and a kilt, took her to one side and told her of a loch, not far away, where the water ran warm in a stream. He said no more but knew she needed a special place, and swimming there alone, night after night, she found the will to go on and the songs had poured out of her. Beautiful haunting melodies, exquisite poetry, telling tales of love and loss, easing her pain and healing her heart; nurturing her until she could be reunited with those she loved.

The room was silent. All eyes were on her. Rai leaned across and took her hand.

"After all this time?" she whispered.

"I've been clearing things out," he told her. "Been indulging in quite a bit of clarity recently."

Greer turned the page, reading on, holding on to the arm of her chair to stop the room from spinning.

"I'm due all this money? Shares I never knew I had?"

Joe passed her a glass of water. She had grown pale.

"Ah, well, Rai …"

Rai cut in. "No need to go into the details now. Greer, the money is yours. I hope it's not too late."

She looked into his eyes, the deep blue filled with remorse and as always, his pain touched her soul.

"Should I be angry?" she asked him. "I feel as if I should be angry."

"Maybe not now. Maybe all the anger's been spent."

She gave him a sad smile. "Maybe you're right."

"The documents are ready," Joe announced.

Everyone in the room held their breath.

"Okay, let's do it," Greer replied, as a flurry of paperwork appeared, and she exchanged her signature for just over a million euro.

And Breathe

Following the revelation that Greer Morgan – singer/ songwriter and major creative force behind one of Ireland's most successful bands – was finally to be recompensed for failing to receive her dues, lunch with Humphrey Beaumont was bound to be a jovial affair.

"I'm so pleased you're okay about it," Humphrey said, raising a champagne glass as they sat in the Shelbourne Hotel's famous Horseshoe Bar. "I did think Rai was being rather pushy suggesting he join us, considering the *non parlez* policy you've subscribed to for many years but all's well that ends well, eh?"

Rai chinked Humphrey's glass with his bottle of non-alcoholic beer.

"I'd like to put it all behind us if Greer will. Sure, I didn't know what we were arguing about half the time." He slid Greer a look. Towards the end of their relationship, they rowed about so much, it would be difficult to remember anything beyond the fact they disagreed about every single thing.

But the truth of it was, the longer Rai pursued his career without her, the more he descended into depression and however much he surrounded himself with 'close personal friends' and his 'solid management team' he was lonely, desolate without her.

If the time away at the Scottish boarding school had been Greer's 'black dog' period, Rai's solo career was his. Despite outward appearances, Rai was not what he seemed, for his destiny lay elsewhere and this path was a route he should not have taken. A far different future had been mapped out, a role he might deny but could not renege upon, and although time in that other place moved at a different pace, he could no longer put off the inevitable, he had to fulfil his calling or never return, a scenario he could not bear to contemplate.

And connecting with his thoughts, she remembered one of their many attempts at reconciliation.

"What's that?" She pointed at the base of his throat, where a small pool of liquid shone like ink. He looked away, dark eyes glaring up at the moon.

"High tide, I suppose."

She knew what it was. Too long out of the water, sea-people drowned; drowned in their own skin.

"Come on!" she ordered, hauling him up.

"Not now." He was drowsy, listless. She dragged him towards the door. "Where to?"

"The beach, Rai. Sink or swim. Your choice!"

"Penny for them," Greer whispered, smiling over her glass but she knew that look.

"Another time," he replied, indicating Humphrey, now absorbed in the menu.

"I know," she said. But she did not know. Not everything. Not yet.

Talking with two of her oldest friends, Greer could feel the years fall away, sharing memories, laughing at the many scrapes they had survived, dipping into sombreness recounting those lost, and side-stepping any mention of the tragedy that had touched them all.

"Now, what news of the sisters?" Humphrey asked, deciding his cholesterol could go to hell in a handcart, the Black Forest Gateau laced with damson gin could not be denied.

"Ah, you know my sisters. No change there," Greer declared.

Humphrey laid down his spoon. "I think not. Lots of change there and more to come I shouldn't wonder."

"Oh, yes. The money. That will make a difference. At least

we can get the business back on track."

Humphrey watched her thoughtfully. It appeared Cassandra had not yet shared her deepest concerns with her sibling, something even more pressing than reviving Manorcliff's fortunes. The barrister kept his counsel.

"I'm pleased you didn't storm out when you heard Rai was giving what remained ..."

Rai coughed loudly.

"What remained of what?" Greer asked.

"You didn't tell her?" Humphrey said.

"Er. No."

Humphrey sighed. "May I?"

"What?!" Greer demanded.

Rai sat back, folding his arms. "May as well, I really do have nothing to lose!"

"Rai assigned his shares to you," Humphrey told her.

Greer sat for a moment, taking it in.

"Is this true?"

Rai nodded.

"But why?"

"Time to set things straight, Greer. I'm just sorry it took so long."

Greer sat back. Shocked and yet relieved at the same time, she felt a weight lift. The sliver of steel hardening her heart against the man she loved, dissolving, ebbing away and setting her free. She wanted to cry.

"A fresh start for everyone," Humphrey said, between mouthfuls of dessert. "Will you take the helm at Manorcliff now?"

"Why, is something wrong with Cassandra?" Rai asked, concerned.

Humphrey shrugged. "All I know is Nagle phoned after the do at the Harbour Spa Hotel, said they'd been making plans. He was in great form!"

"Plans? But Nagle's moving away. Sold all his livestock." Greer was bemused.

"I'll say no more. Don't want to break a confidence." He put his finger to his lips.

Greer blinked at Rai. "Do you know anything about this?"

"Unfinished business maybe," he replied, eyes twinkling.

"Ah, that old chestnut," she said, disbelieving. "Is it even true?"

"If you mean the proposal, it is, I was there," Humphrey said. "Well, I was half-asleep in a tent on the beach. But I heard him ask her to marry him and then she dived into the water and swam away, leaving Nagle – and the rest of us – to sleep it off."

"Bloody hell!" Greer drained her glass. "You mean the romance could be back on, after all this time?"

"It *was* a very romantic evening," Rai said. "Chinese lanterns dancing in the air like stars, music drifting across the beach on the summer breeze, champagne flowing, people dancing." He put his arm around Greer, crooning a couple of bars of Bryan Ferry's 'Avalon' as he swayed her gently where they sat. She rested her head on his shoulder, smiling.

"I believe you two brought the house down. I'd have loved to hear you sing together again." Humphrey held his spoon aloft, conducting himself as he hummed.

"Ah, soppy old romantics, the pair of you!" Greer broke the spell, laughing. "It was a wonderful evening, and it *is* a fabulous hotel."

"You must have something up your sleeve?" Rai raised eyebrows at her. "You've always had loads of ideas."

"I have." Greer grinned. "Pass me that menu, Humphrey, I'll show you." She ferreted in her bag for a pen and proceeded to sketch out the front elevation of Manorcliff, complete with a large stone and glass conservatory, stylishly incorporating a restored Moon Room.

"Big investment," Humphrey said.

"An investment in the future. We'll focus on what makes us different, make our place a retreat. People can come to paint, write, learn an instrument, courses in Reiki, yoga, that sort of thing."

"A haven," Rai said.

"Sounds brilliant!" Humphrey declared. "Any help you need from me, just let me know."

Greer squeezed his hand on the table. Typical Humphrey, always there for them.

They were standing on the steps of the hotel. Late afternoon would soon become evening; it had been a long and eventful day but neither Greer nor Rai wanted it to end.

"You'll be back to see Archie before he leaves?" Rai asked, shaking Humphrey's hand in farewell.

"I will," Humphrey confirmed, turning to go. "Rosshaven means a lot to me too, you know. I might have unfinished business there myself."

They stood watching as he strode briskly away, a tall figure cutting a swathe through one of the city's busiest thoroughfares. Rai looked across to the park, sunshine filtering through the leaves, the green laced with gold.

"Can I tempt you to a stroll?" he asked.

"You can," she replied, pleased they were not parting yet.

It was strange how the park, a sumptuous oasis of lawn and formal gardens edged with trees, contrived to weave its spell of tranquillity as soon as they passed through the elegant gates. The horse-drawn carriages waiting patiently gave a sense of stepping back in time, a familiar resonance for the attractive couple strolling towards the lake, for theirs was a long-ago tale of love that could trace its beginnings way back.

Even the air was different as the lake stretched out before them, its silky surface hazy from the heat, rippling gently as the sun dipped behind the buildings. Kneeling at its edge, Greer leaned forward as if to kiss the water and lifting a handful to her lips drank.

"You always did that," Rai said, spreading his coat for them to sit on, another long-held tradition.

"My safety blanket. If the water's in me it won't take me."

"The water won't take you; you know that, Greer."

She smiled, enjoying the sensation as the liquid ran down her throat and into her body.

"But it is going to take you. I'm right, aren't I?"

Rai sighed, pushing fingers through steely strands of hair fallen across his face. He gazed over the lake. A small family of mallards streamed past towards the reed bed and a lone cygnet trailed its elegant parents beneath the bridge. He closed his eyes briefly and when he opened them, she was beside him, their noses almost touching. He breathed her in; she had taken his hands in hers, cool and damp from the lake. He turned her left wrist over, the tiny half-moon tattoo glistening up at him, and his eyes never leaving hers, he placed his right wrist over hers, reuniting the half-moons etched in their skin – making their moon one again.

Minutes later, clothes abandoned beneath a stately willow, fronds brushing their skin as they disrobed, they slipped silently into the water and swam to the centre of the lake. Greer's heart was beating hard, remembering the excitement of being with him like this, when he stopped, turning her to face him as the water swirled about them; a dark, velvet cloak, warm and smooth.

Cupping her chin in his hands, he held her perfectly still, gazing into her eyes. It was dusk, the perfect slice of time between day and night. The sun had clawed farewell across the sky in plumes of amber and as Greer looked up at him, she saw the fire reflected deep in his eyes, and shivered. He watched her, questioning. Beyond this, there was no turning back. Not for him.

"I'm ready," she whispered. "I want this too."

He drew her to him and clasping her naked body he pressed his cool mouth against hers taking all the breath out of her into him. Her eyes closed and she lay limp as a drowned rag doll in his arms. He watched her for a moment, eyes filling with tears as he remembered the first time, she begging to be taken and he terrified it might not work and he would lose her completely, and then surely, he would be lost too. But overcoming his fear he had taken her, as gently as a ripple yet fiercely as a storm and they were one; and so it would be forever.

He wiped a tear away as her head bobbed in the water, hair floating about her like a halo and looking up, he saw a new moon, a sliver of pale gold curved elegantly in a patch of dark sky – a turning tide.

And wrapping her tightly in his arms, Rai began to twirl in the water, slowly at first, then faster and faster, spinning together as he propelled them downwards, deeper and deeper, leaving a torrid whirlpool of bubbles in their wake. And as they dived, he took her mouth to his again and in this kiss gave her back her breath, the breath he had blended with his own.

Like a princess awakening from a sleep of many years, Greer's eyes flickered and she saw in the shimmering, turquoise light of this secret place, her love, her strange and special love and smiling, lifted her arms towards him for he was taking her home, home to where she felt safe and warm. Home where they would make love and every pore of her body would tingle in perfect ecstasy, for she had loved him forever and her soul had been left to starve all the time he had been gone.

Back on dry land, wrapping her in his sealskin coat, they sat side by side gazing at the stars. The last train had long left for Rosshaven and even this vibrant, timeless city seemed to be drifting towards slumber.

"Hungry?" he asked.

"Ravenous, you?"

He nodded. "Booked anywhere?"

She shook her head. He caught tendrils of damp hair in his fingers and twisting them away from her face, smiled into her eyes.

"Come on. Old Paulo's on duty at the Shelbourne." He

stood, pulling her to her feet. "He'll find us a room."

"And a toasted sandwich?" she asked, taking her shoes from him, for the grass was damp.

He laughed; her favourite midnight snack, sandwiches and salty kisses.

If the couple at the desk looked slightly dishevelled for such an elegant establishment, Paulo the senior night porter barely raised an eyebrow. He handed Rai a room key.

"Just sign here, sir. I'll have the sandwiches and hot chocolate sent up."

A young man in liveried uniform appeared.

"It's okay," the older man told him. "Mr and Mrs Muir don't have any luggage, not this evening."

Greer let out the loud Morgan laugh as they stepped into the lift.

"I don't believe you gave our names as Mr and Mrs Muir, Rai, honestly!" She was still laughing as the door closed.

"Not that funny, really," he replied, turning to look at her. "There's something else I meant to tell you today."

She giggled. "What? What did you mean to tell me?" Her eyes shone back at him.

He took her hands. "Greer, we're still married."

Storm Force

Rai's revelation that their spur-of-the-moment Las Vegas wedding, over twenty years ago, had never been legally dissolved shook Greer rigid. But once over the initial shock, she was beyond furious, calling him all the ridiculous, stupid, inconsiderate eejits under the sun, moon and stars – convinced he had always known they were still man and wife and was too self-absorbed to bother to do anything about it.

Had he not considered for one moment she might want to marry again, have a family, build another life?

"If that had been the case, my love, it would have come to light," he said, as she stomped about the elegantly furnished room. "You'd have needed the paperwork to make sure you were free … but it didn't happen, because let's face it, you didn't want to be free, any more than I did."

"What utter rubbish!" she railed at him. "I've had other relationships. Alistair and I were together for a long time … we might …I could …"

"Have married him?" Rai shrugged. "I don't think so. You chose him for the same reasons he chose you, you're tied to another. Your relationship with Alistair was always going to be just an affair, you knew that." He placed his hands on her shoulders, looking into her eyes. "I haven't deliberately kept this from you, I didn't know either. It's fate and you need to accept it."

And as was his way, Rai soothed her fury, explaining they were both to blame for the oversight, because after filing for divorce due to 'irreconcilable differences', they only ever received a decree nisi, neither of them completing the documentation ensuring the decree absolute followed, meaning they were indeed still man and wife.

"But how long have you known?" she asked, as she sat in the vast bed sipping hot chocolate.

"Not long, it came to light going through the paperwork winding up the business. But I needed to tell you face to face, couldn't have you going off in a fit of pique, finding someone to divorce us properly, not yet. Not till you know the rest..."

He was sitting in the window, the chair bathed in moonlight giving a ghostly glow as he spoke.

"There's more?" she whispered, but somewhere in her heart she knew what was coming.

"I have to go home, Greer. It's long overdue and I'm badly needed."

He watched as she sank back into the pillows, eyes large in her pale face. She looked like the little girl he remembered, scared of being abandoned again.

"But why now?"

He turned back to gaze at the park, where they swam, made love, became one again.

"My world is under attack, changing so rapidly it may not survive and if it can't, this world will change too and what's really frightening is, it could be the end, Greer, the end of everything."

"But what can you do? You're just one man." She slid out of bed, and walking towards him slowly, she folded her body into his, a perfect fit. He embraced her, kissing her forehead as she nestled into the soft skin of his throat.

"Not quite just a man," he reminded her. "They're already working on solutions, new strains of coral to absorb pollution, animals that can feed on plastic, we stand a chance but only if we act now, before it's too late."

"Sounds like science fiction to me."

"Science fact is what it has to become," he told her.

"So that's what you've been doing? Whenever your name crops up in the media you're somewhere obscure working with

SECRETS OF THE SHELL SISTERS

a charity, a foundation researching marine life or something."

"Correct, the 'something' is trying to save the planet."

"But what about me? Us?" There was a cry in her voice; she did not care about the end of the world, not now.

"Come with me, we're still married, it would be allowed, remember?"

She remembered alright. It was something that had entranced and terrified her at the same time. She had seen glimpses of his world, knew the stories and the legends, the rumour that when Rai's father had been lost at sea and her mother had vanished from the shore, they had gone together. He had been recalled and their mother had gone with him, leaving her three little daughters, the half-breeds with nowhere to call home, land nor sea.

It was happening again, Rai recalled to that other place to fulfil his duty, and she – his other half – being given the chance to go with him. Their mother *had* gone, forsaking all her responsibilities, yet could Greer do that? *Would* she do that? As much as she loved him, as much as he made her feel whole again – could she leave the place she had just reconnected with; leave Manorcliff, her sisters, the spaniels – her home?

Now, as they pulled into the station, she felt it. The dread. Just when she had started to feel happy, the endless angst gnawing at her finally giving way to the sheer joy of being with her one true love.

Greer watched the harbour hove into view, the cliffs caressing the curve of the bay, the deep blue dome of sunlit sky. She could see Manorcliff, the edge of the Moon Room, just visible high above the town, the Harbour Spa Hotel's awning billowing, the fishermen's cottages painted pink, yellow and blue. And before it all the sea, the cool, calm, glorious sea, enticing as playful waves sent sparkles up into the surf.

She took Rai's hand. He was watching the sea too, but he could see beneath its beguiling beauty to the chaos and challenges below. There was much work to be done.

He looked at Greer, the beautiful, passionate girl he had loved from the first time he laid eyes on her and he could picture her now, collecting shells on the beach, just five years old, holding each one to her ear as her sisters had taught her, hoping to hear her mother's voice saying she was coming home and all would be well, they would be a family again.

"Little shell sister," he whispered, squeezing her fingers.

She pointed at the sky, a way out to sea; clouds were building, the wind had changed direction.

"It's on its way," she told him, and he nodded, for they both knew what was coming.

If the previous evening had been stormy for the newly reunited Mr and Mrs Muir, it was nothing compared with the freak weather front blowing up just beyond Phoenix Island as a beautiful summer's morning quickly became the stuff of nightmares.

Early risers setting up camp on the beach hastily dispersed as the sea mist turned to a dense heaving fog, belching gusts of wind as it bounced along the shore. Fishermen hurried to secure their vessels, as those already on the water sped back to safe harbour.

High above the beach, as the wind screeched about the cliff-face Cassandra and Orla were chasing across the terrace, seizing tablecloths and napkins as they took flight. Nagle and Fudge hauled parasols from cast-iron bases, declaring nothing was safe. Well used to storms this felt odd, suddenly coming from nowhere, taking everyone by surprise.

"Good job it didn't flare up like this yesterday when you were out canoodling with your old flame," Nagle said, handing Cassandra a stack of menus saved from being blown into the bay.

"How do you know where I was yesterday?" she snapped.

"Talk of the harbour," Nagle replied, his colour rising.

Cassandra turned on him. "They've little to talk about!"

"Well, I heard you were gone for hours, the two of you,

alone out there."

"A spin in an old friend's new boat – that's all it was."

"Really?" He pulled at his collar.

"Ah, Seamus …"

He looked up at the use of his first name.

"I spent some time with an old friend who's going away."

He swallowed. "Not unfinished business then?"

"There *is* no unfinished business," Cassandra told him. "And we're never having this conversation again, is that clear?"

"I'm sure we won't need to."

Nagle carried a basket of tableware to the kitchen table.

"The last of my stock has been sold; I'm away soon enough."

"When?" Cassandra was fiddling at the coffee maker; she had never learned how to work it properly.

"End of the season; I won't see you stuck – you know that."

"You're serious then?" She turned to look at him.

"Here, let me do that." He took the beans, putting them to his nose, breathing in the delicious aroma before passing them to her to do the same. She gave a small smile. Nagle released them into the machine. "I am. Time for a fresh start before it's too late." He could feel her eyes on him but continued to concentrate on the job in hand.

"Too late?"

"You know yourself, Cass. I've lived here all my life, done everything that was ever expected of me, took over the family farm, maintained traditions, raised standards, all of that."

"But you love the farm, your cattle and sheep win prizes all over the country. Sure, it's your life's work."

He sauntered across to the sink, watching as the cool, clear water filled the jug.

"Well, my life's work's been sold, and my brother says he could do with me over there in New Zealand – I've always wanted to go …" He was wistful for a moment. "So, there it is."

"But you're needed here." Cassandra twisted the tea-towel in her hands.

"Sure, Greer is back, you're taking on apprentices. The last thing you need is an auld farmer bumbling about the place." He straightened, looking her in the eye. "And besides, loads of ladies of a certain age out there looking for a nice Irish fella with no ties and a full head of hair to make a fuss of, so my brother tells me."

Cassandra stood very still.

"And you have plans of your own. Remember all the famous places you've always wanted to swim? Niagara Falls, the canals in Venice, the Black Sea ..."

"But you're needed here," she said again, hands pressed against her chest.

Nagle stopped what he was doing and in two long strides crossed the floor to where she stood. "Where am I *needed*?" His usually warm brown eyes were burning as he stared down at her.

"Oh, Seamus, I couldn't bear it if you left," she said, and then regretting her plea, "But I understand, sometimes I feel like that ... wanting to take off ... following my dreams before it's too late."

"So, what's stopping you?"

"Ah ... you know ..."

"Fear, Cass," he interrupted her. "Fear, that's all it is. Fear of the unknown. Go on, do a 'Rai' for once in your life." She flashed him a look. "Jump off the cliff. We both know you won't drown."

Cassandra's eyes widened in surprise.

"Cass, I know, I've always known. And when I asked you to marry me, all those years ago, drunk, and stupid as I was, I meant it. Humphrey told me not to bother, I was an idiot, because you loved Archie and I'd only ever be second best, especially as ... you know." He glanced away, then turning back his eyes bored into hers, unflinching.

"What?" Cassandra could barely speak and though Nagle could see she was shocked, he could not stop, he had been building up to this – *now or never* – it was time he said all he had to say.

"You were having his child."

Cassandra let out a small cry. Nagle pulled her to him, wrapping her in his arms, holding her trembling body against his. By the time her sobbing had eased there was a huge damp patch on his shirt and Cassandra's beautiful teal-grey eyes were tinged pink.

"A world tour, that's what this calls for. We'll go swimming in all those places you want to, on our way to New Zealand, how's that for a plan?" Nagle's huge thumbs moved gently across her cheekbones, pushing the tears away.

"But you can't swim," she reminded him, her sad mouth lifting slightly.

"You can't shear a sheep, but I wouldn't stop you giving it a go." And as she looked up at him, he could see the start of a twinkle in her eyes, as standing on tiptoe she reached up to ruffle his hair. "I'll take that as a yes, then," he said, lifting her off the floor until her lips, level with his, could be well and truly kissed.

"Don't get carried away," she warned as he finally released her and seeing the look on his face, laughed the big Morgan laugh, which could hardly be heard above the wail of the wind.

They sprang apart as the door opened. It was Orla with the dogs. The sky had turned dark so suddenly it had disturbed them, the lightning making them bark, even Tone who had witnessed many storms.

Dr James, just returned from ensuring his boat was well moored, was checking the contents of his medical bag. Orla, adding a few drops of Rescue Remedy to the dogs' bowls, watched him.

"I'm on standby," he told her.

"It's going to be bad." The dogs were not hungry. "I can feel it."

"We'll all be okay." He gave her a grim smile.

"We will," she agreed, but Greer was nowhere to be seen

and no one had heard from her either, all Orla knew was she was with Rai, she could sense it.

"Are you going to answer that?" Dr James asked, the landline ringing.

"No, haven't seen him," Orla said into the handset. "I'll tell Nagle, one of us will go, we'll let you know." She rang off. "That was Declan looking for Rai, *The Pirate's* broken free again!"

"Does he need a hand?"

"Some of the harbour boys are helping but one of the boats coming in past Miss Finn's place said the water's up to the windows and she's nowhere to be seen."

Cassandra and Nagle were at the door, Nagle pulling his coat back on.

"I'll take the Land Rover," he told her. "You've enough to do."

The hotel was full and with the storm setting in, guests would need to be fed, watered and entertained.

"I'll come with you." Dr James said, as a gust of wind threw him back into the room whipping through the kitchen sending chairs and plates flying. Wolfe and Tone hiding under the table started to howl, when a loud groan stopped everyone in their tracks.

"The Moon Room," Cassandra and Orla said in unison, staring at each other.

The groan came again, then a slow screech, the sound of metal being pulled apart. Everything started to rattle, a gentle tremble at first turning into a loud throb. Bríd was at the window.

"Look!" She pointed but all they could see was a swirling torrid of black cloud, the whole building encased in the vortex of a tornado and all the time the old house howling in agony as it clung desperately to the cliff. The noise was deafening.

"The paying guests," Cassandra shouted. "I must reassure them."

"Reassure them of what?" Nagle shouted, but Cassandra

was already on her way to reception, an alarm going off just audible above the wind.

By the time Greer was blown through the door at Manorcliff she was soaked to the skin. Nagle was in the hallway, having just returned from Miss Finn's.

"She's gone," he said.

"Who's gone?" Greer shook herself like a dog, as Wolfe and Tone came to greet her.

"Miss Finn. No boat, no sign of her, place is empty, she must have left in a hurry, everywhere open."

"Her place gets flooded, she'll have gone to stay with someone on higher ground, that's all."

Nagle looked doubtful. "That was on the kitchen table, mind you the water was nearly up to it, just as well I spotted it."

Greer peered down at an old-fashioned suitcase.

"What's in it?"

Nagle shrugged. "Didn't look. Not for me." He turned it over. The words 'The Shell Sisters – Manorcliff' were scrawled across the front in large black letters.

Cassandra ran into the hall, throwing her arms around her sister. "What happened to you? Where've you been?" She was deathly pale. "Thought this place was going to blow away, how we're still standing I'll never know!"

"I bring good news," Greer said, steering Cassandra towards the kitchen. "We can finally make plans to get this place shipshape." Greer had wisely taken Rai's advice to deliver only one piece of news at a time.

Orla, who had been helping in the bar, heard Greer's voice and deciding some good news would be welcome, nearly fell over the old suitcase in her haste to follow her sisters. She picked it up; it was surprisingly heavy and something else was odd, as soon as she touched it her hands started to tingle, so much so they were itching like mad by the time she joined her sisters at the table.

Sister Act

D eclan was at the bar, head in his hands when Rai arrived, the vessel listing severely, and although he had managed to prop his stool upright there was water sloshing at his ankles. The brothers embraced.

"I thought you'd gone." Declan gave Rai a bleak smile.

"Not yet. Soon though." Rai glanced about. "How bad's this?

Declan shrugged. "Difficult to say. It's getting harder to keep patching her up."

"You could do with a new boat," Rai advised.

"Ah, I'm sentimental about the old girl."

"Ah, you're talking about Flossy now, I guessed you two would be more than housemates."

Declan smiled, looking wistful. "Funny you should say that, but we do seem to be getting on extremely well."

"Aha! An item then? Romance in the air?"

"I hope so. She's still lovely ..." He coughed. "Anyway, none of your business, and I was actually talking about the boat. We grew up on the water. Sometimes, especially when there's a storm, I hear father's voice through the shrouds, singing us to sleep, telling us not to be afraid, all will be well."

Rai looked at his brother. The elder, but not chosen. He had often wished their roles could be reversed and Declan would be called to the other place, meaning Rai could stay and live a quiet life with Greer. He laughed out loud – *a quiet life with Greer*, a contradiction if ever there was one.

"Let me help, get you up and running in no time."

"There's time?" Declan was doubtful, the storm would

have opened the portal to the other side but who knew for how long.

"Always time for you." And they looked into one another's eyes, wishing they had longer together, regretting the years they had lost.

Back at Manorcliff the eye of the storm had moved on, leaving the building shuddering reproachfully on the clifftop, and although the Moon Room and its spiral staircase had survived, it was leaning precariously away from the main structure. Miraculously, no one had been injured and as everyone went back to their duties, Cassandra was trying to assimilate the family's change of fortune.

"If we weren't so up in the air with everything, I'd say this calls for a glass of champagne," she declared, rereading the paperwork her youngest sister had presented.

"But what does it mean?" Orla asked, frowning, her arms wrapped around Wolfe for comfort.

"It means we can carry out all the work here, with enough to pay the bills, so Cassandra doesn't have to worry." Greer gave a reassuring smile.

"Are you making it ready to sell?" Orla had tears in her eyes. "Mrs Finlay in the town paid loads doing up her cottage and instead of living in it and enjoying it, she sold it. Now only people from abroad come and she's in the nursing home and cries every time I see her because she had to give her cat away." A large tear rolled down her cheek into Wolfe's fur. "Is that what you're doing?"

"No!" Greer put her arms around her. "We're doing Manorcliff up so we can all stay together, it'll be a retreat, a place for people to come and heal and relax. It's going to be brilliant, honestly!"

Orla sniffed, frowning at Greer under her eyelashes. "Are you sure? Things were going to be brilliant before and they weren't, not for me and Cassandra anyway."

Greer gave Cassandra a quizzical look.

"Ah, Orla, that was years ago and Greer's career *was* brilliant, travelling the world and everything, we were very proud of her."

"Were we?" Orla sounded doubtful. Greer looked bemused.

"We were just a bit lonely, that's all." Cassandra glared at Orla. "Any other news?"

Greer seeing Humphrey in Dublin had been niggling Cassandra. Of course, she trusted him implicitly, but Greer could be very persuasive and if she suspected something was being kept from her, she would not let it rest, using whatever means she could to find out the truth.

Greer put the papers away.

"Tell you later, let's check out the damage, we'll have champagne once we know the hotel's not going to blow away." She directed this at Orla, who was being unusually gloomy about everything. "Has anyone done a roll-call of our guests yet? We need to know everyone's safe."

"I have," Bríd confirmed. "The only one I can't get hold of is Mr Petrova, the Eastern European gentleman."

"He didn't check out?" Cassandra asked.

"I saw him on the train going up to Dublin," Greer said. "Maybe he stayed over." She would be relieved if this were the case, in fact, if she ever saw the sneery, leery-eyed Bolshevik again it would be too soon.

"Who the ...?" Cassandra pushed past her; someone was hammering on the door. Leela stood there, hair flattened, mascara streaked across her face, her cardigan sodden. Cassandra pulled her in out of the rain, wellingtons squelching as she walked.

"What is it?" Cassandra demanded, Bríd was already pouring tea.

"Archie." Leela was so out of breath she could hardly speak. "Took ... the... boat out."

"Steady now." Greer brought her to the table. "Where did he go?"

Cassandra gave her the tea, her hands frozen. "Towards the island …" She looked out of the window. The black cloud was so low it was impossible to see beyond the cliff.

"Have you tried the radio? Phone?" Cassandra asked. *Encore* had all the latest equipment onboard.

"No one can raise him."

"There'd be very little signal in this," Greer said.

"Electricity's been off for over an hour," Bríd reminded them, indicating the pots of water heating on the stove.

"Will you go?" Leela asked, eyes pleading.

Greer looked at Cassandra. Orla was watching them.

"How long has he been gone?"

"Not sure, I came up here as soon as I realised, he wasn't back. I tried to ring you but the landline's down."

"We can try," Greer said.

"Are you mad?" Bríd declared, turning to face them. "You can't take a boat out in this, it would be suicide!"

Orla, seeing the look her sisters exchanged, was at the door.

"We'll be fine, Bríd," Cassandra told her. "Give Leela a drop of rum and get her out of those wet clothes. We'll do our best." And Leela knew they would, they had the gift. They were good girls, the Shell Sisters.

But neither Bríd nor Leela were happy about them attempting any kind of rescue in this storm without backup.

"Can you get in touch with *him*?" Leela asked, as soon as the women had left.

"I have his number." Bríd dragged out her old phone.

"Well, bloody well ring it, then!" Leela replied, adding another large slug of rum to her tea.

If the storm had eased slightly inland, it was still raging out to sea with huge waves crashing angrily against the rocks. The coastguard was stretched to breaking point, all helicopters grounded.

The spaniels followed the sisters out and down the cliff

steps to the shore. There was very little beach, a mere sliver of shale, strewn with seaweed and flotsam. They wasted no time running out along the jetty and climbing like spider monkeys to the highest point of Dr James's boat moored at the far end. Their first dive had to be deep, the sooner they were in the slipstream and on their way the better.

Cassandra undressed in seconds; the strongest swimmer, she could go further than the others if needed.

Orla dived next, the fastest, well able to outrace boats if she had to, and finally Greer, more tentative than her sisters, yet the most nimble, Greer could turn and spin in the water, like a butterfly dancing in air.

The dogs barked wildly into the wind, Tone, the elder, had never witnessed so violent a storm. He wanted to follow but the waves were too high, too dangerous. Wolf, with all the fearless, foolishness of a puppy stood too close to the edge and was suddenly in the water, unable to stay afloat, wave after wave buffeting his little body, legs pumping desperately as the swirling current dragged him under. When his head bobbed up for the third time, Tone threw back his head and howled, a pitiful high-pitched wail so piercing it could be heard above the wind.

The tall man in the long coat striding along the beach, stopped. Hardly able to hear Bríd on the phone, he dropped it back into his pocket and turned to where the sound came from, where shielding his eyes from the sand, he could make out a dog on the jetty. Rai knew that cry, someone was in the water, and he took off, coat flapping as he ran.

"Where?" he shouted above the wind.

Tone went on point, looking out to the spot where he had last seen Wolfe surface. Rai dived seamlessly into the water, metres beneath the surface in seconds. He stopped, floating effortlessly, scanning the ocean for one tiny sign and then he saw it, a faint flotilla of bubbles coming up from below. He might just be in time. He dived again.

Dr James struggled out of his bunk, hair on end, as he

stood at the door of the cabin. He blinked at Rai, beckoning him in out of the rain. Tone shook himself heartily once inside; it was fuggy and warm on the boat. Rai held the bundle towards the doctor.

"He's not breathing."

James, now wide awake, grabbed a blanket and taking the limp little dog wrapped him tightly, laying him on the chart table.

"Rub his legs, get the circulation going, I'll try to resuscitate him."

Tone crawled silently away, watching as the men worked on Wolfe.

No response.

"Let me try," Rai said, and taking a deep breath placed his mouth at the dog's nose releasing a blast of air into his nostrils.

Wolfe was still, silent.

Rai tried again, more air, a stronger blast.

The dog sneezed, then coughed violently. Water ran from his mouth onto the table, his eyes flickered, then closed but he was breathing, they could all see that.

"Good work," Dr James said, gazing in awe at his guest.

"I'm an old sea dog too." Rai smiled, as Tone stood on hind legs to lick his brother's fur dry.

"I think you need a drink." James went to the cupboard.

"I won't, thanks," Rai told him. "I'm on my way to Manorcliff, to see how things are there." Not entirely true; he knew where the sisters had gone and was on high alert in case he was needed but Rai could only help if someone wanted to be rescued. There were rules, and all sea-people had to abide by them.

"I'll come with you, storms freak me out, I was sure I heard footsteps running along the deck earlier but there was no one there."

"Maybe you need to cut back." Rai indicated the whiskey.

"You could be right," James agreed, putting the bottle away.

Swimming through the deep caves on the far side of Phoenix Island, the sisters could see Archie's beloved new boat impaled on the rocks, the bow ripped apart, half-submerged and listing badly, her torn sails flapping helplessly against the mast.

Swimming around the boat, Cassandra dived through the hatch into the cabin. Greer watched, fascinated, amazed at the strength of her once she was in the water, the sea re-energising her.

Cassandra shook her head at them. The captain was nowhere to be seen. Aside from the cushions that had floated away, everything looked eerily more or less the same as she had seen it only yesterday. The table where they had shared a glass of wine, the bed where she had lain in his arms gazing at the stars, the only difference now it was all beneath the sea.

She looked up. Greer was at the hatch, someone was coming, they needed to go. Swimming away the sisters resurfaced close by, the current so strong they had to hold on to one another.

"Look!" Orla pointed as a small boat came into the cave, rocking wildly against the torrent. They saw a light flash, then darkness.

"A rescue launch," Greer whispered. "Someone's looking for Archie."

"They don't stand a chance in that," Cassandra replied. It looked like a man and a woman. "They need to get back or they'll be lost too."

"A terrible waste." Orla looked wide-eyed at her sister. "Archie's gone, isn't he, Cass?"

Cassandra closed her eyes briefly. It was dangerous to lose concentration when they were swimming, human emotion made them all vulnerable in the water. Greer watched her sister fighting her despair.

"That boat's in trouble," Greer said, pointing at the launch.

Cassandra snapped out of it.

"Give them a minute, let them find the boat, then we'll help."

It was then they saw the man leap from the launch onto Archie's boat, hanging on for dear life before diving below deck.

A shout.

In seconds he reappeared, arms wrapped around another man – it was Archie alright, limp in his grip, as he swam as fast as he could back to the launch, where the woman helped drag them both back onboard. Suddenly a huge surge of water filled the cave, crashing the little launch against the rocks. The couple were struggling, the current strong, the sea rising fast.

Following Cassandra's lead, the sisters dived below the surface, positioning themselves beneath the launch. Linking arms, they began to spin, slowly at first, then as their combined strength grew, faster and faster, creating a swirling whirlpool of reverse current, the force eventually so strong it drew the little boat away from the rocks. With one mighty shove they lifted the launch up, as the wave they had created pushed it towards the mouth of the cave and out into the open sea.

Bobbing like seals, eyes just above the water, the sisters watched as the bouncing boat steered away, back towards the harbour and safety.

Time and Tide

B y the time the sisters returned to the hotel the storm had blown itself inside out and the electricity was back on. Rai and Dr James had delivered the dogs safely home, helping to restore as much order as they could before going into town. There was much to be done, the seawall had been damaged, and waves had reached Patrick Street, and now with the water receding two able-bodied volunteers were sorely needed.

James was curious to know where the sisters had been, appearing all at once in the kitchen, but Orla distracted him by running to embrace Wolfe, who seemed none the worse for his near-death experience.

"He's fine," Rai assured her.

"I knew he was in danger, then I felt he was safe." She glanced at Dr James. "Thank you."

"Are you okay?" Rai asked Greer, lifting her chin gently to look into her eyes.

"We did what we could."

"You two go and change," Cassandra ordered her sisters. "I'll get some food on the go."

The door opened. Nagle was dressed head to toe in wet-weather gear. "Ready, lads?"

Bríd handed him a flask of coffee as the men left, glad she and Cassandra were finally alone; she had been biding her time.

"Did Leela get back okay?" Cassandra asked, piling food by the range, always ravenous after taking to the deep for any length of time.

Bríd nodded gravely. "She's expecting the worst. How bad

is it?"

"Bad enough. But those needing to be saved were saved, I'm sure of that."

Bríd rolled her eyes. Having spent all her adult life in Rosshaven, she could never get used to the natives' strange relationship with the sea, the acceptance of its cruel, unforgiving nature, the notion that whatever hand was dealt was meant to be.

"The radio said Archie Fitzgerald is missing, they interviewed the coastguard, not everyone has been accounted for yet."

"It's early days," Cassandra answered, placing two frying pans on the burners. "The currents can be very strong around the island. Far too dangerous to be sailing in those waters."

Bríd looked at her boss. "You seem very calm about it all, considering how close you once were."

Cassandra lifted her gaze to the window, the last of the rainclouds disappearing over the horizon, the sun soothing the sea.

"We did our best," Cassandra said, silently begging the universe to save her old love, give Archie a chance to be happy, to enjoy the new love he had found.

Bríd, dropping the tea towel, collapsed into a chair and started sobbing quietly. Cassandra took the pans off the heat. Returning to the table, she poured two tots of whiskey.

"Let's not get maudlin. We'll know what's what, when we know." She passed Bríd a glass. "*Slainte.*"

Bríd sniffed and drank her whiskey straight back; it made her cough, as she had been teetotal all her life.

"How many for dinner this evening?" Cassandra asked.

"Full house. Let's hope it's warm enough to eat outside or we'll be spilling into reception again," Bríd warned.

"Not for much longer. We've the wherewithal to restore the dining room now and lots more besides. Things are looking up!" Cassandra gave a weary smile, the very thought of all that had to be done exhausted her.

Bríd straightened in her chair, shoulders back. "I'm afraid I won't be here to see that."

Cassandra put her glass down. "Why? What do you mean?"

"Retiring. We both are."

"Both?"

"Myself and Fudge. We're moving back to Galway, we always said we would."

Cassandra blinked at her. It was true. Bríd had always promised she would take Fudge home to the best county in Ireland, the place they had left in their teens to seek work. They had been at Manorcliff ever since. When they married Nana had given them a rundown cottage in the hotel's grounds and now they had saved enough to realise their dream.

"Oh." Cassandra swallowed back the lump in her throat, pouring more whiskey. "Well, there's a thing."

She looked at Bríd properly for the first time in many years. Small and sprightly, Bríd was a human dynamo – the cornerstone of the whole operation. She knew everyone, remembered everything. Cassandra leaned forward, taking Bríd's hands in hers, the brow of her sharp, little face lined, her jet-black hair turned silver long ago; Bríd was well past retirement age.

Their eyes met.

"Here's to a long and happy retirement." Cassandra raised her glass.

Bríd took Cassandra's lead, throwing it straight down her throat.

"I must get on," she said, taking the glasses to the sink. "That case Nagle brought back from Miss Finn's is in the office if you're looking for it, I've enough to be falling over."

"Do you know what's in it?"

Bríd shrugged. "Nothing to do with me." She stopped what she was doing. "Funny woman, very odd."

"Such a wonderful teacher," Cassandra defended. "Unconventional, I'd have said."

SECRETS OF THE SHELL SISTERS

"That's one way of looking at it," Bríd replied, bustling out noisily.

And there was something in Bríd's tone, an odd note Cassandra had not heard before, or had she ... now she came to think about it ...?

Cassandra could hear voices at the door. Aware since their grandmother's death that she was head of the household, she went to see who was there.

"I just want to give my condolences, make sure the girls are alright." A woman's voice, well-spoken, with a gravelly rasp. It was Miss Finn, the new teacher at the Mary Magdalene.

"The girls are fine, thank you," Bríd answered sharply.

"May I come in and see for myself?"

"Best not," Bríd replied.

Cassandra stopped. It was odd for Bríd to be unwelcoming; half the town had been calling, leaving gifts and cards for the sisters since the wake.

"You do know who I am?" the woman asked.

"Yes, I do. I know exactly who you are, and you're not welcome here." Bríd went to close the door. Miss Finn placed her foot in the way.

"Please, Bríd," she whispered.

Cassandra watched, fascinated, as Bríd threw the door wide open.

"How dare you! You think now Nana's gone I'm going to let you back into their lives? You broke that woman's heart, all their hearts. Go back to where you belong, take yourself off, go and live with your vanity and your selfishness. Leave us alone!" And with that, Bríd slammed the door in Miss Finn's badly scarred face.

Cassandra's usually immaculate office looked like a raid on Aladdin's Cave by the time her sisters came to fetch her for drinks on the terrace; the sun had reappeared, the wind had dropped, and a show of united calmness seemed like a good idea. But Cassandra's anxious eyes and high colour looked far from calming, as she strained to read what looked like an old journal under her desk.

The room looked like a bomb had gone off, papers in piles, stacks of little boxes here and there and what looked like trails of ribbon hung at the door, shimmering in the half-light.

Orla let out a cry.

"Look! My drawings. The ones I did with Miss Finn." She pointed at a pile of paper, sketches of shells and seascapes, others of princesses and mermaids, all wearing copies of the jewellery she made from her finds on the beach. She ran and gathered the sheaves of paper to her chest. "I thought they were lost." She was grinning but her smile faded as she gazed at her sisters, their expressions a mix of confusion and dismay.

"It seems she's kept all our drawings, they weren't lost at all," Greer said, casting about.

"Maybe better if they had been." Cassandra looked up from the page she was reading. "I can't make head nor tail of this and there's a load of pages torn out from the middle. About the time I ..." She stopped.

Greer peered over her shoulder, checking the date. "The early eighties, you were in England on that catering course. Didn't Miss Finn organise that?"

"Yes, she knew someone at the college." Same old lie, Cassandra had just not told it in a long time.

"Has she written in it every day?" Orla asked, fascinated.

"No sometimes months go by, no mention."

Greer was sitting beside Cassandra now, flicking through the pages. She paused.

"It always seems to feature us though. Sometimes together, sometimes on our own."

"I know." Cassandra pointed at a large, velvet-covered tome. "That's a scrapbook, there's a few of them. You're in that one, clippings from your time in the band, articles, pictures, tickets to the shows."

"Really?" Greer was aghast. "She never once mentioned the band. Whenever I saw her, we always talked about something else. That's why at the height of all the madness, I loved to see her. She couldn't care less about money or fame and seemed to understand Rai better than anybody."

"Understand what about Rai?" Cassandra asked.

"His strangeness," Orla said matter-of-factly. She had felt that with Miss Finn too. She had never treated Orla any differently, just seemed to love her in a special way.

"And so many photos." Cassandra passed a battered shoe box to Greer, who started pulling out old Polaroid pictures.

"She loved that, didn't she, all the kids from the harbour over at her place, barbecues, the dancing and singing. She'd fall asleep in the middle of it all, didn't give a toss what we got up to." Greer was laughing at the clothes, the loon cords, the elephant jackets and hair – lots and lots of hair. "She always wore those huge Jackie Onassis sunglasses and that floppy old hat."

"She said someone bought those for her in Carnaby Street and would go all wistful, remember?" Orla said.

"She's cut herself out of the pictures, always did that, there's bits of her in them but never her face." Greer splayed them on the table. "Probably because of the accident, you know, her scars."

"You didn't notice after a while though, did you?" Orla replied. "Or her gruff voice. I actually liked that."

"Acid. It was acid on her face, some went down her throat," Cassandra told them.

"How do you know?" Greer was intrigued.

"She must have told me." But Miss Finn had not told her – it was one of the first things Cassandra had read in the journal.

'I'm so relieved I can still speak. I'd no choice but it so nearly went horribly wrong. But it's done, it worked, that's all I needed it to do.'

Greer gathered up the photographs, slipping one into her pocket. It was of them all, high on the cliff with Miss Finn behind, her legs and torso visible but her head cut off. A day she remembered well. She had fallen asleep in the sun and Miss

Finn had woken her with a kiss and for a half a second, she was back with her mother … Miss Finn must have been wearing similar perfume.

"Is she dead?" Orla was suddenly fearful.

"No one knows where she is, love," Cassandra replied gently.

"Oh." Orla seemed relieved. "I remember now, the Sea Witch called her, that's what's happened; it was her time to go back too."

"And that's a message from the shells, is it?" Greer asked.

Orla continued sifting through the pirate's casket that had been in Miss Finn's display cabinet; trinkets not unlike the ones she made herself, although these were finer, adorned with precious stones. She lifted the Sea Lord's dagger with the mother-of-pearl handle, smiling at her reflection in the blade.

She could feel her sisters' eyes on her, but she ignored them, they knew the legends as well as she did, rumours of who Miss Finn really was, that she was their mother returned in disguise, not allowed to be their mother again but close by, close enough to watch over them in her own way.

Orla shrugged to herself, let them make up their own minds, she was always shouted down anyway. She knew what she thought, and the contents of Miss Finn's case proved it.

Not that Cassandra would ever countenance such a thing and as for Greer, who always remarked she could not care less who or where their mother was, they had been abandoned and the only Sea Witch she knew was their grandmother and she certainly did not need anyone else to be afraid of.

"Is the dragon's egg here too?" Orla asked.

"It's not really a dragon's egg," Cassandra said, passing the sheeny dome across her desk. Orla put it straight in her pocket. Cassandra gave her their wide-eyed look.

"Well, if it's not real …" Orla flashed the look back

Greer lifted the dress hanging behind the door.

"So pretty, the fabric's very unusual, like it's waterproof."

"It might be," Cassandra said. "She was very

experimental, could be made from anything."

"Seaweed and plankton," Orla told them. "It goes with the tiara. It's a wedding dress."

It was Greer and Cassandra's turn to exchange the look. Orla was off on one of her flights of fancy.

"I didn't make it up. She told me that." Orla gave them a steely gaze back.

"Well, I think that's everything," Cassandra said, closing the book. "Good of Nagle to bring it, some lovely memories. I just hope she's okay, wherever she is."

"Me too," Greer agreed. "What do you want to do with all this, is any of it worth keeping?"

Cassandra was putting everything back in the case but not before she slipped a lone earring into her drawer, an earring the very match of the one she found in the Moon Room, the one now in her jewellery box as if waiting to be reunited with its partner – squaring the circle.

She could not recall Miss Finn ever being here, beyond that one time she called, Bríd sending her away. But she knew who the earring belonged to – Miranda, her mother – and it was time to accept that Miranda and Miss Finn were indeed one and the same, and that Miss Finn had scarred her own face, hoping to be unrecognisable, except to the few who had known her from the very beginning.

"We can go through it all another time, might want a keepsake, the rest either rubbish or charity shop," she told her sisters.

Orla reluctantly gave Cassandra the jewellery back; her hands were still itching though, nothing she had seen or touched had assuaged that.

Cassandra clicked the case closed, shoving it under her desk.

"I could do with a cocktail myself," Greer said, opening the door. It had been another harrowing day what with one thing and another.

Orla called Tone, who had been slumbering on the sofa.

As they left, he dipped his nose behind a cushion, drawing something out. She looked at it. A little mermaid doll, they all had one, each handmade by their mother and the one thing Nana allowed them to keep.

Orla whipped it out of the dog's mouth and stuffed it under her top.

"What was that?" Cassandra asked.

"Just one of his dirty ole toys, I'll bin it before it ends up under a guest's pillow."

Cassandra took a step towards her.

"Cassandra!" Sergeant O'Brien was striding along the corridor towards them.

"Heavens above, what does he want now?" Cassandra said, locking her office door before skilfully steering the guard into the kitchen where his uniform would appear less incongruous.

"You on duty or off duty?" Cassandra was at the fridge.

"Nearly off, you're my last call," Sergeant O'Brien replied. She handed him a cold beer, taking one for herself.

"Is it urgent, Brendan? We've a full house tonight."

"I won't keep you." The guard took a grateful drink. "Just something handed into the station, and I thought … I don't know what I thought to be honest, but you popped into my head, so I'd a mind to show you."

He dug inside his jacket and pulled out what looked like an envelope, made from a strange sheeny fabric like waterproof silk. Cassandra was holding it aloft trying to see through it when Rai slipped into the room.

"The very man," she said when she saw him. "Might need your help."

Rai recognised the material, a composite of seaweed and fish scales turned into mersheet, a type of paper. He unfolded it; the inner surface was filled with ancient oceanic Sanskrit, a language and text long gone.

"Can you read it?" Sergeant O'Brien asked.

"Well, I know what it is." Rai glanced at the right-hand

corner, checking the document's authenticity. It was there, the special symbol, a circle of miniscule golden shells and in the middle a lock of baby hair, sealed in a bubble of sea.

Cassandra's birth certificate, the link to the other place never spoken of, it proved who she was, her birthright – a princess of the highest order – the document bore the traditional codicil together with the date she was to return, take her human skills to the other place, to share, to teach and inspire. It was what she was born to do, why she had been created in the first place. Just as it was for Rai. They might both have been in denial in different ways, but the time had come.

"I think you know what it is too." Rai gave her a serious look as he folded the document, handing it back.

"Where was it found?" Cassandra finally found her voice.

"Dumped in a bin at the train station, station master thought it was odd, kind of glowed in the dark, gave him the creeps." Sergeant O'Brien finished his beer. "Did I do the right thing, bringing it to you?"

Cassandra nodded.

"Good, I'll see myself out, so." And giving them a brief salute, he left.

"Guess that's what was stolen from Miss Finn. No use to whoever took it then, just to be dumped." Rai shrugged.

"Obviously not. But what were they looking for, I wonder?"

"Maybe they weren't looking for anything, maybe that was just supposed to be found and returned to its rightful owner."

"Indeed," Cassandra said thoughtfully.

The Familiar

S tanding in the queue to disembark it was not the first time
she considered making an about turn and going straight
back. It was a mistake, so obvious to her now, a terrible
mistake.

The customs officer waved her through. She stopped,
frowning at her phone.

"There's no postcode."

"We don't go in for them much, everyone here knows
where everywhere is." He smiled. "Where're you staying?"

"Manorcliff Hotel." She pointed at the elegant building
high above the harbour. "That it?" She recognised the view
from the website.

"It is, not sure who'll be around though, Archie
Fitzgerald's having a bit of a farewell party, as soon as he came
out of the hospital, he made his big announcement and now
he's off." He gave her passport a second look, glancing at the
large, professional-looking camera bag she carried. "But that's
probably why you're here, even though it's supposed to be a
low-key affair."

But Ella was not there for Archie Fitzgerald's party, she
was not really sure why she was here, beyond this was one of
the leads the private detective had come up with. Correction,
the *only* lead, meaning it was a good place to start and
probably finish, with the whole issue remaining unresolved, as
Christopher had warned her more than once.

When she told him she did not care what he thought,
she was going anyway, he put it down to her condition and
knowing how stubborn she could be, patiently helped her pack

and drove her to the ferry anyway. She could picture him now, waving a less than enthusiastic farewell from the shore; how she wished he was here, wished she had not come at all.

"They don't have an official bus," the customs officer continued. "But if there's an old Range Rover by the taxi rank, a fella with a red beard sitting in it, ask him if he's going back, it'll be their man Fudge."

"Or I could just take a taxi?" She smoothed her hair, trying to appear less frazzled, the idea of cadging a lift with some stranger making her uneasy.

"You could. But no point if Fudge is there is what I'm saying, in anyway all the taxis will be up at Galty House." He was speaking more slowly now, aware that despite her looks, she was not local and had a very English accent.

The Range Rover was at the taxi rank as predicted, and the red-bearded man spotted her immediately, jumping out to open the door.

"Manorcliff, is it?" he asked gruffly.

"If it's no trouble."

"No trouble." He threw her bags in the back, making her wince even though her camera equipment was well protected, and soon they were motoring towards the coast, turning right at a shiny new roundabout to climb up the cliff road.

Ella sat back, closing her eyes. It had been a long journey and not only was she tired, she felt nauseous too. But the glorious day was difficult to ignore, the heat building as they climbed, and opening a window she rested her head against the door, gazing out as the bustling harbour drew further away, the deep blue ocean stretching languidly towards the horizon, the rich green velvet hump of Phoenix Island glowing darkly as the sea swirled about its base. It all looked so beautiful in the sunshine; warm and peaceful and safe.

"Are you in your usual room?" Fudge asked as he drew up to the entrance.

Ella was surprised at the question. He had driven in silence all the way there and she had been so enamoured of the scenery and the elegance of the building splayed out before them she had not said a word either.

"I haven't stayed here before."

"You sure?" Fudge looked her up and down. "You're very familiar."

"I don't mean to be."

"No, I meant to look at, sure you haven't stayed before?"

She bit her lip, shaking her head. Another familiar gesture.

"I'll take your bag in, you're the last to arrive."

But Ella was not arriving for anything, in fact until yesterday morning she had not even considered travelling all the way from Exeter to Fishguard and then by ferry to Rosshaven. Christopher had wanted her to fly to Dublin and travel down by train, but Ella hated flying and only felt safe close to the sea, insisting the ferry was the only way she could bear to go.

A woman in dark glasses and a flowing black and white dress appeared at the top of the steps. Her lips matched the cerise roses she carried; they looked like velvet, Ella thought fleetingly, the scene shimmering in a haze of heat.

The woman descended.

"Ah, just in time. Let's take the lane to the harbour, that'll be best."

"But …" Ella tried, as the woman took her arm, sweeping her along the path. The view was breathtaking, hewn out of rock the path twisted along the side of the cliff, and she could see a slice of beach below, waves breaking gently onto the shore. As she looked down the nausea overcame her again. She stopped.

"Don't look down is best. This is by far the quickest route. You'll be taking the pictures then." She indicated Ella's camera bag. "Is it for *Hello*? I've always wanted to be in that."

The beach turned into a lane at the harbour and then back to a trail through golden sand, and it was not long before they came upon a stretch of shore filled with people in party clothes, drinking and laughing under a scattering of parasols.

Ella wanted to explain she was not here on a job, but between the nausea, the heat and the woman's incessant conversation, she thought she would wait until she could catch her breath and hopefully make a bit more sense.

"I'll tell them you're here ..." the woman said, when at the same time the legendary actor Archie Fitzgerald appeared smiling in the sunshine.

"Don't tell me, someone called and said they'd like a photograph?"

"Nothing to do with me," laughed the woman in a floating floral dress at his side. "But as it happens, I'd love a photo, it's a big day."

"Are you press?" he asked Ella, lifting his dark glasses, eyes twinkling.

"Not today, I er ..."

"Would you, please?" The woman waggled her finger. "We just got engaged."

Having taken the official 'unofficial' pictures of the actor and his new Australian fiancée, Ella decided to at least enquire about the woman she had come to find, because if Greer Morgan was anywhere, it was highly likely she was here, particularly as she had just recognised the reclusive rock star Rai Muir talking to the actress Fenella Flanagan and another woman, wearing what looked like a sparkly red skirt under her sailing jacket and a pair of sturdy boots.

"Come up to the house." A girl of about her age, with masses of coiling copper hair, stood beside her. "You must be parched working on a hot day like this, and there's plenty of food, please come and join us."

"Oh, I don't think ..." Ella started. The girl turned to go. Ella seized her chance.

"Excuse me, do you know if Greer Morgan's here? I particularly wanted to catch up with her if I could."

The girl looked round.

"She was, that's her sister Orla." The girl pointed at the

woman in the sturdy boots.

"She'll know where she is."

Suddenly given the opportunity to speak to one of Greer's sisters, Ella felt convinced she was making a huge mistake. Maybe Christopher was right, ghosts of the past should stay in the past.

Too late. The woman with the shells threaded through her hair was beside her.

"Hello. You're looking for Greer?" Ella was taken aback. She had the most beautiful turquoise eyes. "Come with me, Leela's serving champagne and we need to be quick before she drinks it all."

Ella stopped, giving the woman a startled look. Reading her mind, Orla let out a huge laugh, making Ella laugh too.

"Only joking. If I know Archie, he'll have bought loads of champagne, so everyone can get scuttered if they want to." She took Ella's arm. "And besides, I prefer ice cream and there'll be loads of that too!"

The party at Galty House was at its height, an eclectic mix of people of all ages from all walks of life, talking, laughing, dancing; yet despite Orla's best efforts to locate her sister, it was not to be, and finally exhausted from the journey combined with such a dazzling farewell celebration, Ella accepted a lift back to the hotel from a softly spoken man called Nagle, who said he helped out now and again.

Having spent the night with French doors wide open to the sound of the sea and her bed bathed in moonlight, Ella felt like a new woman come breakfast time, texting Christopher to let him know the previous day had been truly fascinating – she would explain later – and all was well.

'**And the person you seek???**' Christopher's anxious text back suggested she was being deliberately distracted.

'**On it! X**' she replied and taking a deep breath went in search of the woman she had come to find.

Ella was surprised to find the elegant lady who had taken

her along the beach to the party at the desk. Yesterday she had looked fragile and wispy, with her flowing dress and bangles, today she was very much in charge, silver-streaked hair piled high, wearing a slightly too big navy blazer.

"Excuse me." Ella coughed. The woman looked up. Another pair of beautiful eyes.

"How can I help?"

"I'm looking for Greer Morgan."

"Anything I can help with?"

Cassandra thought the young woman looked very serious.

"I don't think so. I particularly wanted to see her about …" She faltered. What did she want to see Greer Morgan about?

The woman's gaze was disturbing. "About?"

"A query."

"I'll fetch her for you."

"Thank you," Ella replied, gripping the desk, desperate not to lose her nerve.

The woman in the blue blazer returned with someone who looked the same only different. A door opened and another woman came in, who moved and spoke like the other two. Ella recognised her as Orla, from the day before.

"Hello," Orla said pleasantly. "Nagle said you were staying with us, glad you got back okay."

Cassandra looked quizzical.

"We met yesterday at the party," Orla told her.

"Of course, you're the photographer," Cassandra confirmed. "So, you're a friend of Greer's."

Greer came forward.

Ella swallowed, pushing her shoulders back; *now or never*, the voice in her head instructed.

"My name is Mariella Ley."

She held out her hand, then pulled it back.

Greer frowned. "Do I know you?"

"Not really." Ella turned pink. "But I think I might be your daughter."

Greer blinked. Then let out the huge Morgan laugh.

Ella stared at her stonily.

"Oh my! You're serious," Greer said. "I'm sorry, I didn't realise. But there must be some mistake."

Orla gave her sisters their flashing wide-eyed look.

Ella felt the ground shift beneath her feet; now she was frightened, scared she would be swallowed up. This was awful. This was not happening. She felt sick and then remembering, reached into her pocket and pulled out the little doll, old and worn, but they could all see what it was. A mermaid, with a turquoise satin fish-tail and long wire-wool hair.

"This was with my things when I was adopted, I've always treasured it."

A small cry. A thud.

Cassandra had fainted.

Sea Sister

O rla was filling a jug of water at the bar when the young woman who had evaporated into thin air emerged from the shadows.

"I shouldn't have done that," Ella said, tugging at her chestnut ponytail. A gesture reminiscent of Greer, who used to pull at the ribbons painstakingly weaved into her wild mane. "I promised myself I wouldn't, then just blurted it out before I lost my nerve."

"I did tell them you were coming," Orla said matter-of-factly.

"How did you know? Was it the private detective? He was pretty hopeless, but he did find Greer."

"When was he here?"

"Just the other week."

Orla frowned. A detective. She remembered, the guest who said he worked for a production company, researching locations, a good excuse to ask lots of questions. She had sensed the essence of him in places guests were not allowed.

"A special shell told me," Orla explained. "I thought it said 'sister'– a little sister without a family, but you're not a sister, are you?"

Ella shook her head.

She thought for a moment, reciting the words of the poem in her mind, 'a little sister of the sea'. "Do you swim?" Orla brightened.

"I do."

"Much?"

"Whenever I can." Ella gave Orla a quizzical look.

"Go deep?"

"Yes, very …"

"Meet anyone else while you're down there?"

"No." Ella spoke quietly, as if to herself. "But sometimes I feel someone's watching."

"Good or bad feeling?" Orla leaned in, trying to catch the scent of the sea. A birthmark only sea-people can recognise. It was there alright.

"Sometimes bad." Ella had never told anyone this.

"That's the Sea Witch. Best rush back to the surface as fast as you can. If she gets a grip of you, you're a goner."

"I imagine you're right. What does she want, I wonder?"

"Your soul. She can break it up into smaller ones. You can't give a 'beacher' a baby without a soul, it doesn't work, they can tell and throw them back."

Ella was staring at her now. "How do you know all this, are you sea-people?"

Realising she had gone too far, Orla gave Ella the wide-eyed look, breaking the spell.

"Better take the water, she's going to be very cross, if I know Cassandra."

"And what about Greer? Will she be cross too?"

Orla shrugged. "Greer's usually cross anyway."

"I shouldn't have come." Ella folded her arms across her chest.

"You had to come."

And handing Ella the tray, Orla opened the door, pushing her outside.

"I didn't have any choice." Cassandra stared into her lap as she spoke. Greer stood looking at her, the glorious scenery visible from the sun-soaked terrace ignored.

"Please don't apologise for something you had to do," Ella said softly. She had rehearsed this conversation many times.

Ella had always known she was adopted, her mother had been adopted too, it was something they spoke of openly, a fact

SECRETS OF THE SHELL SISTERS

of life. It was certainly no 'happily ever after' fairy tale, but they were a family and having found one another, were bound by love and loyalty the way all good families are. "I should be the one apologising, turning up like this but the letter said come if you want to, we'll take it from there."

"Letter?" Cassandra looked up, hard-eyed. "What letter?"

"When I was told Greer was here, I wrote asking if I could come, I wanted to give it one last try. If I didn't hear back, I was going to leave it." She shrugged. "I didn't want anyone upset, I just wanted to meet her."

"But it wasn't Greer you wanted to meet, was it?" Greer glared at her sister. "It was your mother."

"Didn't anyone know about me?" Ella asked, dismayed.

"Well, I didn't." Greer rounded on her sister. "Why on earth did you put my name on the birth certificate? It makes no sense!"

Cassandra was silent.

"Why didn't I know? Why didn't you tell me?" Greer's voice was rising.

"Keep your voice down!" Cassandra hissed. "Why would I tell you? You were all over the place, only a teenager. I was supposed to be the grownup, the sensible one."

"Is this when you were at that catering college? You were different when you came back, I said to Bríd, more like you'd been in prison."

"It was a long time ago." Cassandra made to leave.

"You can't pretend you don't remember, Cass – you had a baby. You put my name on the birth certificate, then you gave the baby away. Did you really think this would never come to light?"

"I prayed it wouldn't, but I can feel it every day , like a splinter," Cassandra said quietly. "I told them I lost my ID but in the end, I couldn't bear the thought of there being another one in the world with no connection to us, so I gave your name ... and when she was born ... I looked at her beautiful little face ..."

Ella felt someone take her hand – it was Orla.

Cassandra stood. "I don't want this, best she goes away." She turned to Greer. "I made my decision a long time ago, it should be respected." She did not once look at Ella. "I'm going to my room."

"I'll keep out of the way," Ella told Orla. "I'm only here for a couple of nights, I've someone else to see."

She glanced at Greer, sitting white-faced in the chair Cassandra had just left.

"Where're you going?" Orla asked. But Ella did not look back, Christopher was right, she should not have come.

Cassandra was in the same clothes, a strange expression on her face as she stood back to let her sister in. The room was dark, curtains drawn.

"Has she left?"

"For now," Greer said, "I want to talk to you."

"Not now, Greer, I'm too upset."

Greer ignored her. "Sometimes when we're given no choice about something, it's for the best. A bit like you giving up the baby. You felt you had no choice, and it was for the best."

"I didn't *have* any choice and it *was* for the best."

"Well, maybe Ella turning up like this, giving us no choice, is also for the best."

"No! It's not right. It's as if I've been ambushed." Cassandra stood at the mirror. "What am I to say? How can I explain?"

"Who to?"

Cassandra closed her eyes. "Everyone."

"Everyone? It's our family business. Orla and I know now, it's fine. Yes, it's a shock but a good shock if you think about it." Greer was determined to force her sister to come to terms with this new reality, convinced that living with this secret was doing Cassandra real harm.

"I didn't ever want to meet her. Be reminded. It'd all been dealt with."

"Cass, it can't just be dealt with, it's someone else's life."

Greer sighed. "Just tell her the truth."

Greer saw a flash of pain sear across Cassandra's eyes,

"As much of the truth as you can bear, then."

"It didn't feel like lying, putting your name on the birth certificate."

"Considering what you were going through, you probably couldn't feel anything."

"I felt plenty. Shame, anger, fear. I went there to have an abortion, Greer, I was never going to have the baby."

Greer was wide-eyed at yet another revelation.

"But I couldn't go through with it, I knew it was going to be hard, giving her up but it was the right thing to do."

"And the baby's father," Greer pressed. "What did he think?"

"He didn't think anything." Cassandra's face hardened. "He didn't know, I didn't want him to know."

"Is it who I think it is?"

"Please don't speculate, Greer, it complicates things even more. He didn't know, I never wanted him to know, and he must *never* know."

But that was not entirely true. She had tried to tell Archie she was pregnant, telephoning Galty House twice and both times Leela had said she would pass on the message, tell Archie Cassandra had called. Finally, after waiting a week, she went to seek him out, he should know, the baby was as much his as hers.

The sky was full of puffball clouds – summer coming to an end. She decided to go to the back door of Galty House. If Leela was there at least she would see a friendly face.

Leela offered her tea, but she could only drink water at that time, anything else make her sick.

"They're down at the jetty," Leela had said. "Been for a picnic on the island."

"A picnic?"

"A farewell picnic. Archie's landed a role, big deal apparently. One of those films for the television. What do they call it now?

A mini-series, that's it. You must be the only person who doesn't know, he's full of it."

Cassandra shook her head slowly, tried to speak but no words came. Leela's eyes bored into her, before she turned and raced towards the beach.

Fenella was standing on the jetty, red swimsuit, dark glasses, hair swept up. Archie was in jeans, his white cheesecloth shirt open, flapping in the breeze. He leaned over, passing the picnic basket to the woman on the jetty. She was laughing, drinking wine from a bottle. He jumped from the boat, taking her in his arms, she gave him the bottle and he drank too. She rubbed her arms, the breeze getting up, Archie pulled off his shirt, wrapping it round her.

Cassandra dropped the arm raised to wave. They had not seen her. Of course not, they could only see each other.

Archie scanned the beach. Was someone there? Cassandra ducked behind a dune, pushing the nausea back down her throat, suddenly desperate to be home.

Leela had been watching from the summer house, already wearing her painted wellingtons, to her mind the most ungraceful footwear ever invented but a necessary evil; she hated sand. At least the colour gave a notion of gaiety, unlike the look on Cassandra's face as she watched Archie and Fenella.

Glad of the boots, Leela followed Cassandra, making her way back to the harbour. Remembering a short cut, she took a half-loop through a straggle of woodland and arrived on the pathway a few steps behind her quarry.

"Cassandra, wait!"

The young woman stopped in her tracks, spinning round, face blotched with tears. She wiped her mouth, but Leela had seen her vomit and taking in the state of her, feared the worse.

"You phoned last week to speak to Archie – didn't he call back?"

"Doesn't matter. Not important," Cassandra replied, hands on thighs, catching her breath.

"Sure about that?" Leela went to her. Cassandra's teeth were chattering, although the day was still warm. "I'll walk you back. A

nice cup of tea in the Moon Room wouldn't go amiss, no one would hear in case you wanted to tell me anything. Anything at all, you know me, the soul of discretion."

Cassandra swayed a little.

"I've a remedy for that, if it's what I think it is," Leela replied, nonplussed as Cassandra retched again.

"Your guess is as good as mine," Cassandra said, taking the handkerchief offered.

"Probably better." Leela smiled grimly, taking her arm; it was a good walk back to Manorcliff.

Moonlight Farewell

S itting on the ledge at the opening of the cave, Rai leaned in, pressing his forehead against hers, a gesture he used to soothe the confusion she so often felt.

"It's a lot to take in but not uncommon, not for back then." Rai poured her wine; he had come well prepared, an extravagant picnic in his backpack for what he knew would be their last meal together.

She already felt better. Rai's response to her outpouring had been wise, calm and considered. This was the Rai she trusted, emotions under control, no longer relying on weird and wonderful substances to deaden his senses.

"What's she like?"

Greer thought for a moment. "Seems a well-adjusted, likable young woman. No histrionics, just apologetic."

"And Cassandra?"

"Wouldn't even look at her." Greer sighed.

"Cassandra's hardly going to welcome back the skeleton in the closet with open arms." Rai spooned food onto Greer's plate; the wild mushroom risotto and exotic bean salad with seaweed smelled delicious. "Any mention of the father?"

"Nope." Greer gazed at her plate without appetite. "Says it's nobody's business and she'll never speak to me again if I even mention it."

Rai shrugged. "I get that too. It's her prerogative not to talk about it, her story after all."

"She said she gave the baby up for adoption all those years ago and does not expect to be forced into having a relationship with someone she doesn't want to know."

"Tricky, no wonder the poor girl was mortified. What made her think it was okay just to turn up?"

"Said someone wrote telling her to come."

"Do you know who?"

"Some interfering busybody, who had no idea of the ramifications!" Greer was angry again.

"Or someone who had everyone's best – if misguided – interests at heart."

"Oh, Rai, Cassandra's so cut up I'm really worried about her, bad enough the world finding out she has an illegitimate child, but the child's father will never know – and Cassandra says if he can't know, why should anyone else!"

"Fair point. Maybe that's for the best too."

Greer looked up. "What do you know about it?"

Rai sat back. "Only speculation and I'm sure there's enough of that going on, but thinking back, I seem to recall a very passionate affair one sizzling summer in the eighties."

Greer gave him a sultry look. "Wasn't that us?"

"Ours started way before then, my love." He reached for her hand, lifting her fingers to his lips.

"Does this mean our romance is back on?" She traced his mouth with her nail, her eyes never leaving his lips. He drew closer, nose to nose, so he could breathe her in.

"Never ended for me. You're the one," he whispered, taking her face in his hands.

"Yes, I am," she said, drinking in those dark fathomless eyes. "But we're here now for a reason, aren't we? You've something to tell me and my heart is going to break all over again."

Rai looked back at her, dreading what was coming. Questions. Why must he go when they had found each other again? How could anything be more important than their love, the renewed promise of a life together?

But Greer knew the answers, had always known. Rai was part of somewhere else, a significant part and with that world in turmoil, he was needed; he had to go back.

"Will you stay with me tonight?" she whispered instead.

His eyes clouded. "Our last night for a while." He looked up; the moon was rising over the bay, a full moon, his deadline, the portal to the other place would close soon.

She gave him a half-smile. "Duty calls for me too. Before all this blew up Cassandra and Nagle were planning a trip, she wants to travel while she still can."

"I know, Nagle told me. She must go, they should have their time together too."

She flashed him a look. "You mean we've had ours?"

"I think so, for now."

"I can't leave Orla."

"I know that too." And he kissed her, a deep lingering kiss that made every inch of her flesh tingle. "And because we're still married, I can come back, not often and not forever but sometimes. Will that be enough?" His look intensified. "Or do you want to be free?"

"Free?" Her eyes widened.

"Divorced. Finally get our divorce."

"Never, ever, mention that again." She glared at him. "And I mean it!"

He sat back. "That's a relief, I'm getting on a bit to break in someone new, you'll have to do."

She started to laugh; lifting her glass she licked her lips and there it was, the taste of salt, a merman's kiss.

The French doors were wide open, lace curtains wafting like a web in the breeze, the moonlight flittering across his deeply tanned chest. He lifted a strand of damp curls, stroking her cheek with long fingers, the webbed flesh between them barely noticeable. She twisted her naked body, wrapping the silk sheet around her thighs to keep the pleasure of him locked inside for as long as possible.

"Do you think it's true?" she asked.

They had been going over past times, the early days, days when they had fallen so desperately in love with each other that nothing or nobody else mattered. Long, sunny, summer days when they were inseparable, lying languid and lost in one another's embrace in the water, on the beach, in their special sanctuary of the cave. A summer of perfect love.

"What's true?" He caressed her shoulder, tracing the length of her throat with his lips.

"My mother and your father. That she wasn't swept away at all, they ran away together, as simple as that."

Greer held on to a flicker of memory, an image she could only feel. That day on the beach, when the storm blew up and her mother disappeared, someone had come out of the waves and taken her, she was sure of it.

Rai rolled onto his back, hands behind his head. He was there that day too, watching from the dunes. He saw what happened; his father coming out of the waves to wrap the beautiful woman in his arms, they had lain together for a while in the sand and then as the weather changed, he had taken her by the hand, leading her into the sea.

The infant – Greer – crying, alone and frightened, was rescued and once he knew she was safe, he had gone to the spot on the sand to save the little mermaid doll, leaving it on Manorcliff's doorstep so she would not miss it. He had loved her from that day to this.

"Maybe, maybe not. It could just have been his time to go back. After all, he had two sons, one to stay and take care of things here, and the other … well, I have the gift, maybe his work here was done."

"But Miranda had three babies and our father drowned that night, it wasn't right just to abandon us." Greer sat up; he looked so beautiful, lying there on her bed, the moon casting its silvery shimmer over his skin, lighting those dark eyes as he watched her.

"Did you feel abandoned?"

She thought for a moment. Her grandmother, then Cassandra had certainly fulfilled their duty as maternal role models. Had she missed a mother she never really knew?

"Sometimes I wonder if she ever existed at all and yet at times, I felt she was still here, close by, watching over us. Leela says she'd have made a deal with the Sea Witch and when we were grown, she'd be called back because she'd given the Sea Witch the promise of her soul in return for her time here." Greer looked at him, eyes shining with the telling of the tale. Rai knew the legend well enough.

"Ah, Leela makes things up as she goes along. Sea Witch? Honestly, Greer, that's like believing in Father Christmas."

"Or mermaids," she said gravely.

The next time Greer opened her eyes Rai was standing over the bed looking down at her.

"Is it time?"

He nodded, handing her his sealskin coat to take back to the cave, hide in their secret place for his return.

"I've something for you." He passed her a small oddly shaped package wrapped in newspaper. "You've enough money to buy all the trinkets you could ever want now but this is special, this is from me."

Greer took the gift and unfolding the newspaper found a beautiful pearlescent shell, that even in the darkened room shone with the colours of the rainbow in the moonlight. She had never seen anything like it.

"A gift from home," he said, reading her mind. "Look inside."

It opened like an oyster and there lay a long thin chain made from tiny pearls, each exquisitely matched, and hanging from the chain a glass locket, a perfect circle rimmed in gold, a porthole.

"Oh, Rai, it's just beautiful, I've never seen anything like it."

He took it from her and placed it over her head; it rested between her breasts, against her heart.

"What is it?" she asked, picking up the locket to look inside.

"You'll know." And taking her in his arms held her briefly, before turning her about. "Don't watch me go, this part of me doesn't exist, remember."

She had no voice for goodbye but feeling him leave all the air rushed out of her, all the joy and energy and life he gave her, the ebb and flow draining away. It took all her strength to remain upright, clinging to the furniture, barely able to stand.

A breeze fluttered in from the balcony, the air turning suddenly cool. She went to shut the French window and there on the cliff, silhouetted in the full moon he stood, poised, ready to dive.

Greer closed her eyes, unable to watch and counting to ten before she looked again, the silhouette was gone, the moon clouded over. She clutched the locket at her breast, holding back the tears, and lifting it to her gaze saw what was inside.

Sea salt.

Rai had given her his kiss.

Tears came anyway, tears for all they had had and all they had lost. Their time had been, slipping through her fingers like sand and she had spent too much of this precious time, hardening her heart against the only one who had ever touched her soul.

She lifted the locket to her lips, returning his kiss.

Somewhere in her dreams she could hear weeping and barely able to open her eyes, having cried herself to sleep, she listened; there was sniffing under the door.

Hauling herself out of bed, she found Tone lying there, tail thumping as he looked up, soulful eyes saying he knew her heart was breaking and he was there, no matter what. She lifted him into her arms, glad of the comfort of his warm spaniel fur and taking him to the bed sat down. Something rustled beneath her, the piece of paper Rai had used to wrap her gift. She switched on the light.

"Orla, Orla, are you awake?" Greer was staring at the piece of newspaper as Janis Petrova stared moodily back.

It read:

Government Aide Found Drowned

A Latvian national, working as a private secretary for the British government, has been found drowned. Janis Petrova is believed to have been holidaying in and around Rosshaven and was spotted in the water beyond the rocks off Phoenix Island following last week's freak storm. A yachtsman alerted the coastguard who recovered the body but Mr Petrova had been dead for some time. His family has been informed.

"Well, obviously I'm awake, you've just woken me," Orla told her.

"Listen, remember Alistair's bag, the one with the winter clothes in? I brought it with me when I came."

"Yes, you told me to take it to the charity shop ages ago."

"Okay, but what did you do with the toilet bag? You remember, the one with all his vitamins and stuff, can you remember?"

"Of course I remember. I put everything in your bathroom. I know you're not supposed to throw medicines away, besides they were making my hands itch, I couldn't wait to get rid of them!"

"Orla, get up here, quick!" Greer put the phone down.

"Tell me that again?" Orla said, standing in her Harry Potter nightdress, hair in a scrunchie on top of her head.

"The last time I saw Janis was on the train going to Dublin. He was convinced Alistair had given me something he shouldn't have and was determined to get it back."

"I didn't like him, always looked a bit threatening to me, with his square jaw and broken nose. A villain in a Bond movie kind of fella."

"Exactly. A look he deliberately cultivated." Greer stood staring at the plethora of bottles, tubes, and jars. "Anyway, this man got on at Bray and Janis looked scared and here's the thing, the other fella was Russian."

"How do you know?"

SECRETS OF THE SHELL SISTERS

"Because he was speaking Russian to Janis and although he didn't say much, whatever he said frightened the life out of Janis."

"Is that how he died?"

"No, Orla. He drowned. But who's to say he wasn't pushed? Despite thinking he was an all-action hero, Janis couldn't swim. I remember when we were in the hotel in St Petersburg with a beautiful underground pool, Janis never used it because he couldn't swim!"

"Couldn't swim? That's awful."

Greer threw open the doors to the bathroom cabinet. "So, which is it?"

"Which is what?" Orla was still half-asleep.

"The one that made your hand itch?"

"I don't know."

"Orla, think! Run your fingers over them, here!"

Orla backed away.

"I won't be shouted at. It only upsets me."

"Sorry," Greer whispered, holding her hands up. "Just try, that's all."

"But what're you looking for?"

"Diamonds, Orla. Russian diamonds."

"Oh, that's easy. It's this one." She took a plastic tube off the shelf.

"How do you know? Is your hand itching now?"

"No. It says diamonds on the front, look."

Greer read the label, *Diamond White Tooth Powder* and popping the lid, spilled a dozen sizable uncut diamonds into the palm of her hand. "Orla, you're a genius."

"Don't look much like diamonds to me!" Orla said.

"Not like this. Bet they're worth a fortune though, Alistair never did things by half."

"A present?"

"Sort of. In the taxi, the last time I saw him, he told me to take care of my smile." She looked at the rocks in her hand. "He was giving me a clue, just in case."

361

"In case?"

"In case he didn't make it … we didn't make it." Greer gazed at the stones in her hand. "Thank you, Alistair."

"What will you do with them?" Orla asked, taking a seat on the loo. "Haven't we got enough money now you've been paid for your songs?"

"Yes, sis, we have, besides these would be very hard to dispose of, more trouble than it would be worth, as it seems Janis found out to his cost." Greer put the stones back in the container. "However, I know one part of the planet where these would be warmly welcomed and what's even better, they'd be used to do good work."

"Oh, where's that?"

Greer pointed downwards. "Below sea level. Some urgent projects need funding, and their currency system will have no problem absorbing these, let's face it they've always traded in treasure down there."

Orla's eyes widened, sensing an adventure in the offing.

"But how are we going to get them there?" she asked. Rai's already gone."

Greer gave her a quizzical look.

Orla shrugged. "The shells told me."

"*We'll* get them there. We'll swim to the sea chamber and hide them, then you can tell the shells to tell Rai."

"Sea chamber? You mean the one I only dream about, the one that doesn't exist?"

"That's the one," Greer confirmed, kissing her sister's bizarre topknot.

The Mermaid's Secret

Ella was horrified at the reaction her appearance had caused. Bad enough Cassandra never wanted to reconnect with the baby she had given away over thirty years ago, but the woman she thought was her mother was not her mother at all and now she realised someone else knew the whole sorry story and it was they who had written telling her to come.

She dared not tell Christopher what happened. He had warned against the trip, telling her she was raking up a past that was none of her business. What was the point of connecting with her birth mother now?

But there was a point, Ella needed an explanation and whatever Cassandra felt about her turning up, and however much she did not want to speak to her, she had come this far to find an answer and could not leave without it.

Taking her camera from her room, she shrugged into her gilet, pushing the aged envelope into her pocket. She checked the name once more and taking the side door, started down the steps towards the beach, too focused to notice how gloriously the sun shone above a sparkling sea, or how closely she was being followed by a pair of neatly shod feet.

The woman smiled as she drew close, a slash of scarlet pulled back against dazzlingly bright teeth and Ella felt the twist in her stomach unwind slightly, daring to hope the reception at Galty House might not be so chilly after all.

Leela had been expecting the call. A gifted practitioner of the art of Tarot, she was rarely taken by surprise and seeing the young woman at the party, had been immediately struck by her likeness to the Morgans. Apart from the nose – it was

Archie's nose – not too big, not too small, and so straight, haughtiness could be affected with the merest lift of chin. She had his gait too, Leela noticed, standing at the vast Georgian door watching Ella make her way along the drive, hastily weeded ahead of the party.

Leela had opened the summer house, laying out the tray of tea and cake there. It seemed inappropriate to welcome Archie Fitzgerald's child into his home without his knowledge. Leela reprimanded herself, Archie would know in the fullness of time if he was meant to know, the universe had a way of dealing with these things; one step at a time.

Ella was looking out to the beach, the small boat tied up at the end of the jetty bobbing enticingly on the water, the breakers frothing the sand in lacy frills.

"Wonderful view of the island," she said, sipping the powerful tea Leela had delivered with a hefty slice of fruit cake. "Ireland is more beautiful than I imagined."

"You've never been before?" Leela asked softly.

"No, never." She continued to gaze out of the window. "But it's always fascinated me, the myths and legends, folklore, the music ..." She trailed off.

"And your dreams? I suppose you dream of here too?"

Ella spun round. "I always have."

Leela nodded sagely.

"How did you know?"

"Ah, just a feeling. Sometimes people feel connected to a place for no apparent reason. There's always a reason though." Leela placed her ample bottom in a corner of the old velvet sofa, beckoning the young woman to sit. "Now, what can I do for you?"

Ella pulled the missive from her pocket, looking at it doubtfully, then handing it to Leela, slightly surprised at the older woman's electric blue manicure.

"Archie dictated what we wore to the party, demanding lots of colour and none of that awful taupe, thank goodness, drains me something terrible. Anyway," she looked at the envelope, carefully sliding its contents onto her lap. "Am I to read this?"

"I think you wrote it," Ella said. "It was with my parents' papers."

Leela did not need to read the note, even after all these years she remembered precisely what she had written.

Dear Mr and Mrs Ley

Forgive the liberty but I understand you are the new parents of a beautiful baby girl. I am delighted for you and wish you all the luck in the world as you begin your new life as a family. However, if you or indeed she, at any stage, would like to learn more of her background, please do not hesitate to contact me. I am the soul of discretion and have only your best interests at heart.

Yours sincerely, Leela Brennan.

And a phone number, the landline for Galty House.

"They never did get in touch," Leela said, putting the letter back. She smiled at her guest. "So, you're the baby girl?"

Ella nodded.

"I wondered when I saw you. Come far?"

"Devon. My parents didn't travel much, didn't see the point, it's so beautiful where we live." Ella glanced out of the window; an antiquated veranda wrapped itself around the faded clapperboard building, perched so precariously on the edge of the land, it seemed to lean towards the sea. "Similar in many ways and familiar too, somehow," she said, half to herself.

Ella was also a shore dweller, no surprise there.

"I'd like to know more ... if the offer still stands. It didn't seem to matter when my parents were alive, but things are changing ... I just ..." Ella slumped back into the sofa, white-faced.

"Tell me the story so far and if I can fill in any gaps ..." Leela offered, along with more tea. "I can't break any confidences, mind, but I'll help if I can."

Half an hour later, Leela knew all about Ella's childhood as the adored adopted daughter of an elderly schoolmaster and his eccentric, artistic wife. Their life in a sleepy Devonian village, her time at university in Exeter and her career as a freelance photographer, taking pictures of everything from landed gentry in stately homes to tots on ponies at local gymkhanas – which was how she had met Christopher.

Commissioned by a magazine to attend the county show, Ella was in position at a particularly complicated jump, when Christopher came thundering towards her, misjudged his take-off and parted company with his mount in mid-air. Abandoning her post, Ella rushed to the aid of the fallen horseman, who upon opening his eyes, promptly fell in love with his ministering angel, wooing her doggedly until she had no choice but to succumb to his relentless charm. That was Christopher's version of events anyway, Ella explained.

"I like the sound of your Christopher," Leela told her, as she finished her tale. "Is he the one?"

Ella gave a quizzical look. "The one? Oh, yes."

Leela pointed to the ring on her left hand. "You've set a date?"

"Not yet. Christopher has a new job in Australia, we're leaving next month … and I just wanted …" She tailed off, not for the first time wondering exactly what she did want.

"Australia? Imagine that." Leela smiled, folding her hands in her lap. "Can I ask *you* a question?"

Ella nodded.

"Have you a special gift? Something you've always known, yet don't understand?"

Ella's green eyes widened. Leela had always suspected, especially when she knew Cassandra had given birth to a girl, that she would be special in the way all the Morgans were.

"You're able to breathe under water, am I right?"

Ella nodded again.

"And would I be right if I said you could swim – I mean *really* swim?"

Ella's worried mouth broke into a grin.

Leela narrowed her eyes. "Are you pregnant, Ella?"

The young woman gasped. "How did you know?"

"We all have special gifts, love, if we choose to acknowledge them but we must use them wisely and for good, always for good." And striding as purposefully as her painted wellingtons would allow, Leela went to throw open the door.

"May as well come in and hear the rest of this for yourself!" Leela called to the figure huddled in a sailing jacket beneath the window.

The eavesdropper stood, pushing back the hood as a rope of golden hair streaked with silver broke free.

Leela stepped back. Cassandra Morgan stood gingerly in the doorway.

"I don't know what to say," Cassandra whispered.

"Shall we start with an apology?" Leela said. Cassandra gave her a wild-eyed look.

"I'm the one who's sorry," whispered Ella.

"Just such a shock … I …" Cassandra's voice broke.

She glanced around the room, faded rugs on the bleached wooden floor, the mahogany bookcase, a battered sea chest bearing crystal decanters. The scene of so many summer rendezvous, the aftermath of picnics on the island, barbecues on the beach, early morning swims and sea salt kisses. And she could picture Archie, torn jeans and Rolling Stones tee-shirt sitting cross-legged by the record player, his beautiful, rasping voice singing along with one of their favourite songs and as surely as if he were there, she felt the warmth of his arms about her and heard him say, quite clearly,

"You can do this, Cass. It's time."

Orla and Greer left at dawn, convinced they would be back in time to help with breakfast but they ran into Bríd on the way, who looked less than impressed as they hurried by; she could see they were excited, lit up from within and knew only too well what that meant.

Sometimes they were gone so long she wondered if they would ever return, but she made no comment. She had given her solemn oath to their grandmother and would sooner rip out her tongue than tell what she knew, and Bríd knew the worst of it, keeping her counsel all these years, holding the hardest of secrets in her heart, for better or worse.

They found the slipstream quickly, it was easy at this time of day, the heat of it casting a haze of steam as it wound across the bay towards the island. Diving in, the sisters instinctively closed their pores forming a natural wet suit as they swam, the gills at the base of their spines fluttering to life drawing the oxygen up into their lungs.

Orla sped ahead, a trace of golden bubbles in her wake. She stopped to check Greer was behind, indicating the diamonds were safe in the sealed pocket of her Alibaba silk pants. Greer nodded, laughing as a shoal of mackerel danced around her sister's waist, hoping she had come to feed them titbits as she so often did.

Orla ducked out from the circle as Greer joined her, and holding hands they swam together, Greer taking the lead to swerve in and out of the rocks, Orla propelling from the back, pushing them onwards through the water.

Finally, they came upon the fluttering fall of glittering green-grey water that hid the tunnel leading to the chamber. Inside a cluster of candles in a barnacled candelabra burned brightly in a corner, beside it a small chest, open as if awaiting treasure.

"You sent a message?" Greer asked.

"Told my special shell. For something so important, thought I'd go straight to the top."

Greer gave a small shrug; who knew what Orla was talking about half the time, especially when it came to her shells.

"Be quick, we don't want Cassandra asking any questions, you know what she's like, she'd make us give them in to Sergeant O'Dien," Greer said anxiously.

Orla knew she was right, and she also knew they did not have long to pass the treasure on, as the earth and tides turned so did the chasm to the other side, it was closing and could be shut off from this world for many years. She hoped she had got through and the sea-people had made arrangements, as she had not yet received a message back.

Counting the diamonds into the chest, Greer closed the lid, almost dropping it to the seabed as bolts slammed shut behind the bronze clasp. She gave Orla one of their wide-eyed looks and placing the chest beside the candelabra, went to start back. Orla stopped.

"What is it?" Greer asked.

"Someone's here, I can feel it."

Greer froze. "Who?"

"I'm not sure," Orla replied.

Turning quickly, Greer blew out the candles, and swamped in darkness, the sea chamber became a cave once more. "Let's get out of here," she said. But Orla was already racing towards the waterfall and back out to sea as fast as she could.

In the summerhouse, Leela was explaining that Ella had the gift all the sisters had inherited and as she was soon to be a mother herself, she was anxious to know if this would also pass to her child.

Leela was watching Cassandra closely as she spoke.

"I wonder if you've always thought this might be the case, Cass?"

Cassandra was silent, unable to meet Leela's quizzical look.

"You two need to talk," Leela concluded, taking the tray to the door. "I've a mountain of housework to get on with, I'll leave you to it." Leela knew there was only so much Cassandra could reveal in the presence of a 'beacher' and despite her own special gifts, that is what Leela was after all.

Later, watching anxiously from a high window at Galty House, Leela saw them together on the sand. She watched as

Cassandra stopped at a rock pool bending to take a shell from the water, her heart lifting as Ella held out her hand to receive the gift. She glanced at Archie's handsome portrait in its silver frame, giving it a dust with the cuff of her sleeve.

"There you are now," she told him, and deciding she deserved a very large glass of wine, swished triumphantly downstairs. The newly ever-present green-eyed cat followed in her wake, an imperceptible tilt of its head signifying he snootily agreed.

Greer and Orla were ashore; they had been gone far longer than promised and knew Cassandra would be frantic because not only was the hotel busy but she hated when they swam without her.

"Look!" Orla was the first to spot them.

By now, Cassandra and Ella were strolling side by side in the sunshine, Cassandra stopping to point out this and that as Ella took photographs.

"Now that is a sight to see," Greer grinned. "Who'd have thought it, mother and daughter."

"I did say she was on her way, but no one ever takes any notice of me ..." Orla moaned, wringing water from her hair.

"Come on." Greer lifted her skirt. "Let's get back and give Bríd a hand. With so much going on, maybe Cass hasn't noticed we're missing." And they ran, dipping behind the rocks and up the stone staircase as fast as they could.

Of course, Cassandra had sensed them coming out of the water and wondered fleetingly what they had been up to but she had been so enthralled talking to Ella, hearing about her plans and dreams, that for once the welfare of her sisters was not paramount.

As they arrived at the foot of the steps, the sun was setting, streaks of amber cloud flittered across the horizon as gulls wheeled lazily above, and all was calm and warm.

Cassandra turned to Ella as they admired the view. "Could I ask a favour? Would you stay an extra night, we could have dinner, talk some more if you like?"

And for the first time since she arrived Ella's face lit up, and in that moment Cassandra saw Archie's smile and her own shining eyes and she felt a wondrous joy, deep in her heart, that she had been given this very precious gift, at last.

"I would like that very much," Ella said, and not knowing what else to do shook Cassandra's hand and they started to laugh, that very odd Morgan laugh; something else they all shared.

Cassandra looked across the table at the attractive young woman who was herself pregnant and wondered if Archie had known she was pregnant, would he have stood by her, married her even? Probably. But would she have been happy knowing she had given him no choice, would he have changed direction, never had his wonderful career … so many ifs and buts.

Cassandra chose not to tell her newfound daughter too many details of her time at the home for unmarried mothers in Manchester, yet Ella seemed to sense her thoughts.

"Mum told me lots of girls came over from Ireland to have their babies. She always said it was terrible, instead of being cared for by those who loved them, they were frightened and lonely with no one to turn to." Ella shook her head. "If I ask you a question, you don't have to answer … but did you know who my father was?"

Cassandra had been dreading this.

"I did and we were in love." Cassandra wavered. "That crazy, passionate, wonderful feeling that takes over everything. In love, for just one special summer and then it was over. Choosing not to tell him was completely my decision, it was for the best and I've never changed my mind about that."

"But having your baby on your own …" Ella reached to squeeze Cassandra's hand. "What made you go through with it when you didn't have to?"

"I guess I wanted something of us, our love, to go on.

Selfish, irresponsible perhaps but I wasn't prepared to wipe you away and I'm glad about that. He never knew and that's how I want it to stay."

Ella sat back looking directly at her. "I understand that and totally respect your decision. It must have been really tough but you're a woman of principle and I admire that." Her face softened. "And I'm so pleased you loved him, really loved him in that mad, reckless, wonderful way. Some people live their whole lives and never feel it. My mum always said when it hits you like a brick, grab it and start building, even if it crumbles to nothing, it's worth it."

Cassandra laughed. "Your mum sounds a very wise and wonderful woman. You were blessed. Which is pretty much how I feel too." She gave Ella a bright smile. "I'm so glad you came."

"So am I," said Bríd, who had been hovering with their coffee.

Cassandra blinked, surprised she was still on duty, it was late. "Bríd?"

"I wrote and invited you," Bríd told the young woman. "The time had come."

Family Ties

E lla was packed and in reception, and neither she nor Cassandra could believe how much, despite rocky beginnings, they had enjoyed their time together.

Having given Cassandra her first experience of a video call when she contacted Christopher to tell him all was well and would he like to meet Cassandra who was sitting beside her, she asked Cassandra to promise they would stay in touch, ensuring that when the new baby – her grandchild – arrived she would see her for herself.

Greer came to join the farewells, bringing Ella a gift, a signed vinyl of the band's best-selling album, the one that featured her own songs.

"I have this," Ella declared. "But not on vinyl of course." Greer was surprised. "When I thought you were my mother, I did loads of research, know all about the pop star days."

"Don't believe everything on the internet!" Greer flashed her with one of her wide-eyed looks, which Ella replicated back.

"I'm very proud to have you as an aunt."

"And I'm delighted you're my niece. I can see you're a spectacular woman just like your mother and extremely beautiful and intelligent, just like me!"

"Where's Orla?" Cassandra asked. "Ella mustn't miss the ferry!"

Orla appeared skipping down the right-hand staircase, Wolfe and Tone at her heels. She stopped when she saw them, checking her pockets.

"Now." She held out a closed hand to Ella. "This is from

me to you." She opened her fist, and in her palm rested a cluster of shells threaded into a necklace with a silver seahorse at its clasp.

"Orla, that's exquisite, did you make it yourself?"

Orla grinned. "I've been working on it since I heard about you. All my sisters have shell necklaces."

Ella was just about to take her leave when Cassandra stopped her.

"Your mermaid doll, have you packed it?"

Ella pulled it out of her backpack.

"Good, just checking."

"I think this is yours too." Orla handed Ella the new mermaid doll, the one she had taken from Tone in Cassandra's office, the one he found in Miss Finn's case.

"Did you make that too?" Cassandra asked.

"No. I think another member of the family made that one," Orla said cryptically.

"But this one's been with me forever." Ella smiled fondly at the old doll Cassandra had insisted went with her when she was adopted.

"Then take the new one for the baby," Cassandra told her.

"Oh, that's perfect," Ella said, a choke in her throat. "Can I ask a favour? Can we have a photo?"

And they gathered on the steps of the Manorcliff Hotel – the family seat – as Ella, the youngest of them, handed Nagle her precious Pentax camera and he took a slightly wonky picture of a most unexpected but gloriously happy family gathering, nonetheless.

Greer was just about to join her sisters in the kitchen when her phone rang. She did not recognise the number but took the call anyway. It was Sergeant O'Brien. Her heart sank; *what now?*

"I thought better for me to call, than nip up to see you. Cassandra's not mad about me cluttering up the place with me squad car."

Greer sighed. "What's wrong?"

"Nothing, nothing at all. Just ringing to put your mind at rest. We had the results of the post-mortem on that fella Janis Petrova. And he was dead before he hit the water, wasn't drowned at all. Poisoned."

"Wait a minute, I don't know anything about this!" Greer exclaimed.

"Not saying you do. But I sent Inspector Crosby-Jones a clip from the train station's closed-circuit TV and he came straight back saying your man who was on the platform with him is a well-known international assassin. What do you make of that?"

"And?" Greer's heart was thumping, she really did not want any more surprises.

"And all I'm saying is the dead man's body has been repatriated and the inspector is taking over proceedings, so just wanted you to know it's all been dealt with. Different department. Different country. End of."

"*Really?*"

"Really. Done and dusted, were the inspector's exact words ... oh, 'and please give Greer my best wishes', his wife had the photo framed and it's on the mantelpiece." He chuckled, ending the call.

With chores done and all guests either retired to bed or in the bar, the three sisters sat at the long kitchen table, Wolfe and Tone slumbering on the armchairs, a whiskey apiece for Cassandra and Greer and a massive ice cream for Orla.

"Well, that was something, Cass, your daughter after all these years. Such a huge secret to keep, I don't know how you did it." Greer was gazing at her sister in awe; seeing everything coloured by Cassandra's experience explained so much. Shouldering all the responsibility, keeping their special sibling safe and always pushing Greer on to bigger and better things.

Greer often felt that Cassandra's ambition was far greater than anything she felt herself and now it all made sense.

Cassandra had made sacrifices for the family, the business, her own child and even for Archie, so busy caring for everyone else, she had no time for herself.

Cassandra gazed out of the window. "At times it was very difficult but having given her up, it would have been wrong to interfere in her life."

"But you never told anyone, even me," Greer chided.

"It was enough of a secret for me to keep. Best no one else knew. I've thought of her every day though, and now I can think of her with pride and the promise of a new life, another Morgan coming into the world."

"And tell me this." Orla looked serious. "Can she swim?"

"Oh yes!" Cassandra lit up. "We went swimming together last night and she ducked and dived and flew beneath the waves just the way we do. She said she could hear the baby laughing at the joy of it!"

"I told you!" Orla said sternly. "Another sister, the shells told me so."

"And that's one of the reasons she was so eager to find me. With the little one coming she wanted to know where the gift came from and what it means."

"Because the baby will have the gift too!" Orla declared.

"It might not be all down to us – Ella's father could have had it too." Greer took a sip of her drink. "But of course, we'll never know."

Cassandra slid Greer a look. "No, we won't, not ever."

But Greer had noticed the rich, flat ruby back on Cassandra's finger and when she had asked where it had been, her sister replied that it had been in the pocket of her sailing jacket all the time. Nearly true, Cassandra had discovered it after the last night with Archie on his boat, he must have slipped it into her pocket. It was wrapped in a note.

'Humphrey reclaimed this from the auctioneer in Dublin on my behalf.

It's yours, always will be, as a part of you will always be locked in my heart.'

Signed with his flamboyant A and one big kiss.

"You're full of secrets aren't you, Cass?" Orla said, finishing her ice cream with relish.

Cassandra did not comment. These past few days had touched on a lifetime of secrets, some safe to resurface, the time had come but others needed to stay buried, buried in the darkest recesses of the deepest ocean, and if there was one thing she was sure of, she was sure of that.

As the glorious summer began to seep into autumn, the wind of change whispered around Manorcliff's foundations. Greer, immersed in the refurbishment of the hotel, was busy meeting architects, preparing briefings for planning and generally bossing as many people around as she could. With work underway, there were fewer guests than usual, and the opportunity for Cassandra to finally take off on her much-fabled trip was not so much presenting itself as giving her an almighty shove in the back.

She was just making final arrangements when a letter arrived from the consultant she had seen all those months ago. He wanted to make further tests, as the previous results had been inconclusive. It was Orla who got hold of the letter first, giving it immediately to Greer.

"I'll go with her," Greer reassured. "You mind things here." Which was how she came to be sitting opposite a very distracted Cassandra on the train.

Circling the bay heading north, Greer remarked on the activity in the harbour; the Harbour Spa Hotel had been temporarily closed due to subsidence and the beach was out of bounds, it had been a very disturbing summer all round.

"You'd better go on your trip and get back," she told her sister. "If the rumours are true and that place is to be turned into apartments, we'll be the biggest hotel in the area and busier than ever. You'll love that, won't you?"

No reply.

"Cass?"

"Sorry." Cassandra dragged her gaze back from the disappearing outline of Phoenix Island. Greer reached across, taking her clenched fist in her hands.

"Try not to worry. We'll know what's what soon enough."

Cassandra returned her smile, but she very much doubted the consultant would know any more than last time. How could he? What ailed Cassandra was extremely rare and there was no remedy on earth to cure it.

Arriving at the clinic they were greeted by not one but two consultants.

"Mr Kelly has shared all the test results and I agree with him, this is very unusual indeed." The man stroked his dark beard, pulling spectacles away from glinting eyes. Greer was fascinated by him – all he needed was an earring, he was the nearest thing to a pirate she had ever seen. "Instead of something lacking in your blood, there appears to be something added, something of marine extraction, you appear to have sea water in your veins, Ms Morgan. Don't drink it, do you?"

"I do not!" Cassandra replied, shocked.

"Well, because we've nothing to compare it with, we can't really work out what's wrong. All we know is it's not normal." He turned to Greer. "For a human." Then he laughed as if this was a huge joke. "Are you full sisters?"

They nodded.

"Might I take some of your blood for a comparison?" he asked Greer.

Greer shrugged. "Sure, I don't mind." Then she looked at her sister; she had never had blood taken before, who knew what it would reveal. Greer's sample was sent away immediately but the dark medic with the glinting eyes was not satisfied, he wanted to examine Cassandra.

"I'm just a bit tired, that's all," she told him.

"You don't sleep, do you?"

Cassandra gave a slight shake of her head.

"At all?"

She flicked him a look. She had never told anyone this. It had been years since she had slept properly, she hardly even dozed now, just sat, night after night in the corner of the Moon Room watching the ghostly galleon of a planet sail across the black sky, hurrying down the spiral staircase before anyone else was awake. Except maybe Bríd, who sometimes left tea or a tot of whiskey outside the door.

"I'll go and chase up those results," Mr Kelly said, taking his leave.

"Let him examine you, Cass," Greer said gently.

The medic walked slowly to stand behind her, asking her to lift up her top. Cassandra froze. He knew what he was looking for.

"Is that sore?"

Greer saw him reach out to touch the small of Cassandra's back.

"It's the throbbing that keeps me awake."

"And does it weep?"

Cassandra nodded. He was looking at a large patch of delicate, translucent skin at the base of her sister's spine. They each had the same, a feathery, lightly veined scar that lay flat covering a cleverly designed gill that only fluttered to life when they swam, opening and closing, allowing oxygen up into their lungs, so they could breathe effortlessly.

Greer could see something was wrong. The doctor lifted the homemade dressing and instead of her beautiful, fragile gill, the flesh was raw and weeping, the edges of her pearlescent skin crusty and dry.

Greer gasped. "What is it?"

The pirate shook his head.

"Have you seen enough?" Cassandra asked hoarsely.

By the time Mr Kelly returned the three of them had retaken their seats.

"Very similar blood. Only a trace of saline though. Nothing to cause any concern."

"Can anything be done for my sister?" Greer asked the

dark man, Cassandra sitting in sullen silence, as if she had been caught in a lie.

"I'll write a prescription." He took the pad from the desk, scribbling furiously and handed it to Cassandra.

Later, on the train Cassandra pulled the piece of paper from her bag, squinting at the handwriting.

Your other home is calling, you have been too long out of water. Go back before it's too late, the ocean is your life-force, you need to go back for your own sake and all our sakes. I wish you well. Professor Adrian LeMar

"And?" Greer asked, frowning.

"Nothing I didn't expect," Cassandra replied.

"Is it your time?" Greer asked. They were too close for her not to know.

"How can I leave now, with so much going on, you home … and then there's Orla?"

"Now is exactly when you *can* leave, I'll mind Orla, take care of everything, it's my turn. You have another calling, I know that, I've always known that … we've *all* always known."

Cassandra turned to the window, the train rattling reassuringly along the track. "I love this journey, the view, the way we follow the sweep of coast all the way home. I always feel on the very edge of the world, right here."

"Cass, you *must* go back!"

"But it's not back for me," she said sadly. "This is home, this is where I belong."

Greer wanted to scream.

"But we don't belong *here*, do we?"

"We don't belong there either – if you thought that you'd have gone with Rai."

"I don't feel the way you do. The gift is just an oddity to me, like an extra finger or something."

Cassandra thought for a moment. "What if I did go back, you know how time works there, I could return, and you'd all be gone." Cassandra was right. There were no guarantees either way. "I'll talk to Nagle, see what he thinks."

Greer blinked. Cassandra had never brought Nagle into anything before. Her sister could see her surprise.

"We've never had our time, Greer, and we'd like to have it now, just some time for us … you know before …"

"Before it's too late?" Greer whispered.

"I was actually going to say before the baby's born and I'm officially a granny, but yes, before it's too late."

"Alright, have it your way. Maybe the big fella can talk some sense into you. Because I surely can't!"

"Have it my way?" Cassandra exclaimed, slapping her thigh with her hand. "Ha! I like the sound of that." And she laughed her mighty laugh, so powerful that people on the train turned to look. But Greer was not laughing, her sister had a massive choice to make, while Greer had no choice at all, she knew that now.

Greer was watching from her balcony as Orla and Dr James strolled on the sand, the dogs tripping in and out of the shallows beside them. She could see Cassandra on the terrace watching them too. Sensing Greer she turned round, signalling her to join her.

"They're close, aren't they?" Cassandra said.

"Hmmm. Seems so," Greer replied.

"What should we do?" Cassandra frowned.

"Why should we do anything?"

"You know full well. She might tell him things."

Greer shrugged. "Orla's different, James accepts that, maybe that's enough."

"But what if it went further, you know, intimate."

"Shush, Cass. Our ancestors will hear you!" Greer placed her hands over the ears of the nearest Italian bust. "She *is* a grown woman."

"With the mind of a child."

"Not always, and we should make allowances for that too."

"I feel so responsible," Cassandra said.

Greer gripped her sister by the arm.

"You're *not* responsible. What happened to Orla was an accident. You were too young to be babysitting her, you were only a baby yourself. She fell."

"Out of the window!"

"Yes. Trying to catch the moon, I know what happened and there was no evidence it might have damaged her, changed her in anyway. Orla's just Orla. Our mother was responsible, for leaving two babies on their own!"

"Orla thinks our mother left because of her, because she *is* special and can be difficult to manage," Cassandra confirmed.

"That's not true at all. Our mother left because of me. She had two little ones already, having me tipped her over the edge. Nana said I was very needy and didn't sleep, she just couldn't cope. Happens a lot."

"But ..." Cassandra had tears in her eyes; she was about to tell Greer it was all her fault their mother had left. She had found her with her lover in the Moon Room, her screams bringing Nana to the scene, who had more or less thrown Miranda out that night, telling her never to darken their door again.

"Anyway, Orla's Orla, if she's fallen in love, so be it. You can't control everything, Cassandra, try as you might."

Cassandra flashed her a look. "I'm not that bad, surely?"

Greer laughed. "Oh, but you are, sister dear, you so are!"

A Final Swim

C assandra kept walking, the water getting deeper and deeper, the waves instead of pushing her back, swirling around her in an embrace.

"Cass, it's freezing, come back! Come back!"

She turned to look at him, the turquoise gown billowing out in the surf. Her hair had broken free in wild, damp curls and her eyes shone.

"Now, if you want to come with me, you're more than welcome and if one word of your declaration of love was true, you will come."

"But, Cass ..."

"I'm having one last swim. Nagle, go home and pack, I leave in the morning with or without you. Now let me be." And giving him a broad grin, she turned and dived beneath the surf.

Her sisters, sensing where she was, were soon at the shore. Wolfe and Tone ran straight into the water, forming a doggy guard of honour swimming at her side.

"Is it a mermaid?" Orla whispered.

"It's Cass," Greer stopped. "Swimming in Miss Finn's dress." She looked closer. "And the tiara."

"Is she drunk?"

"Probably." Greer was already shrugging out of her jacket. Orla pulled off her boots.

They were in the water in seconds, the setting sun daubing the surface in molten light as they slid beneath the drowsy waves, resurfacing beside their sister who sang as she swam. It was an old sea shanty, a sad song of a lover lost to the ocean and a heart that could not heal. A lullaby their mother had gifted them, a soft lament she would croon when they were safe and warm in their beds.

Orla and Greer joined in the singing, their voices blending naturally into the half-octave harmony of siblings, twirling in languid circles as they swam, the warmth of the slip stream caressing their bodies like a lover. And though the song was sad, the sisters laughed as it ended, the delight of swimming and singing together an ancient mermaid tradition that always filled them with joy.

"You've decided then?" Greer indicated the glinting tiara. The crown their mother had left for her favourite, the one she wished to reclaim as her own.

"There's no point in our existence if we don't provide a link between here and there. I'm needed in that other place now. So, I'm away with Nagle tomorrow and then after that …" And as they bobbed in the water like three, elegant silky-headed seals, Cassandra took each sister by the hand. "Will you let me go?"

Orla gazed wide-eyed at Greer. Greer looked back unflinchingly.

"You'll never really leave us, we know that."

And hand in hand they zig-zagged regally through the Celtic Sea, an unrivalled display of seamless, synchronized swimming, as playful as dolphins; the mysterious, magical, shell sisters' last dance.

By the time they landed back, the moon had turned the shore to silver, and they had missed drinks on the terrace and dinner.

"Bríd will kill us," Orla called out, running ahead with the dogs. "Where will we say we've been?"

"Bríd knows full well where we've been," Cassandra replied.

"Always has," she and Greer said together and started to laugh, the big hawdy Morgan laugh that just made them laugh even more.

After dropping Bríd and Fudge at the station to finally leave for Galway and their long overdue retirement, Greer and Orla drove straight to the airport. They stood at the fence with the spaniels; the plane looked as if it were encased in a wire cage, and it had to muster all its energy to tear down the runway before taking that huge leap into the sky and finally break free.

Their remarkably similar faces were pressed so hard against the mesh it scarred their skin, but they did not care, they were desperate to see her, watch till the very end.

They spotted Nagle first and then a flurry of colour as she sat at the window, waving wildly, a cascade of shell bracelets – no doubt jangling the nerves of the other passengers – accompanying her bittersweet farewell.

The sisters held on to each other, watching as the jet stream faded into twirls of smoke, a broken chain across the sky, the victorious blue of escape sucking the froth and Cassandra away, free at last.

"Will we ever see her again?" Orla asked, squeezing Greer's hand so tightly Greer had to physically release her fingers one by one to let the blood back into her veins.

"Definitely." Greer smiled into her sister's worried face.

"Not just when the moon is full?"

"Then, but other times too, special times, the shells will tell, just like always." And Greer took Orla's face in her hands, widening her eyes so Orla could widen hers back, mimicking the connection, the one they had always shared; as if they were staring into the depths of one another's very soul. "She's free and in love and I've never seen her more alive, have you?"

Orla's face lit in that wondrous way it did as every thought passed through her, making her eyes even wider.

"We're all more alive!" she told Greer with a grin. "Because of her joy, all more alive because of it and now we must go because James is waiting for me and there could be someone special waiting for you."

Greer blinked, breaking the spell.

"Is it Rai? Is he back?" She started towards the car, pulling Orla behind her, the spaniels already on board. "Why didn't you tell me? How do you know? Was it the shells, was there a message?"

Orla stopped and tapped the side of her nose with her finger.

"I can't tell *all* my secrets, Greer, then there wouldn't be any secrets left, now would there?"

"But I'm your sister," Greer replied, starting up the Range Rover.

"Oh, Greer, that's not a secret, everyone knows that," Orla confirmed, and they let out the loud Morgan laugh that once started was difficult to stop and would surely rock the car and lift their hearts all the long and winding way home.

THE END

Acknowledgements

The acknowledgements for this novel are something of a kaleidoscope. Ideas, influences, and memories absorbed from many angles; colourful, clashing and at times fantastical.

Firstly, thanks to Charles Kingsley's glorious children's novel *The Water Babies,* which having read at a very early age, I re-read as I began writing the shell sisters' story and fell in love with it all over again.

Thanks also to Kibworth Antiques Centre, where I found the Mermaid ragdoll with crinkly hair. She sits on the sofa, gazing at Mary the Mermaid, a beautiful silver sculpture – a gift from my sister Reta – who watches over my desk and, who in turn, can spy a tiny bronze of Copenhagen's Little Mermaid, rescued from a charity shop, on my bookcase. And then there's the huge, porcelain pink Conch and my shell collection – precious reminders of so many places and memories …

I'm grateful to my early career as a pop journalist, when watching a hugely enjoyable gig starring The Boomtown Rats in Moran's Hotel Dublin, I'd no idea how in awe I would be of the amazing Bob Geldof and Ultravox's Midge Ure in just a few short years. This formidable duo instigated the global phenomena, Live Aid, raising millions for famine relief. The outdoor concert on the island is a nod in recognition.

I love hotels. The sisters' Manorcliff is inspired by many. The Bolt Head – a cliffside hotel on the edge of Salcombe, South Devon. Brook Lodge, Wicklow – with its sweeping double staircase and pale stone floor. The Falcon, Uppingham – sumptuous sofas before the fireplace; Manor House Farm, Norfolk – scrumptious breakfasts, shared with fabulous hosts.

I pinch snippets from many others including Stapleford Park in Rutland; The George at Stamford; The Castle at Taunton; St Pancras, Renaissance, London; The Three Swans, Market Harborough and of course, The Shelbourne Hotel, Dublin. We stayed at the incredible Grand Hotel Europe in St Petersburg – no sign of Pierce Brosnan & Robbie Coltrane though (James Bond – Golden Eye – 1995) and that entire, magical trip inspired Greer's high-octane Russian experience. (I still have the hat!)

Special thanks for always believing go to my close family and friends. Especially Marion, Reta, John, 'one's aunts' and sisters-in-law – Carol and Libby.

The Rosshaven books would still be scrappy drafts on my laptop without my incredible and insightful literary agent, Lisa Eveleigh, who totally believed these charming, quirky stories need to be told – and in mermaids too, of course. Thanks to copy editor Julia Gibbs, colleagues in the Romantic Novelist's Association, Society of Women Writers & Journalists and my solid 'always there' writing chums/beta readers – you know who you are.

Spaniel inspiration – past and present: Wodehouse; Wallace; Winston; Wellington; Wignell and Watson.

And finally, to the captain of the ship, Jonathan – for teaching me to swim like a pirate and being my absolute hero.

This novel was a joy to write – and I dearly hope – a joy to read. Thank you. X

PS We writers just love when our readers get in touch! You can find me on Twitter @adrienneauthor or email adrienne@adriennevaughan.com Let's catch up soon!

Books by the Author

The Hollow Heart
Heartfelt Series Book 1

A Change of Heart
Heartfelt Series Book 2

Secrets of the Heart
Heartfelt Series Book 3

Summer of Secrets
A Rosshaven Romance Book 1

Secrets of the Shell Sisters
A Rosshaven Romance Book 2

Fur Coat & No Knickers
A collection of short stories and poems

Author researching
the Rosshaven romance series,
Wicklow Harbour

Printed in Great Britain
by Amazon

37657891R00218